Brandon Twp Public Library
304 South St
Ortonville

MW00582628

ACADIA
FLAT EARTH BOOK THREE
BY
BRENT GOLEMBIEWSKI

Acadia © Copyright <<2020>> Baba Jaga Publishing

Copyright notice: All rights reserved under the International and Pan-American Copyright Conventions. No part of this book may be reproduced or transmitted in any form or by any means, electronic or mechanical, including photocopying and recording without permission in writing from the publisher.

This is a work of fiction. Names, places, characters and incidents are either the product of the author's imagination or are used fictiously, and any resemblance to any actual persons, living or dead, organizations, events or locales is entirely coincidental.

Warning: the unauthorized reproduction or distribution of this copyrighted work is illegal. Criminal copyright infringement, including infringement without monetary gain, is investigated by the FBI and is punishable by up to five years in prison and a fine of $250,000.

Edited by: JLMG
Cover Design: Tom Edwards Design
Ailerons Font Design: Adilson Gonzales
Additional Artwork: Crystal Fiss

ISBN: 978-1-7348875-9-4 (eBook)
ISBN: 978-1-7348875-8-7 (Paperback)
ISBN: 978-1-7354018-1-2 (Hardcover)
ISBN: 978-1-7354018-0-5 (Audiobook)

1st Edition

For more information, e-mail: babajagapublishing@gmail.com

For my two boys and loving wife, thanks for the inspiration everyday

"Mankind without Earth is Humanity without a Home."
—*S.G. Rainbolt*

PROLOGUE

In the dank and dreary dusk, he watched the comings and goings as the rain drizzled down on his head. Grey clouds covered the sky like a wool blanket. *How'd he get stuck with Sector 2?*

A black Alvis-3 drove by, dousing his freshly pressed dress pants; he grimaced. Finding a pair to fit his large frame had taken some time. Glancing at his Datacle, he saw that the screen read "five-thirty". His stomach growled. *Doubt there's anywhere around here still serving breakfast.*

He threw an arm into the air, a taxi pulled up splashing more water. Wasting no time, he climbed in out of the rain.

"Where to govn'a?" The driver eyed him through the rearview mirror.

He returned the blue-eyed gaze, removing his fedora. "The university...Biology department."

"Very good. Picking up a kid?"

He peered back at the driver in the rearview. *A kid? He never could find anyone to settle down with because he was always on the move. At least, that's what he told himself. But then, maybe once this was all over, he could settle down...be a husband, a father.*

"No, just business."

"Very well."

The driver sped off down the road, the rain heavy on the roof. The light faded as evening took hold. Zane looked down at his Datacle, the name of the doctor glowed back at him reminding him why he was there. He needed the information it provided, being on his own again. It was something he was familiar with, yet he'd been growing fond of J and the others' company. The past few months encompassed the most time he'd spent in the company of the same people and it was beginning to feel like a family. That was something he'd not had in a very long time. His eyes refocused on the stone buildings as they passed by. He took a deep breath, settling into the seat then began to think of the others again, out there without him. *Ariel would do just fine and J was becoming more competent by the day. He was glad J would accompany V, he'd be able to protect her if need be. She was such a little thing, little but fierce...and amazingly loyal. She always took excellent care of him...and the others.* He chuckled. *He couldn't recall a time when she wasn't rushing to patch him up or bring him back from the brink of almost certain death. Her smile warmed something inside him, but then again, even her ire endeared her to him.* His whole countenance lightened, thinking of her.

"We're here govn'a."

Zane reached up over the seat, his hefty hands exchanging money for the ride. The driver twitched seeing the giant hand reaching for him, but the tip more than adequately covered the scare and he nodded to his customer as Zane slipped out into the rain. He scanned the streets. A few people walked around, most resembling college students, books in hand, umbrellas popped overhead. *Man, he could have used one of those.* He stared up into the daggers of cold water pummeling his face. Through the endless drops of water he observed a large stone building with two massive, solid wood doors. Each was carved with intertwining vines and flowers. Despite the rain, it was enough to make him stop and admire their intricacies for a moment. He grabbed his hat as a brief gust of wind attempted to dislodge it from his skull, then ran toward the door realizing it was asinine to stand in the rain. After all, he wasn't there on holiday. He jiggled the handle. No luck, locked. His head swiveled from side to side. Ensuring no one was watching, Zane pulled a device from his pants pocket, an auto-lock pick, then straightened up as if someone congratulated him for bringing such a useful tool. He grinned as the device unlocked the door and it swung open.

Zane shrugged out of his heavy, rain-soaked jacket and placed it on the coat rack next to the door, then glanced down at his Datacle. If the information was correct, the doctor was in the building now. The trick was to find him. He surveyed the main entrance. The hall was three stories tall with eight doors in total, two on each wall, and enormous pillars held up the roof while skylights lined the ceiling. One of the doors to his right was open and he decided that would be the best place to start. Peering through, he saw a long hallway running for what looked like one-hundred feet with doors on one side, the stone wall from the main entrance lacing the other. One of the doors was open, lights flickered into the hall. Zane noticed shadows moving about and muffled voices could be heard. He shuffled over, silent as a cat. As he neared, an argument hit his ear, two men going back and forth, one in broken English the other with a thick Scottish brogue. Before reaching the door, a book flew into the hallway. Zane quickened his pace, peeked around the corner. Three men stood surrounding another man behind a desk, his armed cocked behind his head with a book, ready to strike. The three men continued to close in on their prey, Katanas ready to strike. Zane grabbed the book from the hall and, lunging into the room, zipped it at one of the assailants' heads, rendering him unconscious. He drilled the second one in the temple with a fist, downing him in one blow. That left the third a body's length away, squaring off, blade at the ready. Zane bent down, his eyes never leaving his adversary's. Feeling the floor, his hand found the Katana still gripped by the second man and snatched it from its previous owner. He took up an aggressive stance, one hand on the handle the other outstretched, balancing himself as he awaited the attack. He glanced over at the man behind the desk who stood stock still, his eyes wide, mouth parted. Zane worked his gaze back to his opponent, assessing his environment as he did. The attacker thrust forward with his blade and Zane side-stepped, engaging, steel clanging. He saw an opening and attacked, the man blocked it; they tangled, their blades engaging in an elegant battle. Zane's moves were so fluid even Ariel would've been impressed, but his opponent's were as well. A book flew in, hitting the attacker and distracting the man long enough for Zane to make a quick strike, the man's body dropped lifeless to the ground.

Zane turned around. "Dr. Geddes?

"Yes, but who are you?"

"Name's Zane. Arcturus sent me to gather you and a few other scientists. Seems like I'm not the only one searching for you. Any idea who they were?"

The doctor examined his desk, his eyes panning back and forth, his long grey beard flowing down his chest. Zane thought that in another life the doctor would've been a wizard and pictured him wearing a grey pointy hat. He laughed at himself, still studying the old man, awaiting an answer.

Dr. Geddes finally raised his eyes. "No, but they did not seem friendly. They threatened me straight away."

Zane explored the room, considering his options. *How many had they sent and who were they?* His mind wandered, compiling questions. "What did they want?

The doctor gazed back at Zane, leaned into the desk, his arms straight, hands planted on the smooth wood surface. "Access to Project Duracell."

CHAPTER ONE

Beads of sweat rolled down his forehead as he raised the cold steel blade into the air. His hand swung down aggressively, slicing the vine which had previously impeded their progress.

"Tell me again why we're walking there on foot?" J wiped the sweat from his brow, the relief was temporary as more rolled down, hanging on the hairs of his eyebrows.

"I've told you already, the facility we're searching for is off the grid. Atlantis isn't connected."

J peered down at the freshly cut vine then back up in the direction they were travelling. More lay ahead of him. As he stared through the endless jungle, tropical plants littered the forest floor and trees climbed the sky above them reaching incalculable heights. J had never witnessed such grand natural wonders, but the majesty was wearing off as his body fatigued. They'd been trekking through the forest for over a day now and the first night was not kind. His body was sore from the rough, eternal climb and the rocky ground on which they'd set up camp. It seemed that his new world was making him soft; his body longed for the conforming beds, endless technology, and small comforts far from the farm life he'd known on Earth. His ears perked up, hearing the call of a bird. Searching the trees, he identified the voice as coming from a black-bodied bird, its head adorned with a fantastic plume of orange feathers. He smiled; it was the most colorful bird he'd ever seen. But his joy was short-lived as he gazed back at the path before him. He took a deep breath, steeling himself for the journey ahead, then took the next step onward. The backpack straps dug into his shoulders as they inched forward, hacking away at the jungle's infinite supply of vines.

"Why couldn't we take any roads?"

Ariel stopped mid swing, her eyes lasered in on J's, eyebrows high on her head as she growled, "I'm not really enjoying this either so let's not add complaining to the list of today's annoyances."

She slung the machete into the ground next to her foot. Grabbing a water pouch from around her shoulder, she slipped off the cap and took a swig. "You need to drink; I know you're losing as much water as I am. This place is ridiculous hot."

"Are you complaining?"

Ariel stuck out her tongue then turned to her task. Spinning the cap back onto the bottle, she snatched the machete and began to hack at the overgrown path once again. "Shouldn't be too much further. Besides, I thought you were a farm boy used to hard work, or maybe I accidentally brought that guy, Rich, with me."

"Low blow." But she *was* right; he was acting like a spoiled, entitled child. The wet heat was something that he'd never dealt with though, even in the warm summer months. The time he'd been in Arcturus' memories experiencing Sector 5 was the hottest he'd ever felt, yet this seemed much more intense, the humid air making it difficult to breath. His focus fell on Ariel who stopped, checking her Datacle, her head swiveled about.

"Says we're only 100 yards from the entrance. Hand me the journal again."

J found a nearby tree and hacked his blade into it then

slipped off his pack. He'd never gone camping before, this was the first time. He could've done without the bugs and the heat, but being away from the steel and metal of the ships and city was a welcome change. He pulled out the journal tossing it to Ariel; she caught it tossing it back.

"Unlock it."

J laughed at her expression, one indicating he should know better by now. Having security measures on nearly everything was becoming tasking, gone were the simple days. The journal opened, displaying the emblem he wished to forget. J tossed it back to Ariel and she swiped through multiple screens, pulling up the description of their objective.

"Yep, should be just up this ridge. Keep your eyes open for a stone structure."

J peered past her through the trees, the ground rose steeply, jagged rocks jutted out from the mountain. Ariel closed the book, threw it back to him, then sheathed her blade and began the climb. He packed the book away and took a swig of water from his canteen before following. They climbed a good seventy feet or so, eventually cresting the ridge. J's eyes widened. Not only was there a stone structure, but an entire stone city occupying the top of the mountain. Its walls in disrepair, roofs missing, the jungle had reclaimed its lands; vines and trees grew throughout making it difficult to see all of the enormous features. He turned to Ariel. "People used to live here?"

"Yep, long before Earth was remodeled. Now nature has reclaimed it, a forgotten section of Earth. The roads gone, the inhabitants ghosts."

She started down the other side of the ridge, hopping from one stone to the next, her steps graceful and elegant. J admired the view a moment; the lush greens against the harder tan of the buildings, like mountains piercing the sky.

"You coming?"

J looked down; Ariel was almost out of view, standing with her hands on her hips at the tree line. Then she disappeared into the overgrowth. He shouted, not sure where she was. He descended quickly, his steps anything but agile; he stumbled a few times, catching himself. Ariel still unseen, lost to the foliage.

"Ariel! I lost you!" he cried, still inching down the side of the ridge.

He continued into the brush, aligned in her last known direction. After a few hundred feet, he found flat ground and, attempting to gather his bearings, surveyed the area hoping to spot something. Nothing. He finally remembered the Datacle, he could call her. Raising his arm, he began to type.

"Boo!"

J jumped back, letting out a scream as he tripped over a rock and tumbled to the ground, his backpack crushing into his spine. He crunched his stomach up as quickly as possible to identify the threat and spied Ariel, eyes on him, hands on her knees, her mouth open laughing so hard she couldn't breathe.

He scowled back at her. "Not funny," he moaned, wiping off the debris from his fall as he gained his stance.

"From over here it was. Come on, I think it's just up here a few more feet."

J grumbled as he plodded toward her. "So, what are we looking for again?"

Ariel scanned the area. The vegetation was dense, but she spotted a bit of stone peeking back at her through the green vines. "Something like that."

She pointed as she trotted over to the find. J stumbled after her, tilting his head to get a better view. It was an imposing stone wall over ten feet high, but there didn't seem to be an entrance. He followed Ariel as she searched, feeling her way along the smooth stone blocks of unique sizes and shapes. They reminded him of the stone walls the farmers back on Earth would build. She finally found an opening that led into a large empty room, untouched by nature except for a grass floor surrounded by four stone walls, all made of the same rock as the outside.

"See if you can find an access panel."

Ariel grabbed the backpack from J. He welcomed it; the weight was wearing on him, the rations, weapons, water, the journal, it all added up. Ariel pulled the book out, holding it up to J. He smiled, thinking of their earlier exchange, then placed his thumb on the screen, unlocking it. She flipped through a few digital pages and stopped on a blueprint.

"Says it should be on the southwest corner. Looks to be on the ground."

Their eyes dropped to their feet, scanning the four-inch high grass. The area seemed peculiar to J, everything else was covered in wild growth, no barriers, no restraints, yet this grass had a freshly mowed feel to it. He bent down to feel it; the grass was soft, like a carpet under his hand.

Ariel knelt down beside him. "Synthetic."

"What?"

"It's synthetic grass, only grows to a predetermined height."

She pressed her other knee down, searching the ground for any sign of their entrance.

"How do they do it? The grass. Does it really only get this high?"

Ariel didn't stop searching as she continued crawling about. "I don't know, it's science. That's all."

J left it at that, joining her on all fours. "What's this?'

His hands brushed against something just below the grass layer. Solid, the texture of stone, not soft like the rest of the floor's surface. He pushed the grass to the side revealing a round indented symbol, a circle with three intertwined lines. He sat back, resting his butt on his heels. Ariel crawled over to examine it then sat back in the same manner.

"Kinda looks like that medallion the Admiral gave you."

J pulled it out from under his shirt. The symbol was identical, the same shape, even the same size. He slipped it off his neck placing it into the indention. The medallion snapped onto the surface as if being pulled to it by a magnetic force, J's hand whipped back in surprise. He eagerly awaited what would happen next as they both stared at the ground.

J peeked over to Ariel, saw her glance his way and shrugged his shoulders. "Maybe some magic words?"

Ariel snickered then placed her hand on the medallion, giving it a gentle nudge. The medallion retracted into the ground, loud grinding hit their ears as the earth began to shake. Ariel grabbed J's thigh, he slid his hand on top of hers.

A thunderous pop sounded and they felt the floor shudder, the entire surface descending. The haphazard stone walls began to be replaced by smooth, metal, featureless ones as the platform continued down. J and Ariel exchanged looks; neither uttered a word as they visually explored their surroundings. J peered up what seemed like hundreds of feet of steel walls surrounding them, the sky only a small spec above. The walls zipped by, increasing in speed. Ariel's hand tightened on his thigh as the walls disappeared leaving only four steel beams at the corners of the platform. Beyond them was a cavernous space surrounded by dark rock embedded with light rods throughout, giving off an ominous red glow.

The platform slowed as the ground approached. J examined its pure steel, guessing that the bottom of the sector's plate was on the reverse side. His thoughts went to Will's bunker, the lift dragging him under the Earth.

In the middle of the expanse sat a half sphere protruding out of the steel flooring. As the lift came to a rest they stepped off. J grabbed Ariel's hand then snatched up the medallion, the platform shot up like a rocket, disappearing out of sight.

"Hope we can get out of here."

"We'll be fine," Ariel reassured him.

He nodded back, leading the way toward the dome in the middle of the room. "What is this supposed to be again?"

"You know as much as I do. It was simply labeled *Project Herodotus.*"

"How many of these things were on that list again?"

Ariel handed him the journal as they continued their trek, her eyes focused on the dome. "Here. Maybe if you take a look at it again, you'll remember."

J reached for the journal, involuntarily shivering. The air was much cooler down below. At first it was a welcomed departure from the muggy heat they had endured the past few days, but now it was actually becoming too frigid. He shook again and watched Ariel do the same. Unlocking the journal, he saw that there were six items on the list. The other five were scattered throughout Earth. They'd sent Zane and Max for three of them, Ariel and J would get the rest. This one, located in Sector 16, had proven most challenging to find, its location in the remote mountainous region of what was once Peru. They reached the dome and found a door embedded in the side of the structure; it was made of metal, jagged, rough to the touch. A control panel hung just off to the side. Ariel waved her hand, palm up, toward the panel and exaggerated a bow expecting that J's touch would be required.

"My liege."

He rolled his eyes as he handed her the journal and placed his hand on the sensor.

"Denied," the screen replied.

J tried it again to the same end.

Ariel scrunched her eyebrows and stared quizzically at the panel, then back at J. She nodded, her open hand insisting he try again. He placed his hand on the scanner.

"Denied."

His arms shot up and he stomped the ground. He attempted to reposition his hand, but still achieved the same result. Ariel looked up out of the corner of her eye, her eyebrow raised in thought. She brought the journal up to her face, examining the page. There was only the text describing the location, GPS coordinates, description of the entrance, and the project name, *Herodotus*. Underneath the words pulsed an image of a fork, turning from shades of blue to shades of green. Her eyes flicked about while J stomped around behind her mumbling to himself, alternately rubbing his fingers together then squeezing them into balls. Ariel approached the control panel and placed her hand on it.

"Welcome Ariel, DNA accepted."

Ariel froze as she heard the door hiss open, J stopped his ranting, and his jaw fell to the floor. He gazed at Ariel who grinned and skipped into the structure. J ran over.

"What?! How?"

"Seems you father wanted to really keep these items safe."

J straightened up, his eyes swept across the room. "Safe, huh?"

The room was ransacked, items strewn across the floor, vials lying broken on the ground, the tables and desks burnt as though someone attempted to incinerate the entire room. J rummaged around, searching for anything not damaged. Ariel did the same at a much slower pace. She noticed cylinders on the walls, at least ten of them.

"Who would have done this? What are we supposed to be searching for?" J asked, frantically moving about.

His movements slowed as he stopped, his eyes stagnant on the floor. He bent down grabbing one of the empty vials. "What was in here?" he wondered aloud.

Ariel narrowed her eyes, still searching. "I think Arcturus did this."

J perked up his ears drawn back. "My father...why? What makes you think that?"

She pointed at the cylinders. "Those are emergency disintegrators, they're programmed to detect a threat then ignite the area, or be set off as set by the installer. I'm guessing there was a threat and they went off or he did it on purpose to make it appear to be useless garbage in here."

J leaned back on the table behind him staring at the ceiling. *All of that work outside, to find this?* Seemed like a cruel joke, not something his father would have done. *There had to be something.* His thoughts continued as his eyes adjusted on the vial.

"What could have this stuff been anyway?"

Ariel walked up to him and slipped the vial out of his hand, examining it. "Maybe an enhancement serum, turn you into a super hero. I don't know. Could be any number of things."

Just then, he noticed something on one of the desks. Squinting, he approached and examined the object. "How did you know you could unlock this room?"

Ariel scrunched her mouth up. "I guessed. There was a symbol of a fork on the journal, reminded me of my name. Why?"

He pointed at the table, a screen faintly glowed under the scorched remains of the plastic above. Ariel's eyes widened as she neared, her name pulsed on the screen, an outline of a hand next to it. J pushed away the melted plastic revealing an untouched glass screen. Waving her over, he pointed at the screen. She placed her hand on the plate and a compartment rose up displaying six vials. Ariel stepped back as Arcturus appeared on the screen.

"Ariel, I'm glad you were able to lead J this far. I have provided six vials of nanotech revitalizing serum. All prototypes have been destroyed and TK made it illegal to use in attempt to keep the technology hidden for all but the council. V will know how to utilize it; you must have her administer the serum to you and J. I look forward to meeting you soon."

The display dissolved, J looked intently at Ariel. "Nanotech?"

She slipped the vials into one of the backpack compartments and rolled her hand in the air, her eyes following. "Think of them as teeny tiny machines that fix stuff. I'm not sure what we're supposed to do with them, but sounds like V will know. Should we find our way out of here?"

She held out the pack and J slipped it on, spinning toward the door. "Yeah. Hopefully it won't be so hot up there, but right now I might almost welcome it. I'm freezing."

Ariel rubbed her arms. The air temperature, while cold initially, seemed to be dropping as they spoke. She stepped out of the dome, J's eyes tracing the floor as he went. He crossed the threshold, running into Ariel who had frozen. He began to apologize then his eyes drifted past her. His jaw locked up, eyes opening wide. "You gotta be kidding me!"

CHAPTER TWO

J's eyes beheld an enormous ice wall growing more massive by the second. His neck twisted around surveying the room as their entrance was nearly covered. At the rate it was growing, it would envelope the elevator shaft in no time.

"Any ideas?"

J spun, seeing Ariel run back into the dome. He wasted no time doing the same. She was busy working on the only operational screen in the building.

J approached, his hands waist high, muscles tensing. "Tell me you've got something, 'cause it doesn't look good out there."

Ariel kept typing as quick as she could, ignoring him. Then, "Nothing good. The whole system's locked down. This must have been a failsafe to protect the vials, but it's been damaged somehow. I can't seem to override it."

J heard the system scream back in loud, angry tones and inferred that she wasn't getting anywhere with her computer magic. He ran back to the door, peeking outside. As he did so, he rubbed his shoulders, the thin long-sleeve shirt was doing little to keep him warm. *What he wouldn't give for one of those heated suits they wore in Sector 21 right about now.* His eyes danced around the cave searching for anything that may lead to their survival. They came to rest on the growing wall of ice, inching ever closer. He glanced over his shoulder, Ariel raised her fists over her head then plopped her palms onto her forehead. Her eyes stared at the screen for a moment before continuing her typing. J headed outside, maybe there was something around the other side of the dome they hadn't seen.

He walked around scanning every inch, his hands still rubbing opposite shoulders, his teeth chattered. Above them, sweltering heat and down here he was going to freeze to death. *What irony.* He made his first jaunt around, still searching the cave. It appeared to be merely a large room, the walls were all the same smooth, featureless rock extending upward a thousand feet. *No way to climb.* He ventured toward one of them, searching for something he might have missed. If Ariel couldn't shut down the system, it didn't seem to matter where he was. He ran his hand along the cold smooth stone, maybe he'd get lucky and find something. He continued around, nothing. Then he stopped, gazing at the ice wall inching toward the dome and Ariel. He threw his head back, staring at the ceiling, a sheet of cold black unforgiving rock stared back, mocking him.

J dropped his head, his gaze hit the floor and something strange caught his eye. The symbol of the medallion. He dropped down onto his knees, wasting no time, and attempted to pull it off his neck. His overzealous movements caused the string to catch his ear, burning the underside. He grimaced. His skin began to ripple like there were tiny insects flowing underneath, the ice wall had almost reached the door. He slammed the medallion into the slot, pressing in a second time. The floor underneath him rapidly slid away, his body falling ten feet onto cold hard steel. He pressed himself onto one knee shaking his head, then rubbed his face. His nose felt wet. Lifting his hand up, he saw that it was covered with blood. In the fall, he smashed his nose. He adjusted his jaw completing his stance.

"Ariel!"

J spun around, there was a ladder on the side of the wall. He was in a maintenance tunnel not unlike the first one he'd found in Sector 11 after the meteor shower. His body shook as a cold breeze hit him like a blizzard. There was no time to reminisce, he had to grab Ariel. He raced up the ladder, eyes focused on the ice wall. It was almost on top of the dome. He bolted toward the door, bouncing off the ice wall and into the structure, Ariel was still typing away. She adjusted her hair, flipping it over one ear, her bottom lip clenched under her top teeth. He grabbed her forearm, she jumped not knowing he was there.

"What are you doing? I was onto something!" Her eyes stern as the words exited her mouth. J knew there wasn't time to argue and didn't say a word, he just tugged. Against her at first, then she relented, taking a deep breath studying him in tow. He threw her out first, the ice only a couple of feet from the door. Ariel grunted as she herself smacked into it, sliding off and away from the door. J followed suit throwing himself out and almost landing on her. She tightened her eyes, judging him and began to open her mouth. He ignored it, yanking on her hand as he got to his feet, and pulled her along toward the open panel.

"In there. I think it's a way out."

J peered over Ariel's shoulder, the ice wall now over the dome. It appeared to be growing at an even more rapid rate. Ariel stared down into the hole, J glanced back at her as she turned to question him.

"No time, just go!"

Ariel slid down the ladder hitting the bottom. Finding a switch to close the hatch, J slid down, his feet thumping the ground, knees buckling.

Ariel was glancing in both directions. "Now where? I thought you said you found a way out."

J shrugged his shoulders. He thought he'd done well, the ice wall would have frozen them in the dome by now, but Ariel's look told him otherwise. "You pulled me out to this? I almost had something."

"Almost or you did? We'd be stuck in that dome thing if I hadn't dragged you out."

Ariel scrunched up her nose, turning away to focus on the endless tunnel. "You know these things stretch for miles on end, we could be walking for days before we find something."

J studied her, watching her shift her weight as she placed her thumb and forefinger on the bridge of her nose, letting out a slight groan.

J perked up remembering the device on her wrist. "What about the Datacle? Can't we call for help?"

Ariel dropped her arm studying it. She scrolled through menus, then tapped it off. Her eyes slid to J as she threw her hands in the air. "It's Jamming our signal just like up top, there's no way to communicate with the others."

He paused as he stared at Ariel's beautiful face, a cold breeze blew past him from behind and his skin tightened. He thought of the heat, the mountains, the bugs, the forest of trees and never-ending vines.

"It may be miles, but at least it's not mountainous. I think this'll be an easier walk...and a lot cooler."

Ariel raised an eyebrow. He did have a point, the trek to the site had been a difficult one. She glanced up at the ladder. "I suppose we should get walking." She glanced both ways, then back to him. "This was your plan. Which way?"

J examined both directions, had he a coin, he would have flipped it to choose. The breeze had come from behind him, much like when he first found his new world. Maybe they were close and, like the tunnel in Sector 11, it would flow out into the underbelly of Earth. He raised his arm pointing toward Ariel.

"This way."

He stepped off toward Ariel, hoping he was right. She watched him walk by, beginning her strides as he passed.

"Do you have a map on that thing?" J pointed to her wrist then took her hand. It was cold, much like his. The air was frigid, but not as cold as the cave they'd just exited. A smile rose on J's face as they walked. He was lost, but holding her hand steadied him and took him away from their troubles. After all, they weren't being chased or shot at... and that was a welcomed change of pace.

Ariel watched J from the corner of her eye. She too was enjoying the stroll, seeing his smile and feeling his hand intertwined with hers. She drew in a slow deep breath then released it the same way and turned her head to look down the tunnel, chin up. "Of course I have a map, but it's of the surface. We didn't exactly know these tunnels were down here, did we? Not until his royal highness, the boy wonder, discovered them." She winked to let him know she was teasing.

They walked in silence for a bit, simply enjoying the company. J thought the only thing that would have made it nicer would be to experience it outside on a warm fall day.

The lighting in the tunnel stretched the entire length, making it easy to see even though they were thousands of feet underground. The breeze seemed to come in waves, his body shivered as they passed, he felt Ariel join him in the ritual. J began to think about their charge. Stop Cyrellia, save Earth. Her very name gave him the creeps and he tried to push her out of his mind, but it was now there. She was just so cruel, he didn't understand why or what would make someone that way. J tried to think of something to get his mind off of her.

"What was your uncle like?"

Ariel shook herself out of her reverie, searched the ground as they continued. "He was a very good man, a military man. He was kind...*family*."

Family. Something he thought he'd had, but had found out the true nature of his situation. The facts told him one thing, his heart another. His Earth parents *were* family. They raised him, helped to shape him into the man he was, yet he was chasing after a father he'd never known. The drive for answers continually pulled him along. He wondered how Ariel felt, she was in a similar situation, an orphan.

"When did he go missing?"

"A few years ago, not long after they disbanded the military. I was at the Academy when he sent a message informing me of TK's decision. That decision came with strict guidelines which threatened my uncle's life. He said we'd meet again and I've held out hope, but I'm not sure these days. Like you, I hope to finally get answers. With TK still in power, that will never happen."

J nodded in agreement TK would have to fall and they would have to be the ones to do it. A breeze hit him again, he felt Ariel's arm shake as she pulled it away from him. His initial reaction was to grab it again, but stopped when he noticed what she was doing. She held up the Datacle. As he peeked over, Zane appeared.

"I thought we were being jammed?"

"We must've walked outside of the blackout zone."

She opened up the comm channel, Zane smiled back at her.

"Hey, kid. How'd your search go? Find the item?"

"Yeah, something V will want to see. You?"

"Yeah, but there seems to be a problem with one of them."

Ariel's eyebrows crunched together, her lips hardening. "Problem, what problem?"

"Best if you see it for yourself. Where you at?"

She let out a groan, throwing her head back. "We're stuck in a tunnel under Sector 16. Any chance you could shoot me a tunnel map?"

"Sorry, kid. We don't have those. Only the caretaker does."

J placed his hands on his face as they stopped walking, ran his fingers through his hair, the straps of the backpack hanging heavy on his shoulders.

"What about tracking us?"

Zane looked away, playing with something off screen.

"I could do that. Looks like you guys are a mile or two from a small town. If you keep heading that direction, I'll figure out some way to pick you up."

Ariel nodded, closing the call.

"I guess we're still walking," she quipped, taking his hand again.

J relaxed a bit more. Making contact with Zane helped him feel at ease. *At worst they may have to walk for miles, but being alone with Ariel made it worthwhile.* They continued on for a bit, Ariel asked about his childhood. Baseball was interlaced with nearly everything he remembered. Ariel explained how it was run on Atlantis, the rules had changed to speed up the game and make it more exciting for the fans, other sports came and went, but baseball lasted the test of time. J reminisced about farming and working on the harvesters, not knowing how technologically advanced they were. Ariel recounted a few academy stories which ended with serious laughter. Though her time there had been stressful, she couldn't help but think of how her life would be different if she hadn't gone. After all, that was where she first met Zane. They'd stopped a few times for water and a snack. J didn't mind the rations, they were flavored well and the texture was like his mom's fruit cake. Ariel's wrist buzzed indicating a call.

"Hey kid. I was able to get a hold of J's friend, Will, and he sent me the schematics. Looks like there are access panels every five miles or so underneath the tunnels. Continue walking another mile and we'll be able pick you up."

Ariel acknowledged the good news. J smiled. *A mile on a flat surface? Easy peasy.* They sauntered on, knowing that they'd soon be able to leave the cold tunnel and gain the coveted warmth of new, unsoiled clothes. Ariel pulled up the distance counter on her Datacle, marked about a mile, and began the countdown to their pickup location. Arriving at the designated point, Ariel plopped down, resting her back on the wall. J followed suit, removing the pack and setting it aside.

"Can I see the journal?"

J dug into the pack, rummaged around, finding everything else before presenting the book. He handed it to Ariel, she opened the cover and held it toward J to unlock. Access granted, she flipped through, searching for something.

"What are you looking for?"

Ariel continued shuffling though menus. "I was hoping to find something new, something important that we might have missed. There are so many items, discoveries, theories, breakthroughs, you name it in here, it's pretty overwhelming. Your father seemed to have an endless amount of ideas."

J watched over her shoulder as she flipped through the project names, one caught his attention.

"What's that? Project Cybermantis?"

Ariel tapped on it bringing up an overview sheet.

- Project Cybermantis
- Company designer - Cybertronics
- Chief engineer – Dr. Keel
- Oversight – Commander Zebulon

Ariel's eyes focused on the bottom line, her lips parted. The Datacle came alive and Zane appeared once again as they watched the screen.

"I think you guys are in position. It's a bit spotty to locate, I'm getting a lot of interference and the clouds are pretty thick here. I've had to switch to infrared, but I think I've got it. I'm going to open up the hatch now. "

J glanced at Ariel, his forehead wrinkled his chin tucked into his neck. "What does all of that mean?"

She shut the book, handing it to him. J grabbed the backpack and turned to put the journal inside.

"It means—"

The floor shook, dropped down and slid out from under their feet. J grasped for the edge, managing to get a hold of it with one hand, the other strangling the backpack strap. The journal plummeted out of sight into the clouds below. Ariel had managed to grasp the tiny ledge near the wall and was hanging on for dear life. J disobeyed the cardinal rule when dealing with heights, he looked down. The dark clouds swirled while the cold wind penetrating his clothes whistled in his ears. Zane continued on the comm, muffled from the austere environment.

"I see you, this is going to be tricky. Let go when I tell you."

J didn't like the sound of that. *Let go? With nothing but clouds underneath him?* His gaze turned to Ariel, her hair whipping around her face, then he glanced down to see that lights glowed behind the soft layer of clouds. They grew brighter as a craft appeared, hovering up toward them.

"Okay. I've got you. Let go."

Ariel glanced down and let go. The craft had maneuvered to within a few feet and she hit the top surface planting a knee, hand down to stabilize herself. A gust of wind hit the craft shaking it violently, she steadied herself with both hands on the roof. Spotting J still dangling from the bottom of the

21

Earth, she yelled, "Let go J! I'll catch you."

The craft, which had descended during the gust, approached J again. He locked onto Ariel who came to her feet, arms up awaiting his actions. He continued his focused attention on Ariel, his fingers released and he hit the surface. The craft rocked again, knocking them off their feet. They slid away from the center. J scrambled for her hand, his fingers stretching to connect. The craft tilted further and Ariel flew off the edge, but J managed to grab her at the last second. He scrambled for a surface to hold onto, but the craft was so smooth his hand couldn't find purchase. He slid off the craft after Ariel, both plummeting into the cloudy abyss. His stomach leapt into his throat as the sensation of falling overtook him. J glanced up and saw the craft disappear above.

CHAPTER THREE

The wind rushed around their bodies. Ariel grasped for his other hand, J struggled to do the same. He pulled her tight to a hug. Had he been able to fly, he would've felt like Superman holding Lois Lane as he flew her through the air. He gazed into her eyes. If this was the end, at least he got to spend his last moments with her. Suddenly, J's ears picked up one of his new found favorite sounds. His head whipped around, searching for the source. The craft appeared beside them, engines humming, cargo door open. It slid toward them, sucking them up like a salmon feeding, their weightless bodies floating in the center of the bay. Gravity returned and they slapped the deck hard. J lay there a moment groaning while Ariel sat up rubbing her head. The cockpit door opened and their eyes drifted up toward Zane who stood with one hand on the door jam.

"You guys okay?"

J continued to wallow on the ground, attempted to roll over onto his side, the backpack impeding the process.

"The book!" J screamed out.

Ariel massaged her face while Zane took a few steps toward them.

"What do you mean "the book"?"

Ariel, sitting legs bent, torso upright, dropped her hands onto her knees. "We lost the journal when the floor unexpectedly opened up and dropped us into space." She threw her head back, eyes fixed on the ceiling.

J slipped out of the backpack, straightening himself up with one arm. Zane took a few steps toward them.

"So, other than the book, how are you guys doing?"

They looked at each other then focused back on Zane. Ariel took a deep, calming breath, the kind she was prone to take when she was irritated with someone but didn't want to focus on the negative, then replied, "Fine. We're fine. We still have the list, right?"

Zane nodded, extending a hand to her. She ignored it and leapt up without assistance. Zane frowned, turned to help J.

"You still have the item?"

J bent down, both hands digging into the back, and pulled out the vials. He handed them to Zane.

"Nanotech, huh? Thought this stuff was outlawed. I guess Arcturus kept some for you, J."

"What do we do with it?"

Zane spun one of the vials in his hand, the liquid swished around.

"You inject it. I'm sure V can do it, she can do just about anything. There's a sequence to be followed and they have to be activated and adjusted to your body or they'll simply be flushed out."

"How do you know so much about this?"

Zane quirked his lips in a secret smile. The ship rocked causing them to brace themselves on the craft's walls. "Better get out of here, the air's very turbulent. I'll get us to V and show you our newest problem." He handed the vials back to J and stumbled into the cockpit as the ship rattled again, Ariel followed before realizing the craft was actually extremely small. The cockpit only had two seats, so she turned around, walked back to the cargo bay and sat down next to J. He'd already placed the vials securely back into his pack and was resting his chin on his hands thinking of the book. They'd gone through so much to find it, to protect it, now it was gone.

Ariel placed a hand on his back. "We still have the list. That should be enough to get us to Acadia."

His mind shifted. *Acadia. An entire planet far from Earth. He'd seen it in a dream, from space, but what was it really like?* His mind wandered, the prospect of travelling to uncharted space was enough to get it off the book. J sat there, deep in thought, while Ariel absently slid her hand comfortingly around his back. Neither spoke as the ship departed the atmosphere toward Atlantis.

Zane piloted the craft onto Atlantis near V's research facility. J recognized the landing pad and was becoming more proficient at locating himself on the inverted planet. The pads had distinct markings making each one unique. He hadn't noticed them initially, but recently little details had begun standing out to him. Once inside, V reached for each of them, gathering them in a hug, holding Zane's a little longer than the other two.

J wasted no time producing the vials. "This is what we found. Ariel and Zane both thought you'd know what to do with them."

She took a vial, held it up to the light, examining the translucent liquid.

"Nanotech."

Her eyes flicked over toward Zane. "You already have this, don't you?" Her one eyebrow raised, a slight smirk rested on her lips. She knew the answer but was drawing it out for J.

Zane sent a pursed smiled back at her. J watched the exchange, attempting to figure out what she meant. Zane didn't utter a word. "How many do you have?"

J showed her the other five resting in the bag, V peered down at them.

"I know I'll be injecting you, J, and I'm sure you'll want to use one on Ariel, but who would you like to have the others?"

J was still puzzled. *What was it going to do to him? Who else would need such an item and why?*

"Inject? Choose? I don't even know what it does!"

V pointed at Zane. "The big galoot was lucky enough to get an injection from Arcturus before this whole thing started. Didn't you ever wonder why he never seems to age? Why TK have lived so long?"

J really hadn't given it much thought, the actual years had been something he hadn't paid attention to. But she was right. In his dreams, TK always looked the same, yet years had passed in between some of the scenes. Cyrellia never seemed to age a day and Zane still looked the same as the day he and Dillon helped his father launch him to Earth. His eyes brightened as he thought more about it.

"Is it like the Fountain of Youth?"

Ariel snickered, but the smile remained on her face.

V adopted that look she got when she was in explanation mode, her eyes bright and eager to impart knowledge. "Inside this vial are nanotech bots, tiny robots that repair tissue. They, in essence, *are* the Fountain of Youth, as you called it. After developing the science behind them, TK locked it away. Any attempt to replicate them was met with a death sentence. I venture to guess that Arcturus planned to have just enough for a select few, namely you."

J ran through it all in his head. *His father did mention having he and Ariel take it. It was a no brainer to give one to V. Zane seemed to already be infected. No, not infected. Inoculated? Injected? Max...well it remained to be seen if he should have one. He had proven himself useful on more than one occasion, but J still felt uneasy around him. Grant had also proven to be a valuable part of the crew, but J had to be careful, the vials were like gold, actually better than gold, more rare.*

He eyed V. "Okay, so how do we do this?"

V looked back at him still smiling. "Simple, I program them to recognize your DNA then after putting you under, I'll inject it while simultaneously running tests to ensure they're operating normally."

J didn't have any more questions, he trusted V, she'd saved all of them more than once. "Alright, for now, if Zane's already injected, let's just use three of the vials. One for me, one for Ariel, and one for you."

V, flustered, replied, "I'm not certain if I need one. I'm never really in the thick of things like you three are and I already look much younger than my age—"

"If J is offering it, you're taking it. No arguments. I...we can't afford to lose you." His fists and jaw clenched, Zane's body language spoke volumes.

V studied Zane a moment. "This treatment can't fix everything. Yes, it keeps a person young on a cellular level, but the technology is only strong enough to begin repairing cells damaged in battle. It may prolong the amount of time an injured person has before treatment is necessary, but severe trauma still requires a gifted surgeon... Something you know a little bit about." She waited for him to return the verbal spar, her eyes hard, body rigid. She had no problem injecting herself with the nanotech. What she did have a problem with was an overbearing, overlarge, overprotective man thinking he could tell her what to do because of her size.

Zane held her gaze a moment before lowering his head, shoulders slumped. She nodded sharply, her point made, and quickly ushered J into the operating room, which at this point felt like his bedroom. He'd spent more than enough time being patched up by V. Still, it seemed like a lifetime ago when she had somehow replaced his broken back. Thoughts of dressing in front of the girls entered his mind and he involuntarily blushed. If she noticed, she didn't say anything. His mind shifted to the scene in the hall. He didn't understand what that had all been about, but chalked it up to just one more thing pertaining to life on Atlantis that he'd have to figure out. V laid him on the table and a small tray floated out of the wall and hovered next to him. On the tray sat a large needle and syringe. J was glad he was going to be under during the procedure, the needle didn't look very comfortable. V grasped an electronic pad in one hand, typed with the other then set the pad down and placed a mask over his mouth and nose.

"When you wake up, you'll be immortal. Well, sort of." She winked at him as she pressed a button on the pad, his eyes rolled under his eyelids.

He found himself in familiar surroundings, his father's

body stood, surveying space and the Earth beyond through a large glass window. A small ship zipped from overhead toward the engineered planet, its glowing engines dancing off the glass.

"Sir, Cyrellia has arrived. She would like to see the prototype."

His gaze focused on the ship shrinking out of view, his arms wrapped around his back one clasping the other at the wrist.

"Very well, I'll meet her in test cell 14. Ready the equipment."

His assistant nodded then took off toward the door. The room was small, twenty by twenty, the large window covered an entire wall while the other three housed various sleek shapes contoured in plastic and metal. In one corner housed a desk with a large screen covering its surface. A small chair rested underneath, dark fabric stretched over a metal frame. The Earth, like a giant puzzle, floated in the distance. The departing ship disappeared, nothing left. He turned to exit, walking out into a hallway, and was met by a man J recognized.

"Zebulon, I'm glad you made it back from your last trip. How's the prototype? Cyrellia is very anxious to see it in action."

Zebulon's head stood tall, his broad shoulders jutting out of his torso, uniform unblemished. He clenched his jaw. "She's always anxious to see the destructive power of our systems. Today she'll be disappointed to find no test subjects. We've found some old battle armor to demonstrate on, that should suffice."

J turned to walk down the hallway, Zebulon followed keeping pace with his stride.

"Any word on funding? Our budget is getting tight. I've been informed that more money and resources have been redirected to the Exodus, something about adding extra resource containers."

"That's true, nothing we can do about that. The council wanted more stores of valuable goods from Earth instead of building equipment needed for the construction on Acadia. We'll have enough, but their greed and fear of losing Earth's resources is great. Today's demonstration will ensure that you have your funding... provided it goes as planned."

They entered an elevator, exiting a few hundred floors lower. After multiple security checks they walked into a room the size of a football stadium labeled "Test Cell 14". Inside stood a giant, eight story tall, four-legged robot. Steam rolled off of its legs. Large cables were affixed to the body in multiple places, including one on each leg. The top of the body held multiple cannons and a protrusion which looked like a cockpit. Cyrellia stood underneath, running her hand along the device's leg.

She turned, spotting them. "Ah, Arcturus. Zebulon. I understand this is a fully operational prototype."

J extended an opened hand from Zebulon to Cyrellia. She continued sauntering toward them, her long dress dragging behind her, a devious grin on her face.

"Ma'am, if you'll follow us to the observation deck, we'll demonstrate its capabilities with one exception, the LFEX100B cannon."

Her eyebrow raised as the smile slipped away, her eyelids became heavy, her head bowed toward them. "I was informed that it was *fully* operational."

Zebulon maintained his composure, his eyes locked onto hers. "It is. Due to the power of the cannon, we can't test it in this facility. If you'd like, we can pre-position it outside and execute the shoot there."

"You're saying that these armor enhanced walls won't be able to contain it as they do the other weapons?"

Zebulon nodded, his eyes still fixed on hers, his posture strong.

She stopped a few feet in front of them. "You will fire it in here or the funding will be revoked."

Zebulon turned to J. He nodded in agreement. Zebulon chewed his cheek, his eyes assessing the machine.

"Sir, if you could please escort our guest to the observation bunker, I'll ready the area for the demonstration."

He spun on his heel, marching off, shouting orders to the troops and test scientists on the floor. A flurry of activity started as men removed the umbilical cords, evacuating the floor. Two pilots rode an elevator from the belly of the ship into its body. Cyrellia's face remained unyielding. J turned toward the observation deck extending an elbow, she slipped her hand onto it as they began walking.

"We've invested a pretty penny into this project, I'd better see some fireworks."

J glanced over reading her face. Its tight features stared straight ahead, her body floating as they approached the bunker. The door hissed open.

"You'll get what you paid for Cyrellia, the entire council will."

Cyrellia's eyes darted under heavy lids, out of the corner of her eye she glared at him as they entered the lift. After a brief elevator ride, they emerged onto a balcony producing a bird's eye view. They stood hidden behind armored glass resistant to nearly all ordinance available.

Cyrellia approached, placing her hands on the window sill as she scrutinized the machine. "And this...Cybermantis will be capable of defending Tremessos?"

One of J's eyebrows lifted. "Is that what the council has chosen for the name of the capital of Acadia?"

Cyrellia smirked, still surveying the project, the rest of her a statue. "They will soon enough."

J spun back to the machine, footsteps echoed behind them as the systems in the room continued a low hum.

"Sir, Ma'am, the Mantis is ready for the demonstration. With your approval we will begin with the new AN/23AAM anti-armor missiles."

J's head turned to the ice sculpture standing next to him.

"What's the target?"

"Ma'am, it's an M6A8 hover tank, factory built, all systems operational."

She nodded. Zebulon approached the viewing area, ensuring the target was positioned.

"Ready thunderbolt missiles. Fire when ready."

An acknowledgement came over the speaker in the room, then a muffled hissing sound, followed by a plume of smoke from the fuselage of the Mantis. The tank, a few football fields away, nearly disintegrated. Parts flew into the air, shrapnel bounced off of the walls and floor. J glanced over at Cyrellia. Her nose crinkled, lips broke apart as a crooked smile grew in between them. Her eyes danced glossy, flickering in the light of the explosion.

"If you are ready, anti-personnel cluster bombs up for demo," announced Zebulon.

Cyrellia raised a hand, her long oversized sleeves hovered around her wrists, her fingers extended indicating for him to stop. Zebulon remained quiet awaiting a command. She exposed a Datacle on her right wrist, tapping commands into it. The two men watched silently. Two doors opened off to the side in the test area and twenty people were ushered through, the door closing behind them. The people scratched and clawed at the door attempting to be let out. Their silent screams could be seen, but the glass muffled all but the most intense noise.

"Those are your targets," Cyrellia declared, her head turning to J.

"You can't do that, this is a weapons demonstration not a mass murder scene."

Zebulon remained silent behind the two. J felt his heart pumping overtime, his chest squeezed, his fists clenched. Cyrellia stared back, the same smile locked onto her face as if it were a wax figure.

"If you want your funding you will utilize the targets I have provided you."

"I will not allow murder during a demonstration, we are better than that here."

Cyrellia stood tall, her whole body bent toward J, her nose twitched as her face tightened. "If you want your funding, you will attack these convicted criminals, these enemies of the state. They are condemned men and women already. If you don't initiate the test then I will."

She pointed a hand toward Zebulon her head snapping after it. "Commander Zebulon, commence the test."

Zebulon scrutinized J, awaiting direction. He felt his jaw clench, his head bob up and down.

"Fire angry hornet swarm, lock onto all available targets."

J kept his eyes fixed on Zebulon, the muffled sound of ordinance exploding reverberated off the glass. Zebulon returned the stare, nodding slowly. Silence filled the air. He twisted his body to their guest, her eyes large, dancing about, her mouth continuing the devious grin. She turned toward J, her eyes locking onto his, her dress flowing over from her aggressive body motion.

"I'm satisfied with the project. You, however, had better step in line. Once we land in Acadia, things will be different. If you desire to remain on the council you will follow my lead."

She sashayed out, her dress flowing as if in a gentle breeze on a warm summer's day, then disappeared into the elevator.

"This is the only prototype?" J asked, actively avoiding the carnage below.

"No. The request was for five. All have been completed and there are another ninety-five on order. They are in the queue, ready to be started."

J stepped toward Zebulon, his motions slow as he held his chin, thinking. "Suspend the others indefinitely and re-task the workers on the new project. You'll need to ensure that this doesn't reach the council. If there comes a time where you are compromised, these are your orders." J handed Zebulon a disk as he marched by. "Take care of that niece for me."

CHAPTER FOUR

What project was he talking about? J awoke with a start and sat up to find Ariel sitting across from him on a table similar to his, swinging her legs, her palms planted on the edge, fingers wrapped around gripping the table.

"How's it feel to be a Highlander?"

J reached up, rubbing his face with both hands. His body sagged and his head felt groggy like he didn't get all the rest he needed. He stretched his arms out. "Highlander?" he asked through a yawn.

Ariel laughed then yawned herself. "Stop it, no yawning. Someday I'll give you a history lesson on Earth pop culture, and then you'll look back and find the humor in our conversations."

J smiled back. She always said that, but he was okay with not understanding. His ignorance produced the sweetest laughter from her and that was worth the embarrassment of being clueless.

"You sleep well?"

J scratched his head hopping off the table. "Not really, more weird dreams... or memories I suppose."

Ariel stopped kicking her legs and hopped down. "What about this time?"

"A weapons test with Cyrellia, it was pretty horrific. I'd actually like to get my mind on something else. Did the procedure go as planned?"

"You're alive, right?"

J scowled, drug out the word, "yes."

"Then it did. Had V messed something up, the nanobots would've attacked your body, shutting down your heart and killing you."

J's head pushed back, his eyes widened as he approached her. "Oh." He took a step past then stopped. "Zane said they'd just be flushed out of our systems if something went wrong. Why didn't you tell me this before?!"

Ariel shrugged her shoulders, pushing him out the door. "Didn't want to scare you. Besides, V's an excellent doctor, she wouldn't have messed it up."

V *was* a great doctor. She'd never made a mistake on his watch. He only hoped that would stay true, something told him there was going to be trouble ahead, her expertise needed once again.

They walked into a common room filled with a pool table, multiple couches and other electronic games that J didn't recognize. Zane was catching up on sleep while Grant fiddled with one of the machines. Max played a game of pool by himself and Tara was reading one of the multiple screens along the far wall.

"So, didn't Zane have something to show us?" J asked as they entered the room.

"Hey, J. Nice to see you're done with the procedure, looks like you're no worse for wear."

Max sauntered toward J setting the cue on the rack, his face sported a big grin as he eyed Ariel who crossed her arms. He pushed his neck sideways, tilted his head down, tightening one eye.

"You guys up for a challenge?"

J studied Max, Ariel huffed out a breath and turned her eyes to the ceiling.

"How about you and Ariel play Tara and me in a little game of Crud?"

"Crud?"

Ariel's head snapped down, stepping in front of J. "We're not going to play your silly pilot's game. Besides, we have work to do, we've only picked up half the list. We still need to finish collecting the items so we can get to Acadia."

She spun around and strode toward Zane, Max followed her.

"You're just scared you're going to lose to me and an android... a synthetic."

Ariel snapped her head around, fire burned in her eyes.

"Okay, fine. You wanna play? Let's play."

Max smiled, collecting his teammate. Ariel stomped over to J, her shoulders pinned to her ears.

"What are we playing?"

Ariel watched Max as he engaged with Tara then her attention snapped to J. "Crud. You play pool, right?"

"Yes."

"It's nothing like that."

J's face scrambled as he attempted to figure out what she meant.

"Main rules are simple in our case. Team of two vs. two, each team plays one player at a time. You're either the blocker or the shooter then you alternate. For you, just remember "blocker, shooter, out". The game is played with two balls, the cue ball and striped ball. The shooter uses the cue ball to try and sink the striped ball by throwing it on the surface of the table. The object of the game is to sink the striped ball when you're the shooter and stop the shooter from sinking it when you're on defense. That's the basics. There're more rules I'll teach you along the way, got it?"

"But—"

"You guys ready to go down in flames?"

Max approached the table typing commands into a small control panel on the long side of the table. Rails rose up blocking the side pockets and a hologram of a score sheet glowed above.

"What are those for?" J raised his hands, staring at Ariel.

"Oh, you only use the four corner pockets. When you shoot, you have to be on one of the short ends of the table. Be ready, this gets physical. I'll go first."

Ariel pushed past him and approached the table. She leaned past the edge and over the table on the short side opposite side from Max, firmly planted her hands on the felt surface and winked at Max. "You shoot first?"

"Naw, we'll flip on it, make it fair."

He pulled a silver coin from a pocket and swaggered over to Ariel and J. He held out the hand with the round metal object planted in his palm, the TK symbol glimmered back. "This side's heads." He flipped the coin over displaying a crouching tiger, the words 1st Squadron and Tigers wrapped around the rim of the round surface. "This side's tails. J, you wanna do the honors? Call it in the air."

Max placed the object on his thumb flicking it into the air, the saucer flipped end over end. Tara had made her way to the table and stood at the far end watching the shiny coin flip.

"Tails."

The four of them watched the coin bounce and dance on the table, spinning momentarily before coming to a rest. J leaned in examining the coin, the ugly TK logo stared back at him.

"Ha, we'll shoot first. Tara it's all you."

Max stepped aside while Tara grabbed the cue ball, adjusting her hand for the opening shot. Ariel placed herself on the other end, one arm hovering over the table like a wall between her and Tara. She placed the striped ball behind her arm, her tight eyes flipped toward Tara.

"On your time princess."

Tara tilted her head like a dog questioning its master, Max stood just behind her his arms crossed. Tara's eyes searched the far end for the ball, Ariel's arm was doing a good job of hiding it.

"Stop calculating and just throw the ball. Plenty of time for that later," Max instructed.

Tara zipped the ball toward Ariel, she raised her arm, bolting toward Tara. Tara's roll missed, bouncing off of the far end and zipping back toward her. Ariel slid around the corner bumping a hip into Tara, sending her off the side of the table. Tara blinked up at Max who was smiling.

"Get the ball! Turn's not over, that was legal."

Legal? Full contact? His eyes found Max who began shouting at Tara to shoot again. The ball came toward the end; Ariel shifted her weight, boxing out Tara. Tara attempted to push past her then rolled over her back to the other side, her arm scrambling for the loose ball. Ariel thrust her body backward knocking Tara to the floor. Max yelled with more intensity than J had ever seen at a non-sports game. Tara gained her feet and ran to the far end of the table, Ariel slid in front of her blocking her approach. The cue ball stopped its roll. Tara finally slipped by Ariel, grabbed it and tossed it toward the striped ball. She nicked the side causing the striped ball to spin, the cue ball floated to the far end.

"Dead ball, she loses a life!" Ariel called out as the ball stopped spinning.

J gawked at the table, his eyes wide and incredulous. *What just happened?* He turned to Max who was consulting Tara about her poor performance. His eyes snapped back to Ariel. "What was that?"

Ariel ran over to J, excitement and challenge in her eyes.

"The cue ball stopped before she got it. Also, if the striped ball doesn't move more than six inches when you hit it, then you die."

"Die?"

"Lose a life, a point. You start with three, now Tara's down one."

Ariel hopped back over to the table, sinking the ball instantly. Max and Tara turned to look, Max screamed, realizing what had just happened. He sprinted over, grabbing the ball.

"Quick! Get in there, you're on defense."

J hesitated a moment as Ariel flicked her head and eyes toward the table. J bolted over, but it was too late. Max already tossed the cue ball hitting the target ball. He began to gloat as he stepped around the table. Ariel yelled at J to shoot, it was his turn. J grabbed the cue ball and slung it toward his target. As the two balls clashed, Max's ears perked up realizing Tara hadn't jumped in. He shoved her over now as the attacker. Ariel intercepted her blocking her approach with her body. Tara pushed and shoved Ariel causing her to hop on one foot coming down strong like a rock. She released the tension, slipping behind. Tara's arm strained to reach the ball pushing it toward the striped target. She hit her mark, the balls split apart, zipping around. Ariel obtained the cue ball instantly as Max came flying in with a hip check. Ariel dropped the ball, her body tossed to the ground. She scrambled to her feet and attacked again, the two tangling like rams in a battle for supremacy.

"You always did like to play rough," Max said through a grunt.

Ariel dipped a shoulder. Acquiring the ball, she threw it at the other sinking it then spun around the side of the table taking a life away from Max on the counter. Hands on her hips, she gloated, "Down one."

Max grabbed the ball as J jumped in, his turn to block. Max drilled him, his body flying sideways. He caught himself in time to see Max sink the ball.

"And the chosen one loses a life," Max cheered as he removed a life on the score board. Tara slipped in to become the defender, her feet shoulder-width apart like a linebacker awaiting the play.

The game continued, the two teams pushing back and forth. A few more obscure game infractions were called by Max or Ariel. J was doing his best to learn all of the rules, but several of them seemed downright silly. *No pointing with your finger, only with your elbow? Who thinks up these things?* Tara was a formidable foe and difficult to get a clean shot on while Max was easier to deal with as they played on. The shouting between the two teams became more intense, even J found himself adding a few choice phrases. After some time passed, it came down to Max and Ariel, J and Tara had lost all three of their lives and the two remaining only had one each. The next pocketed ball would determine the winner. By now, the commotion had stirred Zane who was stretching and scratching the back of his head as he crept up behind J.

"Crud, eh?"

J turned his head around as Zane yawned.

"Yep, quite an intense game. I think I'm going to have some bruises tomorrow."

J rubbed his thigh as he moved his eyes back to the game, Zane smiled down at him.

"So, what's the score?"

"Next point wins, they each have one life left."

Ariel eyed Max as he walked around the table, she had just knocked a life off of Max and it was now his turn to shoot.

"Why don't you just walk away? You're good at that." Ariel's eye twitched as she taunted him.

Max glared at her as he strutted around the table toward the cue ball. "Don't give me that, you know why I left."

Her eyes fixated on Max, her arms flexed as she stabilized herself on the rails of the table.

"Because you swore an oath to a monstrous organization. You were scared, scared to go against your parents, your destiny. That's no excuse, not good enough. You broke your promise to me."

Ariel's eyes burned through him as he approached. His walk slowed, eyes drifting to the ground. He brought them back to Ariel as he rounded the final corner.

"There's more to it, I—"

"Just shoot." Ariel turned, focused on the cue ball, the striped ball at the far end. Her lips quivered, her body tight.

"Ariel, I—"

"Shoot!"

She steadied herself as Max grabbed the ball, threw her body into him. He released the shot, missing the target. Scrambling to the ball, gaining possession, he searched for an open shot. Ariel mirrored his movements, following him around the table, her jaw clenched. He slipped the cue ball out of his hand, hit the target ball. Ariel rolled off his back, digging in an extra hard elbow. Max winced in pain causing him to stumble, she grabbed the ball shooting it at the striped target ball. The throw hit its mark, propelling the game ball into the corner pocket. Ariel sneered at Max and stormed out of the room. J watched on, not knowing if he should follow or let her go. He rolled his tongue on his teeth as he glanced over at Max. Max flopped down on the sofa and began to stare at the ceiling.

Zane grabbed J's shoulder. "You, go talk to Ariel, I'll get Max. Still need to show you our issue."

J aimed one more searching look at Max then stepped out of the room, his thoughts jumbled in his head, his heart aching. *Did she still want to be with Max?* He felt the blood flowing through his body as he searched for Ariel, she was walking down the hall outside of the game room. He ran to catch up, but she disappeared into another room tapping the controls to shut the door. He was too slow as the sheet of metal hissed to a close.

He knocked on the cold steel. "Ariel, are you alright?"

No answer. He tried again with the same result. He spun around to face the hall, leaned his back against the door and tapped again, still no reaction.

"Zane wants to show us the issue he mentioned."

The door opened and J fell back onto the floor, catching himself just enough to not hit his head. He gazed up. Ariel stood over him with a small laugh, rubbed some moisture out of an eye, extending a hand toward J.

"Klutz."

She smiled, her face still red. J took her hand and hopped to his feet. He wrapped his arms around her, she returned the gesture.

"I'm not sure what that was all about, but I'm sorry for whatever is bothering you." J said, holding her tightly.

J felt her inhale and exhale, she intensified her grip. "You said Zane has an issue?"

He released her.

"Well, he actually said *we* had an issue."

Ariel tilted her head to the side. "I guess we should go see what the problem is then."

They left the room and headed back finding Zane still in the game room with the others. Max seemed his usual self, while Grant had Tara's back plate open with several wires running from it to a device he held. Zane spotted them as they walked in.

"You guys ready for the bad news?" He didn't wait for a response as he stepped toward the door. "Follow me."

He walked past them and they all followed. Ariel did her best to ignore Max while he did the same. Tara and Grant fell in last, he worked quickly to close up her back panel while they walked. Zane led them into a massive storage room. Front and center sat a large two story device resembling four cylinders laying on their side, all fused together by welded rectangular plates. The parts were sleek and the metal spotless with a white matte painted finish. J walked up and touched it, the shapes of the panels reminded him of the harvester from his Earthly home. His gaze swept back to Zane.

"So what's the issue?"

Zane approached him, pressing a few panels on the side. They popped open exposing the interior of the object. Frayed wires hung out of a hole where there should have been a panel, creating the visual of a rat's nest.

"There's supposed to be a controller here for the warp drive. Without it, we can't use it."

"Is this what you went to find?" Ariel asked.

"Yep, the first were the suits I believe you two are already familiar with, this was the second one. Based on the list we have, I'm assuming the controller should have been in it. Looks like someone or something ripped it out."

"Did you find anything else with it?"

"Just this."

He flipped a coin over to Ariel and she caught it, displaying it in an open palm. J peeked over her shoulder. The coin had a relief of a seashell on one side, she flipped it over and displayed a TK emblem on the other. Words wrapped around the contour of the top, "one credit".

"What's this?" Ariel asked. "I've never seen this currency before."

"Neither have I, any ideas?"

Grant waddled over, Tara behind him. "Let me see."

Ariel handed the coin to Grant who in turn passed it to Tara. She lifted it up to the light. "It's a Nauru water island coin, Sector 17."

"Nauru?" J's questioning eyes landed on Ariel.

She shrugged her shoulders pointing to Tara. Everyone focused on Tara, she glanced around at each of them.

"Nauru is a small island in Sector 17 utilized for water acquisition. It doubles as a beach resort retreat for prominent Atlantean families. This coin is the currency used exclusively on the island."

Ariel smirked at J. "Guess we need to pack our swimsuits."

CHAPTER FIVE

The lights on the ship's control panel reflected in Max's eyes, he twisted his head, addressing Ariel. "They're requesting a landing code?"

She flicked her eyes to Grant. "Can you help with that?"

He grunted and bent over his machine, fingers flying over the keys typing in code. His eyes never leaving the screen, tongue slightly exposed as he chewed on it.

"Any luck with those codes?" She already knew the answer wouldn't come from Grant, but tried to get him engaged anyway.

A moment later, the request on the screen switched from "pending" to "approved". Max continued his landing pattern and set down the Omorfiá onto the landing pad. J found it unique that they didn't use a hangar underground or in the side of the plate like every other sector. He was also taken back by the view he'd seen while they were inbound; water as far as he could see, only a single island breaking up the sparkling dark blue. He'd never seen a real ocean before. As the ramp opened, two men clad in blue flowing robes greeted them.

"Welcome to Zion," they said in unison.

"I am Michael and this is Samuel. We will be your guides for the duration of your visit. Do you have any luggage you would like us to transport to your rooms?"

J's big eyes whipped to Ariel for direction, hers sported the same bewildered expression. Zane, V, and Grant just stood there staring at the two men. Tara remained in the back of the group, her eyes assessing the situation, ready in case she was needed. One of the men stepped forward followed by the second.

"If you do not have any luggage, we would be glad to show you to your rooms."

J fiddled with his hands then whispered to Ariel, "Shouldn't we be searching for the missing piece?"

She scrunched up one of her cheeks then addressed their welcoming party.

"Thank you for your kindness, but we have business with your..." Her eyes rolled around searching the skies for the correct word. "...employer."

The two men shared a look, then together responded, "*Lady* Capella?"

"We must see you to your rooms first," said Michael.

"Then we will have to set up an audience with her," Samuel finished.

Ariel stepped out of the craft, waving for the others to follow her. "Then by all means, show us to our rooms and set up an audience with Lady Capella."

The two men bowed, extending their robes out, then turned and began walking toward the large metal structure J had noticed on their arrival; it was peculiar to him in that it resembled a partially opened clamshell. Upon entering, they were relieved of their weapons as the resort was a weapons free zone. The two ushered them into a small transport vehicle which hovered over a metal track embedded in the ground. Light glistened through the shell, the entire opening made of stained glass, most of the panels were blues and reds with yellows and purples interspersed between. At both ends, stained glass doors adorned in the same pattern covered the tracks. J, Ariel, V and Zane had climbed into the front transport while Max, Tara and Grant boarded the second. Michael took a seat next to Ariel.

"How long do we have the pleasure of your company?"

Ariel rolled her teeth over her bottom lip. "A day or so, depends on how our audience with Capella goes."

"Is there something I can help you with so as not to bother the fair Lady Capella?"

Ariel sat up straight, surveying the path ahead, the doors opening as the transport approached. "I'm sorry, but our business is with Capella."

Michael made a few hand motions in the air, the cart accelerated. The warm sun rays glistened off of the ocean as waves crashed onto the beach only a few feet from the track. J smiled, taking in the colorful blues and greens the sea made as they rode along, the sandy beach almost as white as snow. A few dolphins jumped out of the water in the distance and colorful birds fluttered above. The journey continued for a few more minutes until a series of thatch roofed buildings came into view. As they neared, the transports slowed and came to a stop. Michael climbed out, waving for the others to follow. The path was built of smooth stone and led toward several small buildings.

"This is your room Sir and Miss." He eyed Zane and V, pointed to the open entranceway of the first building. V peeked up at Zane, her face red. Zane glanced down then toward Michael.

"I'm sorry, but do you have any other accommodations,

just..."

"You are Zane, judging by the entrance scan, and are you not Vasalis?"

The two looked at each other then back at Michael slowly nodding their heads.

"Then this is your accommodation. See here."

He held up a small pen-like instrument which projected a screen into the air, the page displayed the reservation request. Zane and V were together, Ariel and J, Tara and Grant, and Max had his own quarters. At the bottom of the page under "requester" the name read "Grant". Everyone's heads swung toward Grant who returned there querying looks with a devious grin. It was the most emotion J had ever seen come out of him.

"I can place you with Mr. Max if you desire?"

Zane eyed Max, who was in his own world searching the beach, then held up his hand, declining the suggestion. V did the same, a slight smile briefly flashed on her mouth. Zane and V headed inside, turning at the last minute as they heard Ariel call to them.

"Meet out here in thirty minutes."

Michael then showed Ariel and J to their quarters, guiding them in to explain the layout. At a push of a button, a fully automated kitchen would swing out. Another section held a bathroom that did the same, with a large shower surrounded by glass. A third section revealed an inviting king-sized bed. On command, all three would somehow disappear into the transparent walls, only the beach and the scenery beyond were in view. Toward the beach was a wooden dock, small jet boats lined one side. On the beach surfboards and other water equipment lay about, appearing brand new. J focused on the ceiling and found a similar view, the roof transparent but slightly dimmed.

"Is there anything I can get you before I leave?" Michael asked.

"No," Ariel replied, admiring the room. "But we do need a time for our audience with Lady Capella."

"I will provide a time to you shortly. If you need anything press the blue button on the far wall."

"Thank you," J nodded as Michael left them.

"This place is ridiculous," J exclaimed, exploring the room.

"Should be, only the extremely wealthy could afford to visit."

J walked outside as he left the room, the warm air hitting his face. An invisible wall kept the conditioned air inside. J jumped back and forth a few times, his eyes wandering, taking everything in.

"You goof! It's just the climate control system. We should meet up with the others and see if any of them have any ideas on where to start looking or how we're going to deal with Lady Capella."

J landed outside one final time, spinning around to face her with a giant grin on his face.

"Sure, but first let's go look at the ocean. I've never seen one in real life before." He lightly bounced on his toes, eyes pleading. Ariel crinkled her nose and, with a smile, strolled over toward him.

"I did tell the others thirty minutes. Let's go show you

the ocean."

She stepped out, grabbing his hand, and led him to the shoreline. The sand glistened as the sun's rays bounced off the pristine grains, sparkling like gems. They stopped only a few feet from the waves. J felt Ariel's shoulders rise and fall as she sighed. His eyes latched onto her profile as she stared out into the endless blue sea.

"You enjoy the ocean?"

"Yes, I've only been a few times with my uncle, not something we had on Atlantis."

J's eyes drifted over the water watching the waves crash into the beach, the sand washing up and down, a few small crabs scattering about, small shells dancing on the bubbling wave tops. A voice came from behind them.

"Nice view."

Zane trudged through the sand, V next to him.

"Any luck getting an audience?" V asked.

"Not yet, Michael said he'd return and let us know. Have you seen the others?"

Zane didn't have a chance to answer, almost on cue Tara, Grant, and Max wandered up behind them.

"This place is awesome. I say we stay a bit before we get down to business." Max kicked the sand with his bare feet.

J narrowed his eyes and frowned as he released Ariel's hand, stomped a few paces toward Max. "This isn't a vacation; we need to find the missing piece to the warp drive."

Max crossed his arms, adjusting his stance to lean back on one leg. "Well I haven't seen a schedule, and last time I checked, we aren't being chased, the Earth isn't going to blow up, and nothing on the list is time sensitive as far as I can tell."

J took another step toward Max, raising a finger with a bent hand and continued up to him. "Cyrellia's out there, TK is out there. They're on their way to Acadia, we can't let them get a foothold. You should know them better than most, you were one of them weren't you?"

Max pulled away, his head dropping into the sand, voice quiet. "I never took the final oath."

Ariel's head perked up. Leaning toward Max, her eyes fixed on his reflective sunglasses, she focused her eyes trying to see past them.

"What do you mean you never took the final oath? I saw you leave, I saw you enter the auditorium."

J's aggressive stance loosened as he watched Max's reaction, it was the first emotion other than anger or a general disregard for anything important that he'd seen from him. Max stared at the ground biting his lip, J could tell his eyes flickered around under the glasses. Ariel walked past him, resting a hand on Max's arm.

"What happened?"

Max picked his head up, glancing around at the six of them scrutinizing him. J tried to make sense of the situation, his knowledge of Max was very thin, only bits and pieces from the last few weeks. Max kicked his jaw forward before he spoke.

"I had my reasons. Let's just say TK didn't have what I wanted."

Ariel pulled off his glasses, Max stared back through glossy eyes.

J's body tautened. "So should we go see about that audience?"

Ariel and Max turned toward J, he raised both eyebrows. Ariel released her hold on Max and spun toward their rooms. Zane grabbed J's shoulder, tugging him toward their accommodations.

"I'll take J to have a look around; we'll meet back here in two hours if I don't hear anything from you."

Ariel nodded while J struggled to free himself from Zane's grip. He spit out some words, but nothing came across as a meaningful sentence. Once they reached Zane's room, he released him.

"Best let them talk it out, no need to interfere. Besides, I hear you've never seen a real ocean, so let's take a little bit to enjoy it."

J crossed his arms, leaning on a palm tree near the building. That wasn't the type of walk on the beach he'd imagined after arriving. Leaving Ariel with Max felt even more wrong. He clenched his fists.

"That right there's what I'm talking about. Relax, J. Ariel's a big girl, she can take care of herself. Heck, she saved your life a few times...mine, too."

Zane's eyes were fixed on J's fists so he noticed when J released them. J's body tingled as his mind wandered, playing out scenarios of what they were doing together on the beautiful beach. Zane snapped him out of it with a strong slap on the shoulder.

"I saw a lookout not too far down the tracks we came in on. Let's see if we can get into some trouble."

"What? Shouldn't we wait for the audience with Capella?"

Zane leaned down toward J. "She was a TK loyalist, I'm

surprised she didn't leave with Exodus. Also noticed a few replicants in the tower and I'm pretty sure Michael and Samuel are as well."

"How can you tell?"

"Just call it a hunch, something about them seems off."

"Lady Capella has decided that she will see you now."

J jumped at the voice, snapping his head around. Zane straightened his spine, his gaze turned back toward the entrance. Samuel was approaching them, his walk very proper; his body seemed to float over the sand.

"Are your companions ready as well? She requires all of you to be present."

J didn't hesitate, he began the walk to the beach not uttering a word. Zane addressed Samuel, informing him they'd be back with the others. The setting sun rested atop the ocean waves, J squinted to see the silhouettes of their friends. They sat on the sand watching the sunset, two absent. J spotted Max and Ariel on the dock, their figures tiny as they stood on the edge.

"I'll get Ariel," Zane offered, overtaking J. "You get the others."

Zane trekked off toward the dock, J grumbled to himself, his footsteps labored in the sand. V turned her head hearing the sand slinging off of his toes.

"That was quick, everything alright?" She stood up, her eyes focusing on Samuel behind him.

"Yeah, Capella said she'll see us now. You guys ready?"

"Of course we are, J. That's why we are here," Tara replied.

Grant didn't say a word as he rolled his little plump body

upright and headed toward him.

"How's everything here?" J asked.

His eyes flowing over to Ariel and Max who had begun to walk back down the dock, his jaw tensed. *What did they talk about?*

V turned to see what J was so focused on. "Don't worry about that, everything's fine here. This place is pretty amazing, don't you think?"

"Yeah," he said with a bit of a grumble.

"We're all here and ready," Zane announced as he walked within earshot of their host.

"Very well, if you will kindly follow me, I will escort you to Lady Capella."

They all followed their guide back onto the transport, it sped off as it did before silently hovering over the tracks. It was putting more distance between them and the Omorfiá. J had hoped they'd be closer to the ship. If anything were to happen, they'd need her to escape. The situation with Ariel and his conversation with Zane had his mind reeling, he decided to focus on the less stressful of the two. He studied Samuel, attempting to find clues to his robotic nature. Other than his incredibly proper posture, nothing else seemed out of sorts. J had taken a seat next to Ariel who was in her own world, staring out at the dimly lit beach. The sun had set and the sky glow was all that remained. J felt uneasy, the water making the horizon disappear, fading into stars. He thought of the sheer drop-off on the outside of the wall, his first brush with an unlimited horizon. Somewhere past the water, the same thing occurred out of sight. J's eyes adjusted to the front of the transport, a city of lights appeared, the tracks leading directly to them. Their ride sped on as individual buildings came into view. J reached over, placing his hand on Ariel's thigh, she rested hers on top of his. His shoulders unknotted. Breathing in the fresh scent of the sea, his eyes danced over the passing buildings. They were stone castle-like structures, it was hard for J to determine their use. Most were square, adorned with glass windows. Inside, lights glowed, but the interiors seemed to be empty, faux buildings for aesthetics sake. The transport entered an immense tunnel of stone, the archway intricately carved with palm trees, birds, and other tropical items. A few hundred feet ahead, J saw an entourage of fifteen to twenty men all dressed in white pants and flower print shirts. They had dark tan skin and were heavily built, not anyone J would want to tangle with. As the transport stopped, they were escorted into a long entertaining hall. The ceilings were three stories tall, all stone and painted white. Eight columns supported the structure, four on each side. Samuel led them through the grand hall, the twenty men following. At the far end sat a woman, a large stone chair engulfing her, its shape mostly rectangular making it appear very uncomfortable. J examined the woman, her features birdlike and thin, her dress purple with a large collar flared out behind her head, her bleach blond hair flowing around both sides of her neck.

"Lady Capella these are the guests who requested an audience. I was informed you were ready to see them. May I present J, son of Arcturus."

J stepped forward, hoping the others would be introduced shortly. Capella examined him, her eyes running all over his body, her mouth twisting into a smile as she did.

"J, son of Arcturus, why have you come here? Is it for business or pleasure? We have both."

Her speech was slow and calculated, level and mellow. J looked over to Ariel for guidance. She stepped forward, Capella's eyebrow lifted.

"And you must be Ariel, your reputation precedes you. Am I to talk to you or J? I don't care which, but would prefer one or the other." Capella leaned back in her chair awaiting the response.

Ariel began. "Lady Capella, we're searching for a piece of equipment we believe may be somewhere in this sector."

Capella held her head up, peering down at her. "What is this piece of equipment you seek?"

Ariel's eyes danced around searching for the words. "It's a control panel for a sensitive piece of equipment needed for our mission."

"And what mission is that?"

"Helping Earth."

Capella began to cackle, the sound making J's skin dance. "You mean leaving Earth."

J and Ariel looked at each other, their faces mirroring one another, eyes tight, lips pursed. Both focused back on Capella as she continued.

"I know what you seek, I know your mission, and I know what your plan is. Now tell me what is in it for me? What do I get in return for your precious warp drive control panel?"

CHAPTER SIX

Capella rose to her feet. Her robe dragged on the ground as her long legs kicked out from underneath, her stride flawless, a resting smile on her face.

"So, you plan to leave Earth and I plan to stay. I would like to make you a deal that will be beneficial for both of us."

J's eyes fell, his mind searching. *How could she know?* He didn't even know the plan; he'd hoped there would be more information. Capella froze, her eyes fixated on J.

"You know your father always has a plan and Earth was a stepping stone. I can help you achieve your destiny. Walk with me."

She turned, taking a few gliding steps. J glanced back at Ariel who moved toward him.

"Just you, J," Capella insisted. Her eyes still on J, appraising, she instructed her minion, "Samuel, please make J's companions comfortable. We will be back shortly."

"No, he's not going anywhere without me," Ariel protested.

Capella gracefully whirled around, turning her back on them all, beginning her stroll once more. "This is a conversation for royalty, my dear. J, please follow me."

Ariel scrunched her nose as she huffed, incredulous. J mouthed the word "sorry" as he moved to join their host. They ambled out of the great hall into a smaller corridor, the floor and walls made of white marble, columns laid out every six feet, and both sides open to the outside. Starlight entered, twinkling on the glossy surface. A small torch on each column lit the way, the surfaces flickering in reds and oranges.

"You mean to go to Acadia, don't you?"

J toyed with his hands as they continued down the corridor, his mind still searching for the source of her information.

"I take your silence as a "yes". I know you are curious as to how I acquired this knowledge. It is fairly simple really. Do you know what this place is?"

J glanced outside, the sound of the ocean filled his ears, the stars dancing on the water's surface. "A resort for the wealthy of Atlantis."

"My dear boy, you are partially correct. In addition to this lovely resort, we supply the fresh water required to sustain Atlantis and Earth. The weather system needs our water to operate. Without it, the engineered planet could not function."

They entered a room at the end of the corridor, men stood in each corner, their hands clasped in front of them. The center held a massive, ornately carved, marble table with a glass inlay in the interior of the horizontal surface. Capella approached it, rested a hand on its smooth surface. An image appeared above, floating a few feet in the air, a square box with wires protruding from it. J realized it was the missing piece. *She had it, or an image of it, but how did she get it?* He stepped up next to her, his arms crossed.

"Is that the control panel?"

Her intense observation compounded with her growing smile made him uneasy.

"Yes, J, and I will give it to you so that you may continue your journey. But, I require something in exchange."

J watched the image floating around. *What did she want*

and would it be something he could give her? "What do you need?"

"I will be named to the new council for planet Earth."

J's jaw dropped open, his eyes moved about and his chest became tight. Somewhere in his mind he knew that someone would have to oversee Earth, ensure that the systems continued operating and that each sector received that which it needed to survive. Ariel had said it'd be him, but recent events made that more complicated; he had to leave to go to Acadia. *Who would watch over Earth? The scientists they gathered? Capella? Someone he hadn't met yet? Would he come back after facing Cyrellia?* His head pounded as he tried to focus on her demand, it spun out of control. *He didn't even know Capella, her character, did he have the right to offer that?* He stared warily toward Capella.

"I'm not sure I can grant that request."

Capella's smile dropped. She focused on the spinning panel, her body rigid, arms stiff as she leaned on the table. "You are the last remaining member of the TK bloodline and the heir to Earth, you can grant any request. This one is fair. Do we have a deal?"

J had dropped his arms and begun to fidget with his fingers, they shook as he addressed her once again. "How did you acquire the panel? It was in a secure location."

Capella's eyes tightened, lips pursed. She gathered a deep breath then stared straight into J's eyes. "That is of no consequence. I have it, you need it. Do we have a deal?"

J felt the tension building. He rolled his shoulders in their sockets, repositioned his feet multiple times. "May I have some time to think it over?"

Capella clenched and unclenched her jaw, her nose twitching, still staring at J. "I am afraid not. I require an answer immediately."

J surveyed the room, contemplating options. The four men stood as still as statues. He had no weapons, they had been confiscated earlier. He straightened up, placing his hands behind his back as he remembered his father doing at such times.

"You require an awful lot," J quipped. Ariel was definitely rubbing off on him. "Tell you what, *I* require a visual confirmation. I'd like to see the panel first before I grant your request."

Capella balled her hands, knuckles whitening. "Very well. I will send you out to the facility. Your friends stay here."

J thought about the proposal. *Ariel.* He wanted her advice, her expertise.

"Ariel must accompany me," he replied, his voice unwavering.

"I am afraid that is impossible. I know who she is, what she can do. You will journey there without any of your companions, but I will send Michael as your guide. You will see the device and, upon your return, you will sign a contract electing me to the new Earth council."

J relented, it seemed he was out of options and this was the only chance he'd have to get near the missing piece. He nodded. Capella signaled to one of the guards and he left the room, Michael appearing almost instantly.

"Please follow me, Master J," he said, sweeping an arm toward an adjacent door.

J moved toward the door and looked over his shoulder at Capella who was straightening her stance, watching him go. She crossed her arms, the long sleeves flowing around her body, her eyes heavy, peering back at J. He thought about that look then turned back to follow Michael out into the darkness guided by rows of torches; his feet shuffled over smooth stones cut so precisely that the seams were nearly invisible. The pathway led directly onto a dock where a great wooden ship was moored, gently rocking along with the waves. J studied it as they approached, it reminded him of the ship in Moby Dick. Three masts stood tall overseeing the deck and the rear housed well-appointed captain's quarters resembling something out of Treasure Island. They walked up a plank onto the deck, J's head swiveling around, taking in the extravagant features of the ship. Ropes were tied along nearly every vertical surface, the railings were carved with flowers, the deck planks all fit seamlessly together and the captain's door was a work of art. Michael walked through them holding one open, waving him in.

"You are more than welcome to explore the ship, but first let me give you a tour of the cabin."

J was greeted with just as much extravagance as from the outside. Everything was made of a rich, dark wood, a desk sat in the back, glass windows stood behind crisscrossed metal rods creating diamond patterns. J walked over, admiring the dancing specs of light as he peered down to the water below.

"If you are ready, we will set off."

J spun around searching for sailors. *Surely there would be more people to sail such a large vessel?*

"Where's the crew?"

Michael placed a hand on the wall and a seventeenth-century ship captain appeared. "Good evening, sir. Where would you like to make off to?"

J jumped back, attempting to understand what just happened. The middle of the room had been empty, but now before him stood a captain who looked as real as him. He crept over to the captain, who turned to face him. They eyed each other. Michael took a few steps toward them, his hands behind.

"He is a hologram, the ship is automated so there is no need for a crew. We do have a holocrew for the resort guests, do you prefer to sail with the royal navy of old or do you prefer..." He pressed the wall once again, the captain dissolved reappearing as a pirate captain. "...pirates."

J took a step back the pirate appeared so real.

"Where be ye headin'?"

"Facility 8. Please take us there directly, we have a schedule to keep."

"Aye," said the captain, walking out the door onto the deck.

J looked past him, an entire crew moved about all dressed in seventeenth-century pirate attire. Mesmerized, he leaned forward to watch the show. Men danced along the rails releasing ropes, others carried buckets about, and somehow the sails unfurled.

Michael stepped out of the cabin. "If you need anything, the cabin acts as your accommodations did; the controls on the wall will adjust the setting of the room should you require food or relief. We will arrive within the hour."

He walked off toward the pirate captain, J stood in awe still watching the commotion, the wind whipping through his hair. His eyes tracked up the deck above his quarters, a sailor with a parrot on his shoulder manned the helm, turning the large wooden wheel to and fro. J climbed the stairs to gain a better view, the wind continued to pick up as the ship bobbed up and down over the waves. Behind them, the shoreline shrank in the distance. J leaned on the railing, a half-smile on his face. He felt like he was on a high seas adventure with a band of pirates off to find treasure.

But the feeling was fleeting, his mind snapped back to their mission. They needed the controls, they needed to save Acadia. He had once felt relief when they saved Earth from total destruction, now he was tasked with saving a planet he'd never known. *Would he ever come back to Earth? Capella had mentioned such a scenario. How long would it take to get to Acadia? Who would take care of Earth while he was gone? Zane seemed to be under the impression the "new world order" would be the caretakers. But, was that the plan?*

He was becoming entirely sick of being in the dark, only finding out information as his father or one of his cronies doled it out or when he had a dream memory. Something didn't feel right. He tapped out a message on his Datacle, hit send, then took a deep breath watching the shoreline disappear into the horizon. The ship sped along faster than he'd antici-pated; he doubted they were getting all that speed from the sails. Still leaning against the rail, he swung around, eyes now fixated off the bow. A small rectangular building grew as the ship sailed ever farther out to sea. J squinted to get a better look. The top flashed a bright blue light alternating to red, he watched the beams rotate around in the air as a projected wheel of light spinning horizontal to the Earth's surface. The ship slowed and the holographic pirates ran about shouting at each other as the sails rolled up into their stowed positions. The pirate captain strutted along the deck, eyeing his sailors, hunting for anything out of place. The ship docked next to the large structure J had seen from quite a distance away. The plank slid out from the side of the ship touching down onto the stone dock at the base of the lighthouse. The pirates dissolved as Michael stepped out from the captain's cabin, his head rotating left then right before settling on J. "If you are ready, sir, I will escort you to the object in question."

J stumbled down the steps, the ship swaying, rocking against the dock. The air was eerily quiet, waves slapping the stone walls the only sound. He followed his guide off of the ship and down into the building, they stepped into what J thought of as a service elevator, sparse but sizeable. He felt oddly comfortable, the metal walls reminding him of Atlantis.

"Confirm identity," the elevator demanded.

Michael leaned forward toward a small mirror just inside the lift, a ray of light shot out into his eye.

"Identity confirmed Michael, state destination."

"Floor 15."

The elevator started down and J felt his body become light as they accelerated. The walls disappeared around him and they were instantly surrounded by water. J spun around taking in everything he could. Lights flickered in the distance, reflecting on the glass surface of the elevator walls. As he gazed down below, a sea of lights glowed, illuminating several buildings. They raced toward them and soon the sea disappeared, nothing but walls surrounded them again. His feet felt heavy as they slowed to a stop, the doors hissed open.

"Follow me."

They exited out onto a catwalk inside of a cave, pipes lined the walls in various sizes. Huge vat-like structures sat in the middle of the room, pipes the size of small houses ran into them.

"What is all this?"

"The water treatment facility. At the end of those pipes is collections and dispersion. This way, not too much further."

After the catwalk, they entered another elevator and descended again. J felt they were going to pop out of the other side of the plate. The elevator stopped and when the doors opened, they were greeted by two replicants guarding a formidable looking steel door. J's initial reaction was to run, but he kept his nerve as they approached. Michael tapped a series of codes into the door, unlocking it. After the thick piece of steel slid aside, they stepped in. A control panel hung above a table in the middle of the room, two more replicants stood motionless holding plasma rifles, their eyes fixed on the panel. *Don't think she wanted anyone stealing this.*

As they moved closer, Michael closed the door behind them. "The item in question is there, as you can see. You may inspect it as long as you like then we will be on our way."

J walked around the table, his eyes moving around the room then back to the device, his body tingled as he saw Michael's eyes locked onto him. He approached the panel and

CHAPTER SIX

reached out for it.

"I am sorry, but you must not touch. There is a field around it."

J retracted his hand. "When the deal is finalized, it'll be mine. Can't I take it now?"

"I am afraid not. My instructions were to show you the panel then escort you back to the resort for the signing of the contract. You will receive the item after it is signed."

J hunted the room, his mind coming up with possible solutions. He needed the panel. The ship's voyage, the holographic pirates, made him question whether the panel was real. He eyed the piece again.

"How do I know this isn't a trick, a simulation like the ship? I have to feel the device in my hands or no deal. Tell Capella."

"You can inform her of your decision yourself."

Michael opened his hand in which rested a small cylinder resembling a flashlight. He ran his thumb along the ridge. Capella appeared with 100 percent accuracy as if she had been teleported into the room with them.

"You have seen the device, now it is time for the contract."

J placed his hands behind his back, something about it made him feel comfortable, confident. He rounded the corner of the table. "I must be able to physically touch it and bring it back with me before we complete the agreement."

Capella tilted her chin up, her eyes calculating, fixed on J. "Very well. You may hold the item, but it will remain there until your signature is complete."

J could sense that this was the best deal she'd make, watching Capella's lips squeeze together. "Okay, let me hold the panel."

"Michael, unlock the device and allow J to inspect the item then replace it and bring it to me."

Her hologram disappeared, Michael turned, tapping on a control panel. The panel lowered down resting on the table. J approached, picked it up. The lightweight metal felt cold in his hands as he spun it around studying the back. He examined the wires and it was at this point that he wished he knew exactly what he was looking for. It could have been a prop, a toy. It sure as heck looked real enough for him.

"Are you satisfied with the item?" Michael still had his hand on the controls.

J spun around, tripping over his feet. The control panel flew out of his hand, skipped on the floor toward one of the replicants.

"Bless it!" J exclaimed, scrambling to his feet to reach the panel, the replicant didn't move.

Michael's stoic expression didn't waiver. "If it is broken, Capella will still require the signature. The item is being bartered in "as is" condition. Now please, recover the item and place it back onto the stand."

J stood above the item, the wires splayed out. His body tense, his fingers wiggled. He took another look at Michael still standing there, eyes fixed on him. J peeked out of the corner of his eye at the replicant. "This is going to hurt," he muttered under his breath. He reached for the weapon, thrusting a knee up into the replicant's body, J left the floor as he did, twisting around. His movements quick enough, he rotated the rifle letting multiple shots fire into the replicant then twisted the rifle around firing on Michael. He prayed Zane was right. The rounds struck his body, exploding on impact. His body, like the first replicant, falling silent in a heap. J took a shot in the shoulder, wrenching in pain, then pulled the barrel around shooting four shots at the final replicant, three of them hitting their mark. He slid down against the wall emitting a growl. The item lay next to him, Michael's body sparked near the entrance.

J flopped his head back smacking it onto the wall. "Now comes the fun part."

CHAPTER SEVEN

He dropped the rifle, examined his wound. He grunted as he tried to lift his arm; it functioned, but wouldn't be much good in a fight. He had to make a plan to get out, there were more replicants outside. He knew it would only be a matter of time before they came looking for him. He was surprised they hadn't heard the commotion. *The walls must be thick.* Glancing over at Michael, he realized he would need him, at least his head. His focus turned to the panel; it would be a challenge to carry.

He looked at his pants. "Guess you're going in here." He stuffed one end of the panel into his waistline.

Staggering over to Michael, he was glad Zane was right. He hoped he was done with killing, it wasn't something he ever thought he'd be capable of and it definitely wasn't something he strived to be good at. He placed the plasma rifle on Michael's neck and, turning away, pulled the trigger. Through a spray of sparks, he found Michael's head severed at the neck, it would prove much easier to carry than the whole body.

"Two more outside."

J dropped the rifle, searched the room for anything he could use. He slipped the other replicant's rifle over his shoulder, he didn't know when he might find another one, but otherwise his search proved fruitless. The room was like a vault, the only things in it were the table, device and the two, make that three, sparking replicants. J picked up his rifle and positioned himself at the door control panel, took a deep breath and worked his injured arm to the controls, his other holding the rifle fixated on the far side of the door. He pressed the door open, the steel exposed one of the two replicants awaiting him. He fired, downing the target, lights began pulsing, a loud siren wavering. The other replicant peeked around the door, his weapon aimed high. J crouched down and planted a shot in his chest. The door began to close, J released the rifle, letting it hang from its strap. He snatched Michael's head as he slipped out, ran into the elevator and asked for the top level.

"Lockdown initiated. Please confirm identity."

The elevator started scanning for the suitor, J held up the head allowing it to scan. He felt like Perseus holding up Medusa's head, completely grossed out but slightly triumphant. The ruse worked and the elevator ascended. He exited out onto the catwalk, sirens blaring, and gazed down to the far end. He gritted his teeth against the throbbing in his arm. Mediators marched toward him single file, it was their only option due to the path size. *What was Capella doing with Mediators?* He released a volley of fire. The first two went down as the third stumbled, shooting over his head. He lay down, stabilizing his weapon and taking out two more, then scrambled to his feet and sprinted down the walkway into the final elevator. He executed the same procedure with the still sparking skull, the elevator sped upward. He backed into the corner, tossing the replicant's head aside. *What will be waiting for me at the top?*

The elevator came to a stop, the doors opened and the night crept, stars still lighting up the sky. He inched out, searching right and left, nothing. The boat rocked, bumping into the structure's base. J kept his head on a swivel as he approached the ramp. He wasted no time boarding and proceeding into the captain's cabin. He smacked the button with his good hand, the hologram pirate captain appeared.

"Aaargh, where ye be off to?"

"The resort, make haste."

J laughed at himself, it sounded like something a pirate would say, but was silly at the same time. The captain walked out shouting commands. J noticed the button on the wall just like at his room in the resort, he pressed it. The desk sunk into the ground and a bed slid out from the wall along with a sofa and love seat. He pressed the button again and a bathroom replaced the bedroom, once again and a kitchen.

"There's gotta be a med kit around here somewhere."

He scoured the kitchen drawers and cabinets eventually finding a tin with the Red Cross emblem on it and cracked it open. His shoulders relaxed, his throbbing arm almost stopped at the mere sight of it, a medical wand. He ran it over his shoulder then heard a loud pop. He dropped the wand, felt his shoulder, then heard another pop. This time the window lit up as if daylight suddenly appeared. More pops and fizzles. He glanced out the widow and saw four ships heading straight at him, the first firing balls of lightning. His ship's lights flickered, darkness surrounded him as the ship fell silent. He glared out of the window, the approaching ships were nearly on him. His shoulder could have used a couple more passes of the wand, but would have to do; he was running out of time and ideas.

His eyes swept through the cabin. *What would a resort ship be carrying that he could use?* He had two rifles, a medical wand and a disabled pirate crew. There were no cannons or weapons. *What was any of that going to do against four weaponized ships?* He hit the button again; the floor dropped and became stairs that folded out into a room below, the cargo hold. J navigated the stair, his steps too quick, stumbling in the swaying tides. He bounced off of a wall, tripping and stumbling onto the ground, his face plunged into the ocean. He snapped back scuttling to the stairs on his butt. *The hull under the ship was empty...not there! It led straight into the sea below.* He spied a familiar sight as he panned his head around. Two racks of spacesuits hung on a wall, backpacks next to them. He hopped up, shuffled over, his eyebrows raised in a question mark. He pulled a suit off of the wall, studying it closer. The letters "AWS" were embroidered on the chest. His head shifted to the underwater pool, he smiled finally realizing what they were. *This could be his chance to escape.* He heard something hit the hull. *They must have boarded his vessel.* His attention focused on slipping on the suit, donning one of the backpacks. It was nearly identical to the one he'd used in space. He slapped on a helmet, locking it into place, then stared into the inky depths. He heard footsteps and voices up above. No time to think, he ran and jumped into the water, sinking down to his shoulders. He twisted his head back and forth but continued to float. *Why wasn't he sinking?* His fingers began to dance, his eyes zipped about as a menu appeared in front of him. The footsteps grew closer, they were in the cabin. He quickly read the menu items. He was right, it was an automated wetsuit. One of the menus read "depth zero".

"Depth one-hundred," he whispered.

He spotted legs appear, stomping down the stairs as the suit began to sink. The menu in his eyes glowed bright, blinding him against the surrounding black ocean. The suit continued down, he looked up the at the boats above, outlines breaking up the starlight beyond. He wiggled his fingers in the glove, his thumb rubbed against the familiar controls.

"I've got this," he reassured himself, initiating forward thrust.

The sound of tiny fans buzzed in his ears as he began forward. He realized that he had no idea where he was going; he only knew that he needed to get away from there. Sounds of muffled slashes entered his suit, beams of blue light bounced beside him, one coming to rest on his shoulder. His eyes moved about, picking up nothing but darkness. He commanded "lights on" from the suit. Beams shot out of the darkness to light a thousand yards in every direction. He increased speed, thrusting the control full forward he descended. The suit announced his passing every hundred feet. His shoulder still lit up, but the pain had begun to fade. He switched off his lights, scanned his surroundings, hoping the assailants had gone. Lights flickered about, grazing over him. He kept the descent up the suit still informing him of his depth, then it occurred to him maybe the suit had a tracking system, a map. He requested one and a diagram of the sea floor showed up. His joy diminished quickly when he realized that the enemy may be able to track him as well. He went through menus as rapidly as he could, trying to figure out how to disable the function, if there was one, his eyes reading as fast as ever. He continued down as he worked the menus.

"Aha."

He found the setting and disabled the tracking system, he was swimming blind but at least they wouldn't be able to find him.

"Warning, maximum depth reached. Please ascend."

J searched, realizing that in his haste and due to the darkness, he couldn't determine "up". He rotated around, hoping to find clues. The suit screamed again.

"Maximum depth reached. Suit will fail at this depth in five minutes. Ascend, ascend, ascend."

J muted the suit, reached deep for a solution. His pursuit was nowhere to be seen, but that was the least of his worries, the water was the highest priority. He felt his foot clip something, he snapped it back, then his shoulder bumped off something else and his back smacked something solid stopping him instantly. Pain rushed through his body and he realized he couldn't determine his speed; it must have been quick to cause that sort of pain. The suit flashed in his eyes, visually attempting to coerce him to the surface. He ignored the flashes, they weren't helping. He snapped his head around, searching for any sign of lights, movement, anything. Nothing.

"Lights," he announced.

Lights flickered on, a large steel form shaped like a crescent reflected some back. The suit read "three minutes", he'd have to figure something out fast. He found himself engulfed by the rusty remains of a ship. He spied a smoke stack and an assortment of twisted metal, bulkheads, riveted steel, it was like something out of a book, but not one he'd ever seen or heard of.

"Oxygen 20%," the suit bellowed.

J rolled his eyes, shutting off that warning as well. *Great.* He needed to figure something out and fast. He spun around searching for anything to orientate him, the light picked up something out of the corner of his eye. A couple of bubbles floated away from his body, his mind clicked, it was a race to catch the bubbles. He pushed the thruster forward, the suit flashed less than one minute, oxygen at 15%. He knew he had to stay with the bubbles and not overtake them or he could get disoriented again. The bubbles inched along. J cheered for them to speed up, they had to win the race in record time, he was low on oxygen, the pressure building. The timer ticked down to zero then disappeared. He stayed focused on the bubbles, they were life.

The suit crackled, he felt a cold drip run down toward his left foot, the drip called in more friends and an army of drop-lets began rushing in. He stayed focused. *Don't panic.* His chest tightened as he stared at his two new friends leading him to the surface. The suit flashed red, the oxygen dipping below double digits, he held his breath. *Maybe he could conserve air.* The two tiny bubbles spun around each other, dancing to a melody he couldn't picture. Suddenly, their dance became illuminated. The water beyond transitioned from the dark black abyss to a deep blue, he was getting closer, his fingers played the piano. He breathed out, the oxygen now at 5%, maintained his focus on his saviors, his friends.

His head burst out onto the surface, his two new friends gone. They'd given themselves up for him and he was grateful.

He let out a long sigh, closing his eyes. A bright light nearly blinded him through his eyelids, he raised a hand to block the intense beam. His suit flashed 1% oxygen. The hum of engines danced around in his helmet, he struggled to see the light as he lost consciousness.

CHAPTER EIGHT

"Dr. Arcturus, your transpo awaits you on landing pad five."

J was staring at a list of names as he sat at a small desk. "Very well, inform them I will be there in a moment."

He looked up to see his assistant nod then leave the room. J tapped on the screen, ejecting a disk which he placed in a pocket on his coat. After shutting off the screen, he stood up and grabbed a book, then stepped out of the room into a busy hallway. Scientists in lab coats moved from one end to the other ducking into rooms, one ran by yelling for someone to hold a door. J turned his head to follow for a moment then proceeded to the elevator. It let out on the 62nd floor where J found himself outside in a courtyard, a TK transport awaiting his arrival, the door slid open as the driver stepped around to greet him.

"Lovely day for a Monday, I would say."

J nodded then slipped into the back seat next to another man. J kept his eyes front, never acknowledging the other man.

The driver called on the intercom. "Where to today, sir? I'm afraid I wasn't able to get the location ahead of time."

"My home."

The driver took off meandering through streets, stopping for pedestrians. J watched out the window, never looking at the man beside him. They passed shops and restaurants; he watched a small girl drop an ice cream cone after an attempted lick. The drive went on for some time eventually stopping at Arcturus' building. J heard the door slide open and the man

exited. He came around and J watched him walk away from
the transpo toward the building, he appeared to be wearing
the same outfit as J was. The driver started off again, through
parks, by shops, then a peculiar turn unexpectedly brought
them into an alleyway. The driver continued through the alley
and down into a tunnel which let out into an underground
structure barely tall enough for the vehicle to fit into. The
transpo came to a rest.

"One hour, sir. Or should I wait longer?"

"One hour will be plenty."

He stepped out into the open structure, his head ducking
as he walked toward the lone door.

Dillon opened it, greeting him. "They're all here, the
scientists you requested."

"Thank you, Dillon. You stand watch, I'll be out shortly."

He ducked through the door, following the path into a
room. Metal chairs sat strewn around, in each one a person.
J recognized them as the scientists he and his team had been
tasked to gather. J stood in front of them, their initial chatter
dying down.

"You may be wondering why I called you all here today.
Like me, you care about the Earth and its inhabitants. There
are others who don't. You know who they are. But I'm not
here to talk about them, I'm here to talk about Earth. There
may come a time when I call on you to help me govern Earth. I
need to know today if you will follow through to ensure Earth
and its inhabitants are cared for. When you arrived, you found
a tablet on your seat with a list of questions. I'll assess the
answers and assemble a team to govern Earth should the time

arise. If any of you cannot, or do not wish to, fulfill this duty, the last question on the sheet stated such. This is your last chance to change your answer. J surveyed the room, his eyes shifting to each of the scientists. Nobody moved.

"Very well, please hand over your tablets to Dominik and meet Dr. Mallow in the back of the room. For your safety as well as Earth's, she will wipe the last two hours of your memory. I wish you all well."

The scientists stood up without saying a word and made their way to the back door. J saw V's mother standing next to it, waving each of them in. He turned to see Dominik collecting the last of the tablets and moved toward him, his hand rummaging through his pocket. He extended the disk to him.

"At another time, I will give instruction on what to do with this. Until then, keep it safe."

Dominik smiled. "And what do you want to do with these?" He held up the tablets.

"Destroy them."

J's eyes flickered open, the soft white light above him glowed in his eyes. He squinted, trying to determine where he was. He blinked hard then sat up, his head hitting something solid, invisible. V's face came into view.

"Careful, J. You had generalized barotrauma and need to stay in the chamber for another thirty minutes clear the bubbles out of your system."

J's eyes went crossed. *General what? What was she talking about?* His head rolled over to the other side, Ariel was sitting with a big grin on her face, recovering from the sight of watching him conk his head on the glass.

"How ya feeling?"

J couldn't help but smile back. He remembered his arm wound and moved it around. There was no pain, it felt as good as new. V must have patched him up. *How did he get in the chamber?* "I'm good, where are we?"

Ariel stood up, placing a hand on the glass. "Atlantis. We plucked you out of the ocean like a dying fish."

J rubbed his head, his eyes snapped wide open. He frantically felt his waistline.

"J, you really think we would leave it on you?" She chuckled then continued. "Grant has it, he's been working on the warp drive since we arrived. You did good...took me a bit to translate your message. That was a nice call sending Max for the Omorfiá, still had some trouble with the boats, but we all made it out."

J rolled onto his side, his skin touching the table. He was in his underwear...again. His hands shot down trying to cover himself, he attempted to distract. "What uh...what happened with the boats?

Ariel snickered starring at his hands. "I'll tell you what, you take me to dinner sometime and I'll tell you all about it."

J's face turned red, he gnawed on his bottom lip. So, thirty more minutes?"

V stepped into view, referencing a tablet, she looked at Ariel. "I set an automatic sequence, when his levels reach normal, the chamber will open. I'll leave you guys to it. Zane's making a late dinner, you two should head on over once he's dressed."

"Thanks, V," Ariel said, her hand still on the glass.

J admired her small hand, thought of how incredibly capable those hands were. He placed one of his on the glass, wished he didn't have to wait. They talked about nothing, waiting for the chamber to release. After getting dressed, Ariel led J toward the dining hall. Luckily it wasn't too far of a walk because J's stomach growled hungrily; he could definitely use some food. When they walked in, Zane was sliding a fresh plate of pasta over to V, her short legs swinging in the chair. She greeted them with a wave.

"Whadya kids have?" Zane asked. "Got some fresh pasta whipped up."

"Pasta sounds great," J replied, taking a seat a couple down from V.

"Do I have cooties now?"

"No...I was saving a seat for Zane."

V blushed and did her best to try and hide it. She dug into the pasta, stuffed a large bite into her mouth.

"So, what do we do about Capella?" J asked.

"That's a decision for the NEC," replied Zane, dripping with sarcasm.

Ariel fanned a hand at him. "Don't mind him, he's just upset they didn't go with "New World Order"."

Zane slid a plate over to J. "It's better than the New Earth Council."

J sat back, his chin tucked into his neck. "New Earth Council? How long was I out?"

"Just a few hours, V stabilized you pretty quickly. Escaping the sector proved to be the longest part. The scientists we rescued have agreed to oversee Earth. While Zane's name was a fine one..."

"Thank you." Zane slipped a plate in front of Ariel.

"...they decided to go with NEC. I believe the first few items on their agenda include Capella, security, and terminating MKUltra2X."

"MKUltra2X?"

"The mind control chips."

J's mind flashed to the time he cut one out of Carol's head, he'd nearly forgotten about her. He hoped she was doing okay. He stared at the pasta, mind wandering. So much change in such a short time. Back then he'd been worried about whether he should go to college or stay to help his folks on the farm. *What a silly trivial thing.* He stabbed a piece of pasta and popped it in his mouth, reminding him of Giovanni's back in Sector 11. Thoughts of Capella and the tasks ahead of him filled his mind, unwelcomed. He sat back, his hands behind his head, and closed his eyes.

"Should we go check on Grant?" Ariel pushed her plate aside.

J half-hoped he'd have a moment to relax, but it seemed Ariel had other plans. "Sure," he sighed, opening his eyes.

Zane lifted his fork, he'd silently moved to sit next to him, raised an eyebrow at J and looked pointedly down at J's mostly untouched plate. J shrugged his shoulders and followed Ariel to the hangar where the warp drive resided. They found Grant yelling at the machine from atop a short ladder. He punched in a code, the sounds of errors rang back at him. He hopped off the ladder then kicked it over and stormed off. Tara was standing a few feet away not knowing how to respond, she waved to them as they approached.

"Hi, Tara."

"He's been having trouble with the connections and the programming. He'll return."

She flashed a small smile then her lips straightened. J stepped in next to the toppled ladder and peered into the compartment. It looked familiar, like something he'd seen before, but couldn't put a finger on it. He reattached some of the cables in different locations, reenergizing the control panel. His attempts were met with the same obnoxious tones. He stepped back. *Who was he kidding? He was a farm boy from Earth, he'd never worked on systems like this. All he'd ever worked on was their harvesters.* His eyes lit up and he placed his hands on his forehead.

Ariel leaned toward him. "What did you figure out?"

"We gotta go to Sector 11."

"Why?"

"Just trust me, we do. Come on." He ran off toward one of the ships, bounced on his feet. "Come on!" He ran into the Omorfiá, all the way to the bridge, Ariel trotting in behind him.

"You want to take this?"

"We won't be gone long. Besides, the other ships are too small for both of us."

"I don't know, I recall you enjoying the last ride together." Ariel smirked, while J's eyes danced on the floor turning away.

"Can you get us there?"

"Keep your pants on." Ariel slid into the pilot's seat. "Or not. You seem to have a problem keeping them on around V and I." She laughed to herself.

J blushed furiously. "You think you're so funny."

"That's because I am," she winked as she flipped a few switches and manipulated the menus. "Okay, Sector 11 here we come."

The hangar doors opened on her command and she pushed the thruster forward, accelerating through the approach tunnel, shooting out the other side into space. A transmission came over the screen.

Max's veins bulged out on both sides of his neck, his eyes shot daggers. "Where are you taking my ship?!"

"Don't get your panties in a twist, we'll be back shortly. I'll take good care of her."

"You'd better, she's—"

Ariel switched off the feed, J silently chuckled with satisfaction. Earth came into view off the nose. J stared, counting the plates. He wondered how many more times he'd see it, his future was a mystery. They zipped between the plates into the skeletal structure. Ariel engaged the auto-land, sliding them into Sector 11's hangar. After touchdown, they hopped out and grabbed clothes from the dressing area, they felt it best to keep up appearances. Up top, they hitched a ride out of town to his parents' house. J stepped onto the farm, his legs locked as he eyed his childhood home.

"You okay?"

"Yeah, it's just been a bit of a whirlwind. There were times I didn't think I'd ever be back here."

"You still haven't told me why we're here."

J's eyes remained locked onto the house, he opened his

hand for Ariel to take it. Her eyes flicked down then obliged.

"When I was younger, much younger, my father was working on one of our harvesters. I didn't know much and hadn't seen any blueprints or schematics before. While I was playing, I spotted one on his work bench. The words were gibberish, I couldn't read at the time. I asked him what they were and he simply told me that it was a project for a friend. I kept trying to place why the warp drive controller looked so familiar, then it clicked. The images I saw on the table that day looked like what we were just staring at hours ago. My father, my Earth father, must know something."

Ariel squeezed his hand, her ice blue eyes stared back at him not saying a word. They strolled toward the house, his father stepped out onto the porch.

"James...James, is that you?"

J almost looked behind him, the name sounded so foreign. They walked up and J released Ariel's hand, grabbing his father, squeezing his arms around him.

"I missed you," he said, squeezing even tighter, a tear ran down his cheek.

"There now, boy. We missed you, too. Why don't you come on in? Your mom would love to see you. And don't leave your..."

"Girl friend, her name's Ariel."

"Well don't leave Ariel out in the cold. Come on in."

J reached for Ariel, pulling her inside. His mom nearly dropped a dish she was washing when she saw him. She ran over, showering him with love. Her arms locked him in a big hug, she released him still holding his arms.

"Where have you been? Your father said you went off to college, but I thought you were off flying around the world or something. No note, no letters."

"He's at college, like I told you. See? He even met a new girl there." His father winked.

J's mom eyed Ariel from head to toe. "My she is a pretty one, but what happened to Carol?"

J explored the ground, his eyes searching for an answer. "Mom..."

His father jumped in. "Let me show you the new harvester I just received. I decided to finally replace #2, come on out."

J's father pushed them toward the side door, his mom still trying to get some words in.

"Honey can you whip up some sandwiches? I know it's a long way to college, a very long way."

He escorted them to the barn; J shook his head looking at the unburned wood floor. They stepped inside, J's father shutting the door behind them. "How's college?" he asked, turning and walking over toward his workbench.

J raised his eyebrows, not knowing how to respond. He opened his mouth, inaudible sounds escaped, more of an exhale than words.

J's father pulled a brown tube from under a cabinet and popped the top off. "What, you haven't been at college?" His eyes focused on J as he continued to study him.

J looked away, hoping the judging stare would go with it.

"Is she from Atlantis?"

CHAPTER NINE

J's head shot up, his eyes wide as his father pulled a roll of paper from the brown tube. Ariel stood there as dumbfounded as J, silent.

"Well, Arcturus said this day would come and, like many parents, I've come to realize that time passes too quickly. I suggest we keep this a secret, you going to college will be easier for your mom to take. I believe you'll need these."

He handed over the papers, J unfurled them examining the images. The drawings sparked his memory, it was as he remembered. "But..."

"I used to live on Atlantis myself, but as I know you've found out, there were plenty of us who didn't enjoy it there. My specialty was interstellar travel, even planned Exodus' warp drive. This one's faster." He smiled letting it all sink in. "So, Ariel. Who are your parents?"

Her shoulders sagged as she looked away. "Dougald and Natia, they passed away when I was still a baby."

"I'm sorry to hear that. I didn't know them, but if you're here it means Arcturus trusted them with his life." He turned to J. "You making the rounds? Saying goodbye to any of your other friends?"

J was entranced by the blueprints so it took him a minute to hear what his father had said. He blinked quickly. "No, should I?"

"Well, it's going to take a minimum of fifty years to reach Acadia. And that was based on the last system Arcturus was searching in, I'm not sure where he actually found it. I'm afraid even if you decide to come back, nobody you know will still be alive."

J froze. *Fifty years?* That seemed like an eternity. His mind started going through the names of his friends, acquaintances...his parents. If he went on the journey, he'd never see them again. Yet, something poked at him, something even more than curiosity burned in him. The desire to meet Arcturus, to end TK. He knew what had to be done. His throat felt tight as he rolled up the papers, handed the blueprints to Ariel.

"Father, what day is it?

"Friday, why?"

"Can I borrow the truck? There's something I have to do"

"Sure, it's yours until you leave."

J placed a hand on Ariel's, his eyes gazed into hers.

"Can you stay here with my father, there's something I need to do, alone."

Ariel opened her mouth to speak then retracted, pressing her lips together. She nodded, understood. J walked out of the barn and hopped in his truck. He took a deep breath inhaling the familiar smell of worn leather, burnt oil and grease. He placed a hand on the dash, he'd miss this broken down old truck. The ignition fired up. He glanced in the rearview as Ariel stepped out from the barn and gave a small wave then pulled into the road, the dirt kicking up. He smiled thinking of the pure fear he felt the night of the meteor shower, it paled in comparison to what he'd faced since.

Continuing down the road, his arm hanging out to catch the air, the wind rushing through the open windows blowing his hair around, the warm sun glowing through the wind-screen...it all brought back memories. The fields of wheat rolled past him. He wasn't in a rush, knew deep in his heart that this would be the last time he saw them, maybe the last time he saw Earth. The town came into view, passing through it was like looking at a time capsule, never changing, always the same, it made him feel comfortable, reassured that he was doing the right thing. He pulled into a parking spot next to a yellow Chrysler Windsor Highlander, shook his head at the flawless shimmering clear coat, it was all so trivial now. His gaze moved toward the diner. The front was empty, though he half expected to see Will taking a drag on a cigarette. Through the window he saw that they were all there, in the booths they'd shared for as long as he could remember. He watched Carol stand up and lean toward the clear glass, he smiled back. She ran through the diner as J sauntered up to the main entrance. Flinging the door open, she stepped out.

"You're back? I thought you were gone for good! Where's Ariel?"

Her eyes dropped, for a brief moment she remembered. The thought of Ariel brought back reality. J continued toward her, his stomach constricted, their last moments had been hard on her. Looking back, J wished he'd handled it better. He reached out, grabbing her hand.

"I'm sorry...so sorry for how I left you."

He could see her eyes welling up. She took a deep breath, wiping her eyes before the tears could release.

"Seeing you brings back memories...memories I will always cherish. But in my heart, I know you have other things you must do. Other people to love—"

"I'm so—"

She placed a finger on his lips eyes locking onto his. "You're destined for greatness. This is my home and life feels new again without the restraints. The knowledge of Flat Earth, that there is more out there than our little town, being able to think for myself...it's like a new life. You gave me that. There is no need to be sorry."

J smiled at her, he'd almost forgotten how sweet she was, his new life consuming him. He drank her in knowing this would be the last time he saw her, rubbed his thumb on the back of her hand.

"How are you doing?" he asked softly.

She smiled back at him, rubbing her neck with her free hand. "Much better. Jason asked me to the movies tomorrow night, seems he's had a crush on me for a while now." She grabbed his other hand. "Oh don't worry, I told him we were through, so don't think he was trying to pull one over on you."

J gave a slight chuckle. *To think, his best friend had hidden it from him this whole time. Jason had always been a good friend.* J took a breath, his stomach loosening at the thought.

"So, have you been on any more crazy adventures?"

J's mind zipped through all of them, the highlights that is. "A few. You tell everybody the truth?"

She laughed, tucking her hair over her ear. "Definitely not, they would think I'm crazy...no, I think it's best left for me."

J tightened his eyes as if concentrating really hard, he needed to say goodbye...for good. He shifted his weight between each leg, his one hand still holding hers.

"I'm going away for good. I came back to say goodbye, make amends."

Carol smiled the same sweet smile she always had for him, placed her free hand on his cheek. Her warm palm made his face tingle.

"Thank you, James. Are you going to say goodbye to the gang?"

"Yes, can you help me with that, keep the true nature to yourself? Like you, I think it best for them to not know... for now. It's simpler this way." *Maybe someday they would know, when NEC terminated the mind control.*

Carol nodded, taking him into the diner. Sam bellowed out a big welcome as he always did. He looked past the first few booths to his old stomping ground. Jason stood up next to the table, his eyes moving through Carol to J. Rich turned his head.

"Look who it is, big college man. You come to gloat?"

J walked up and leaned down placing a hand on his shoulder. "Nope, that's your thing."

His eyes turned to Jason at the same time Carol grabbed his hand. Jason flinched, his face turning white.

"Relax, Jason. Carol told me everything. I'm happy for you."

Jason still stood there speechless, looking as though he was about to faint.

"So, how's college? Went a bit early," Barbara asked.

J nodded, placing his hands behind his back, his eyes flicked into the air preparing his thoughts. "It's been...enlightening."

He glanced at Carol who held back a giggle.

"I've been accepted to a new program, one in which I'll be studying abroad. I'll be far away and won't be able to come visit for quite a long time."

"Like, in New York?" Barbara asked.

"No," Rich scoffed. "Like Florida, right?"

J kept his composure, he wanted so badly to laugh at them. It wasn't their fault, he knew. He'd lived it. Their world was so small, he'd forgotten how small.

"A little farther than that, Rich. I'll be out of the country and traveling all over. I just wanted to say that I wish you all the best of luck. I've treasured you as friends."

"Aww." Barbara increased her hold on Rich's arm.

"When do you leave?" Jason finally piped in.

"Today, actually. My ride leaves this evening."

Jason walked over, giving him a huge hug. J returned it.

"I'll miss you, and that rocket of an arm." Jason stepped back, slapping J's throwing shoulder. A tear popped out of his eye, slipping down the curve of his face, resting on his lip.

J leaned into him. "Treat her like a princess, she deserves it."

Jason nodded. As J started to leave, he threw a hand in the air, turning to get one last look at his friends. Carol beamed at him though her bottom lip quivered. The doorbell rang as he walked through one last time. He slipped into his truck, taking it all in one last time. His friends gazed out toward him, he waved as he pulled out of the parking lot. The sun set as he drove home, his stomach still hadn't settled. As hard as it had been to say goodbye to his friends, saying goodbye to his parents would be harder. They'd raised him, taught him everything he knew, loved him unconditionally.

He stopped the truck, the windscreen full of his child-hood home. The truck door squeaked open. "I really should fix that," he smiled to himself. His nose twitched. The smell of steak and potatoes, one of his favorite meals, wafted out from the kitchen. He walked over the threshold, his father at the kitchen table reading the newspaper, Ariel busy setting the table, his mom mixing the mashed potatoes.

"Everything go okay?" his father asked as J entered the dining room.

J thought about it, his mind at ease over the exchange with his friends. Now it was time for his parents, he hoped it would go as well. He sat down across from his father, Ariel placed the last fork and headed to grab the pan of potatoes.

"Yeah," he said, sinking into his chair.

His mom grabbed the frying pan, steaks sizzling on top. "Ariel says you met in college, that she was your campus guide."

Ariel placed the potatoes on the table, J's mom followed with the steaks. His father said grace then the meal began.

"So, Ariel tells me she's into athletics, swimming, right?"

Ariel placed some corn onto her plate then handed the platter to J. "Yes ma'am."

"Not much swimming around here. There is that lake you used to go to, right James?"

J nodded plating a cut of steak. He took in the aroma closing his eyes, garlic, butter, salt, and pepper absorbed into his nostrils, his mouth watered. That night his mom was a chatterbox. Her questions ranged from the campus layout to the food, the professors. She spent some time on Ariel, he could tell she had some reservations, but found her to be a sweet girl. Ariel did her best to play along. Between her and J they'd made up a whole school from scratch down to the finest detail. J's father would chuckle occasionally knowing none of it truly existed. J caught himself staring at him a few times. *All this time, he was an Atlantean, he knew all of it.* He wondered what he would have said had he found the round metal object that started his journey. *Or did he see it?* He zoned out a few times, his mom or Ariel pulling him back. He tried not to think about it, but every few minutes his mind went back to this being the last night with his parents. He studied his mom and father; he wanted to remember their faces, their smells, their laughs. The night wore on as there was more talking than eating, eventually coming to a close with some apple pie. J devoured his piece, it felt like ages since he'd had any sweets. The sugars tickled his tongue as he savored every bite. He helped with the dishes while Ariel chatted with his father in the living room.

"She seems very nice," his mom commented, polishing a plate and handing it to him.

He dried it placing it in one of the cabinets. "She is..."

His voice trailed off not sure what else to say. He wanted to tell her about all the times she saved him or he saved her, the sights they saw together, the things she taught him. But he knew that must be left out.

"Well you take care of this one, I have a feeling she's something very special."

J dried another plate, stacking it on the first. "She definitely is." He gazed out at the moonlit field behind the house.

"Did you know the world is flat?"

His mom set down the dish laughing and grabbed him up with both arms. "What am I going to do with you? Of course it is! But you know what's a funny thing? There are people who believe there's a whole other civilization that lives on the moon."

His mom looked up at the celestial object laughing, J laughed too. *If only she knew.* They finished up the dishes and J meandered into the living room. He stopped and looked down at Ariel who looked very comfortable tucked into the sofa, her knees curled up into her body.

"I think it's time we get going."

Ariel peered up as J leaned on one leg, looking at his father. His father pressed his lips and nodded back, J's mom walked in.

"Go now? But it's late, you should stay the night." His mom moved about, tidying up the tables and furniture in the room.

J protested, "No, I think we should get going. Besides, there's nowhere for Ariel to stay, it's not like we have a guest bedroom."

"Nonsense, she can stay in your room. It's too late to be driving tonight, I don't want you falling asleep at the wheel."

"But there's—"

His mom waved her hand in the air walking back into the kitchen to put away her cleaning rag. "I don't want to hear it. You're staying one more night," she shouted out of sight.

Outmaneuvered, they looked to J's Father for assistance. He shrugged his shoulders, eyebrows high on his head. J relented, plopping down next to Ariel. His mom walked in holding a deck of cards.

J's father laughed. "Seems your mom wants to keep you prisoner here forever."

"Oh, stop it. Just one game then they can get their sleep."

She gently slapped him on the shoulder as she moved past, sitting in a chair across from him. J leaned toward the small coffee table situated in the center of the room.

"One game mom, then we need to get some sleep."

She smiled, shuffling the deck.

J twisted his head to Ariel. "You know how to play?"

"Depends on the game."

"Euchre," J's mom replied, her face glowing as she dealt the cards out to the four of them.

Ariel's brow tightened, slowly shaking her head. "Can't say I know that one."

"It's fast, you'll like it." J picked up the pile of cards in front of him.

For the next few hours they laughed, made small talk about the farm, the town, church; everything his mom loved to gossip about. They taught Ariel how to play, which in hind-sight was probably a poor decision as by the end of the night she couldn't get enough. The game was quick and she was getting good at it. Finally, after two games, J's father turned in. His mom gave J and Ariel a big hug, leaving them for the night. Before turning in, she made him promise he'd say goodbye in the morning before they left. He agreed without a fight. J led Ariel to his room, stopped short as he opened the door, almost not recognizing it. It was spotless, not the way he left it. He was a typical teenager, clothes on the floor, books strewn about. His mom must have cleaned everything. His bed sat perfect, the sheets tucked, the top straightened and smooth, the pillows fluffed. Ariel walked past him bouncing onto the bed. J studied the floor, the wooden floorboards uneven and hard, appearing less than inviting.

"You're not sleeping down there." She extended a hand, curling her pointer finger at him, invitingly. J moseyed over, sitting down next to her. She crawled on the bed forcing him down on his back, rested her head on his chest. J closed his eyes as the sunflower and ozone scent that was uniquely hers touched his nose.

"Your parents are nice. I know you'll miss them."

J's chest rose then fell, ending in a long exhale. He kept his eyes closed; it felt good to rest, to have Ariel so close once again. "I will," he answered, drifting off into sleep.

CHAPTER TEN

The sound of birds chirping filled his ears, letting him know they were still on Earth. He drew in a long breath, his chest rose feeling pressure as the night before. His chin tickled from Ariel's hair, fluttering from his breath. Still groggy, he opened his eyes. The plain white ceiling stared down at him. He wiggled his way out from under Ariel who grumbled a bit when her head kissed the mattress. J stretched as he entered the kitchen, the smell of bacon permeating his nose. His mom was at the stove flipping bacon and working eggs in a frying pan.

"Morning, mom," he greeted, mid yawn.

She dropped the spatula, running over to give him a hug. His father tipped the newspaper, pursing his lips. J slinked over swiping a piece of bacon.

"Thanks for the breakfast, mom."

"Of course, dear. I wish you could stay longer, it seems like you just got here. I'm just not used to you being gone so long."

J sat down, his mind trying to think of the last time he was away for an extended period of time… he couldn't remember any. He did stay over at Jason's a few times, but that was only one, maybe two nights tops. *How would things be after he left?* He shook his head, his attention focused on his father. The world had been rough on him; his body was torn, broken, he'd mentioned finding help after J left, but he still worried. Yet, knowing he was Atlantean somehow made it better, something told him they'd be okay, that he'd experienced harder times than simply running a wheat farm. J gazed out the window at

ACADIA

the blue sky. *What would Acadia be like?*

His mom slipped a plate of bacon and eggs under his stare. "Where's Ariel?"

J thought of a number of things to say. She loved her sleep, but who could blame her? While she was awake she'd be going a mile a minute, anyone would need rejuvenation after that amount of energy expenditure. "Still sleeping." He stuffed a forkfull of eggs in his mouth.

His mom smiled, going back to build a plate for his father. J looked back at him, his paper covering his face as though it was any other day. Ariel appeared above his shoulder, walking with a purpose stopping at his side and bouncing on her feet. J glanced up, about to slip some bacon in his mouth. Ariel's eyes darted around the room then back to J, she bit her bottom lip.

"What?" he finally asked as she started tapping on her wrist, her Datacle hidden under her dress sleeve.

"Um, we need to get going."

J's mom spun around, she jumped making a slight gasping sound. "My dear, I'm sorry I didn't hear you. Good morning, can I get you some breakfast?"

Ariel smiled placing her hands behind her back, her fingers twirling around each other. "No, thank you. Something has come up and I really must get J...ames back to college."

She flicked her eyes around attempting to come up with a good cover story. J could see something wasn't right and that they needed to leave. He looked at his plate hoping to help with an answer.

"The...train...the train is leaving early, isn't it?"

J's Father bent the corner of the paper, one eyebrow raised,

102

a smirk on his face. His mom set down his plate of food.

"You have to go? But you haven't had any breakfast, you could really use some breakfast."

Her eyes strolled to Ariel's hips then back up as she pinched her mouth. Ariel followed them and smiled back trying to keep the mood light. She knew it'd be the last time J saw his mom and, though they had pressing matters, she didn't want to spoil it.

J stood up, reaching for his mom. "Thanks for everything mom, I owe you so much. I love you."

He left it at that, he didn't want to throw too much out making a scene. He clasped his arms around her as she did the same, squeezing him tight.

"You be careful out there, only swing at the strikes," she said through tears, her voice shaky. It had all hit her at once. She squeezed him one more time, knowing it was time to release, J followed suit. He slipped away.

Ariel was already at the door waiting for him. "It was a pleasure meeting both of you."

J's father stood up, J grabbed him in a big hug. "Thanks... thanks for everything."

His father locked his eyes with him. "You'll do well, it's in your blood. Trust your instincts."

J smiled then turned to leave. He raised a hand, looking back one last time as he took a deep breath. His mom ran to the door, her eyes red. His father stood behind her, a proud smile on his face.

"I'll leave the truck in town at the diner." As they pulled away J waved out the window, getting one last look in the rearview at his house. From now on, he didn't have a home, but was determined to find one. He placed both hands on the steering wheel.

"So, what's going on?"

Ariel pressed her sleeve up revealing the Datacle. "Zane and Max ran into trouble in Sector 5, they need our help."

J tilted his head, eyes still on the road, his eyelids twitching as he narrowed them. *Sector 5. Why did that sound so familiar?* He accelerated, driving as fast as he could into town, only slowing to make the few turns needed. They left the truck, scrambling back to the hangar. Ariel wasted no time lifting off, J buckled up knowing the flight would be aggressive, albeit short. Ariel careened through the structure, not slowing for the turns. J held onto the chair, his chest constricted, fingers crushing the leather armrests as Ariel nearly missed multiple structure beams. She executed the landing sequence on manual control, it was quicker that way.

She bypassed the changing room. "No time for that now."

They stepped out of the elevator, J covered his eyes as the light blinded him. The intense heat hit his throat like a hot campfire, his face burned in the searing sun.

Ariel pulled out a blaster as she glanced at her Datacle. "This way. I suggest you arm yourself."

J didn't waste any time pulling out a small blaster from a hip holster he'd donned in the Omorfiá. Uneven, poorly laid concrete flowed underneath them as they ran down a wide street. Brown stucco and concrete buildings lined both sides, their impoverished construction was evident as the mortar squished out from between each brick, the overlying stucco missing and broken. Men and women in tattered robes ambled about, a few tents were set up to sell dates and other foods. J was piecing it together, he'd been there once before, in a dream. Ariel crawled into an old rusted out truck, slid her head and shoulders under the dash. J realized what she was doing and knew it was pointless to argue. He bounced into the passenger seat. "Ariel..."

"What?" Her voice was muffled by the dash board. She swung hear head out, J was pointing at the ignition, the key with a leather strap hanging from it. She tensed her jaw spinning upright.

"How far is it?"

Ariel's eyes surveyed the road and the surroundings. There wasn't much movement, it was the middle of the day. Every piece of the truck smoldered, J's butt was sweating in the seat along with every inch of his body. She started the truck pulling into the street.

"Not far, maybe a mile."

She stomped on the accelerator and the vehicle lumbered up to speed, the truck slow and the engine underpowered. They passed similarly broken down trucks hauling large wooden crates and barrels, J stuck his head into the breeze hoping it would cool him down. The wind rushed around his body giving slight relief, but the added energy wasn't worth it. He plopped back into his seat.

"How can people live in this heat?"

Ariel snickered. "But, it's a dry heat."

She veered off the main road, heading away from the buildings. Dust engulfed the truck as the road changed from concrete to dirt. J wiped his eyes, the fine-powdered sand sticking to his face, his sweat attracting it like a magnet. Ariel wasn't fairing much better, running her arm over her brow, the soaked sleeve dripped as she pulled it away.

"This place sucks," she announced, blinking hard.

J wasn't going to argue, it was completely inhospitable. Even breathing was difficult, he could feel the sand in his nose clinging to the hairs. He reached for the window handle, thinking that closing off the pesky sand would provide some relief. His fingers touched the knob, but he was quick to retract them. The shiny chrome metal burned at the touch. *Fighting with the sand was the better option, it couldn't be too much further.* He gazed out the windscreen, hunching his back as he neared the glass. A large pyramid-shaped structure he'd seen once before as Arcturus came into view. Ariel kept the truck chugging along, its shot suspension squeaked and rattled above the whine of the engine. It was worse than his pickup back home, much worse. J stepped out, his eyes drawn to the top of the structure. The foundation and walls were comprised of tan, hand set bricks. The steps leading up to the top, empty. The stone, crumbling. Ariel stopped the truck, got out and started walking toward it.

"Where are they?"

Ariel kept a quick pace, her arms swinging with her determined strides. But J didn't have trouble catching her, his longer legs managed to eliminate any speed advantage.

"Inside. Seems they tripped a security system."

J's eyes rolled skyward. *What could be going on? And why did they have to rush?* Ariel stepped past the entrance to the stairway, making a beeline for the corner of the stone where the two walls met. She slapped her arm on one of the smooth stones shoulder high, a panel underneath flipped out. She tapped a code utilizing her Datacle as a reference. J stepped up next to her, leaning on the dusty wall. His eyes drifted to his chest, hands brushing some of the dirt off of his clothes. Ariel pressed the final number sequence and J tumbled into the structure, rolling down a smooth metal ramp. As he hit the bottom, lights clicked on lending a soft orange hue to the room. Lying on his back, he propped himself up and watched the shadow of Ariel enter the structure, her laugh echoed around him as she marched down.

She approached, extending a hand. "You're always falling for me. Better be more careful, Zane said there're traps in here and that wasn't even one of them."

Still covered in dirt, Ariel yanked J to his feet. He attempted to brush his pants clean, it was a losing battle which racked him with coughs from sucking in the fine powder.

"So, which way?" He'd noticed three different corridors from the platform he had landed on, four if you included their entryway. They all appeared identical; metal floor, stone walls sheltered from the elements and in much better condition than the ones outside. Ariel checked the map, it seemed easy enough but the warning she received from Zane told her otherwise. She flipped it open again, showing J. He attempted to read it out loud. "t__p_d in z_g_r_t cel_s m__s___g n__d h_lp tr_ps ev__w__re"

He flicked his eyes to Ariel, "Who wrote that, a kinder-gartner? I can't understand it, can you?"

Ariel chuckled, shaking her head no. She clicked a switch on her blaster, a beam illuminated one corridor. J gazed down the hall; the end looked empty, dark and uninviting. J clicked his on as well, staying close behind her, his head still trying to decipher the message. He watched as Ariel stepped lightly. He attempted to speak, but was met with a sharp, "Ssshh." Lips pursed, eyes on the ground, he focused on not tripping any booby traps. He felt like Tom Swift on an expedition through Mayan ruins. His feet lifted and sunk with grace, the pressure on his soles light, like a cat in the night. Ariel continued forward, stopping as the last of the light faded to darkness. She bent down, examining the floor. The metal stopped and became stone once more, they were generally round or oval, with cut blocks to match the empty spaces. The blocks had letters on them for twenty feet, or so. Ariel glanced at the Datacle then placed a hand on the stone wall. A hologram shined onto the floor, a question glowing in soft green, raised letters.

"What is Greater than God, More evil than the Devil, Poor people have it, Rich people need it, If you eat it you will die?"

J placed a hand on his head, the other on his hip. *Now we're doing riddles?* He watched Ariel stare at the question. Her head swiveled to him and she shrugged her shoulders, raising her hands. J mirrored her movements. *We're still playing the quiet game?* She turned back, placing a finger on her lips. J's gaze caught on her lips, momentarily losing focus of where they were and what they were doing, then his mind snapped back to the question. *If Zane and Max figured it out, surely they could.* He stepped up closer to the hologram and shining a light on the ground, peered past it onto the floor. He felt a hand caress his shoulder. J's eyes swung to her as she mouthed the words "I've got it". He stepped back as Ariel approached the stones. She searched the ground reading the letters, neither of them knew the repercussions if they were to get things wrong. She looked at J, her chest rising as she took in a large amount of air then placed her foot down on the first letter.

J's eyes widened, his arms reached out as he watched Ariel disappear. He frantically searched for her, the floor disappeared, her flashlight beam flickering as she plummeted away from him. He stumbled to the edge and landed hard on his knees, shouting her name. His hand slipped off the edge, the loose gravel from the remaining rock creating an unstable surface. At the last second, he caught himself, face and shoulders hanging over. Ariel's light went out, her screams tapered off, nothing but darkness stared back at him, laughing. He stared in disbelief, his eyes unwavering. *Maybe she'll reappear, flying boots?* Nothing. A few moments passed and he pushed himself up, slid on his butt resting his back on the stone wall behind him. He stared at his boots, the metal plated space boots he'd acquired on Atlantis. His vision shifted to his hands as he contemplated what just happened. *Ariel was gone. Was she dead?*

He answered himself quickly. *No, she's not dead, she can't be. He wouldn't accept that.* Ariel, Zane and Max needed his help, he must find them. He stood up, looked at his Datacle and tapped on the screen attempting to call someone...anyone.

No luck, something was interfering with the operation of the device. *Worthless bracelet.* He thought about throwing it down the hole, but caught himself, thinking better of it. He remembered all of those times it would have come in handy. He examined the walls, the floor, the riddle still shining in his eyes. *The riddle.* Something about it made him feel it was meant for him. He stood up, stared at the letters. *It had to be simple, right?* His head tilted as his finger tapped his lips. His eyes lit up seeing the letters from that angle, there was a word he could spell with them. *Would he plummet to his death if he chose poorly?* He took a deep breath and slipped his foot past the question, repositioning it on a stone labeled "N". He placed his body weight on it, nothing happened. He released the breath he hadn't realized he was holding. *One down six more letters to go.* He worked to the next, the "O" block, then the next block and the next, working his way across the stone walkway. He took the final off of the stone walkway and exhaled, bending over and placing his palms on his knees. *Nothing.*

Glancing back at the defeated obstacle, he turned back toward his objective. Ariel had chosen this path for a reason, he had to continue. He held up the blaster as a miner would a lantern, the path ahead of him was straight and long, the end out of the light's reach. He marched down the hall, his body tight, movements stiff. Sweat ran down his forehead even in the cool underground air. A steel wall glimmered back at him as the light pierced the darkness. Nearing, he found no hinges, no handle, nothing indicating he'd be able to move past. It was a blockade. He spun around searching the dead, black air behind him. *Ariel was heading this way, there must be something I'm missing.* He twisted back to the smooth, featureless surface, the light grey wall uninviting and cold. He placed one hand on it then the other, feeling around for something, some evidence, of a way in, around or through. He took a step back after failing to produce any results, ran a hand through his hair, the sand rubbing between his fingers. *What was he going to do?* He placed his hands on his hips, staring. *Maybe force was needed.* He pushed with his hands then his shoulders, his feet slipping on the smooth ground. He kicked it, but only managed to hurt his toe.

"Come on, just open up!"

"Voice print recognized, J, son of Arcturus. Place your hand on the screen for DNA verification."

After the soothing female voice concluded, a small plate slid out from the side wall, the impression of a hand etched onto it. He did as requested and the door slid open, the voice ushered him in.

"Welcome, J. Please make your way into the proving room."

J's eyebrows drew down. *Proving room?* That sounded strange. He looked past the opening and saw a door leading into an empty room no larger than a bedroom. His steps were light as he continued, the door closed behind him. The wall in front of him illuminated and an image of a woman appeared before him. J's jaw clenched, his fingers curled. Cyrellia.

"Welcome, J. I believe you are here for the fusion cells." She walked to the window of the Exodus, stars flew by like street signs on a summer night, and the camera followed her as she positioned her back to him. "I'm glad you have come. As you know I am on my way to Acadia. Once there, I will rule with an iron fist and no one will stop me. I will create the new world in my image, by my rules, my desires." She turned to face him, her lips tight as her face became stern. "I wish I would be able to see you make your decision in person. You see, I arranged all of this. Arcturus is not the only one pulling strings, I too have people in place to do my bidding. There are people whom you call friends that are, let us say, not. And in the right moment, they will turn on you as Dillon did."

J's knuckles whitened as his chest flexed, he slid his hands behind his body interlocking them, his chin tipped up in defiance.

"You will fail, Cyrellia. Your reign is coming to an end."

Her smile began small and grew into a haughty laugh, one which J wished he'd never heard. His entire body shivered. He attempted to calm it, a brief hum shot through him. Cyrellia's laugh tapered off as two images appeared beside her. J's eyes adjusted to the new pictures, unbelieving. Zane, Ariel and Max stood in a box much like the cargo container in which he'd once ridden. The other image showed a container labeled "Fusion Cells". Between the two, numbers counted down.

Cyrellia smirked as she watched his expression. "You see, I have your friends and now you will make a decision. You stay on Earth and I let them live. Choose to pursue me and they will die."

J's gaze flipped between his friends and Cyrellia, his breathing labored as he continued to hold himself high, his mind taking it all in. Two panels slid out under the screen.

"When the countdown reaches zero, you have to make a choice. Continue after me or save your friends. Simple enough. What is worth more to you? The lives of a few or a world you've never seen?"

J stared at the countdown, the numbers spinning down. They'd just dropped below one minute, the last two digits flipping by ever faster. He weighed his options, there wasn't much time to think. His eyes jumped from his friends to the fusion cells, his chest hurt, his heart felt as though it was colliding with his ribs. *He must save Acadia, his father needed him. But, could he handle losing his friends? Losing Ariel?* His bottom lip quivered as he watched the clock tick down to fifteen seconds.

"You must make a decision, your friends will die if you do not."

J's eyes fell on the two panels. One read "Earth", the other "Acadia". The clock hit 5 seconds. He made his decision, nearly jumping onto the plate, his hand coming down hard. The screen switched off.

CHAPTER ELEVEN

The light emitted a dim hum as he stared at the blank wall, his hand still locked onto the panel as if stuck by an unseen force. His head remained high, attempting to take in what had happened, what the results were. *Did he make the right decision? Did he make a decision at all? Was he too late?* His chest expanded, he held it there a moment before the slow exhale came. The screen flickered on, his hand fell back to his side as his eyes alighted on the image of a man on the screen. He wanted to smile, but the recent events, the unknown, held it back.

"My son, I apologize for the theatrics, but I had to test you. Even with the advances in science, we still cannot determine a person's true intent. I have made mistakes and I know one of them has affected you greatly. As you move forward, be vigilant, think your actions through. Today you were forced to an expedited decision between your friends and the lives of millions you have never meet. You have done well and I'm proud of you. Your greatest and hardest task will be ahead of you, I look forward to meeting you soon. Remember, you are the key, Godspeed."

The image faded and a small platform extended from the wall, presenting him with a data disk. He raised it to his eyes. "Acadia, launch plan?" His arm fell, he still didn't understand what just happened, where his friends were. Just then the door behind him hissed open.

"J?"

He didn't hesitate, he twirled to see Ariel, and a smile drew

up on his face reaching his ears, arms shot out as he ran for
her embrace. He hugged her, squeezing her body tight, a tear
slipped out of his eye.

"Oh, get a room," he heard Max groan as he walked in
behind her. "Guessing you found the fusion cells."

J pushed back from Ariel, cocking a head to meet Max's
query. "Well...no."

J hadn't thought about it, he was still trying to make sense
of it all. *Was that really Cyrellia?* His eyes moved past Max as
Zane entered.

"Thanks for breakin' us out. Not much of the confine-
ment type myself."

His large arms stretched above his head as if he'd been in a
dog cage and released after days of torment.

Ariel slipped her hands onto J's forearms, her eyes locking
with his. "So where are they...the fusion cells?"

J pursed his lips, he wanted to give her the answer she
desired, his eyes rolled side to side like a child thinking of a
story. "I'm not sure, I'm still trying to figure out what just
happened. Where were you?"

Ariel kicked her head back, her chin pressed into her
throat as she examined him.

"Well, I suppose we should start looking for them." She let
go of him as her eyes drove over his shoulder. She smiled, raising her eyebrows. "You sure you don't know where they are?"

J scratched his head. *Was there something he'd missed?*
Ariel pressed two fingers on his cheek forcing his head around.
A large door at the far end of the small room had opened to
reveal a storage room. Multiple cases of cylinders the size of

fifty gallon drums sat stacked neatly on platforms.

Zane stepped by them, his body a dull shade of blue picking up the light emitted from the glass bodies of the canisters. He examined the supply then turned. "Looks like it's all here. Good work, J. Now we can prep the Parádeisos."

Ariel checked her Datacle, it didn't respond. "Zane. Max. You guys good here now? J and I have still have to pick up the last item before we launch."

Zane was already manipulating the platform control, his actions bringing the steel-built structure to life. The cylinders hovered on a cushion of air. "Yeah, we got this. See you on the Parádeisos."

Ariel headed out a separate door that J hadn't noticed before, he was beginning to think he was losing his mind. He quickened his steps, heading off to catch her. She wasted no time moving through the structure and J did all he could short of running to catch her. They popped out into the sunlight, the oppressive heat hitting him like a flaming wall, sweat instantaneously spilling out of his pores. He wiped his brow.

Ariel adjusted her wrist. "Let's get back to the Omorfiá."

She didn't have to say that a second time, he was ready to be rid of this sector. Being trapped in a dream was bad enough, physically being there was unbearable. They jumped into the rusty truck and made their way back to the hangar. J felt as if everything was in slow motion, he couldn't get out of the heat quick enough, sprinting to the elevator when Ariel stopped the truck. This time he didn't care where they left the truck, his body was desperate for relief.

After a ride in the elevator and through the tunnels, they

were back on the ship. Ariel processed the start sequence and the ship bolted out of the hangar. J sat near Ariel as she piloted the ship.

"I'm glad to be rid of that heat, that was horrible. I'm hoping the next sector is much cooler than that hell on Earth. Where are we going again?"

Ariel began laughing.

Her smile was infectious and J stared back at her, his mouth grinning as well. "What?"

Ariel's laughter tapered off, her face dwindling into a devious smile. "You'll see."

J didn't like that answer, but felt he couldn't press her for much more. He'd find out soon enough.

Ariel landed the ship. As they exited the craft, he noticed that the hangar bay sign over the equipment room read "Sector 20". Ariel disappeared in the aisles of clothing, she was forever disappearing. J called her name multiple times. His chest tightened as a heavy object collided into it; instinctively he grabbed it and held the object in his arms. He glanced up at Ariel who stood a few feet away still sporting the devious grin then examined his catch.

Unfolding it, his shoulders sank, jaw dropped. "Seriously?"

Ariel chuckled as she began undressing, the same outfit near her feet. "You said you wanted somewhere cooler."

J gawked at her as she slipped off her shirt.

She caught him staring. "Might want to get dressed, there'll be time for that later."

"When?"

She just winked.

His jaw still hung loose. He dropped his eyes to the suit, he'd worn one before and yes, it had been cooler than Section 5... much cooler. His mind flashed to the bear attack. He wondered if the same threats would be here. At least they could have weapons this time, or so he hoped. After squirming into the suit, Ariel tossed him more clothing, leather and wool over-garments. Navigating the corridors and an elevator, they stepped out into the brisk air. This time, J wasted no time activating his suit. The warming sensation flowed around his limbs like a heated blanket. He shielded his eyes, it was midday and the sun shone brightly, the snow was nearly unbearable to look at.

"Here, take these." Ariel slapped a pair of dark tinted goggles onto his chest, his body retracted from the impact. She went back to searching her Datacle. He slipped the strap over his head, the tint reducing the glare of the fresh white powder. His eyes swept the landscape; small wooden homes lined a single empty street, mountains rose up around them higher than he'd ever seen. He paused, awestruck as his eyes danced on the jagged rocks above, the snow blanketing the flat horizontal surfaces.

"Time to find the last item." Ariel tugged him along. Like him, she was enjoying the colder weather. They made their way to the edge of town and Ariel stopped, triple-checked her wrist, then glared at the steep rocks a dozen yards off. Her head spun toward him. "Looks like we climb."

J's eyes moved to the rock, the jagged stones interlaced with snow tops, platforms only large enough for a single foot.

This was not going to be easy. "Couldn't we just use the flying boots or something?"

J couldn't see her eyes but the rest of her body told him enough. "Climbing it is," he said, walking past her.

He quickly realized his mistake and relented, allowing Ariel to pass him. She immediately began dragging her body up the mountain. J worked hard to keep up, he imagined what it might be like to be Ariel's size, smaller, lighter, more agile. Though his arms proved to be an asset, his long reach allowing him to grab holds Ariel couldn't. His breath was short, Ariel's was as well. They took frequent breaks resting on different levels, never together, the mountain wouldn't allow it. J slipped once, almost losing his footing, his focus jumping sharply down to the ground below. By then, they were a thousand feet above the ground, his vision blurred and swayed. He blinked hard, tilting his head back up. *Don't look down.* He grabbed a rock face, pulling himself up. As his eyes peeked over the cold hard surface, he saw Ariel sitting cross legged staring at the mountain wall. He stood behind her, staring at a wall that was flat and smooth, too flat.

"Is this it?"

Ariel continued scrolling through menus on her Datacle. "That's what it says." She stood up taking a deep breath.

"Any ideas on getting in?"

He figured she'd tried the usual, there wasn't a panel or any other exposed control. She continued scrolling through more information while he stared at the wall. He approached, arm held out, muscles tensed as he placed a hand on the stone. Nothing happened. His shoulders sagged as he took a deep breath. He had to think. Everything was set up for him, for Ariel or the others. His father had planned all of this, there had to be something, a secret block, a password, something. His eyes wandered, never focusing. His mind raced back to his father, his last encounter. He faced the wall.

"J, son of Arcturus."

The mountain growled, a deep sound rumbling from beneath, heavy gears grinding, spinning on one another. The wall cracked open and snow tumbled off the ledge above, the daylight shining in. His eyes darted around searching for what lie behind. Ariel grabbed his arm, almost hugging him. She coaxed him inside, the wall closing as they entered. The sound of grinding stone filled the room then finished with a loud thud. The tinted lenses displayed a dark abyss ahead. Ariel popped her goggles up, J didn't hesitate to follow suit. Their eyes were greeted by four giants. J scanned the area, the walls were stone, another cave buried just inside the mountain, four large pieces of equipment he'd never seen before yet felt oddly familiar with.

"What are they?"

Ariel smirked, walking toward the one in front. The four long, metal legs like that of a large lizard spanned over fifty yards, the rest was a bionic tank-like structure similar to the mechs he'd seen. Ariel grabbed a hold of a ladder at the base of one of the legs.

"They're mechs, though I've never seen any quite like this before. I'm guessing they're one of your father's prototypes."

She continued her ascent, waving him up. He glanced around searching for a better way, the ladder less than inviting.

The mountain had given him enough fear for the day. His eyes focused on Ariel, watching her smooth graceful movements.

She stopped at the top, peering down at him. "Come on, it's not that high."

"Says the girl who's not afraid of heights."

She shook her head, turning to climb into the machine. J studied the ladder. He paced over, grabbed the rungs, and hand-over-hand he climbed. Halfway up, a hum hit his ears. He looked up, the lights on the machine illuminated, brightening with every second. He felt the ladder vibrate and quickened his pace. Three quarters of the way up, the leg took a step forward; he clung tight to the round metal pole. It came to a stop, he took a deep breath then scrambled up the final few rungs and onto the top of the machine. Ariel had left the hatch open, he dropped in. Ariel laughed as she hit a few switches.

"Not funny," he said, his eyes stern and focused on hers.

"Oh relax, you were fine. Besides, your father's stuff is amazing."

He could tell she was excited by the way she sang the last word as she continued playing with switches, her smile permanent. He found a seat next to her. His controls mirrored hers, a large display acting as a windscreen, a control stick, and pedals on the floor near his feet, a lever to his left.

"So, how are we going to get these up to the Parádeisos?"

"That's the trick, right?"

Ariel hit a switch cutting off the engines, the systems faded, the hum extinguished. She stood up facing him.

"I think the best bet is to load each one on a KracKen,

they're the only ships large enough to carry these. And only one in each at that."

J's eyes wandered around, it *was* an amazing piece of equipment. Four seats were laid out in the small cockpit, but it was large enough to move around even with his tall stature. Ariel climbed out, standing atop the giant, J popped his head up and rested on his elbows. He could see what she was looking at and he had the same question.

"How do we get these outside? That door was barely big enough for us."

Ariel crossed her arms shifting her weight to one leg. "There's gotta be a way out, Arcturus would've planned for it."

In his mind, he knew the same. There had to be a way out, they only needed to find it. They climbed down, J's head up all the way to the last step. His muscles relaxed as he hit solid ground. He walked underneath the giant machine, gazing up as he did. Its body was surrounded with rugged panels, all pristine, direct from the factory, or wherever they were built. He spied multiple cannons and weapons racks under the belly, a round oval protruded underneath its opening, facing forward. From his vantage point, he could have stood up in it. He stopped his visual search, wondering what it was for.

"Hey, need to find a way out, remember?"

He observed Ariel tilting her head, standing a few feet away. "Right," he said, his eyes searching for something.

He made his way toward the back of the room examining the wall. Between him and the vertical stone face sat a pedestal not much taller than waist high. He continued toward it, calling to Ariel. As she approached, he found a familiar glass panel on top and placed his hand atop it.

"DNA recognized."

The ground shook, J stumbled grabbing onto Ariel. They steadied themselves as the whole floor began to rise. The walls slid away, metal screeching as it dragged along the stone face, small pieces of rock popping onto the platform along the edges. Hearing the sound above them their eyes scrambled towards the ceiling, their necks tightening to their traps. The ceiling folded open revealing a shaft up the entire mountain. J's eyes dropped back to Ariel.

"I think we found our way out."

She called Zane on her wrist, his image glowing back at them in the dimly lit tunnel.

"What's up kid?"

"You get the fusion cells out okay?"

"Yep, Grant and Titov's crew are working on modifying the Parádeisos. What'd ya find?"

She looked over to the giant mechs, a grin appeared. "New toys. Need transpo though. Got four KracKens handy?"

Zane looked off screen, speaking with someone, then he came back. "They've got one. Guess we'll have to make multiple trips."

Ariel shook her head, she'd hoped they would be able to do it in one go. Still, at least they had one. "Copy that. Can you get it down here ASAP?"

Zane nodded, the comm cut out. The platform continued its crawl upward. *Four trips then they'd be on their way, on their way to a new world.* His mind was brought back as the top of the mountain came to view, the metamorphic rock jagged, uneven rested above them, unmoving. His initial thought was that it would open as the previous ceiling, but this was not the case. As the platform came to a halt, the giant four-legged mechs stopped mere feet from touching. His eyes focused back to the pedestal, a symbol flashed next to it with the words "hangar door". Ariel pressed it and the sandstone rock wall split open. A gust of wind and snow snuck into the room. J's body shivered, he had switched his heated suit off upon finding the interior of the mountain much more comfortable. The cold harsh reality of the true nature of their location revealed itself as more snow flowed in, beginning to cover the ground. A snowstorm must've developed while they were gone.

"Hope Max can get in."

"Oh he will. For all his flaws, he really is one helluva pilot."

J made a face at the comment, something about her giving praise to Max made his skin crawl.

"Let's wait it out in the mech, this weather sucks."

He had to agree with that. The cold, the snow, he could've done without either. Climbing out of the elements sounded like a great plan, even if meant climbing again. After a slow trek up the ladder, J found himself seated next to Ariel. She fired up her new toy, her face glowed as she tapped through menus, hit switches and manipulated the controls. J inspected his surroundings then began to fiddle with the screen and controls at his seat. It felt much like the Tetriack, the menu locations, the status sheets. He came across the weapons load-out and flipped his attention fully to Ariel.

"What is Smoczy Ogień?"

CHAPTER TWELVE

The steel grey hangar doors opened exposing the unforgiving space beyond. His eyes zeroed in on the inbound ship, seemingly small against the gaping opening in the Parádeisos, though the KracKen was anything but. They'd transported an entire satellite holding the Earth's core inside, with room to maneuver. J's focus shifted to the stars beyond, he was mesmerized. It never ceased to amaze him how many there were. And somewhere, out there, a new world awaited. The promise of a new life. They'd soon be traveling beyond the stars he could see now. His thoughts went to the day he first saw it on the screen. Acadia, its green landscape littered with forests and lakes. Would it hold more humans or something different? The movies he grew up watching taught him there'd be giant monsters, blobs or some race of killer robots. *Was any of that true?* Had he been asked the day of the meteor shower, he would've dismissed it. But now his perceptions of reality were skewed. The KracKen came to rest next to the three giant mechs previously delivered to the Parádeisos. He surveyed the deck, a veritable army of ships were scattered about. He hoped it would be enough, or not needed at all. *Father must have a plan. I*t was growing on him, *father.* He knew him, yet he didn't. Max popped out of the ship, Zane behind him.

"Where's that pretty little thing at?"

J sneered back at him his eyelids heavy. "If you're referring to my *girlfriend*, she's on the bridge with Dmitry going over the final preparations."

J had initially been on the bridge with her, but decided

he was only getting in the way; military planning was more of her thing than his. He'd taken a stroll to admire the equipment, the ships, the devices only a child of his past could have dreamed up. He found them fascinating, especially now that he wasn't being shot at, admired the craftsmanship, the contours, the shapes they made. Max walked past him placing a hand on his shoulder, J shook it off glancing back at him, his lips tight.

"Still not fond of him, eh?" Zane was a couple steps behind. J nodded, not wanting to verbalize it quite yet. Zane grinned, stopping beside him. "So, whatcha doing down here? Shouldn't you be on the bridge with Ariel?"

He frowned down at his feet, crossing his arms, then watched the hangar doors as the gap closed. "No. I felt like a third wheel. They've got it covered."

Zane turned to see what he was gazing on. "Beautiful, right?"

J nodded, it was beautiful. He never would've imagined the colors he'd see from space. His preconceptions had visualized space as a black void with white stars. It was proving to be more diverse than he could've ever imagined.

"You eat yet?"

J smiled tilting his head up at Zane. "No. I'm guessing you haven't either."

They strolled to the dining hall. Zane wouldn't be cooking this time. There was a flurry of activity. People littered the seats, the counters buzzed with activity. *Where did all of these people come from?* He followed Zane up to the counter and they ordered. After grabbing his tray he turned, a small voice called to them. "Guys! Here, I saved you a seat."

J chuckled initially, he felt like he was back in high school, saving seats. He surveyed the room and realized it was a good thing she had, not an open table anywhere. Zane lumbered over, plopping down next to V.

"Where did all of these people come from?" J asked, adjusting his food tray.

V stuck a spoon in a cup of white pudding, lifted it up examining it, then flipped it back into its dish, her lip curling as she did. "Earth. It seems that there were more Atlanteans there than we thought. Most came from Sector 13. I've been running them through screenings since you guys left."

She turned to Zane holding up the spoon. "You need to teach them how to cook, this rice pudding is inedible. It tastes like powdered mush."

Zane chuckled, glanced back at the kitchen staff. "I'm sure they're doing the best they can with what they have."

V pushed the tray away, sitting back. "So much for an incredible last meal."

J's eyes darted over to V. "Last meal?" What was she talking about?

She crossed her arms, her back pressed against the seat. "We're going into cryosleep for the trip, didn't Ariel tell you?"

She'd mentioned something to him before, but he hadn't thought much about it. *It was just sleep right?* "She told me we'd be sleeping, is there more?" He leaned in, his thoughts dancing around the possibility of not waking up.

V's expression lightened. "No, J. It is just sleep. It's perfectly safe as long as there's no sabotage."

J's shoulders tensed, he sat straight up.

Zane's body bounced with the effort of hiding his laugh. "Don't scare the kid, V." He turned to J. "It'll be fine, completely safe. You probably won't even dream."

"Oh, he'll dream alright," V predicted as she went back to playing with the rice pudding.

He stared down forlornly at his tray, a burger and fries suddenly didn't seem so appetizing. "What did you mean about sabotage?"

V grabbed a metal cup and took a swig. "Titov. I still don't trust him. What if he sabotages the sleeping containers?"

This time, Zane laughed out loud. "Since when did you become the paranoid type? This isn't one of Ariel's bootleg movies, we'll be fine."

V wasn't convinced and let him know with a look.

Zane shook his head, still sporting a grin. "Okay, what makes you so sure he's up to no good?"

"It's not anything he's said, it's what he hasn't. There is something going on behind the scenes that we're not privy to. I just can't put my finger on it."

J picked up his burger, bacon and lettuce hanging out of the sides. He was determined to enjoy it, last meal or not and had stopped paying attention to the conversation.

V stood up, tray in hand. "Sorry to run, but I have to prep the cryochambers for the trip. It's going to take me a while as we added so many last-minute passengers. Keep an eye on Titov." She slid a hand over Zane's chest and up his shoulder as she walked away, he turned to watch her leave.

J dug his teeth into his meal, it didn't taste too bad, though he'd had better on Earth. They finished their meals in silence. J was lost in his own mind, adding V's paranoia to the ever-growing list of his concerns. He searched his memories for any indication that Dmitry could be a turncoat, but none came to mind. From Zane's reaction, he knew he didn't feel threatened. Still, something seemed off.

"I'm going to go check on Grant, see if he could use a hand. You wanna come?" J needed to occupy his mind with something, left to nothing his mind would focus on the oncoming unknown, something he knew was going to hit like a freight train regardless of how prepared he was for it.

They dumped their trays, headed toward the engine room. Zane showed off his new mastery of the ship, he'd spent more time onboard than J. They hopped on an elevator which not only moved vertically, but horizontally as well and arrived in no time at all.

Tara was standing behind Grant twirling her hair between her fingers. "You think red or purple would look good, I'm thinking purple, can you do that?"

Grant mumbled a reply, he was on his knees, neck deep inside a cabinet. He reached a hand back palm up, flicked his fingers out. Tara placed a tool in his hand and it disappeared into the cabinet, more grumbling shot out. The room featured multiple cabinets, all metal construction, in various shapes. J could see the tops of the fusion cells just behind the two protruding above the floor. Tara spotted them, bent over and tapped on the small of Grant's back. He groused about being interrupted, but his body slid out backward. His head snapped to the intruders, his face obscured by large glasses that resembled binoculars, his eyes huge in the lenses staring back at them.

"Almost done, just a few more lines to connect." He flipped up his ocular device. "Oh, it's you. I thought you were Dmitry again."

He disappeared back into the cabinet, Tara strolled over to them. "I'm sorry, he's been pretty stressed lately."

"Anything we can help with?" Zane asked.

Tara looked back at Grant, his butt wiggled as he worked, still on his knees, waist deep in the ship.

"No, he said he's almost done."

On cue, Grant crawled back, a triumphant cry leaving his lips as he stood staring up at Zane. He adjusted his glasses, flipping them off of his face, and worked to reset the tool to its original configuration. Grant's head stayed buried into the tool, the awkward silence lasting longer than J could handle.

"So everything's set for the flight to Acadia?"

The little mole of a man completed his tool manipulation and handed it to Tara. "Yes. 220,474."

J's eyebrows furrowed. "What?"

Grant waddled over to the fusion cells, leaned on them, his face nearly touching the glowing blue glass. "That's the best I can do, we don't have enough fuel cells to make it there any quicker."

J's eyes rose over the equipment rested on Zane. *220,474 years? Was that how long the trip would take?*

"Grant, simplify it. That's days, I hope?" Zane asked.

Grant fiddled with one of the cells, turned to another accomplishing the same task. "Yes, days."

Tara walked over to help, handed Grant another tool.

"54 years, that was the best I could do. The cells will overload from too much stress if I push it to 50 years as Dmitry required."

Required? Why would Dmitry require 50 years exactly? J's eyes wandered, watching Grant manipulate each cell.

"You sure we can't help?" Zane asked, taking a few steps toward the containers.

Grant popped up, finished with the cell under his hands. "No, that was the last one." He waddled over to the cabinet shutting the door. "We should tell the Admiral the new timeline."

J turned to Zane, his lips tight together as he placed his hands behind his back.

"Did he say why he needed to be there in 50 years?"

Grant shrugged his shoulders, walked past them.

Tara followed, but stopped, briefly addressing J. "You like girls with colored hair. Do you think I should go purple or red?"

J stared at her a moment. It seemed like an odd question, but then again, she wasn't human. Maybe it was in her programming to want to change her hair color. "Purple," he blurted out.

She beamed, it seemed she was already leaning that way and only needed confirmation. Just then an announcement came over the ships speakers.

"Attention on the ship, this is Admiral Titov speaking. Our systems are fully operational and are in the final stages of preparation for the jump to Acadia. Make your way to your cryochamber. If you have not been assigned one, see your commanding officer. Admiral Titov out."

"Commanding officer? What are we, the Army?"

Zane shrugged, walking after the others. "Guess we better go get a ticket for this ride."

They made their way back to the bridge. *Why would he be so specific about the arrival time?* J tried to work it out in his mind, finally resting on the fact that they were attempting to get there sooner rather than later. Cyrellia already had the jump on them, they needed to close the gap. They stopped in front of a room he was very familiar with, the briefing room. Zane went in first, hopping into one of the cush leather seats to the side. The table sat empty, the window open to the stars. He walked around the table, hands interlocked behind his back, then stopped to gaze out the window. The moon hung in the distance, juxtaposed with the Earth behind; they were putting space between the two. The Earth looked like a normal round planet, the structure, the plates hidden in the swirls of clouds and the inaccurate details increased with distance. The moon, he corrected himself internally, New Atlantis, glowed brightly. The contours of the craters, the shades of grey all met his eye in high definition, details he never believed he'd ever see. In a few short hours it would be a memory. He lightened his focus, dragging it over the moon's surface.

"You look just like your father."

J turned to see Dmitry standing inside the doorway, his square jaw dominating his face. He stepped around Zane as he circled the table.

"I remember this view in a similar situation. Standing next to him, gazing upon his creation, a creation some days I felt he wished hadn't come to fruition. Still, there it sits, nearly empty."

Empty? Hardly. He prayed the new governing authority would prove honorable and just caretakers for the innocent inhabitants. His shoulders lightened as he exhaled. "Why did you ask Grant to adjust the power so the trip would only take fifty years?"

Dmitry twisted his head, his eyes focused on him. J's posture remained solid, his vision locked on Atlantis.

Dmitry turned to mirror his posture. "Simple, really. We need to get there as quickly as possible, we can't let Cyrellia gain a foothold on Acadia."

J heard footsteps at the door, twisted his torso and leaned back. Ariel sauntered in with half of the officers he'd previously met on the bridge. Their faces were recognizable, though none of their names came to mind. Not even the Lieutenant's, as pretty as she was, her blond hair tight in a bun behind her head. They all positioned themselves in seats around the table. Dmitry extended a hand indicating for J to take a seat.

Dmitry faced the table, the screen behind him becoming opaque, a nearly entirely green planet materializing. "You all know that this is Acadia. Thanks to J, we have the launch plan and the equipment needed to make the jump. Getting there will only be half the battle, the other is to remove Cyrellia and TK from power. You all have your tasks, any last questions before we enter cryosleep?"

J looked around, everyone remained still. He had so many

questions, but felt he would get a chance in a more private setting to ask them. The blond Lieutenant called the room to attention, Dmitry dismissed them immediately and the room emptied leaving Ariel, Zane, and J watching Dmitry. He lowered his head a few inches, his shoulders following as he placed his hands on the table.

"This is going to be nothing short of a miracle; even with what we have, we're still out matched in every category. Ariel, brief J and Zane on the way out. I have your crew on the quarter deck, we'll rally on the bridge after we exit cryosleep. You're dismissed."

Ariel stepped out of the room waving for J to follow.

"So what are we doing?"

Ariel marched down the hall toward the quarter deck, Zane took up position behind, his heavy steps vibrating the ground behind J. She grabbed his hand and tingles danced up his arm, his muscles loosened. He matched her strides.

"Sleeping together," she winked at him.

He blushed, she knew that wasn't what he was asking. Zane didn't say a word, just continued on. J followed suit, he didn't want to be a nuisance, her touch was enough for him at the moment. They arrived at the quarter deck's cryo-sleep chamber. Tara was sitting on the floor against the wall, her eyes wandering around while Grant hunched over her. J looked closer to see that her neck was open, two tiny screw-drivers pinched in his small hands working on her.

"Hi, J!"

Her voice was jovial and a smile came to her face when she spoke. J surveyed the room. Ten drum-like contraptions lined the walls. They were half-covered in glass and leaned at forty-five degree angles. He shuddered thinking that they looked similar to the escape pods he'd not fared well in. Max had slipped off his clothes and was down to his underwear, he pointed at them giving Ariel a grin. She rolled her eyes in response.

"Ready for a long sleep?" Tara queried.

Grant continued his adjustments, spun the screwdriver one more time and Tara's head went limp. He realized there'd be no use for a robot to cryosleep. He turned to see Ariel begin stripping, Zane was doing the same.

She locked eyes on him. "Don't just stand there, I get to watch too."

J looked down, pulled off his shirt, then slipped off his boots, pants and socks. He bounced on the cold floor. "Heated suits but no heated floor?"

"I know, right?" Ariel grinned, pressing a button to open the canister.

J skipped over to the adjacent one, pressing the same button. He continued his dance, bouncing as he shifted his weight from leg to leg, hoping the movement would warm him up. In reality it wasn't that cold and he knew it, he was trying to preoccupy his mind. He was basically naked and so was everyone else. He took another peek at Ariel as she climbed in, adjusting her hair behind her head.

"Wait. Dmitry said you'd brief us."

Ariel pressed the button, the canister began to close. "There'll be time when we get there, sleep tight."

His jaw hung open as he watched her smile. The chamber

locked shut, the device hissed and he watched Ariel close her eyes.

"Well, get in there."

J's head spun around as V walked in. She was fully dressed, once more in her trusty lab coat, and holding a tablet.

He opened his mouth, still dancing on the floor. "What about you?"

"Don't worry about me. I convinced Dmitry to let me check on everyone before I myself go under. Now hop in, it's a long trip. Grant said that the fuel cells couldn't get us there any quicker than 54 years."

J's eyebrows raised thinking about the statement. He climbed in, laid down on the comfortable cushion that conformed to his body and depressed the interior button to close the device.

As the glass shut, V walked up tapping on the tablet. She peered in giving him a smile. "Have a great sleep, see you on Acadia."

CHAPTER THIRTEEN

The Earth looked back at him, its beautiful greens, blues and whites all blending into a collage contrasting the darkness behind. A grey desert lay in the foreground obscuring the bottom third. J knew it was a dream, he was more aware than he'd ever been before. In the back of his mind he knew that he was on the way to Acadia and this was but a fleeting moment in the life of his father, Arcturus. He felt the comfort of his hands behind his back as he shifted his weight to one foot, his chest rose then fell, footsteps echoed in his ear. He waited for the question, shifting to the other leg.

"Sir, it's time for your appointment with the council. Will you be driving or flying?"

He placed a hand on his chin, tapping, the other remained behind his back. "Flying. Ensure Zebulon joins us for the inspection."

"Yes, sir. Anything else?"

J turned to see his assistant standing with his tablet in hand, adjusting his glasses.

J dropped his hand and sauntered toward Jeffrey. "No, that will suffice. I'll meet you on the pad momentarily."

His assistant left out the door and J turned, again appraising the Earth. He walked up, placed a hand on the glass, his fingers spread out. Cold rushed though them, shooting down his arm. "All of this because of us."

He dropped his hand as he spun on his heel, stalked out into the hall and onto the elevator, riding it up to the interior of Atlantis. As the doors opened, the false sun scattered beams of light around him, he squinted. J had never felt comfortable under the intense glow. The hum of engines permeated the air as a large ship came into view, the docking ramp lowered as it touched down.

His assistant walked up beside him. "Zebulon has been notified, he will meet us at the inspection."

J nodded as they boarded then took a seat, his assistant next to him.

"Is everything still on time?"

"Nearly everything. We had to push the weapons storage to the right, there is a steel shortage again."

"Have you advised the council to melt down their metal monstrosities, those Mediators?"

His assistant fiddled with his tablet, swiping through a few screens. He adjusted his glasses once more. "I have, but they would rather acquire some from other sources."

"Where?"

"Economic housing in Sector 23."

J felt his jaw clench, he shifted it back and forth, leaned his head back. "What are they doing with the people there?"

His assistant hesitated before answering. "Removing them."

J felt his chest and legs contract. He lifted his head and rolled it toward Jeffrey. "You mean murdering them."

His assistant didn't move, just stared at the tablet hoping for the moment to pass. The engine noise changed indicating that they were on approach. They walked out onto an empty pad, the ship departing to another task, and worked their way into the conference room. The council was already seated, he was the last one to enter.

Cyrellia stood up, her lips holding a tight smile. "I am so glad you could join us. We were just discussing the steel shortage, but we have found a solution."

J felt his nose crinkle as he slipped past her into his seat.

"Now that the illustrious Arcturus is here, we can attend to important matters. Solon, you have the floor."

Cyrellia sat down, glancing at J. A man at the far end of the table stood up, his appearance young, if slightly overweight, ears large with a nose to match.

"As you know, the Exodus is a major undertaking. The construction requires all of the resources we can muster, resources which are in short supply. We have already displaced a section of housing, but that will only supply us for so long. We simply need more steel."

J looked around the room, the council members nodded their heads in agreement. Cyrellia stared back at Solon.

"I believe Sector 14 has a similar situation we can capitalize on."

"What about the Mediators? You have thousands of them and we don't need that many to keep the peace. By my calculations we only need an eighth of what is already in use, if that. Atlantis is safe, secure and you have cameras everywhere. There is enough security without them."

Cyrellia's eyes snapped back to his, her lips curled. She straightened up, her head tall. She leaned it back, eyes glaring down at him. If J had been in control, he would've shivered from the icy cold glare.

"The Mediators are off the table, they will be kept as is. I suggest you find another solution."

J felt his tongue flick the back of his teeth, he placed his arms on the table one hand on the other. "Let me reinitiate project lantern and I will—"

"Stop with all your project names. If I remember correctly, that is the one where you pick up space trash, is it not? Just call it what it is, trash collection."

J tightened his grip on his hand, he shifted in his chair. "I'm confident I will acquire more than enough steel to finish Exodus, I will just need the funds and approval to reinitiate... trash collection."

Cyrellia watched him intently as he examined the room for approval. Solon, still standing, was the first to speak up. "I second that."

His eyes paced around as did J's, more voices could be heard in agreement. J relaxed, not enough for anyone to see, but J felt it.

"Very well, you get your wish. I shall have the funds deposited immediately and you will give me weekly status updates on the progress." She looked around the room, her lips tight forming a small circle. The room remained silent. "Any other issues to be brought to the council?"

J surveyed the room once more, not a single member stirred.

Cyrellia stood up, her hands firm on the desk. "Arcturus, the floor is yours. We eagerly await the inspection and expect nothing but good news."

J stood up, addressed the council. "Members of The Kontrolery, I am pleased to announce that we are on schedule.

And with the previous issue addressed, we have no further issues. We are working feverishly to produce results showing a life-sustaining planet. We have narrowed it down to three solar systems, one of which is very promising. Now, if you will join me, I'll walk you through a finished portion of the Exodus."

The council murmured excitedly and he noticed many of them smiling as they passed, some shook his hand. His eyes moved to the door where his assistant stood awaiting his approach.

"Is everything prepared?"

"Yes," his assistant replied, nodding to council members as they strolled past.

"And Zebulon?"

"He is at the worksite, prepared for all questions. Shall I notify him that the council is on the way?"

"Please do and ensure they do not begin without me."

His assistant turned and walked away, J continued to stand by the door shaking hands and addressing members as they left. After a few moments, the room was empty save for one. Cyrellia pushed her chair away from the desk, her presence looming in the room. It felt small, as if her spirit flooded every crevice. She strutted over to J. "Are you not coming with us Arcturus?" Her eyelids hung low as she finished with a half smile.

J gathered himself, felt his body stiffen, his feet lift in his shoes as if asking for more height.

"Yes, I am. I have some business I must attend to before."

She raised one eyebrow, attempting to suss out what nefarious business he might have and whether or not it impacted her

141

plans, then dismissed him and glided away. "Don't be late, we have schedules to keep."

The elevator door closed and she was gone. He explored the room, verifying it to be empty. After his careful search, he raised a wrist tapping in commands, watched and read.

Meet at location 5BE in one hour, new assignment.

He proceeded down the elevator and boarded his ship, his assistant standing at the ready at the top of the ramp. "Cutting it a little close, sir."

"No way around it this time. Please expedite travel."

He proceeded to sit down as the ramp closed and the engines hummed to life, his body pressed into the chair as if a person sat on him. His eyes shifted out the window, the city flew by, building after building as the craft picked up speed. They traded edifices for underground structures of pure steel and shiny metal as they careened down the approach tunnel. The light flickered ever faster as they accelerated. The stars glimmered and twinkled back at him as they exited into space, the craft adjusting course, keeping the moon just out his window. The glow of the sun bounced off of craters and uneven terrain. A solid line of light instantly disappeared as they transitioned to the dark side of the moon, the sun's rays nonexistent. He felt the craft slow, saw the build site appear below, the skeletal structure of the Exodus illuminated by millions of work lights sitting motionless on the moon's surface. The craft descended, landing in a hangar near the largest section, nearly complete. The ramp dropped down and he stepped out meeting Zebulon.

"Jeffrey informed me that you wish for me to assist you on

the inspection today."

He walked past, his stride quick and deliberate, Zebulon followed. "Yes. He passed you the information?"

"Yes, sir. I will guide them through the battlements and the battle cruiser Houzeau."

They continued their march, still at a brisk pace, up a ramp onto another floor, then rounded a corner into a briefing room. A few members of the council had arrived, he sought out particular faces, ensuring they were in place. "Has Cyrellia appeared?"

"I have not seen her, sir. I believe she is still in transit," replied one of the council members.

His assistant rushed in, his breathing labored. He tapped on his tablet, handing it to J. "The presentation is ready."

J handled the device, moved to the front of the room. He turned around, his face full of Cyrellia. She had just walked in, her arms crossed, expression awaiting a show.

He adjusted his stance, confidence flowed through him, his shoulders back, head high. His hands, in the familiar pose behind his back, both gripping onto the tablet.

"TK council, we are here today to witness firsthand the solution to our growing problem. It is no secret that Earth is failing and we must find a new planet, a new home. Until now, the technology to move an entire planet was out of reach. Today I tell you otherwise and am proud to give some tangible evidence of your plentiful credits at work."

He held up the tablet. Tapping a button, a hologram popped off of the screen displaying the skeletal structure of the ship. He manipulated it with his hand, pulling a piece of the ship away from the main portion.

"This is battleship Houzeau, housed inside Exodus, ready to detach from the main ship once we arrive in Acadia's solar system. Last week it was completed and today, Commander Zebulon will take half of you through a select section of the ship. The other half will join me as I detail the construction site and the timeline going forward. As you have heard, we are fully on schedule. Now, if the right half of the room will follow me, I will be happy to discuss any questions you might have."

J's body loosened as he stepped to the back, half of the room following him, including Cyrellia. His nose twitched when he noticed, he massaged his chin continuing past her and she turned to follow. He strolled out into a large opening in the center of the ship, tapped the screen as the rest of the council filtered in. A projection of the final product, a large maintenance hangar, displayed in front of them. He took a few questions, closed the program and continued on. He accomplished this a few more times as they toured through various parts of the ship until they came to the final finished bulkhead. Cyrellia approached, her long strides smooth and graceful. She stopped directly in front of him, merely a foot away.

"You have done well. Ensure the timeline stays intact or there will be consequences." She marched off, her show was over and the construction progress was as briefed. She had no reason to lash out and, to J, she seemed almost disappointed. He guided the rest of the council back to the main entrance, switching with Zebulon. The second half proceeded as the first and came to a close where they started. His assistant met him as the council members dispersed, he handed him the tablet.

"Tell the pilot to drop me off at building 525, I'll find my own way home."

His assistant scurried away.

J took his time, gathering in the construction of the Exodus one last time. He felt his teeth rub on his upper lip as he headed out. After arriving in his ship, he was dropped off as requested atop building 525. J had never seen it before. The structure appeared older than the others on Atlantis, the metal not as polished, as if left to rot. Black soot was caked on half of the entranceway and he manually opened the door. The smell of smoke hit his nose. He turned his head, hoping to reduce the effects, but it was too late. He coughed, covering his mouth with his forearm. After a few minutes, he found a set of stairs, the first he'd ever seen in Atlantis, and began to climb. Everything seemed from a different time, a different place. The building's interior was worn, tattered paintings and other wall decorations hung randomly with no care. Four flights up, he exited the stairwell into a lobby. Well-worn leather chairs sat facing a steamer trunk, a tattered deck of cards atop it. He continued in, the lighting dark. Hard shadows fell across the room, his eye detected movement.

"You know they're tearing this place down. We'll have to find another place to meet in the future."

The voice came from the shadows across the room, his eyes struggled to see in the darkness. He took a couple of steps closer. "This will be the last time we meet in person."

A sparked flashed near the shadowy man's face, the red orange glow slightly illuminating his features as he lit a cigarette. "I'd offer you one but I know you don't' smoke."

Will stepped out from the shadow, his appearance just as J remembered him. Had he been in control he would have shaken his head to make sure he was seeing okay.

J took a step toward him. "Here, I have something for you." J reached into a pocket displaying a carton of cigarettes. "I'll send encrypted instructions when the time is right. Is your brother here?"

On cue, Dominik stepped in, his cigarette already in his mouth.

J turned his attention to Dominik. "I have reactivated Project Lantern, there's a specific task I need you to accomplish with regards to a certain satellite."

Dominik took a drag on the cigarette, holding in the smoke a moment before exhaling it out of the side of his mouth. "What did you have in mind?"

J crept closer, tilting his head as he leaned in. "I need you to produce a meteor shower."

CHAPTER FOURTEEN

He slapped his hands on his face, dragged them down. His skin felt like mush, his eyelids pulling away toward his cheeks. He ran his fingers through his hair finishing over his ears. The blaring sound that had awoken him still rang out like an ambulance. He rolled on his side, his free arm searching for a pillow to block out the awful noise. Failing to find anything, he shot his arm straight out hoping to find his alarm clock, his fingers smashed into the glass enclosure. He instantly retracted his hand, wincing at the throbbing pain in his fingertips and knuckles, then thrust himself up and drilled his head on the upper glass. He fell back in a heap rubbing his head and moaning in pain, the wavering tone making things worse. He shook his head, attempting to get his wits about him and peeked out from under heavy eyelids. The room flashed red in time with the pulsating sound he wished would stop.

He finally remembered where he was, why he was in the cryochamber. Fumbling around, his fingers found and depressed the release button, his glass prison began to lift, its metal straps and hinges reflecting the red light into his eyes. He squinted, attempting to see better and slipped out onto the ground. His head snapped around searching for Ariel. She was in a similar state of disorientation; he watched her nearly collapse on the floor. The room shook, he'd felt that before when they'd attempted to rescue one of the scientists from the Reprobi Angeli, heavy cannon blast. He steadied his feet, held his arms outstretched, ready to brace for another impact. Ariel was holding her head with one hand, the other searched for something, anything, to help with the sudden violent motion that had just occurred. The ship rocked again, he stumbled over to her grabbing her hand.

"You okay?" he shouted over the deafening siren.

She rubbed her head then another wave hit, knocking them into her canister. She ended up on top of him, any other time he would've enjoyed it, but under these circumstances he needed to do something quick. His eyes swept toward Zane's capsule, he was out grabbing Max who was having the same difficulties they were. J gently pushed Ariel back to her feet, his body following. Over her shoulder he could see Grant attempting to get Tara up and running again. That meant...

"V. Where's V?"

His eyes darted around, Ariel did the same, searching. He realized that neither of them knew where she was. The ship rocked again. Zane stumbled, still trying to help Max. The siren silenced as the speakers came to life.

"This is Admiral Titov, the Parádeisos is under heavy attack. Every able body to the launch hangars, launch the fleet. Standby for further orders."

The speaker cut out, the sound of heavy blasts replacing it as another large cannon hit the hull, rocking the ship again. The lights continued to flash but reduced in speed.

"Do you know where V is?" J asked Zane as they braced themselves on the same canister.

"No, she was supposed to be in the Admiral's cabin. She said she would be the last one to go down after him."

"Where's that at?"

Max stumbled into them as the ship rocked. "Up one floor."

He glanced at Ariel then back to Zane. "Ariel. You, Zane and Max get to the hangar, I'm going to find V"

Ariel stepped up next to Zane, blocking J's exit. "Not without me!"

J glanced over and pointed at Grant. "I need you to help Grant. Get him and Tara to the hangar."

Ariel stood firm, her shoulders tensed as her fingers tightened. "I'm—"

"There's no time to argue, you need to help them. I promise I'll meet you in the hangar." J reached up and placed his hand on her cheek, looked into her eyes. "Please, Ariel. Grant needs your particular set of skills."

Ariel growled, pushing off of him. She ran toward Grant, sliding in next to him, pulled a blaster out and aimed it at Tara's head. J's eyes grew as she locked onto his then clicked on the tactical light illuminating Grant's access to Tara's head. J exhaled sharply as he took off running down the hall that housed the elevator. He pressed the up button and waited for the ride to be over. The ship continued to periodically shake, each time throwing J around. He constantly braced himself, but stumbled a few times on his way to Titov's quarters. Once inside, he stopped in his tracks. All of the capsules were empty.

The speaker system sounded, "This is Admiral Titov. The ship has been breached, all access to the forward portion has been cut off. Anyone still in the aft cabin must access hangar bay #4. All personnel aft of bulkhead 94 must evacuate, the breach is too great to contain. The system will be jettisoning the aft portion. I—"

The transmission cut out. J stopped staring at the ceiling

and continued his search. *Nothing, no trace. She must be with Titov.* The ship rocked longer than it had before, the sound of metal screeched through his ears. He fumbled with the elevator switch. The hangar was down, he knew that much. He navigated the corridors and hallways until reaching the hangar then stumbled, a blast hitting the ship as he reached the entrance ramp. He lost his footing and rolled down toward the spacecraft. Picking himself up, he realized that the hangar was nearly empty. All he saw were soldiers running into the KracKen, the last two fighters taking off and exiting the hangar bay. Flames and sparks flew from the walls and ceiling. His eyes snapped to the KracKen's ramp. Ariel spotted him at the same time and began running toward him. Looking past the ship and out the hangar he saw ordinance flying in every direction. A colossal craft seemed to hover in the distance, he witnessed multiple blue glows along the ship's side. Cannon blasts hit a few seconds later, the ship rocked and he stumbled forward into Ariel's arms.

"Where's V?" she shouted.

"I don't know, the cabin was empty. The Admiral said—"

She grabbed his hand, tugging him toward the KracKen. "We heard, there's no time, this is the last ship. I pray V makes it out alive."

She dragged him onto the ship, the large mech greeted them as Ariel slapped the loading bay door switch. She raised her arm, screaming into it, "We're on board, punch it."

J felt the craft shake as it lifted off, the hum of the engines spooling up. Ariel reached for a handle near the wall, but it was too late. Their bodies flew into the rear of the craft as

Max went from zero to full thruster. J groaned when his back smacked the uneven metal wall of the cargo ship. *For being so large, it sure packs a kick.* While his body hated it, he knew that it was better than being dead. The pressure alleviated, Ariel and J slid down onto the floor. He winced and groaned, pushing himself up, feeling as if he'd just been in a car accident.

"You okay?" he asked Ariel, rubbing his head.

She rubbed the small of her back with both hands, her chest out as she wiggled back and forth. J continued rubbing his head, using it as an excuse to stare. His ears picked up the distinct sound of ordinance hitting the ship's shield. Ariel stopped licking her wounds and ran toward the bridge, J in tow. The sight that greeted them left them momentarily mute. A large planet sat directly off the nose. Ariel bolted toward the screen. Stopping, she placed a hand on the headrest of Max's seat. "Is that...?"

"Acadia," J finished, stepping up next to her.

He feasted his eyes on their new home, observing the greens and blues he remembered. It looked just like his dream. They'd made it.

"Where's V?"

Maybe not all of them had made it. He'd been dreading the question, knew that Zane in particular wouldn't be satisfied with the answer. "She wasn't there. No one was there. I couldn't find her."

Zane straightened away from the wall he'd been leaning on, fists clenched. "You couldn't find her? I wouldn't...none of us would be here if it wasn't for her. Why did you leave if you didn't find her? Did you even look?"

"That's not fair, Zane. We all love V. You know he went after her and..."

The shield percentage flashed on the bottom of the screen...50%.

J's eyes cut to the planet then back to the percentage. *How could it be so low already?* His gaze was drawn back to the screen. Multiple fighter ships engaged each other. The mammoth battle cruiser floated above them, its cannons pummeling the Parádeisos behind them.

"What are we going to do about that?" J pointed to the dwindling shields. Ariel assessed the scene on the other side of the screen, her palms together, forefingers on either side of her nose and thumbs below her chin; she pinched the bridge of her nose between her forefingers. J looked over at Max who was systematically tapping buttons, adjusting thrusters, shields, attempting everything he could think of to keep them afloat a bit longer. J's eyes danced around the screen while thinking about the ship, it was a cargo ship, no weapons. He stood up straight, ran toward the cargo bay grabbing Zane on the way. His adrenaline pumped as he threw Zane through the door, shutting and locking the bridge.

"What's going on? Are we having it out away from the others?" Zane stood erect, his eyes narrowed, judging J.

"No time, get one of the spacesuits."

Zane's mouth hung open slightly, he watched J hop off the deck sliding down the emergency stairs to the cargo bay floor multiple decks below. J bolted over to the emergency space-suits, tossed an extra-large suit toward the stairs. He worked at donning his own. Dillon came to mind while he slid it on, something he'd said during his weapons training. "Slow is fast, fast is slow." He worked at an even pace, his movements fluid. No energy wasted, no fumbling with the equipment. He finished, tossed the larger suit to Zane as he ran toward him.

"What's going on?"

J didn't answer initially, he just ran to the ladder embedded in the mech's leg.

"No time, just get the suit on and follow me."

Zane watched him scale the metal giant, there was no hesitation in his climb. J slid down into the cockpit. Remembering that the controls were programmed like the Tetriack, he initiated the start sequence, the engines hummed to life.

Zane flopped into the seat next to him, putting V out of his mind, compartmentalizing so that he could focus on the mission...for now. "Okay kid, looks like you're running the show. Whadya need?"

J flipped switches, ran through menus. He grabbed the controls, moving them as he'd seen Ariel do earlier. While waiting for Max, she'd let him drive it, albeit only for a few minutes, but it was enough.

"Call the bridge. Tell Max to open the hangar doors."

J slipped on the helmet locking it in place, the screen appeared, menus flashed. He extinguished them and concentrated on the task. Zane called Max and Ariel on the bridge, they appeared in his helmet visor.

"What are you doing, J?"

"Remember the flight in the mountains when we were running from the Russians?"

Ariel raised one eyebrow, leaning into the screen, her hand

still on Max's headrest. "Yes," her response slow.

"Same thing...but with a mech."

Ariel's grin was infectious. "Okay, I hope I gave you good enough lessons. Shields are at 20%, you're only going to get one shot at this. Max, place all power into thrusters, get us to Acadia as fast as you can. J, I'm opening the hangar bay doors, good luck."

Her image disappeared from the visor. J organized his weapons, placing them at the ready. He armed the missiles, cannons, and anything else he could find in the menus.

"Zane, you take the rifles. I'll work with the missiles. When those bay doors open, shoot at anything hostile."

Zane's lips curved into a smile, his fingers tightened on the controls. "I can do that."

The hangar bay lights flashed, warning them that the bay doors were opening. They were slow and cumbersome. He stepped the machine forward, his fingers rubbing the controls, he gnawed on his bottom lip with his teeth. The stars began to emerge and a fighter craft zipped across followed by another, its weapons engaging the first. He lurched the mech forward to the edge of the ship's doors, now half-open. He felt the ship rock when a heavy blast hit. His body pressed into the seat as Max banked the ship. Two more fighters flew across, one conducting a return-to-target maneuver to engage them, its rounds inbound. J opened fired, letting two missiles slide off the rack, smoke trailed as they exited the KracKen. Zane added rifle rounds and the enemy ship popped like a firecracker, the sound inaudible. Another fighter engaged, the KracKen turned, the g's pulling his cheeks toward his chest. He tensed his body attempting to combat it. Zane fired first as J crept closer to the edge, the giant mech almost hanging out of the KracKen. The battlespace became clear, ships littered the stars. The colossal battle cruiser he'd seen earlier was engaging what was left of the Parádeisos, their cannons exchanging volleys of ordinance. His eyes were drawn toward Admiral Titov and the Parádeisos, the ship continued to be hammered by the enemy, explosions popping on the skin of the behemoth. He saw the battle cruiser break apart as the final blow landed mid-ship. The Parádeisos drifted apart, the aft section dropping toward the planet. His mind turned to V, his skin tingled. A blast blinded him momentarily, snapping him back to the battle. Another fighter was engaging, pieces of the KracKen broke away, the picture of dark space began to lighten and the pursuing ship broke off. His eyes snapped around searching for more dark space now morphing to sky, a thin haze built as the stars continued to fade. The hangar doors began to close and J glanced over at Zane. He sat back into his seat, his shoulders relaxed.

Zane looked back at him. "We made it, kid. Good thinking."

J took a deep breath, watching the black sky fade into a white milky substance, the stars completely gone. Ariel popped up on his visor, frantically tapping buttons, Max was doing the same. She slipped into the seat next to him engaging the restrains, straps flipped over her shoulders and waist.

"Not in the clear yet, boys. I suggest you buckle up, hull's breached, hangar doors are jammed."

J focused on the half-closed doors, the edges glowing

orange. The color spread as one of the doors began to bounce open, the whole craft shaking. Zane flipped on the restraints, J followed suit, the buckles tightening around his chest, waist, and thighs. Both cargo doors began to shudder, the upper one departing the craft. He watched it flip away, completely engulfed in flames, melting right before his eyes. The bottom door didn't fare much better, clinging to the ship as if it were alive. The door fluttered away, disintegrating. The edges of the ship continued to glow red, some of the items in the hangar combusting. He pressed the controls into reverse. Glancing at the small screen displaying the rear view, he walked the mech back until it made contact with the KracKen's interior. Flames danced about the open bay in front of him, obscuring most of the white clouds engulfing the ship. The white opaque layer vanished. He squinted to see beneath the chaos. Green began to emerge, he guessed it to be vegetation, though the ship's speed made details indistinguishable. The ship shook violently, rattling his brains.

Ariel's voice came over the comm. "Brace for impact!"

J released the controls, his hands moving onto the chair arms. His fingers squeezed, muscles tensed making him immobile like a mannequin. He closed his eyes, another shudder of the ship, this one even more violent. His head bobbed around, flailing as if attached to a spring. He held tighter, if that was possible. He was thrown backward into his seat at the same time the sound of metal crushing found his ears, then silence.

CHAPTER FIFTEEN

J groaned, rubbing the back of his neck, stretching it to the empty seat next to him. He wiggled his jaw, his sockets cracking.

Zane reached for him, unstrapping his restraints. "How you doing, kid?"

J continued rubbing the point where his neck met his shoulders, his fingers grazing the helmet's clasp as he climbed out of the seat. His legs wobbled as he stood up.

"I've felt better. You?"

"Yeah, there's nothing quite like a spacecraft crash to get the blood flowing."

Zane had already removed his helmet, but J fumbled with the globe over his head, his dexterity shaky. Zane reached over, clicked it free and tossed it to the side.

"Better find the others."

J agreed. He needed to ensure Ariel was alright. The mech, on the inside, was still intact; little to no damage could be seen. He thought about the flames on entry to the planet's atmosphere, the heat melting objects in the KracKen's bay. He'd felt none of it, the mech's life support systems must've been able to handle the intense heat, keeping them safe and cool. He reached up out of the hatch, placing his palms on the flat exterior of the giant, pressing himself up. The sun's reflection off of the metal surface hit his face causing him to squint, he turned his head surveying the damage. The mech sat in a pile of rubble near the KracKen's bulkhead and bridge entrance, its legs folded underneath itself. A beam of sunlight peeked through the upper half of the KracKen, its hull broken open in multiple locations, pieces of twisted metal hung from the walls and ceilings. Sparks flickered as cables and wire swung, grounding each other as if saying "hello". The air was silent, enhancing the sound. J finished climbing out and moved out of the way for Zane who plopped himself on one cheek an arm supporting half his body. He didn't say anything, but J could tell what he was thinking, he too hoped the bridge had fared better. They climbed through the wreckage, trudging along, careful to avoid the sparking wires and jagged metal pieces resembling sword blades. He jumped to the bridge door over a chasm, the floor split open from the high energy impact. J pressed his hand on the control panel, his head snapped back as the door hissed open. They crawled into the bridge, the muffled sounds of electricity flowed around them, the main screen flickered, its picture static. He heard a moan, then saw a hand creeping over a headrest. *Ariel.* He rushed over to her, dodging the damaged equipment. She was clutching her chest with the other hand, her teeth clenched tight, face in a grimace.

"Hey, you," she gritted out, her voice weak.

J couldn't answer, overcome by the sight of her in such pain. He just released her restraints, wrapped her arm around his neck and lifted her out of the seat. Zane scrutinized the bridge, searching for the others. J carried Ariel toward the cargo bay, it was the best way out. He gently set her limp body down next to the door, she moaned as he did. He whipped his head up, spotting what he was hoping for. A medical kit hung on the wall only a few feet away. He placed a hand on her head, her heavy eyes gazed back at him. Quickly grabbing the kit, he flipped it open exposing the gun-like device. He configured it for "auto-detect" and scanned her body.

"Internal bleeding, punctured lung, bruised ribs, head contusion."

He shook his head, changed the setting to "repair". Ariel coughed up blood as he started working his way around her body.

"You'll be alright, I've got you."

Ariel smiled up at him then passed out. J dropped the medical gun, holding her chin up to make sure she was still breathing. He heard the device skip off of metal as it plummeted out of sight into the wreckage below. J's head snapped down, stared at the gaping dark hole amongst the twisted metal.

"Bless it!"

His head whipped around looking for help. Zane's head bobbed above a console, Grant on his shoulder, Tara climbing the wreckage behind him.

"Ariel alright?"

J looked down at her. Most of her external wounds were healing, but he had no clue about the internal ones. Max popped up just behind Zane, his movements sharp and quick. He hopped from the deformed metal flooring toward the bridge like he was playing hop-scotch. J sensed urgency in his steps.

"I know we all like to be sentimental, but the energy cell has destabilized. I'd advise we move quick."

J didn't have time to contemplate what all that meant, but

one thing was for sure, he needed to get Ariel out of there. Zane approached, stumbling over the wreckage, his movements hindered by Grant's unresponsive rotund little frame. J hoped he was just passed out, but from his vantage point he couldn't tell. He lifted Ariel once more, propping her head on his shoulder. They followed Max out into the hangar. J paused, his gaze shifting from watching Max bolt out the back of the ship, to the view beyond. It was the first time he saw it in detail. The vegetation, trees, bushes, vines lay just outside the gaping cargo bay where the doors once hung. Max disappeared into the foliage.

"Come on, J. You heard Max, this thing's gonna blow."

J figured that was a possibility, what with Max's sense of urgency, but now he knew it to be true. His eyes searched for a path. Tara and Zane hopped down following the same line that Max did. J hesitated, his eye caught a glimmer of light reflecting off the giant mech. He remembered how safe and secure it was inside and the exterior of the machine looked as new as it had the first time he laid eyes on it. He skipped, over careful of his footing, trying not to jostle Ariel, but it was difficult with the state of the cargo bay. He slipped, balanced on one leg, and pressed his arm out shifting his center of gravity. The movement worked, his free foot finding a stable platform. He climbed onto the machine. Letting Ariel down first, he climbed in, shutting the hatch. He placed Ariel in a seat, strapped her in then hopped into his own and fired up the machine. The giant metal mech came to life, its legs straightening, body growing tall. He threw the thruster forward and drove toward the opening. The first leg reached out into the jungle below. The terrain was mountainous and they'd crashed in a valley. He spotted a river a great distance below, but couldn't tell for sure how far it was, the screen distorted his perception. It could've been a thousand feet for all he knew. The second leg of the machine stepped out, planting onto a large flat stone. He manipulated the controls to drive the mech forward—

J's ears rang from the explosion, his body pressed unmercifully into the seat. His head spun as the machine was tossed into the air like a dandelion on a summer's day. It tumbled, flipping down toward the river below. His initial thought was incorrect, it was only a hundred feet below. His eyes focused on the screen, the pristine blue-green water accelerated toward him. Reaching for something to hold, his hands found the rail of the seat, his knuckles keening from the tension in his tendons. He closed his eyes as the craft plummeted into the river, the restraints tightened around him. He peeked out, turned to Ariel who hung lifeless, her arms dangling. He released his deathlike grip, glanced at the screen and tapped the menus to bring up the system status. He couldn't believe it, all of the systems were fully functional.

He grasped the controls, commanding his equipment forward. The sound of actuators filled the air, robotic joints moved, but nothing happened. They still hung there still upside down. He exhaled slowly. *How was he going to get them out of this?* His eyes bounced around the screen before settling on an icon flashing in the bottom corner. It resembled a turtle on its back, legs walking upside down. He tapped on it and rockets blasted, he felt a kick in the pants. The metal giant flipped to its feet, planting solid on the bottom of the river, the hull of the ship peeking above the water. He moved it forward and out of the greenish blue liquid. The comm flashed.

"J, you alright? Saw you flip off the ledge, that was quite a fall."

J glanced over at Ariel, her body flopped over the side of the seat. "I'm okay, but Ariel's not doing so well. How's Grant?"

"Not sure, he's in pretty bad shape. You got a med kit on that thing?"

J hadn't even thought about that. He visually searched the cockpit with renewed hope. Near the back wall, he found it.

"Yeah, I've got one."

Unbuckling, he couldn't get to the kit fast enough, nearly ripping it off the wall. Opening it, he dispersed the medical gear. Zane rattled in on the comm, he had Grant and was on his way. J ignored it, he had more pressing matters to deal with. He scanned Ariel's body. The system read back the stats, her body was healing but it would take time, her punctured lung still showed. He raked over her again on the "repair" setting, but the device flashed, indicating that the wound was too deep to treat. He wanted to throw it against the wall. *What good was all of this technology if it couldn't heal her?* He thought about V, what she'd said about the nanobots being more of a stopgap measure than a complete treatment. He wished she was there, not only so that she could do her doctor thing, but because then he'd know she was still alive. He placed a hand on Ariel's thigh. He heard her cough, bits of blood spat out of her mouth. She curled over at the waist and J

162

helped her sit up.

"Hey."

"Hey babe." He caressed her cheek, she slid her soft hand onto his, eyes closing. She took a short breath, the sound of gurgling accompanied it. J pressed his forehead onto hers.

"Babe, huh?"

"You're my girl. You'll be okay, promise."

She lifted her eyelids enough to lock eyes with him. "Don't make a girl a promise you can't keep."

She turned her head, coughing up more blood. J ran a hand through his hair, there had to be something he could do. His mind went blank trying to find a solution. *If the wizardry of this new technology wasn't enough, what could he do?* Ariel had passed out again. He double-checked her pulse, his heart raced, senses heightened.

He stood up, searching. Something had to help him. He bent over, picked up the medical gun, twisted it around. Examining the screen, he flipped through menus, nothing. He found the box and repackaged it, then slumped down in his chair. He tapped on his head with the fingers on one hand, his other swatting at the control stick. He placed his hand on a control pad, swiping up then down. As he continued fidgeting, his eyes stared out, unfocused, at the jungle beyond. His mind was imprisoned by thoughts of Ariel's health; the planet meant nothing to him, the river rushed underneath, the beautiful blue-green water flowing like mountain runoff in the spring. He picked up his finger, leaving the screen, placed it back down attempting to continue his mindless toying. It pulled up a map, most of which was empty. J squinted, readjusting his hand to go back to the previous screen. A red dot flashed. A line from the icon ran to a label beside it. Tremessos.

J stared at the ground, then back to the image. He knew the name. Cyrellia had said it before.

"Hey, J! You in there?"

Zane was calling on the comm, he'd reached them and was standing on the shoreline. J repositioned a camera, Grant was draped over Zane's shoulder, Tara and Max stood beside him.

"If you are, it'd be nice if you could keep us dry. Don't feel like swimming with a barrel on my shoulder."

Tara punched him in the shoulder, Zane winced giving a slight chuckle. Tara's face stayed tight as she eyed him.

J maneuvered the mech up to the beach, its legs spanning over them, and Zane trudged up the ladder, his progress slow with the added weight. Tara and Max followed, piling into the mech. J greeted them by handing the med kit over to Zane.

Opening it, his eyes drifted to Ariel. "How's Ariel?"

J's shoulders drooped. "Not good..."

Zane placed a hand on his shoulder, taking in a deep breath. "We'll get her some help."

Help? Where? Who? He didn't even know where they were. Some planet, somewhere. He opened his mouth to combat the optimism, but was cut off.

"What's that?"

J's mouth snapped shut, his head twisting. Max pointed at the little red dot flashing on the screen as he climbed over the back of the seat, his butt coasting down the backrest, landing with a thud. J sneered. *My seat.* Max manipulated the controls. J clenched his hands into fists, flexed them until his wrists popped. Max zoomed in on the dot, it flashed back twice the size, the letters much easier to read. Max turned his head, his eyes wide as they met J's stare. He pointed again at the dot. "How did you get a lock on that?"

Max's eyes stayed large, his jaw hung open. It was the first time J had ever seen surprise on his face. J investigated the screen once more. Truth be told, he had no idea. He worked his eyes back to Max, still locked onto J. He shrugged his shoulders giving a sigh. "I haven't the slightest, it just appeared after I exited the KracKen."

Max manipulated the controls, typing in commands quicker than even Ariel. He shrank the display, the dot nearly invisible, only the data and the word "Tremessos" glowed on the screen. Max hit the last button sequence and the screen read "downloading" on the top right. The percentage grew. J leaned forward, pressing both hands on a steel plate, awaiting the result.

CHAPTER SIXTEEN

Contour lines appeared on screen, the mountains, valleys, rivers all visible as a topographical map reflected in J's eyes. Max tapped another button and a satellite image overlay appeared under the contour lines, the heavy vegetation visible, the rivers bends and twists easily seen from the God's eye view. He adjusted a few settings then drew a line from a blue dot J hadn't noticed before to the red one. A distance marker appeared, 15.62 kilometers.

"You say it just appeared?"

Max twisted more controls, zooming in on the red dot. The color dissolved as it approached, the outline of a small metal futuristic city became visible and continued to grow until it filled the screen.

"It's—"

"Tremessos, the capital," J said, running his teeth over his lips.

Zane pointed at the screen, one eyebrow raised. "The capital? You mean the capital of Acadia? Are we talking aliens?"

"No, not aliens. It's the capital of Acadia."

Zane stared at him in disbelief, his bottom lip jumping about, finally he formed words. "There's no way! How long have they been here?"

J scratched his head. "Not long or I think it would be bigger."

Zane's head rested on his traps, his huge shoulders rising toward his ears. "Bigger? You see the size of that?"

"Not much smaller than Exodus..."

"Yeah, not much...wait. Are you saying *that's* Exodus?"

J nodded. His dream had shown it to him as TK had prepped for the briefing. Distracted, his eye caught a glimpse of Ariel. *That's it. He needed to get her to Tremessos, they'd have medical facilities, ships, everything needed to help Ariel.*

"How far is that?" he asked Max, his eyes focused on the number 15.62.

Max chuckled. "15.62 kilometers."

"I can see that jerk, in miles."

Max stood up, he pressed his shoulders back, chest out. His eyes burned through J. "Okay, so what's your problem? You've been out for me since we met."

J flexed, he stepped toward Max, staring him down. His nose twitched as he revved up his verbal assault.

Zane looked on. Finding a seat, he kicked up a foot over his knee, propping his arms behind his head. Tara was in the back working the medical device on Grant who was still passed out.

"You're my problem, TK supporter."

Max tilted his head. "TK supporter? What're you talking about, I'm here aren't I?"

J balled up his hands then placed one in the other rubbing his knuckles. Blood rushed to the skin, his massage warming it, he dipped his head. "You left Ariel to run off with TK."

"What? No I didn't, I wouldn't be here if I did."

"You would if you were a traitor, a spy."

Max clenched his fists.

Zane chuckled, leaned toward Tara. "Might need your

help with this one."

Tara looked up. Setting the device down, she stood up and watched the situation play out.

Max retorted, his voice heavy. "You think I'm a traitor? What makes you think that?"

J jumped him, landing a right hook to Max's nose. Max stumbled back hitting the controls, his hand slipping on the thruster. The machine began crawling forward. Zane's eyes grew big, he levitated out of his seat landing in the pilot's seat. J swung again, missing as Max ducked, his body dumping onto Zane. Max countered with a shot in the kidney, J growled his body retracting from the blow.

"Stay away from Ariel!" J shouted.

Max attempted a light jab, missed. "I see. That's what this is about."

He swung again, missing as J ducked and countered with an uppercut. Max's chin snapped up, blood sprayed into the air splattering on the screen. Zane pulled the thruster back, stopping the machine. He turned to the brawl as the blood hit.

"Ahh, keep it clean! We're gonna have to use that."

"Yeah, that's what this is about. You've been all over her since you returned."

He threw another punch, missing. Max tackled him, giving a shot to the kidney as they fell. They hit the ground hard, bouncing on the cold steel grating. Max planted a palm in J's face, pinning it to the ground. J flailed his arms, one latched onto Max's arm the other became a projectile, drilling Max in the ribs. He slipped a knee up pinning the arm, his free hand held down J's other hand.

"Listen farm boy."

J struggled to get free, but it was pointless. Max's body weight and strength made it impossible for him to create enough leverage, but his mouth still worked.

"Don't. Call. Me. Farm boy. And stay away from Ariel."

Max shook his head. "Listen to me, because I'm only going to say this once. We're just friends."

J's body struggled, his hearing impaired.

Max repeated himself, breaking his promise. "We're just friends, anything we had is in the past. We discussed it, so chill out."

J stopped fighting.

"We cool?"

J's cold eyes glared back at him, his lips wrinkled. He tried to think through his emotions, wanted to believe him. He nodded and exhaled heavily through his nose.

Max released his hold. Standing up, wiped his bloody nose taking a step back to give J room. J climbed to a knee gaining his strength. Max tapped on Zane's shoulder, motioning for him to evacuate the seat, he obliged. Max hopped in, adjusting the controls. J still didn't like him taking his seat, he felt attached to the ship somehow, like it was his.

Max swung his head to J smiling. "She does have a great body."

J lunged for him, Zane intercepted him. "I think you've had enough of a warm up. Let's save the rest for TK."

J stepped back throwing out an arm at Max his jaw dropping.

He heard Max continue. "I'm just messing with you. You

ACADIA

need to get some thicker skin."

J relented, taking a deep breath and Zane stepped aside, keeping close to him as he approached Max.

"You got me good," Max begrudgingly declared, rubbing his nose. "I don't think I'll be winning any beauty contests anytime soon."

J chuckled, a smile eked out the side of his mouth.

"I'm guessing you want your seat back?"

J nodded.

"Figured as much. Want me to teach you a few things? Could come in handy when we meet up with TK."

The tension in J's shoulders loosened. *One less thing to worry about, only 99 more to go.* He sat down in the seat and felt at home, Max behind him.

"I think we should get you to Tremessos as quick as possible, your girl could use a fix up."

J glanced over his shoulder.

Max's cheeks rose. "A little over ten."

J drew his eyebrows together.

"Miles. You asked how many miles fifteen kilometers was."

J grinned, readjusting to the screen. He pressed the thruster forward and the machine's long legs crushed the ground as it moseyed along. Max leaned over, tapped a few buttons to adjust the system settings, while he explained what he was doing and why. J thought about the head-spinning turnaround in their acquaintance. A few minutes ago they were, in his eyes, enemies. Now he was taking instruction from Max. His mind and heart felt lighter as if he'd defeated a mighty foe. The mech continued along the rock littered shore of the valley.

J glanced over to Ariel as she stirred, his face drawn with the thought of losing her.

Max pressed a hand on his shoulder. "I can drive for a bit."

J didn't hesitate, his mind was on Ariel and controlling the mech was a distraction, regardless of his macho drive. Switching, J grabbed her hand, her breath gurgling as her chest rose and fell.

She slipped her arm free, holding her side. "I feel like an alien ripped apart my guts."

J leaned in close. "We're getting help, it's all going to be alright. Promise." The last word ended up sounding more like a plea than a pledge and he didn't know who needed to be reassured more, him or Ariel. *He'd thought he'd lost her before and it nearly killed him. Now that he knew there was nothing standing between them, how would he ever live without her?*

Ariel rolled her head over on her shoulder, her weak eyes falling on him, trying to maintain their connection. She closed them again, groaning, and fell asleep once again. J held her, shifted his gaze to the screen. The forest, seemingly untouched, climbed the mountainside. The trees were tall, but unable to tell the scale, they appeared as skyscrapers extending for hundreds if not thousands of feet, their branches like platforms high above. Other assorted plants were scattered underneath, shaded by the populous vegetation. A bird-like animal with an inordinately long beak swept down into the river, dipping into it, but coming out empty, its prey elusive. He watched and wondered what the wildlife was like on this new planet. *Would it all be like Earth?* The bird had proved similar.

171

Max adjusted the map the red dot continued to flash. "So, I'm not sure how you did it, but that's an encrypted location beacon we're picking up and we're tapped into one of TK's satellites. You sure it just appeared?"

J ran through his memories, his eyes shifting to the ceiling. He stood up slowly, as to not disturb Ariel, and moved toward Max.

"Yeah, it was just there. You said it's encrypted. So if we can see them, can they see us?"

J was hoping the answer was no. He looked back at Grant, but Tara was still working on him. J knew he'd have the answers, he just didn't know whether or not Grant would ever be able to give them. J watched as Tara finished with the medical treatment. Taking up a seat on the floor next to him, she placed his head in her lap; Grant still wasn't doing well.

Max zipped through several menus. "I can't tell, still not sure how you got the signal. Knowing TK, they're going to have border sensors set up. I'm thinking we stop about five clicks out and proceed on foot, it'll be easier to blend in as opposed to this walking building."

Max had a point, the mech was quite the sight, a veritable walking tank. *Mech, it needed a name, and what was a click?* He was about to ask when he heard Tara.

"Come on, Grant."

Her voice quivered as a woman losing hope. J's attention shifted to her rocking Grant in her arms, a tear ran down her cheek. *She was just a robot, right?* Shifting to Grant, he knelt down, placing a hand on her shoulder. She reluctantly lifted her eyes away from Grant, tears streaming down her face.

"The medical equipment was insufficient."

J's head fell, eyes resting on Grant's face. Motionless, cold and pale, his eyes closed, lips slightly parted. Other than animals on the farm, death was something still relatively new to him. His hand trembled, resting below his nose and over his mouth and chin. He patted her shoulder, no words came to him, he felt silence was more important than saying the wrong thing. Tara continued to hold him, her eyes closed, dropping tears onto Grant's face. Zane stayed at his position knowing she needed her space, the cabin fell silent, the only sound the vibrating floor as the mech continued its trek. The machine continued drawing closer to their objective then Max reduced the thruster, bringing it to a stop. The engine hum cut out. J stood up, pausing a moment as he saw Tara still holding Grant.

"Five clicks, the terrain's not to steep, but it's going to be tasking. That's about three miles, J."

J nodded understanding, his eyes fell on Ariel. As small as she was, carrying her three miles would be no simple task. Zane approached Tara, kneeling down next to her. Having the same thought, he placed a hand on her shoulder, her still watering eyes gazed back. "Tara, we're going to need you to carry Ariel to Tremessos. Can you do that?" his voice soft as if talking to a child.

She glanced down at Grant taking a deep breath then stood up, holding Grant in her arms like a sleeping baby. "May I bury him first?"

Zane stood up. "Of course." He depressed the button opening the hatch, Tara adjusted Grant in her arms and climbed out. The cockpit fell into silence once more.

J turned to Ariel, she was still sound asleep, her head resting on her shoulder.

Zane stepped over to Max, leaning toward the screen. "It will probably take you about half a day with this terrain. I'll help you get Ariel down while Tara's...grieving. Max and I will stay here; the two of you get her medical attention then call us on comm."

Grieving? They were all grieving in their own way and their situation didn't allow for much of it. Ariel needed help quick or she could end up like poor Grant. J's skin tingled at the thought. He climbed out onto the top of the mech, the light from the planet's sun was low on the horizon, its blue-white ball just visible over the terrain. He looked up both sides into mountains. They were still in a valley, the river running next to the giant machine. Zane popped up with Ariel on his shoulder, he stopped surveying the environment.

"This is the most green I've ever seen...and that includes Earth."

J agreed. The colors were exceedingly vibrant, like an over-embellished painting. The greens and blues popped, the enormous trees blanketing the hills. He could only imagine what lie beneath. Save for the bird they'd seen earlier, there'd been no sightings of animals, no sounds, only the river. Zane disappeared down the ladder, but J remained there a moment, scouting their path. He shook his head. *It wasn't going to be easy. At least it wasn't through the snow.* He hopped off the ladder to find Tara walking their way, wiping her cheek, clearing it of the drops clinging to it. Zane handed Ariel to her. She grumbled, her eyes peering up at Tara.

"I know you don't trust me, but I'll take care of you."

J stepped over to her, staring down at Ariel. He heard a voice yell behind them.

"Forgetting something?"

He turned in time to see a rifle flying at him. Max had two more strapped over his shoulder, J caught the first one slinging it on his own. Max approached, handing him the other two. "You're probably going to want these as well."

J looked over at Tara holding Ariel, realized why he said it, and slung the other two on as well. Zane laughed at him as he fumbled with the weapons. J attempted to adjust them, their sheer size causing problems. His shoulders were already beginning to burn. He exhaled sharply, this wasn't going to be an easy trip. Zane tapped on his wrist displaying a communications screen.

"Channel 971, like we discussed. Should be encrypted. We'll let you know if anything happens here."

J nodded. As he turned to face their path, Tara walked up next to him, both staring at the enormous tree line.

"We're not in Kansas anymore."

CHAPTER SEVENTEEN

Wind rushed through the leaves reminding him of a warm spring day. They were finally somewhere nice, not stuck in the scalding heat of Sector 5 nor the icy chill in Sector 21. He plopped down on a fallen tree, the bark dug into his butt and he wiggled, attempting to get comfortable. He leaned forward peering over the side, a ten foot drop stared back at him. It was amazing how big the trees were, their circumference like a small house. Tara laid Ariel next to him but remained standing, viewing their pathway. It was along the downed tree, much easier to traverse than the floor below. They'd been traveling for hours, navigating the forest, the smaller brush a nuisance as it tripped and grabbed at their feet. The downed tree happened to be pointed in their direction of travel and J was glad for it, and the rest. Ariel coughed, rolling on her side and spitting up blood.

"I know you're tired, J, but we will need to be moving soon. Her body is failing."

J winced at her choice of words. *Failing*. He remembered that she wasn't human, a fact that he kept forgetting until she made a statement like that. He caressed Ariel's shoulder.

"Are we there yet?"

Ariel's voice was weak, barely audible. The sounds of animals flowed through the tree as the leaves continue to rustle. There were plenty of animal noises since they'd entered, yet only a few birds crossed their path. Albeit much larger than those on Earth, their bodies very similar, in colors of gray and brown. He ran his fingers over her cheek, Ariel still had a sense of humor even on death's door.

"About a mile left."

He lifted his wrist, checking the map. Less than half a mile actually and he was glad of it. His shoulders burned from the rifle straps that lay next to him, it was the first thing he'd done when he crested the top of his perch. Tara bent down to pick up Ariel once more. She attempted to raise her eyebrows, coughing up blood again.

"We need to get going, J," Tara said.

He raised a hand indicating he understood, pushed off of his thighs as he blew air through lips puffed out like a mdoka fish. He hobbled along behind Tara, the solid uneven bark crunching under his footsteps. At the end of their path, they reached the root system. Enormous pieces of underground branches now reached up into the sky and hung exposed in the air, dry dirt covering the majority of them. J heard a light hum, Tara stopped, her head twisted about on a swivel. She spun around taking a hold of the bark, the grooves large like an enormous truck tire, and let herself down to the forest floor using the bark like rungs on a ladder. The hum grew louder. J scurried down the tree, staring up at the sky. His feet touched the floor just as his eyes caught a ship zip by overhead. Tara wasn't wasting any time, she'd disappeared into the forest ahead. J scrambled to catch up, finding her just on the other side of the brush. The floor opened up into a glade; lush, purple, waist-high grass covered the entire surface. He stared a moment at the unique sight, but the sound of another engine hummed overhead snapping him out of his reverie. He caught up to Tara who was hugging the tree line. She had the right idea, being spotted now would be a mess. Tara stepped into the tree line at the far end of the glade, the sound of humming engines whistled overhead. The sound increased in intensity, he twisted his head around to see a large ship descending down into the purple grass, the blades flowing outward. He quickened his pace still peering back. He twisted around ducking to avoid a tree limb, relieved he hadn't smacked it with his face, continued through the forest. *Who knew what would've happened to them had they been spotted.*

He found Tara only a few yards up ahead standing still, Ariel hung in her arms. He watched as she placed her on the ground. J's brows drew together as he squinted to try and make sense of the situation. Tara raised her hands as she stood back up. J was almost at a full sprint by this time then planted both feet, sliding to a stop. Four men sporting rifles stepped toward Tara, their approach tactical, their bodies small, knees bent, eyes focused down the gun sights. J threw his body behind the mass of a tree next to him, knelt down, his breath quickened. He peeked around the trunk. One of the men dropped his rifle, walked up to Tara, her arms still reaching to the sky. He could tell they were talking, the discussion going back and forth. J raised a hand feeling the synthetic rifle strap, the bane of his existence, maybe the hours of carrying it would now pay off. He slipped one of the rifles off his back, carful to not make a sound, and raised it, aiming at one of the men. He stopped analyzing the situation, it seemed clear enough. Ariel was dying, there were four targets, and Tara was in their custody. He pressed his cheek to the cold metal of the weapon, his eye stared through the sight. He focused on the far solider, that one would be the hardest to hit. The nearest one had his weapon lowered, he'd have more time to engage him. He pressed his finger onto the edge of the trigger.

"I wouldn't do that."

J's head snapped back. Another solider stood over him, a rifle pointed at his head. J pressed his bottom lip tight to the top, his face drew into a scowl. He tossed the rifle to the ground raising his arms up as he climbed to his feet. A voice came from behind him.

"What'd ya find?"

The soldier looked at J, his grizzly features pressed through his tightly trimmed beard. "Just a kid."

J's eyes dropped. *Just a kid?* He didn't know if that was a good thing or not, some anonymity was relished, especially in their current situation. If they knew who he was things would be different, very different. The bearded soldier looked back at his companion.

"You?"

"Same. Two kids, one's in pretty bad shape. We'd better get them to the medical bay ASAP."

J heard his footsteps fade away, his captor picked up the rifles throwing then over a shoulder. They were captured, but his shoulders where singing praises.

"You get lost or something?"

Something. J thought not saying anything was better.

"Not the talkative type, huh? Well, you're going to see Xander, maybe you'd like to speak with him."

The solider grabbed underneath J's arm, coaxing him toward the purple glade. J didn't resist, his eyes darted around examining his surroundings, thinking of Ariel and what the man said. *Medical bay.* His priority was getting her medical attention and it sounded like cooperating would accomplish that. He trudged along, pushing through the brush, his captor occasionally nudging him as his walk slowed. He parted the final branches, exposing a large ship resting in the center of the glade, its ramp lowered, engines silent. After a few paces into the waist-high grass, he looked back over his shoulder to check on Ariel. Tara was in the same situation as him, a rifle pointed at her back. Ariel was carried by the largest of the five men. J turned back to the ship, continuing his march. It was of modest size, smaller than the Omorfiá, but not as small as the fighters he was becoming accustomed to. A woman stood near the top of the ramp, her pose stoic, hands on her hips, hair in a single braided pony tail. J approached, her eyes judging him, locked on his, mouth wanting to smile. She shifted her weight onto one foot, looked past him toward Ariel and her expression changed, growing more serious. The solder directed him toward her, her focus shifting back to J.

She tilted her head to the side as if examining his profile. "Have you scanned him yet?"

"No, I was waiting until we got on board to confirm what we were doing with them."

She appraised him from head to toe then her attention snapped to Ariel who topped the ramp still being carried, the watery cough grabbing her attention.

"Place them in the holding bay, give that one an anesthetic. We'll deal with them when we get onboard the Houzeau. We'll need all hands for the trip."

She turned and walked toward the ship's bridge. His captor marched him to a holding cell about six by eight feet. After pushing him and Tara into the cell, they brought in Ariel who was now fast asleep and laid her on the bed. J leapt over to her, falling to his knees to hold her hand. One of the men made the sound of curiosity as they left and the door closed.

"They gave her some medicine to slow her heart reducing the blood flow. With medical care, soon her systems will be able to be repaired."

"Systems, huh?"

"Isn't that the proper term?" Tara leaned on the wall of the cell, her large eyes pondering his question.

He thought about it. *Systems. It could work, but wasn't something a human would say.* He thought about how he would have termed it. "If you want to be human, we need to work on your phrasing. Instead of systems being repaired, try...she'll pull through, or heal, or, better yet, recover. Try recover."

Tara paused, he could tell she was processing it. "With medical care, she'll recover?"

J chuckled. It sounded like a question, but was definitely more human. "Yes, but next time make it more of a statement."

He examined the container, trying to discern who their captors were. They had to be Atlantean, highly unlikely the technology he was familiar with would be in the hands of life from Acadia, but other than that, he had no clue. "Any idea who they are?"

J stood up, ran his fingers along the edges of the smooth walls. The ceiling was low, only a few inches higher than him.

Tara looked down at Ariel, her expression blank.

"They are Atlantean. The ship is a T19 Scout designed for long, minimally-armed excursions. That is all I can gather."

"Well that's better than me. Any idea on where they're taking us?"

"The medical bay to see Xander, that's all I was—"

"Able to gather. You don't have to be so formal and...and who am I trying to kid? I'm the last person who should give advice on how to be less formal. Not so long ago, I was the one out of place, trying to learn what everyone was saying. I still don't understand half the things Ariel says." J smiled to himself.

"You do just fine, J. You truly are one of the crew, an integral part of this little family."

"Thanks, Tara, that means a lot. It's all Ariel's doing, she must be rubbing off on me. Alright. Maybe try loosing up your speech patterns a bit. You might even fool anti-replicant over there."

"I'll try. Grant hadn't finished programming my speech system fully."

A tear came to her eye, J stopped his search and grabbed her hand.

"I'm sorry, he was a good man. We'll work on it, okay?"

Tara nodded.

J sat down next to Ariel on the bed, he felt the ship shake as the engines roared to life and the craft lifted off. Where they were going was unknown to him, but a medical facility was a good start. J focused on Ariel, caressed her hand then looked up at Tara. "So I hear you have some memories."

"Yes." Tara sat down next to him and the delighted smile on her face made her look younger, carefree.

He spun toward her, his hand still in Ariel's.

"A lifetime of memories, some of the most beautiful things you can think of. Running in a park, rolling in grass, school, friends, hiking in the mountains. I enjoy remembering. They are all good, no violence, a perfect world."

J watched her as she talked, her eyes sparkled, her posture straightened. Her face glowed, the words coming out through smiles and giggles. She was like a child, cheerful while she recounted the stories, something J wished he could have now. He remembered what it was like playing ball as a kid without the pressure of winning, just playing for the love of the game. The days when he went on a picnic or down to the market with his mom to trade livestock or maybe chicken eggs. His body relaxed, muscles loosening as his mind was swept back into his childhood. He wondered if it would ever be that simple again. Those times seemed long gone, a lifetime ago. He had another life now. J squeezed Ariel's soft hand, his new life was much more difficult, challenging with more to come. Maybe someday. Someday he'd have a simple life again...with Ariel. He snapped from his daydream, refocusing on Tara, her stories beautiful and jovial still filling the air.

"Once we get through this I'm sure V can adjust your vocabulary."

J stopped, realizing what he'd just said. *V.* He had no clue where she was or if she was even alive. His stomach sank thinking of the worst and he dropped his chin to his chest.

Tara squeezed his hand. "Thanks, J. You're a good friend."

183

He looked up and she smiled back at him, his dark cloud lifting. The ship shuddered, the engines changed tone. The hum became more powerful and mechanical noises echoed outside their prison. They rocked one final time, inferring they'd landed. He heard voices outside the cell and the door opened. Two men with a stretcher rushed in, J moved out of their way as they loaded Ariel and hustled out.

"You two will be coming with me."

The female that greeted them as they boarded stood in the doorway, her hair tight pulling her forehead back, not a single hair out of place. She turned without a backward glance and walked out, confident in her position that they would do as they were told. J glanced at Tara who shrugged her shoulders then followed.

"What were the two of you doing out there?"

J glanced again to Tara as they continued their march. He opened his mouth, about to spit out a terrible lie, but Tara cut him off.

"We were scouting building locations for our parents."

The woman looked back over her shoulder raising an eyebrow. "Is that so, how did your...friend get injured?"

"Fell off a massive downed tree," J replied. Eager to help, his words shot out incredibly fast.

The woman didn't turn, simply stated, "I see" as they continued. After some time, they reached an elevator and entered. The woman spun, announcing their destination. J and Tara adjusted their stance, facing the entrance as the woman stood behind them.

"Might want to come up with a better story than that for

Xander."

The doors opened to reveal a long hallway. J felt his back nudged forward and he obliged, strolling through the tight space. Doors lined each side of the hall, all closed off to prying eyes. They reached the end of the corridor and the woman scanned her hand and eye, the door hissed open onto the bridge. A man stood in the center of the room, his arms behind his back, seemingly focused on the screen. A bright blue moon glowed in the distance taking up the screen, a sliver of stars peeked out from the side. Multiple people occupied various levels, moving about, having discussions. They continued into the room the woman grabbing their shoulders before reaching the puppet master. J's eyes spun around the room, searching for any indication of who his captors were. His eyes focused back on the man frozen as a statue before them.

"Xander, the package has been delivered."

The man slowly rotated around, his eyes peering out of the corner. J drew back, his eyes as large as the moon outside.

CHAPTER EIGHTEEN

Arcturus stood before him, hands still pinned behind his back. J's jaw hung open, his lip quivered as he exhaled. Questions flooded his mind, his eyes danced over every inch of his father, his fingers tapping on his thighs.

Arcturus ambled toward him, his face loose, his cheeks pleasant. He stopped a few feet away gazing into his eyes. "I know you have questions, but they will have to wait. The situation has not gone quite as planned and I've had to accelerate a few steps quicker than anticipated. I apologize for the secretive nature of your retrieval and the use of an alternate name, but I assure you it was necessary. We have had trouble with a few spies."

He turned to their escort. "Commander, were you able to retrieve the others?"

"Yes, sir. They are in the medical bay."

"Very well. See J and...Tara, I believe, to the medical bay. I'll meet you in the briefing room when I'm ready."

She nodded. As J stood there, his feet locked into the steel grating, the commander cleared her throat. J turned. The commander nodded for him to exit, raising her eyebrows. J looked back to his father, now back at the helm overseeing... something. Dismissing him, after everything he'd done to get there, to ensure that his father's vision came to fruition. The commander grabbed his elbow and escorted them into the hallway, J was too numb to fight.

Arcturus' assistant came running toward the bridge, trusty tablet in hand. J twisted his head, watching his long stride disappear into the bridge as they reached the elevator.

The commander selected the floor. "So, J. We'll get you to the medical bay to check on your lady. I'm Kiska." She extended her hand.

J shook it, studying her face, determining what to say next.

"And you're Tara. Glad to have a replicant on our side, helluva fighter."

Tara beamed at the comment, her emotional programming had made her care about such things. It was times like these that he had trouble telling she wasn't alive. They exited the elevator and turned down the hall.

"So what went wrong?" J finally asked, his steps quick to keep up with Kiska.

She exhaled sharply as she glided through the halls. "Well, to start, you guys are late. TK has established themselves on Acadia, their defenses are fortified. Alphonsus was overrun..."

She kept going, but J's mind wandered. *Late? Is that why his father was so distant? Because he was disappointed in J? Had he somehow made things worse?* Enough negative thoughts. He had more pressing matters, namely Ariel. He regretted asking the question. Kiska didn't seem distraught about Ariel's condition, which meant one of two things: Ariel was going to be okay or she just didn't care. He hoped it was the first. They reached an entrance, the doors opened to reveal a clean white hall, walls glowing as they reflected the light. Color was absent, even their clothes appeared bleached out. Multiple rooms sat on the outskirts. The commander marched over to one. Opening it, she stepped out of the way, ushering them in.

Ariel was lying asleep in a bed, an IV bag hanging next to

her. As J approached, a chair rose up out of the floor and he sat down, taking her hand. Tara and Kiska stood in the doorway. Ariel's eyes blinked, finally opening halfway, still groggy from the procedure, her icy blue eyes locked onto his. "Don't look at me I'm hideous."

J laughed in relief, leaning back. Ariel gave a slight smile, closing her eyes. Her hair was pulled back under a cap, her body covered by a surgical gown.

"Everyone make it out okay?" Her voice was strained as if she'd been up all night and was trying to operate on an hour's rest. J glanced at Tara still standing next to Kiska. He leaned in close, whispering, "We lost Grant."

A heavy sigh came after.

Ariel's eyes opened a little larger, she spied Tara at the door, looked down at J's hand in hers. "Zane and Max?"

"Yeah, they're fine. I don't think Max had a scratch on him..." J snickered remembering their fight and Max's broken nose. "Well maybe a bit more than a scratch, but he's just as pretty as he was before. What's the last thing you remember?"

She turned her head, stretching and sitting up, her legs shooting out, shaking as they did.

"Warning you of impact, nothing after that."

J looked back at Tara. She'd hauled Ariel for a little over three miles, there was no way he would've been able to do that.

"We crashed in a valley and I used the mech to get us out. Tara ended up carrying you through the forest, now we're here." He looked up a Kiska. "Where is here, exactly?"

Kiska sauntered in, nodding to Ariel. She stood with her hands clasped in the small of her back, legs shoulder width apart. "Battle ship Houzeau. Flagship of Xander's Royal forces."

Ariel sat up, removing the IV from her wrist, her next words drug out. "Right...and Xander is?"

"Arcturus," J answered.

She raised her eyebrows, her nose crinkled a bit. She looked around the room as if he was somewhere around. "Arcturus...the Arcturus? As in your father? What did he say? How's the rebellion going? Where is he?"

J pressed his hand on her thigh, it was the fastest he'd ever seen her speak. He waved a hand up and down. "Slow down, you know about as much as I do. I needed to see you first... and, he kinda kicked me out."

Kiska was quick to come to Arcturus' defense. "He didn't kick J out, there is a skirmish he is attending to on Acadia. He has a task for you two, he needs your skills."

"He did kick me out, but he was also busy." J still didn't know how he felt about that. Or the fact that his father thought he had skills. He hadn't really thought about it like that. Ariel and Zane had skills. Even Max had some skills. He was just, well, J. He looked back at Ariel. "Don't worry about that. How're you feeling?'

Ariel stretched her shoulders, blades nearly touching causing her chest to push out. J pulled his head back, staring.

She raised an eyebrow catching him. "I could use some food."

J's stomach growled as if it had simply needed reminding. He placed a hand on it, turned to Kiska. "Do we have time to eat before the briefing?"

She glared at J. He returned it, unimpressed.

"I'll have some food brought to the briefing room. You may have a moment to get dressed then we'll get going."

Kiska stepped out of the room and Tara spun out as well leaving J with Ariel. He searched the room and found a pile of clothes on a table in the corner, hopped up to grab them. He turned to see Ariel standing, facing away from him. She dropped the gown and he snapped his eyes to the ceiling using his peripheral vision as reference. He heard Ariel snicker and he offered up the clothes.

"Always a gentleman, thank you." She took the clothes. Pulling on the pants then the shirt and jacket, she sighed. He could tell it was a pleasant one and glanced over. She was done dressing, but the sight gave him déjà vu. He didn't pay attention to the pile of clothes before handing it over, but it was the same style outfit she'd been wearing when they'd first met. He remembered her utilizing her signature move on him, a shoulder drop tackle, then using him as a chair as they escaped the Mediators in the Tetriack. It was the first time he'd smelled the peculiar combination of sunflowers and burnt ozone that was purely Ariel, though he hadn't realized what it was at the time. He smiled goofily.

She ran her fingers through her hair, loosening the tight mass from the surgical cap. "Ready."

J couldn't tell if it was a question or a statement, either way worked. He moved out into the bright hallway, Kiska began walking as Ariel stepped out. As they made their way through the ship, J filled Ariel in on what she missed, breezing over Grant, not wanting to upset Tara. Kiska showed them into a briefing room very similar to the one on the Parádeisos. On the table were some rations, J lunged at the bars, unwrapping one and taking a big bite.

"Mmm, steak. I still can't figure how you guys get this stuff to taste like real food."

Ariel shook her head taking a bite of a chicken flavored one. She could've done with never eating a ration again, the Academy had made sure of that, the constant training exercises emphasizing field conditions. She'd endured too many training events to count, all focused on possible hostile alien encounters. Yet, here they were, fighting the very government that trained her.

A loud voice came from the doorway. "Hey, kid."

Ariel stood up and flung her arms around Zane, nodded at Max. Max grabbed her up in a hug. She pushed back immediately, eyes stricken as she looked at J.

He smiled reassuringly. "We're good."

Ariel's head whipped back and forth like a cat chasing a toy, then stopped, sat down. "How'd you guys get here?"

Zane flipped a seat around, slid down onto it. Max did the same next to J, leaned in wanting to hear.

"After we contacted you the last time, a scout ship flew over. We attempted to hide that thing, but it was just too large. We almost engaged them, but they sent a transmission. Seems Arcturus had a homing beacon embedded in it. They picked us up and here we are."

"What about the mech?"

Kiska made her way to the other side of the table, tapping on the window, turning it opaque. "We sent a salvage team for it. It should be onboard by now."

She pulled up a map of planets, something J had never seen before. Acadia's solar system. Acadia was depicted as the fifth planet from the sun, four more past it. Three moons orbited the planet making J feel like it was something he would've seen in Hollywood, impossible in real life. She zoomed in close to one of the three moons and he could see that a ship floated hidden from Acadia's surface. A few dozen people flooded in to the briefing room. Most were in their thirties, all wore military uniforms and about half wore flight suits, maroon with the TK emblems removed. They gathered around the table, taking seats until it was standing room only. Kiska spun, snapping to attention. J whirled around as the room collectively stood up and Arcturus strolled in, walking purposefully to the display.

"Thank you, Commander."

She moved away to a seat off to the side. Arcturus stood in the center facing the members who'd taken a seat. The standing members relaxed their stance. Arcturus released a hand from behind his back, lifting it toward the moon.

"As you know, first contact with the enemy did not go as planned. Due to unforeseen circumstances, we lost Alphonsus and Parádeisos to TK. We have shielded ourselves from Acadia, out of range of their sensors. Half of the Parádeisos contains an object I require."

The screen adjusted focus, centering on a visual of the Parádeisos wreckage. A line danced from their position to the target.

Arcturus continued. "It is secured in a vault which only J

has access to as it is coded with his DNA. J, Ariel, Zane, Tara. I need you to retrieve it for me. Max, you will pilot the ship. The item is not large so you can use a scout craft. The others will need to provide cover. There is no way to disable their sensors in our current situation and they have patrols currently orbiting the wreckage."

He dropped his arm, strolling back around the table. J watched his movements, remembered what it felt like to be him, the bond between them was strong even though they only just met.

The room stood up as he sauntered out. J attempted to follow, but Max grabbed his shoulder. "Sounds like I'm giving you guys a lift, any refreshment requests?"

J's mind was on his father, so he responded automatically. "Yeah, sure."

Max leaned back his chin tucked tight to his chest, he eyed Ariel and she grabbed J's wrist. "There will be time soon enough. Need to focus on the mission."

J searched his feelings. She was right, there would be a better time. It would do him no good to force his father to talk, he knew him too well. He did things on his time, in his own way. There'd be time when this was all over for answers. He nodded, his eyes still staring out the doorway.

Kiska popped her head in. "I'll see you to the ready room."

Ready room? J laughed inside, there wasn't anything that could get him *ready* for any of this, that much he found out the hard way. She disappeared into the hall. The crew made their way to the staging room, a small area lined with lockers, weapons, and an assortment of supplies. Kiska handed them each a rifle and a small pistol. J strapped it to his leg.

"I'd just carry it if I were you, not sure if it'll be a dry dock or a space walk."

J unstrapped the holster watching Ariel. "What's a dry dock?"

Ariel chuckled. Setting her rifle on the bench below her, she handed him a spacesuit. "It means we attach to the ship and can walk onboard, no space walk required."

J took the suit examining it, the rubbery plastic slipped around in his fingers. He flopped it over his shoulder.

"I'd put that on now. You don't want to be trying to do it in the middle of battle."

Ariel had a point. Attempting to don the suit was hard enough with no pressure, the skintight fabric stuck to his skin as he pulled it on. He glanced over at Ariel. In order to make the suit fit, they first had to strip down into their underwear. He couldn't help himself, his eyes were drawn to her. He was mesmerized by her motion, her gracefulness evident even while performing the simple task of dressing. He slipped in the final arm, turning to see Tara putting one on as well. He paused, contemplating her actions. She looked away. *Why would she need a suit?* He shook his head and grabbed a helmet off of the locker shelf placing it under his arm, his other holding the blaster holster.

"You got the right stuff?" Ariel teased.

J pinned his bottom lip up, jutted out his chin as she laughed. He realized he missed something, but relished her laughter, glad to hear it once more even at his expense. The others finished and Kiska led them to the hangar to find a scout ship smaller than the one they'd been retrieved in. Max walked around the outside examining the ship, Kiska ushered the others inside, saying a few words to Zane before closing the door behind them. She gave a quick salute as she disappeared behind the rising ramp. J found a seat and settled in. The cockpit could be seen from the cargo area, two seats facing front, no room for more than Max and one other. Ariel had already taken one of the seats. Max entered a smaller door on the other side, prancing into the cockpit. J watched as he hit overhead switches then plopped down next to Ariel. It was weird seeing the two together and not feeling his chest constrict. He watched as they worked together to get the ship running then pressed his head back against the wall closing his eyes, the ships engines vibrating through the wall. The engine oscillations comforted him like a baby rocking in its mother's arms. He thought about the farm, a universe away, smiled as he thought about his journey. A moment of peace swept over him, but it couldn't last.

Zane nudged him. "Sorry to interrupt your cat nap, but I'd suggest you configure your suit."

J looked at him, his lips parted about to ask why, but Zane finished his thought.

"Sounds like it's a space walk."

Great, a space walk. It'd been some time since the last one and he didn't enjoy them. His weightless body freaked him out, the sensation still new. He dropped his shoulders staring at his helmet visor, the shiny glass reflecting back his image. The lights of the ship pulsed behind. Tara walked in front of him holding her own helmet, her rifles swung on her back as she passed.

J leaned over to Zane, whispering. "Does she need that, I thought she was a replicant?"

Zane's eyes examined her, he talked out of the side of his mouth as she turned away from them. "No, her system doesn't require oxygen to operate."

J sat back, placing his head against the wall again, closing his eyes and thinking. The wall rattled, knocking his head forward. His eyes popped open. Zane was tapping on the suit's controls on his forearm, Tara was doing the same. The ship shook again. J finally realized it was a blast, they were under attack. His eyes snapped to the cockpit, streams of light trails enveloped the screen. He unlatched his restraint, bolting to Ariel's side placing an arm on her head rest, it stiffened as another attack hit. Fighter craft zipped past, weapons rounds filled the battlespace. Ariel felt his presence, turning back she grabbed her helmet with both hands.

"We're about five minutes out, finish getting ready."

She placed her helmet on, locking it in with a hiss. Max continued to fly the craft straight toward the objective, their escort mostly able to distract the enemy, only letting the occasional attack get through. Out of habit, J glanced at the shields. 95%. His rigid arm loosened. He peered back toward Zane and Tara, they were fully suited up. He spotted his helmet resting on the seat as another blast hit, knocking it to the floor, it rolled over to Tara. She grabbed it holding it out to him.

"This is life J, be more careful."

He took it from her, thanking her with a nod. She was right, if he was going out into the void of space, his helmet was a necessity. He must be more careful. He slipped it on, locking it into place, his eyes glowed from the bright menus shining on the visor. Extinguishing them, he reached for his rifle and slung it over his shoulder. Zane walked past about to look out the windscreen, but Ariel blocked his way. She configured her suit and placed a hand into the air, her fingers spread out. J tilted his head, not recognizing the sign. He heard Zane's muffled voice, but the only word he caught was "five". Ariel reached out and grabbed his wrist, twisted him around manipulating the suit's controls.

"You hear me now?"

J perked up as she released his arm. "Yeah, what—"

"I wanted you on secure channel five; remind me later to go over hand signals. No time now, we're thirty seconds out."

The ship rattled more violently than before and his eyes swept up to the screen. The battle still raged, the Parádeisos wreckage coming into view. J pressed his knee forward only seeing half the ship. His ears picked up Max on the comm.

"Area's too hot to stop, this'll have to be a drop and go."

J stared at Ariel his eyes empty.

"He means he'll fly by and we jump out. I'll lock the cockpit door, Zane you prep the cargo door."

Zane strode over to the door panel, pressed a series of buttons. His finger came to a stop hovering over the final selection, he peered back at Ariel. She finished locking the door and skipped over to Tara and Zane.

"I'd hold onto something, J."

As Ariel grabbed a bar near the cargo door, Zane tapped the button. Gravity ceased, he heard the hiss of the door as the cabin equalized with the dead space outside.

CHAPTER NINETEEN

The scout ship zipped away, the weightless feeling enveloped him, his mind working to understand it. His eyes swept around, finding the others, beyond them the wreckage of the Parádeisos, dark and looming. He figured they were fifty yards away and engaged his thrusters, pushing him toward the objective. A beam of light whizzed by him, his head whipped to the culprit. An enemy fighter was inbound. It exploded in a dazzling display of reds and yellows turning into scrap metal, floating listlessly toward them. J increased his speed, the shrapnel barely missing him as he continued. Looking out toward the battle, craft continued their maneuvers, engagements and attacks. He felt his head hit something.

"Watch out!" he heard Ariel yell, running into her as she met the ship's hull. His lips pinched together, his eyes avoiding her. Zane pushed himself along the twisted metal, J grabbed a hold following along. Glancing back, he found Ariel and Tara doing the same. Zane pushed himself into an opening, a long corridor once leading to some of the ship's cabins lay before them. Now protected by the massive hull, the threat of the enemy fighters diminished. Zane continued to lead the way, finding an opening along the way. Doors complicated things, but Tara was prepared and used a small laser tool to cut through the cold steel.

J heard a voice crackle through his helmet speaker. "You guys've got incoming. Looks like eighteen Mediators."

They'd been huddled at the door. Zane unslung his rifle, kicked his feet against the wall floating toward twisted metal using it as cover. Ariel balled herself up, covering Tara as she continued cutting through another door. J floated to Zane, taking up position next to him, all weapons aimed toward the entrance.

"How's it coming Tara?" Ariel asked, twisting her head as if not talking into the comm.

"Almost there, just a few more seconds."

J adjusted the rifle, he tried to press his cheek onto it, the glass ball preventing the contact, bouncing off. He studied the weapon attempting to figure out the best way to aim. Light flashed above his shoulder and Zane repositioned his weapon over the barricade

"Here they come."

J looked up and saw the easily recognizable shape of a Mediator, it opened fire moving from wall to wall, a spider unaffected by gravity. J fired, clipping its shoulder. Ariel and Zane let loose proving better shots than him, the lifeless metal body floated motionless. They braced for more. Tara was nearly complete, her rectangular pattern glowing red hot from the impact of her tool. She kicked the cutout and flew back into Zane, knocking them both into the far wall. Had it been a different situation, J would've laughed, watching them flail about in the zero g tunnel. His eyes refocused on the entrance, still nothing. Tara kicked off of the wall, flying into the door and dislodging it from its melted supports, her body disappearing into the darkness beyond. J had watched the whole thing as the noise drew his attention, he swung his head back around to a face full of Mediators. Three of them had appeared out of nowhere. Zane fumbled with the barricade. Ariel was the first to open fire.

"Into the door!"

Ariel continued firing, her body as small as she could make it. J pushed himself back at the same time that Zane did and they met at the door, Zane floating in first. Ariel eliminated one of the Mediators, but the other two proved elusive, their movements quick, unpredictable. She slipped into the door, darkness engulfed her.

"Keep it off."

"What?"

"Your lights."

J nodded, rolled his eyes realizing no one could see him. His silence would be enough. A small amount of light glimmered into the room, J felt around searching for something to hold onto. He stared at the rectangular opening, raised his blaster. A Mediator peeked in, analyzing the room, its movements smooth and calculating. A light flashed momentarily blinding J. Ariel had fired a shot, hitting their assailant in the head, its body floated out of sight. Another appeared.

"Probably should find a way out," Ariel quipped, firing again.

Zane opened fire as two more appeared. J clicked on his light searching for an exit, Tara did the same, and found another door amongst the debris. She started working on it, sparks flickered off the surface lighting up her face. J spun toward her, his eyes squinting examining her face. Her tongue was partially exposed as she bit it, concentrating. J couldn't help but chuckle. He floated over to the door, Tara was making a smaller hole than this last; this one an ugly oval. He felt her

tension as she hastened her efforts. The other two continued
battling the intruders, knocking each one out. Blasts hit the
door above, J's eyes shot up. *That was close.* They needed to
move faster. Tara was almost through. J grabbed a handle
near the side of the door, he wouldn't make the same mistake
as Tara. Before she could completely finish, he pushed his
feet off of the wall, using the bar as a pivot point, and kicked
through the cut metal. The disk whipped into the next room
floating to the far end, a long dark hallway greeted them.

Tara stepped in. "The vault is in the next room."

Ariel grabbed Zane and forced him into the doorway. He
nearly got stuck, but managed to wiggle himself free. She fired
another blast, destroying a Mediator before retreating. She
flipped her rifle back out of her way while grabbing something
out of a pouch. She pointed to the round disk. "Zane, grab
the door!"

Zane kicked off the wall. Zipping past J, he grabbed
the metal chunk then flipped his body around as a swimmer
positioning for the next lap. He kicked again, zipping over to
Ariel, and caught himself on the far end placing the disk over
the hole, the Mediator disappearing behind. J watched as Ariel
welded the plate back on.

Tara was at the far end working on the last door, her task
nearly complete, another poorly shaped portal. J flipped over
to her, kicking it open as she completed it, and they stepped
in. He searched the room. A sofa floated in the middle, a
mattress off to one side, a desk in the corner. "I thought we
were searching for a vault?"

Tara's eyes flicked back and forth as if reading imaginary

text. "You were expecting the type of vault shown in bank robbery scenes from Wild West movies?"

"Yes...wait, what?" J's head tilted in his helmet. *How could she know about a Wild West vault? Or that he was thinking of one? She'd never lived...existed on Earth.* He'd think about that later, they needed to find the objective.

Zane flipped in through the hole. "You find it, kid?"

J searched again, he didn't have a clue what he was looking for.

Tara spoke up. "It's a small two by two metal vault. It should be on one of the walls, about chest high. People used to hide them behind pictures."

It was like she was inside his brain. J shook his head and continued surveying the room, spotting a glimpse of a frame hidden behind some debris. He pushed himself over and relocated the debris. Behind it was a picture of the interior of Atlantis. He grabbed the corner, tugging it away from its home.

"I think I found it."

"Good," he heard Ariel say as she entered the room. "That hack job of mine isn't going to hold them long."

J scrutinized the wall, hunting for a control panel, but only a silver square smiled back, defying him.

"There's no control panel!"

Ariel flew over to him, flipping through the dead space with grace and ease. She landed next to him, feet on the wall, scoping out the vault door. J was befuddled. In a zero g environment there is no "up", but his mind wanted to fix that. Ariel standing ninety degrees from his position threw him off.

"Place your hand on the panel."

He did and the panel lit up. His head kicked back almost pulling him away. He hadn't expected anything to happen, the ship's power was down. The panel pressed toward him, his arm giving in from the force. It slid out of position and he reached in, pulled out a gold brick and held it up to show Ariel.

Her forehead furrowed. "Is that all that's in there?" She bent down, gazed in, the vault was empty.

The room lit up as the Mediators breached the door. Zane laid down fire, knocking a few out.

J stared back at Ariel, his eyebrows pinched together. The doorway seemed to be the only way out. "Any ideas?"

Ariel began firing back at the Mediators, slipping behind floating debris.

Tara scanned the room. "There's a ventilation shaft above that leads to the climate control room. Over there." She pointed to a vent near one of the walls.

J bent his neck forward, his face inches from his visor. It appeared small and he wasn't sure if Zane would fit, though they'd made that mistaken assumption before. Somehow the behemoth of a man managed to mold his body into whatever shape it took to get out of a sticky situation. He fired a shot, the frail metal melted away. "I think Tara's found a way out. Zane, you first. If you can't fit we gotta fight it out." *Please fit.* He took up Zane's position, firing on the Mediators. Blasts zipped to and fro, several missing the targets on both sides. Zane backed up, continuing to fire, his eyes focused on the Mediator-laden opening. J watched, his eyes drifting between the two. He kicked the wall flying back to Zane, grabbed his pack and shoved him into the ducting. Zane's body easily moved in the zero g environment.

Ariel twisted her head back. "Your turn, J." She maneuvered backward calling for Tara to do the same.

J popped up into the vent, his helmet bouncing off the ceiling. It was larger than he'd anticipated with room to twist his body around and see Zane crawling away, his helmet light leading the way. J paused. *Should he wait for Ariel?* He turned his head back and a laser blast exploded on the wall. J eked back, his eyes big.

Ariel's head popped in. "What are you doing? Get going, they're wall to wall in there!"

J scrambled after Zane, following his light as he bent around a few times. He saw a bright flash around Zane before he dropped out of sight. J stopped, Ariel ran into him knocking him forward.

"Keep moving!"

Her voice informing him the Mediators were hot on their tail, that he needed to move, but he was unsure of what happened to Zane. He inched forward. Ariel finally shoved him to hurry him up and he flew forward over a large hole, as he passed he gazed down, Zane's eyes staring back at him. J kicked his hands and feet out, pressing them to the sides of the conduit, and slowed to a stop flipping over. He saw Ariel shoot through the hole, Tara zipped in as well, disappearing. Glancing up, he spied a Mediator crawling toward him. He scrambled for the hole, pulling himself through. Tara reached up and yanked him out of the way, just as Zane tossed something into the opening. A flash of light hit J's eyes as he gazed toward the hole.

"That'll slow 'em down," Zane said as he floated back to the center of the room.

J peered around, all of them illuminating the dark, windowless mechanical room with their headlamps. Multiple square ducts twisted around, entering and exiting large conditioning machines. He watched each of his crew search the room, attempting to find an exit. To him, they were more than a crew. Tara was right, they'd become a family. He stared a moment, just watching, his thoughts broken as Tara spoke up.

"There is a door over here that leads to the dining hall."

Ariel pushed herself over toward Tara finding the door. "You open it." Her head snapped to Zane and J. "You two cover the vent."

Ariel ran, taking up position next to Tara. J did as ordered, raising his rifle toward the open vent, his muscles contracting and loosening while his eyes scanned the square black hole. A mechanical steel hand slipped out onto the ceiling, he steadied his aim awaiting the target, the metal humanoid's head shot out next. It burst into pieces, floating about the room. He recoiled from the shot, hunted for another. The subsequent shots felt heavier with more recoil and he dropped his support hand searching for something to provide a bit of stability. His efforts in vain, he found himself near the center of the room.

Zane stepped up next to him. "Get to the wall, I'll stay here."

J glanced at the wall, it was close enough to provide the steadiness he needed. He took a step forward pushing himself with his thruster. His pack announced 50% reserve. Zane opened up as another Mediator attempted to gain access. Even as he dispatched it, another took its place. J had almost reached the wall when something hit his shoulder. His body spun out of control, the rifle slipping from his hand and bolting toward the wall. A Mediator had managed to take a shot while climbing in. Zane finished him off, slid over to J, his body still spinning. J attempted to stabilize himself, his fingers pressing on the controls. His mind disoriented, his input did the opposite and increased the spin. He smacked into the wall, bounced off. The impact slowed him enough that Zane was able to grab him.

"Gotcha, kid."

A blast zipped over his shoulder and J peered back, his chest tightened. Two Mediators were now in the room, their weapons poised to fire. Zane flipped his arm toward them, letting off a few rounds, his other locked on J. He tossed J toward the far end.

"Get to the door." He took another shot. "Right behind you."

J zipped over using more propulsion than necessary, his readout below 40%. His eyes raked over the numbers, hoping it would last. *How much longer would they be out?* Tara finished the cut, her torch still burning as J approached. He added another hit of thruster and instinctively closed his eyes, kicking out the panel. His body flew into the space beyond and he opened his eyes. Stars gleamed back at him like a clear summer evening sky, a fighter zipped by.

"You guys ready for pickup?" Max came through on the comm.

J swung his head around searching for the ship, spotted it amidst the battle. Fighter craft chased each other, ships exploded. Sheltered from space, J had forgotten about the battle raging outside the enclosed ship. He heard Ariel come up on comm.

"Yep, need a quick exit. Got some metal-heads on our tail."

"I see ya. Coming in hot."

J watched as Max adjusted the ship's vector for the approach, a single fighter engaging him. A bolt came from behind, buzzing over J's shoulder. His head snapped back to see Zane letting loose, more shots buzzed, the electrostatic fuzz ringing in his ears as it passed.

"Careful, you almost hit me."

Zane didn't pay attention, just continued firing, the shots barely missing J. He pressed on the thrusters and his body zoomed out of the way, pressed it again, spinning to see the engagement. Max continued inbound, the ship not slowing as if he was planning to ram them. J pressed the thruster again, nothing.

"Crap."

The ship was incoming and fast. His eyes exploded open, his arms waving, a vain attempt to stop the incoming craft. The ship behind Max exploded and J continued to wave his arms. The scout ship lit up, shining in J's eyes, blinding him. He threw his arms crossed over his face, awaiting the inevitable. There was a moment of silence, then he peeked out one tiny slit. The scout ship sat still, merely a few feet away from him. He floated frozen, half out of fear, half because that's all he could do. He watched Zane float by then Tara.

"Come on, no time for contemplating death." Ariel grabbed him as she zipped by. "Blew our thrusters too quick, did we?" Ariel snickered as she continued pulling him into the ship. Another fighter attacked and a few shots bounced into the cargo bay. She threw J toward the wall, hit the ramp switch. "Get us outta here, Max."

J felt the ship rock as it was hit again. Zane climbed on the wall working an extinguisher, one of the shots had damaged some of the electrical lines. J's eyes shot up feeling the ship come to life. Max enabled all of the thrusters, forcing the scout craft forward. J braced himself, grabbing a seat. Zane grabbed the electrical lines, his legs kicking back toward the rear of the craft. Ariel was temporarily pinned to the aft wall. Once her body caught up to the craft's speed, she tapped a button on the control pad. Gravity returned and J's legs and body felt heavy in the seat, his head spun from the sudden change. Zane hung by his arms on the wall.

"Little warning next time."

J heard Ariel snicker as Zane let go, toppling to the ground. He laid there rubbing his knee. Hearing the cockpit door slide open, his eyes snapped up to see Tara's head pop out from the cockpit.

"There's something you have to hear."

CHAPTER TWENTY

"We need to get this back to Arcturus." Ariel held up the gold brick, its weight now known in full gravity. It was only gold plated, if that, much too light for it to be solid. She handed it back to J who was thoroughly entranced by it. The item resembled a solid gold bar etched with lines like a digital spider web, over a dozen small indents were embedded at the end of each of the lines.

"But she could still be alive!" Zane's hopeful face leaned in through the small cockpit door.

Ariel looked back at him from the copilot seat as Max continued piloting the ship.

"J?"

He glanced up to see Zane and Ariel staring at him. He'd heard the conversation but really didn't want to give his opinion. They'd picked up a distress signal coming from an unknown object near one of the three moons. Its signature resembled the Parádeisos, but the enemy activity rendered the message incomplete. A string of numbers was all they could decode; it was a locator beacon and coordinates.

Zane broke the silence. "You know that's the last place she was. We owe it to her to at least look."

He had a point, V was last known to be on the Parádeisos, but they didn't know if it even was the Parádeisos. His eyes dropped down to the gold brick. It needed to get back to his father, Ariel was pushing that angle. He was the tie breaker, it was his decision, Max and Tara on opposite sides.

Ariel tightened her forehead gazing at Zane. "We don't

know if the ship's even still able to support life. We do know that we need to get this to Arcturus. You know that's the mission, we can check afterward."

Zane jutted out his chin, his eyes flashing as he stared back at her. "What would you do if it was him?"

Ariel stared back, her face softened but resolute. "You know what I would do."

J thought he knew what her decision would be, but he also knew that he'd make a different choice...had made a different choice before and it almost cost them V. There was also something bothering him about this whole mission, the interaction with his father, Tara's odd behavior. He placed his fingers on his forehead, they slipped over, massaging his temples. He took a deep breath and exhaled. "Let's check the beacon. If it's nothing, we'll head straight to the Houzeau."

Ariel's eyes snapped to J and he felt the icy chill of her stare down to his bones. He couldn't bear to see the betrayal in her eyes and looked away, out into the stars. Zane rested a hand on his shoulder, gripped it in gratitude not saying a word.

Ariel turned to face the windscreen. "You heard his highness. To the beacon."

Max watched her out of the corner of his eye a moment before shaking his head and setting the course. Even if Ariel didn't know it herself, Max was pretty sure she wasn't the same girl she used to be. He'd seen the way she was with J, even envied it for awhile, and there was no way she'd have left him out there if there was a shred of a chance he was still alive.

Zane headed back to examine the weapons rack. J gazed down at the item once more before placing it in a pocket. He peeked up at Ariel, her back turned to him, anger and hurt rolling off of her, before he turned and hopped off the one foot platform into the cargo area and slouched into a seat.

Zane grabbed a weapon and dropped in it J's lap. "Thanks, kid."

J looked up rolling his lips together, Zane tipped his head. J's eyes fell on the weapon, another rifle. He pressed the cell's energy stats trying to distract himself from his thoughts. But they were still there in the forefront of his mind. Ariel was pissed that he hadn't sided with her, but he felt he owed it to V. He'd left her once before and needed to atone for his mistake. Zane had also been quite convincing, he seemed very eager to chase the beacon in hope of finding V. He sat there lost in his thoughts, the ship occasionally rocking from enemy blasts.

"There's a 55% probability that systems are functioning."

J lifted his head to see Tara standing over him.

"What?"

She looked down at him, her face almost soft, a smile on her lips. His eyelids twitched as he tried to find any sign that she wasn't human.

"A 55% chance that we find survivors. The beacon was clear about that, the ship's identifier is the unknown."

J slouched back into his seat flicking the weapon with his finger. Staring through it, he didn't answer.

She approached the weapons rack, grabbed a weapon and a couple of helmets, handed one to J.

He took it, stared down at it a moment and saw his face looking back, his eyes bloodshot. He could use some sleep. "What's this for?"

Tara flipped one onto her head, locking it in. "Ship's locked down, it's standard system protocol during a massive breach. We'll have to—"

"Ship's locked down, you'll have to..." Ariel stepped out of the cockpit, her mouth open mid-sentence. "Looks like Tara beat me to the punch."

She turned to Zane and her eyes softened. "You were right, too. It's the Parádeisos. Hope you're right about V. We can't get a status on what systems are operating, but they do have power."

J stood up holding his helmet. "Any word from Arcturus?"

Ariel shook her head, her lips pressed tight together. "It's strange, we're picking them up on radar, but it seems like the comm is jammed. It doesn't make sense."

J slipped the helmet over his head, his body shivered as if stepping into the frigid cold back in Sector 21. The room was warm, it wasn't that. He took a breath, his eyes focused on Ariel, her beautiful body swaying as she slipped on her own helmet. She tapped on the door controls shutting them off from the cockpit.

Zane stood next to the cargo door. "Ready?"

J reached down picking up the rifle, checked it one final time. *As ready as I'll ever be.* He moved to face him. Zane briefly smiled back.

Max came over the comm. "Clear to deploy on my mark. 5, 4, 3, 2, 1, deploy, deploy, deploy."

The ramp snapped open and gravity left, J realized he didn't charge his pack. "Ahhhhh." He screamed as he toppled out of the ship head over feet, Tara bounced off him not realizing his predicament. The stars flipped around him, the moon, the ship, all came and went. Closing his eyes, he tried to steady his stomach. It did, his body was weightless, the spinning constant, his inner ear had stabilized. He opened his eyes.

"Nope." He snapped them shut once more, still in the spin.

"I gotcha."

He felt a body grab his, the light sound of jets firing. His eyes opened, Ariel was holding onto him, their glass helmets kissing. She shook her head, smiling, light glistened off the lens reminding him there was a battle raging in the distance.

"Forgot to recharge?"

J snapped his head away like a shamed dog, his eyes low into his shoulder. "A few things on my mind."

She grabbed his hand, bolting them toward the wreckage. Tara was floating near it, her head and eyes walking over every inch of the ship. She pointed to a section of the ship. "There's a hatch here that I believe we can use for access."

Ariel dragged them toward Tara. Stopping short, she released him and began to work the hatch controls. J sat there motionless, his eyes roving over the ship, its lights flickered showing signs of life. The shattered remains glowed from the moon reflecting Acadia's giant blue star, the shadow of the planet attended their side of the ship. Ariel finished the sequence, the light in the glass hatch flickering red before popping open. The four of them entered, Ariel locking the hatch last. The cabin pressurized automatically, restoring gravity. J caught himself falling a few feet and Tara pointed them toward a door.

"I'm picking up life forms through those doors."

Zane ran forward, readying his rifle. J prepped his with one last look at the cell, it had already become a habit. Ariel approached tapping in the door's opening sequence. J's body tensed, his rifle tight to his shoulder, his heart fluttered. Something didn't feel right. The door hissed open.

Dmitry stood on the other side, his soldiers flanked around him aiming rail guns at them. Dmitry stepped forward. "You can put those down now." He pointed to their weapons, his head high, square jaw jutting out, a small smirk on his face.

"You gonna give us the accent, too?" Ariel asked, strengthening her grip. The fabric wrapping her fingers squeaked.

"No, but you are going to give us your weapons. There is no call for needless bloodshed."

A solider stepped out from behind the others holding V, shackles adorned her wrists and held them tight behind her back. Ariel glanced back at Zane. He lowered his rifle, his jaw popping as he bit down. J and Tara mirrored the others, dropping the weapons to the ground.

"Guys, we have company. TK ship inbound."

Max wasn't privy to their situation, yet and continued trying to contact them.

Dmitry cracked a grin. "It sounds like our ride's here."

He waved his soldiers toward them. Two ran over and grabbed J, snatched his wrists, tightening restraints on them. One detached his helmet, the latch hissed as it came off the suit sounding defeated. Max's voice ceased. J looked up as if he expected words to flow through the ceiling. More soldiers imprisoned the others.

J intensified his gaze on Dmitry, his face still naive. "What'd you do?"

"My job." He turned, walking out of the room. "Take them to the hangar."

The soldiers dragged them toward a separate door.

Ariel struggled, her movements sharp, elbowing one of her captors. "Get off of me." She turned around kneeing one of them in the groin, he dropped to his knees wincing in pain. She attacked the other captor, her efforts met with a stun staff. She crumpled to the ground in a heap. The solider picked her up, threw her over a shoulder.

Any thoughts of an attempted escape left J's head. He'd have to wait for a better opportunity. His eyes roamed about, multiple soldiers followed them as they proceeded through the ship. Zane and Tara walked in silence, J followed suit, being as vigilant as he could. They soon exited an elevator into one of the large hangars, a green ship adorned with a golden TK emblem sat in the center. Two rows of Mediators lined both sides of the boarding ramp and a man stood at the bottom, his feet shoulder-width apart, hands behind his back. They continued their march, their captors pushing them along. J squinted, his eyes locked onto the man.

"We really need to stop meeting like this. How are you and your little girlfriend doing?" The man pulled the hair out of Ariel's face, stepping toward him. "Not so well by the looks of it."

J's eyes flashed, his mouth turned down in a scowl. "Dillon." He'd almost forgotten about him, pushing him out of his mind. The first one to turn on them. His eyes searched the ground attempting to draw up some witty comment. "Happy with your decisions?"

Dillon laughed derisively, his head snapping back, his chest bounced under his green and gold shirt adorned with ribbons.

"You get one for each betrayal?" Zane sneered.

Dillon slowed his laugh, dropping his chin to his chest to glance at his medals. He chuckled again. "If that was the case, I'd have more." He laughed again, pointing to the ship. "Put them in the holding bay."

He watched Ariel bobbing on the soldier's shoulder and thought better of it. "Put that one in a separate cell. She tends to get...ideas."

He chuckled again watching Zane walk past. Tara didn't even engage, staring straight ahead, her expression that of a disapproving teen. They moved his crew onto the ship. The interior was well-maintained, decorated with elaborate patterns, something royalty would travel in. Not a warship. The soldiers threw them into rooms more like hotels than cells. Zane and J were in one while the girls were separated in two others. J attempted to unlock the door panel after the soldiers left, to no avail. He turned around. "How could Dillon betray everyone?" He implored Zane for the answer. He'd been with Dillon and Arcturus from the beginning, he had to know something.

"I don't know, kid. Dillon was an arms dealer, an underground one at that. He's always has been a little shady, going after the deal that'd make him the most profit."

"You were there with my father...and Dillon."

Zane walked around examining the room, exhaled with a heavy breath. "Yes, I was there. Never really knew him, though. That was one thing about your father, need to know basis. I only needed to know my part."

J banged on the door, kicking it caused him to wince in pain. He gritted his teeth. "What part was that?"

"Watching out for Ariel...and you."

J turned around, his eyes searched Zane's face. "Me? What did he tell you?"

Zane laid down on the bed, it bounced then sagged. J popped his head back as it sprang back up contouring to his body.

"Just to help you when I could, but to let you make your own decisions. That's it, that was what I..." he popped his hands into the air, fingers making the quotes sign. "...needed to know."

J leaned on the door as he stared at the ceiling, the floor trembled underneath his feet. The ship was lifting off, he would soon be facing Cyrellia once more. He let his feet slide out from under him, his back skimming the wall with just enough friction to not fall. His butt hit the floor and he placed his hands palms down on the cold metal surface. How he wished it were wood, on Earth. He stared at the ground trying to remember. It felt like a dream, a movie, something that was a lifetime ago. He ran through his friends' names. *Would he forget them? Would they always be somewhere in his head?* He focused on the town, the diner, and his mind shifted to Will, the Earth's core. He took a deep breath, Zane noticed.

"You should get some sleep if you can. Who knows the

next time you'll be able to."

J twisted his head. Zane laid there, eyes closed. He seemed so calm after all that just happened. "How do you do it?"

"Do what?"

J stood up, stared down at him. "Sleep. After what just happened, how can you be so calm?"

Zane didn't stir, his eyes remained shut, only his lips moved. "Feelings come and go like clouds in a windy sky. Conscious breathing is my anchor."

J tilted his head, pressing an ear toward Zane. His eyes pinned on him, brows tight.

"Now stop staring at me, kid, and get some rest. Tap the wall over there."

He twisted around in slow motion walking over to the wall. Smacking his hand on the wall, nothing happened.

"A little higher."

J snapped his head around attempting to catch Zane peeking, no luck, his eyes were shut tight. He moved his hand and a bed rotated out. He looked down on it.

"Now sleep."

J flopped down, the soft surface contoured around his body. *Conscious breathing.*

CHAPTER TWENTY ONE

The door rattled then slid open.

"Wakey wakey." Dillon stood smiling in the doorway.

J rubbed his eyes, rolled over to see Zane slowly gain his feet.

Dillon motioned impatiently for them to climb out. "C'mon, let's go. Don't want to keep her highness waiting."

J passed Dillon, whose face rested in his perpetual smirk. A soldier slapped a set of shackles on his wrists then Zane's and they headed down, out of the ship. The clean air hit his lungs. J closed his eyes, taking it in. Until now, he hadn't noticed that the air was different, fresh, unlike the ship's which had an electronic "fake clean" smell to it. J dragged his feet attempting to slow them down, but his captor wasn't having it, shoved him in the back.

"It'll be much easier if you cooperate... Lady Cyrellia would prefer you in one piece."

J shot a scowl at Dillon. The same expression as before shot back, his head swiveled to the trek. He walked on smooth steel flooring just as in Atlantis. A light mist gathered underneath, dissipating as it rose into the trees lining both sides of the steel walkway. Up ahead, a vast metal city emerged out of the forest, its buildings replicated from those on the moon. A central structure towered over the others, its glass-domed top reflecting the sunlight toward J. He blinked, trying to gain more details. His head trailed down the buildings to the ground in front of them. A vehicle hovered with a single driver in front, the back seats empty. He thought it resembled

220

a sleek looking spacecraft crossed with a sedan, the rear door rotated up toward the sky.

"Get in. No games."

Dillon pushed him toward the door and J ducked his head, slipping into the seat. Zane was pushed in behind him, the vehicle dipped before bouncing back to its original height. Dillon entered, sat down in the middle seats which faced aft and a soldier climbed in last, shutting the door.

J eyed Dillon and his help sitting across from them. "Where's the other traitor?"

Dillon raised an eyebrow as he thought about the question, his face morphed in understanding and a chuckle escaped. "You mean Dmitry? He's with the others, you'll see him soon enough." He turned and looked outside.

J's head followed. Rows of Mediators stood frozen, their cold lenses peering out into the forest. The trees hindered the transmission of light to the ground, enormous trunks extending up hundreds of feet above them, casting a shadow over the vehicle as it began to move. *How long did the sun stay overhead? He'd yet to see darkness on the planet.* Their prison gained speed and the trees began to zip by. He tried to peek past Dillon who fingered a knife, running his large phalanges over the smooth surface of the curved blade. The view behind him obscured by a solid wall, he felt trapped in a moving box. Zane gazed out the window as if waiting for something. For all J knew, maybe he was. The natural beauty drastically changed. Metal structures filled the windows, people walked in the streets, shops passed. With the blue glow of the planet's sun, it reminded him of a colder Atlantis. A few minutes passed and the craft came to a stop. The door hissed open, blue light shined onto his legs once again. His head snapped up as Dillon crawled out with a groan.

"Blasted small XL7s."

The soldier slid out next, grabbing J's shackles and giving them a sharp tug. J's arms extended out, the cartilage in his shoulders popping. He grimaced, not ready for such force. Another appeared, reaching behind him to grab Zane who grumbled as he was forced out.

"Watch it, no need for that." Zane shook his head, his eyes flashed as he stared down at the smaller soldier. His gaze was met with wide eyes. The soldier snapped around, his arms shook. Dillon started off first, J looked past him. A set of steps climbed up ten feet to a secondary platform. From there, a glass opening awaited at the base of a tall steel building.

Dillon took up position to the side watching as his prisoners were pushed into the glass box, he stepped in as it closed. "Throne room," Dillon commanded.

J's eyes met Zane's, his brow furrowing down as his head tilted. Zane shrugged his shoulders, pinching up one side of his mouth. J tilted his head back, gazing up. The ceiling was glass, the inner shaft of the building could be seen, and the floor began to rise. *A glass elevator?* They hung on the edge of the building's wall, but halfway up, disappeared into a shaft. He watched as metal walls zipped by. Coming to a stop, J was forced out the elevator door before he even knew what was happening, it hissed shut. J spun around, his eyes searching. Zane was gone, his chest tightened, jaw clenched. "Where's Zane? What are you doing with him?"

Dillon walked away from the elevator, not acknowledging J's confusion or questions. J froze, his body shook and he felt a shove in his back. He spun around, his arms still tied together, swinging them like a club. His attack landed on the soldier's mouth. Unprepared, he dropped harmlessly to the ground. J swung around, searching for any other threats. His body fell into a heap convulsing, eyes twitching. He tried to move, but found that he had no control, his muscles continuing to flex as vibrations surged through his body. The violence stopped. His body relaxed still unresponsive, his eyelids dropped down and his ears became the only useful part of his body.

"And I thought Ariel was going to be the problem."

Dillon picked him up, slinging him over his shoulder. He holstered the stun blaster onto his left thigh. J felt the swaggering steps of the man as he sauntered on. Where he was going, J could only imagine as his eyelids continued their revolt. The sound of doors opening and closing rang through his head, Dillon's footsteps magnified echoing off of the walls. He felt his body tossed into a chair, his arms flopped over his lap. He took it as a good sign that the feeling was slowly coming back. The footsteps trailed off, whispers from a distance met his ear. He strained to hear, to pick up any words, the sounds of hissing was all that processed, the words inaudible. Sounds of footsteps approached, clicking, much different than Dillon's boots. His eyes still not working, he could only imagine whose they were.

"J, come to visit your dear mother. I'm flattered."

Cyrellia. He wished he could speak, he'd have some choice words for her. His lips twitched, it was all he could manage.

The clicks continued around him like a shark circling its prey, then stopped. He felt pressure under his chin, a soft hand lifting his head up.

"You do look like him. Where is he by the way?"

He felt his head drop, the back of his neck burned, the pain radiating outward. Inside he smiled, the pain was a good sign that his senses were trickling back to him. He fluttered one eyelid, almost enough to see, tried the other with the same result. The presence of Cyrellia towered over him, his body would have quaked had he been able, instead his mind played out events. He had no attachment to her, they shared blood, but nothing else. She was a murderer, an evil witch. He imagined her with green skin and a pointy hat, calling for Mediators to flood in around him.

"I guess that I'll have to do all the talking since you decided it would be wise to attempt an escape in my city, my tower." The sound of her steps clicking as she circled him again. He heard a chair scrape across the floor, his eyes opened slightly. Sunlight beamed in around the shadow of a figure seated across from him. His eyes were beginning to work on command. Cyrellia sat with her legs crossed, a gold and green gown draped over them. She swirled a glass of red wine, raised it to her nose inhaling the pleasant aroma, then pressed the glass to her lips. After taking a small sip, she rested her elbow on the arm of the chair, her fingers caressing the bottom of the glass she held in front of her. She gazed down on him, her lipstick a heavy red, hair pulled up and styled as if she was attending a gala or a ball.

"I guess I really should thank him...your father that is. He did, after all, help create you, find this beautiful planet and build the ship which now stands as the cornerstone of our civilization." She swirled the glass again, her gaze contemplative, as she watched the red liquid swish about, the legs of the wine running down the sides of the glass when she stopped. "And this superb wine. I never imagined that this planet would be so fertile."

By now, J was able to raise his head. His appendages moved or twitched, depending on who you asked. He attempted to move his eyebrows, his jaw still hung loose underneath. Cyrellia took notice and glanced over to the corner of the room, his guess was that Dillon lurked there out of sight. Footsteps approached and J's hunch proved correct.

Dillon leaned in front of him, released the shackles. "Don't try anything foolish." He stood up, tapping the stun gun on his hip, a grin on his face as he moved out of view. "Or do. More fun for me."

J wiggled his jaw and attempted to speak, an unintelligible series of moans crept out making him sound like a zombie. Cyrellia kicked her eyebrows up then again turned to her wine, she was content to wait. His eyes flicked about scanning the room, searching for anything that might help him escape. *He had to get free, find Ariel and the others.* The room must have been at the very top of the tower, its appearance replicated her quarters in Atlantis, the windows surrounding it, the bar in the corner. The view was different, but not the status it conveyed. It still sat taller than the surrounding environment. Even the grand trees below were dwarfed by its sheer size.

Controlled movement returned to his neck, his body

almost mobile he tried again. "Where are my friends?"

Cyrellia squinted, leaning forward to try to decipher the sounds that came from his scratchy throat still recovering from the paralysis. She tilted her head back, a devious grin crossed her lips. "They're safe."

J heard the door hiss open and turned his head, his movements slow and wobbly. Dmitry stood in the door, his posture straight, chest puffed out proudly. He marched over to Cyrellia, she opened her hand toward J.

"Ah, perfect timing. J was asking about his friends, you can brief us together." She stood up, strutted toward the bar.

Dmitry focused on J a moment, his face blank, emotionless, before turning to address Cyrellia. "Of course, my lady. We have them held in the detention block in square four, all are alive, awaiting further orders." He placed his hands behind his back his eyes locked onto Cyrellia.

She set down the bottle she'd been using to refill her glass, her eyes stopped gazing out the window and snapped to meet Dmitry's. "Execute them."

J was momentarily mute, stunned by what he'd just heard. He attempted to compose himself, his mind wasn't strong enough and his heart took over. His voice screeched out, "No!"

Cyrellia smiled, knowing she'd won this round, and held up a hand in the air. There was a moment where the room stilled, J watched as her smile grew. "True love of your friends, but how true?" She sauntered toward him, her dress swaying over her hips, the smooth green silk flowing on the ground behind her. She stopped, still caressing the wine glass, raised two fingers and flicked them up. J felt his body forced in a standing position, he almost tumbled forward. Dillon caught him, pressed him back up as he stood next to him holding his collar. J glared at Cyrellia, his bottom lip quivered, his leg twitched. He couldn't understand her blatant disregard for life. His friends were not merely things to be discarded, not pests to be dealt with. They were humans, like her.

"I have a proposal for you...son."

His mind spun. *What did she want? What could he do to save them?* He stared down at the polished stone quartz at his feet, rugs overlaid throughout, distracting him momentarily from the dire situation he was in. He brought his head up, their eyes met. "What do you want?"

She turned and sashayed to the far window, appraising the city below, then pressed her empty arm straight down flicking two fingers forward. Dillon dragged him to the window and held J's body beside her. He spied down onto her view; the city stretched out for miles before meeting the forest. A glint of light hit his eye from the forest and he leaned forward, focusing on the far off object.

Cyrellia laid her hand out flat, palm up. "Dillon."

He handed her a set of white plastic binoculars she took them adjusting them to her eyes. J witnessed a smile grow on her face then she pulled them away. She took another sip of her wine, placing the binoculars in front of his face. J took them. Spinning them around, he peered out toward the woods. The binoculars outlined a slew of mechanized creatures in the tree line. J tightened his grip on them and the binoculars zoomed even closer, the trees all but dissolving. He popped them off, his eyes snapping to Cyrellia's face. Her body rocked as an inaudible chuckle overtook her. Gazing through the binoculars once more, he focused on the machines he recognized, the weaponry he wished he could forget. "What do you want?"

His voice was elevated, the tension evident in his words. He knew what those machines could do, it wasn't anything he ever wanted to see again. Cyrellia continued to stare through the woods, her eyes unfocused as if in a trance. "Arcturus... down here."

Her answer was laid on the table, it wasn't the answer he wanted... it wasn't an answer he could deliver. J stumbled backward, Dillon strengthened his grip, adding an empty hand. J tried to shrug it off, but his hands clamped down even tighter. Cyrellia pressed the wine glass to her nose again, her eyes closed and a small moan came from her lips.

J struggled with his captor, finally relenting. "What does that have to do with me?"

Cyrellia opened her eyes slowly, placing both hands on the wine glass. "You're the bait."

She waved a hand over her head, the window became opaque and a digital screen flickered then came on solid. The image of a ship's bridge met his eye and a man stepped into the picture, his grey hair filling the screen as he bowed.

"My lady, what are your orders?"

His face came back into view, much too young to have grey hair, his features round reminding J of a panda.

Cyrellia swirled the wine. "Get me an audience with Arcturus, I have a proposal for him."

The man bowed again, shouted orders to someone off screen, and the display flickered again, this time displaying a ship floating in space. The Houzeau. The screen zoomed in then flickered before displaying a man staring back at them. J stepped back.

Cyrellia tilted her head. "Arcturus. You're looking well. Tell me, did you envision me having this young, naive boy in my possession?" Her hand extended out, palm open to the sky, fingers pointing toward him. He pulled his bottom lip up as he glared back at her.

Arcturus pursed his lips, his stance firm, hands at rest in the small of his back. "It would seem that you bested me this time, Cyrellia. What is your proposal?"

Cyrellia laughed, stepped back to pour more wine as she looked up at the screen. "That's the Arcturus I know, quick and to the point, no time for chit chat, right to the big event."

She sauntered over to J placing a forefinger under his chin. Arcturus narrowed his eyes as she did. She flicked her finger off his chin. "I'll admit he's a handsome devil, gets that from his father. He's also incredibly stubborn, that's my line."

She shifted her weight onto one leg, hip sticking out, hand resting on the opposite.

"I'll trade his life... for yours."

CHAPTER TWENTY TWO

Dillon pulled J out through the elevator door, the shackles digging into his wrist as Dillon towed him along. *Arcturus was trading his life.* J tried to wrap his head around it. His father was a smart man, he must have a plan, there had to be something more to it. Cyrellia had made the deal and Dillon was to take J to the designated location for the trade. They exited the hall through a large set of glass doors opening to a balcony. A ship sat motionless, its wings armed with large missiles, cannons hung off the belly and sides, the most sizeable attached to the top. The hum of the fusion driven engines filled the air and J almost stopped to listen, it was steadily becoming one of his favorite sounds. But now wasn't the time to bask in the glories of technology. He'd thought he played an integral part in safeguarding the universe, in bringing an end to injustice and tyranny, but he was slowly realizing that he was a mere pawn in the game of Acadia. *After all, how many times could a guy get captured by his mortal enemy? And what did it say about him, his usefulness and purpose, that he was forever in need of a savior?* Dillon pushed him into the ship, its small cargo bay holding only two of them. He buckled himself in and Dillon did the same, crossing his arms as he rested his head back. J looked away, he didn't deserve acknowledgement.

The ship rattled, the ordinance clanged as the craft lifted off. J felt the vibrations shoot through his body. Something about it comforted him; he could feel again and that was a win. But what he felt now was claustrophobic. Folding canvas strap seats seemed like an afterthought and the windowless prison made it easy to lose orientation, the compartment must have been designed solely for cargo. He wracked his brain to come up with a plan. *Maybe he could incapacitate Dillon.* His eyes fell on the stun blaster and he quickly deleted that from his mind. The ship rumbled on, bumpy for a spacecraft. He was surprised by how much vibration trickled through his body. The engine whine changed, he guessed they were on an approach. The ship rattled more, then he heard three clunks and the vibrations ceased. Muted blue light spilled through the aperture as the cargo door opened. Dillon's hand grasped J's wrist and tugged him outside, a blast of air rushed over J's face and he closed his eyes as tall grass swirled about.

After the wind died down, he looked up, watched the ship ascend out of sight. His head swiveled around, visually exploring in all directions. A gentle breeze swept through creating waves like an ocean. Behind him was a large tree line, in front, rocky mountains extended upward for thousands of feet. Other than the sound of the wind through the rushes, there was silence, they were alone in the middle of the field. His chest rose and fell with his nervous breathing, he bit his bottom lip. Dillon finally let go of his bindings, crossed his arms.

"Hurry up and wait."

J raised an eyebrow and focused on Dillon's face, he stared out toward the mountains and drew in a deep breath, his nostrils flared. "You smell that? Fresh, natural, unfiltered air. Grass and mountains. No synthetic stuff here."

J eyed his blaster once again, his thoughts not on the grass or air, but on escape. Dillon gave a slight chuckle as J searched his face after the commentary. Dillon stared at the mountain-tops. "Paradise...Acadia."

J followed his gaze, surveying the same view. Green covered the mountains from the base to the peak, a few rocky outcroppings broke up the shades of green with a contrasting reddish brown. He spotted something just past one of the peaks, a red fireball. The sound of a weapon sliding from a holster filled the stillness, Dillon raised it into the air.

"Showtime."

J looked him up and down, his eyes tight as he did. He snapped back to the red ball of flame growing in the distance. The flame broke away revealing a ship. Over a dozen more fell in behind, all appearing the same way. The craft began its final descent. J watched as landing gear extended out from under the belly. *The Omorfiá.* The ship landed a few hundred yards from their location, the others fell in behind. J glanced around, seeking an answer as to whether or not Cyrellia had something nefarious planned, a face off in the field. Nothing stood between them and the tree line. The Omorfiá's ramp opened and Arcturus stepped out, his walk proper and slow, his face leveled at Dillon.

Dillon grabbed J's tricep. "Brought a little more than just you I see."

Arcturus didn't acknowledge the quip, just continued walking toward them. J stepped forward, but Dillon corrected him, tightening his grip. J winced as the pain shot up his shoulder, a reminder, no funny business. His father neither sped up nor slowed his pace. J's calf bounced as he waited, his body tense. Dillon tugged on him attempting to settle him down, only making his anxious tendencies worse. They stood their ground awaiting the exchange. Arcturus stopped a dozen feet from them, his head held high. Dillon raised his blaster and, without hesitation, shot him in the chest. A guttural scream erupted from J's throat. Shock, anger, sorrow, betrayal... he didn't know what he felt at that moment, but it was some combination of those. Pulling his arm away from Dillon's fingers, he gained leverage and kneed Dillon, dropping him to the ground. J raised his arms up for a final strike, but a thick green beam glowed overhead. The heat from the ray burned as if he'd been standing too close to a campfire, the light blinded him. Tiny bits of shrapnel exploded outward as the Omorfiá burst into pieces, the blast knocking J back, his body careening though the air. He bounced twice, sliding to a stop. Another blast zipped overhead and the same intense heat spread over his face. He laid there a moment, squeezing his eyes shut then opening them, trying to focus. Everything was blurry as though his tear ducts had stopped working. He rubbed his head, another green blast zipped overhead. His ears rang, sounds of explosions muffled in the air, automatic bursts of weapons began to fill the sky, colors danced about. J rolled onto his side, his whole body hurt, pain radiated throughout. He coughed. Mouth wet, he wiped it absently and his hand came away bloody. Grabbing his chest, he took a deep breath and pain swelled inside of him. Ariel's injuries came to mind. *Maybe he wasn't that bad.* He achingly rose onto one knee. Peeking over the grass, he saw the remaining ships engage the tree line. The green blast continued at constant intervals, hitting their marks, the ships disintegrating like thousand-year-old parchment. He stumbled to his feet, attempted to trudge through the tall grass, searching for his father. His head spun, nothing felt right. He passed the location where he thought his father should be, nothing. No body, no blood, no evidence of the horror he'd witnessed. He held his head, attempting to stop the spinning. A green blast flew over him, his neck felt like it was lit on fire, the skin hot to the touch. He began running toward the mountains. *Arcturus' soldiers were in the mountains.* His progress was slow, the battle raged on above him, the two sides clashing. Ships danced out of sight in a desperate attempt to escape the green lasers cutting them down. A tree the size of a building collapsed hitting the ground with a thud, causing the ground to shake. J made it to the base of the mountain, collapsed and rolled over to witness TK annihilating his father's forces. Resting on a hillside, his back elevated, he tilted his head up to look at the sky. He wiggled his hands. *Still trapped in the shackles.* He took a deep breath, his heart slowed. *What to do?* He closed his eyes as the blasts continued, the cacophony slowly trickling off. The ships destroyed, the lives lost, he began to blame himself. He laid there. *Maybe I should give up.* He coughed again, smearing the blood with his forearm. His head slapped back onto the ground and he licked his lips, the metallic taste of blood flowed through his mouth. A shooting star zipped by as if to mock him. He coughed again. Trying to catch the blood on his arm, his teeth hit metal. The Datacle was still on his wrist. J stared at it for a moment in disbelief then jerkily attempted to reach it with his fingers, the shackles making that impossible. After a few minutes, he gave up that tack. Next, he tried his tongue, but the sensor didn't recognize it, the blood covering the surface making it illegible. His nose fared no better, he couldn't tell what he was touching. He sat back and again plopped his head back onto the ground, his eyes watched the sky as clouds drifted by, some obscured by the branches of the tree. He sat up.

"Aha!"

J climbed to his feet, his eyes searching for the right object. He found it a few feet into the foliage, a bush with a few broken branches like fingers protruding outward. Maneuvering his wrist, he placed the Datacle vertically, tapped the buttons with the branches. A huge grin popped onto his face. *It was working!* He ran through menus, having trouble at first, but soon got the hang of it. The comm was jammed and many of the functions didn't work properly. He flopped down onto the ground, his gaze toward the enormous trees and Cyrellia's tower, looming over him. He pushed his hands through his hair, as far as the manacles would allow; a small beeping sound skipped off his ear as he did and his eyes whipped over to his wrist. A dot flashed on the map display. He recognized the area, it was probably the only place he could remember on this planet. The valley, the river...the mech. He stood up, eyes scanning the horizon. *If he could find the mech, maybe he'd have a chance.*

The sun hung low on the horizon, the mountain's shadow stretched over the valley below. It continued to set quicker than he anticipated. He coughed, spraying blood onto the ground. *The mech had medical supplies, it might buy him some time.* He looked down his path, the green foliage engulfing all.

It wouldn't be easy, that was for certain. He had direction and that was enough, enough to keep his mind off the tragedy he'd witnessed. His eyes welled up, a tear splashed on the ground as he checked his footing. He'd just met his father, now he was gone. Shaking his head, he focused on the task at hand, it would be a dark journey. Acadia's daily cycle was still foreign to him, he prayed it'd be a short night. As darkness fell, the forest came alive with sounds, sounds that weren't present during the day. He wondered if he'd just not heard them or if the majority of the planet was nocturnal. He stepped carefully in the waning sunlight, his feet slipping every so often. He checked the Datacle, Max's voice ran through his head, "It's only eight clicks". Eight clicks it was, but eight clicks in the dark, surrounded by whatever was making the strange sounds.

J firmed his resolve, nodded to himself. "Eight clicks."

He trudged on, the journey replicating the one before, minus Tara and Ariel. He came across a fallen tree, wondered if it was the same. Two of the moons had risen in the sky, their light brightening the forest. It seemed more like a dark, over-cast day, the way a deep thunderstorm cloud smothers the sun. He was thankful for any light and wasn't about to complain. The growl of a creature caught his ear, another attacking it, the fight ensued. J imagined two alien demon dogs fighting like in one of the space movies he watched as a youngster. He hoped he wouldn't run into any of them. A shadow fell over him, the soundless flight of a flying creature zipped over his head, his eyes not quick enough to pick it up. He soldiered on, cough-ing up more blood as he went. The map showed that he was getting close. He could see the river and it triggered his thirst.

His mouth was parched, the feeling of cotton balls filled his gums. He hobbled down to the water, the moonlight flickered off the crests of the river, its gentle sounds soothing his ears. Cupping his hands, he brought it to his mouth and the refreshing, natural water slipped down his throat, a cool sensation accompanying it. He rested on his knees, his palms placed on top, his eyes stared at the river, his focus through it into nothingness. *What was Ariel doing? Was she okay?*

A wracking cough broke him out of his trance, something caught his attention as he wiped the blood from his sleeve. Glowing green eyes stared back at him as he turned up the shoreline, he froze. The growl he heard earlier had come from the shadowy beast. He squinted, trying to determine its makeup. The creature walked on six legs and resembled an Earthly hound. It crept forward, the low growl continuing. J glanced down, only moving his eyes, his hands still bound in the shackles. A stick could have proven useful, he scanned the ground. Nothing but sand and small rocks sitting motionless, the river flowing over, rippling around the objects. His attention snapped back to the creature nearly on top of him. It jumped, all six of its arms spread out wide, claws extended like razors, its eyes locked onto his. J swung his arms as his attacker impacted, stumbled back, the animal bouncing off his strike and landing on its feet like a cat. J twisted around as it circled him, his foot submerged into the water. He glanced down at his leg, ankle deep. The creature was corralling him, pinning him against the water. His eyes flicked about. He had an exit, but he'd have to go now before he became entrenched in the water. He took another step back as the creature crouched, its shoulder blades high, neck and face low to the ground. J took off running along the river, a snarl came from the animal now behind him. He pushed hard with his legs, adrenaline surging through his body, his muscles contracting like rubber bands, propelling him forward. A heavy weight knocked him off balance, he fell down face first into the sand, the creature on top of him. He rolled over, hitting its face with the shackles. Blood spewed into the air from the creature's mouth, its claws dug into J's skin, two of its six paws on his chest. Its head back, eyes glowing, readying for the strike. J reached up, grabbed it by the neck, before its snapping jaws could latch onto his nose. He tossed the animal aside, scrambled to his feet. The creature regained its composure, shaking off the attack. J turned his attention to the tree line. *Maybe if I get there, I can lose it.*

He bolted, his feet churning up the sand, finding it difficult to move in the loose crushed rock. He glanced down, only a few more steps and he'd be on stone and dirt, much easier to move. Much easier for the creature as well. The growling and gnashing increased behind him, but he stayed focused on the tree line, his steps quick, his breath heavy. He caught a glimpse of a fallen branch a few steps away motivating him to accelerate, his legs propelled him forward, the footing more secure on the hard-packed dirt. Pain radiated from his back as the creature clamped onto him, knocked him down again, its sharp claws digging into his skin through the suit he still wore. He was thankful for it, had he been in regular clothes, his body would've been cut to shreds. His hand extended out to the stick and he snatched it off the ground, his fingers squeezing. It felt natural like a baseball bat. He swung, twisting his body violently, knocking the animal into the air. He gained his feet, wrung the makeshift weapon between his palms, the shackles offering no interference. He cocked the weapon back, loading up, his body preparing to strike. The creature growled once again. Shaking dirt from its fur, it leapt toward him. He locked onto the snarling head, took a step forward, unloading, his arms extending toward the target. The branch snapped, splinters spun through the air, the animal's face bowed inward from the sheer force of the blow, its eyes darkened, lids closing. His follow-through left him with half of a weapon just longer than his grip. The creature hit the ground limp, its multiple legs flopped lifeless. J stood staring down on it, his breath heavy, hands shaking.

More growls hit his ears, he focused his gaze. It wasn't coming from his attacker, the creature was motionless, empty, gone. Searching the surrounding area, he found a pair of eyes staring back at him in the distance, glowing, then another set, and another. A sea of lights flickered through his retinas, he swallowed. His body shook and he glanced at the broken, splintered wood, hardly a weapon now. He eyed his wrist, the dot flashed. One click. His eyes snapped back to the threat, the growling, snarling growing louder. Luck was on his side though, his path lay behind him, he had distance between them. *One kilometer, he could do this.*

J dropped the stick, pressed his body weight onto one leg propelling him backward. His body twisted and his second foot hit the ground springing him in the air. He ran. The moons' light dim inside the foliage, he scrambled through the trees, hit a few. The creatures cries grew closer and he turned back toward the river, the interior of the forest proving too dark to navigate. His breathing sped up, heart rate sky-rocketed, he was in overdrive. The pain in his chest disappeared, the immediate threat filling his mind. They were quicker than him, designed for their environment, he wasn't. He struggled through more of the foliage, breaking out into the moonlight. His feet danced across the rocks as he ran parallel to the water, the river muffled the howls, chants and growls of the predators.

Lights beamed up toward the sky as if beacons signaling to some celestial being. He continued his sprint, his legs weakening, the creatures closing in. He rounded a bend and the source of light became evident. Two ships sat on the shoreline, spotlights aimed to the heavens. Soldiers walked near the craft, one sporting binoculars pointed at him. Behind him, multiple Mediators stood motionless, their metal sensors aimed outward providing a perimeter for the ships. J's gaze pushed past the ships to his target. The mech loomed over the smaller craft, his chest loosened, a slight smile popped onto his face. *It was still there.* His joy turned to agony as the strike of teeth bared down onto his heel. He collapsed, turned over. One of the creatures had caught him, its snout snapped at him. J lifted his arms, but the attacker's jaw closed onto it. The creature jerked its head back not finding the juicy meaty prize presented before it. J swatted landing a blow to the head, knocking it sideways, clearing his line of sight. J's jaw dropped, eyes widened. Past its body, two more creatures leapt into the air, he raised his arms in defense.

CHAPTER TWENTY THREE

A light flashed past his hands, heat hit his palms. Another flashed simultaneously and the two creatures fell to the ground dead. Gaining his feet, J pressed his attacker off of him. He ran toward the machine, the men yelling for him to stop, bolts from their weapons zipped over his head and near his legs. The squeals of injured animals echoed behind him through the valley. He dug deep, concentrating on the target. The Mediators came to life, their movements adjusting for an attack, they fired taking down more of the creatures. J didn't look back. He was close enough now to see, the men were soldiers, their uniforms green adorned with gold trim. The one with the binoculars began to shout as J neared.

"You! Stop there!"

J's body tensed, he didn't want to stop, couldn't. He chanced a peek behind him, bodies of dead creatures were strewn about, others retreating back toward the woods. The soldier shouted to him once more. J accepted the command, the immediate threat gone. Collapsing to his knees on the sandy shoreline, his glutes hit his heels as he gazed up at the stars. He absently wondered if one of them was Earth, if people were still going about their daily lives, no fear, no pain, no persecution. The solider stepped into his view.

"Where'd you come from?"

J searched his face, opened his mouth to speak, but a cough cut him off, blood trickled down his lip. The soldier bent down taking his shackles in his hand.

"Doesn't matter, better get you medical attention then you

can talk."

He helped J to his feet and two Mediators approached, one scanned him.

"Prisoner 42651, identification J. Subject must be transported to Lady Cyrellia immediately."

The man squinted, his eyes searching J's face, his eyebrows pressed together. He didn't say a word, just turned and dragged J toward one of the ships. J hung his head, his only relief was not being eaten alive. His body ached, the small puncture wounds stung like bees and the pressure in his chest was becoming unbearable. He stumbled along, his steps slow, his body crashing from the adrenaline high. The solider glanced back multiple times, coaxing him forward. J obliged, his mind elsewhere, eyes scanning for a possible means to escape. He slid an eye to the side as they passed one of the mech's legs, the rungs of the ladder inviting him. Jaw rigid, he lifted his foot, thrust it down on his captor's leg, the soft tendons giving way underneath the immense pressure of his boot. The man's leg buckled, expletives emerged as he crumpled into a heap, his rifle slipping from his fingers when he impacted the solid ground. J rushed to the ladder, climbing as quickly as he could, his arms still married, flying up together, his legs stabilizing his torso. His arms continued releasing and grabbing as his feet accelerated him upward. The men below were shouting commands, there was no time to look down, it would only slow his movements. He continued as a jumping spider, bar to bar. Two of the soldiers scrambled after him, the Mediators crowded around the ladder, their weapons locked on. One of them spoke.

"Halt! Prisoner 42651, return to the ground for transport and processing. This will be your only warning."

J ignored it like a husband reading the paper while his wife is trying to get his attention. His efforts focused on the top, eyes locked onto the last rung. *Four more.* He reached up for the final bar and a bolt hit his leg, pulling him off balance. Another hit where his body once was. He gritted his teeth, kicking upward, his steel belted arms shot over the edge. He pulled himself up, the sky now littered with blaster rounds. His eyes frantic, his chest pounded, the latch lay closed tight as a banker's vault door. His ear twitched as the ladder clanged, he knew there wasn't much time left. Dropping to his knees, he planted his hand on the latch. If this didn't work he was out of ideas. A hand slapped onto the machine's metal roof, a head popped up.

"Hey stop, cease!"

J's ears rang with a joyous sound as the latch slid open and he dropped down into the cockpit, punched the latch closed. He ran over to the pilot seat, his body seeming to hover over the arm rest. His pursuit banged on the latch. Muffled shouts rang out and the sound of a blaster skipping off of metal caught his attention. He didn't know how long the door would hold. He lifted a hand to the controls letting out an audible growl. His hands were still prisoners, the controls required separated hands. He tapped the buttons to fire up the machine. *I'll figure something out.* The engine came to life, the ship saying hello as the screen appeared. He placed both hands on the thruster pressing it full open, the mech moved, its legs stepping forward. The screams above became frantic, filled with genuine panic. The machine stepped more quickly, responding to the thruster now set at full tilt. A leg crushed one of the ships, another nicking Mediators as it rose and fell. His enemy began firing at the ship, the blaster rounds bouncing off like water droplets. J smiled, he felt invincible. The feeling was fleeting. His cough returned and blood dripped down his chin. He pulled the thruster back to 70%. On the display, the enemy encampment shrank as the machine continued its march along the riverbank. He stood up and tapped through a few more menus. The ship spoke, its voice a silky smooth female.

"Voice controls activated. Welcome, J. Please state command."

"Eliminate all incoming hostiles, weapons free."

The ship acknowledged and weapons began firing. Multiple camera angles showing gunsights appeared on screen, J ignored them all, he was on a mission. He searched the cockpit, shifted around, his hands balled up into fists.

"Where is it!"

He stumbled around as the mech continued its jaunt on the beach, he needed to find the med kit. He knew they'd left it somewhere in the mech. *But where?* At one point, he got so frustrated that he kicked the wall. Instantly regretting it, he fell to the floor caressing his foot. Raising his eyes from his foot, he spotted it, lying on the floor behind the ladder. He hobbled over, popped open the kit and wasted no time running the device over his body. The ship rocked as it was hit with a larger weapon, his eyes moved to the screens. Two fighter craft were strafing him, the mech engaged its auto-rifles, littering the sky with dotted trails of light. He finished scanning himself. His external wounds healed, he pulled himself to his feet. He winced as he felt pain radiate through his chest, almost magnified from before. The multitude of wounds had preoccupied his mind, now it screamed at him. His chest was injured like Ariel's, no medical equipment to heal him. A maintenance tool box distracted him and he hopped over to it. The mech shook and his head whipped to the monitor. He watched the attack craft splinter, balls of light flickered down to the ground. He stared a moment reminded of the Fourth of July celebrations in Sector 11. *Sector 11? Is that what is was to him now? No longer home, just a number?* He didn't have a home, but if he wanted one here on Acadia, with Ariel, he'd have to get on it, find help and stop Cyrellia.

The ship sounded off, more ordinance fired against the enemy craft. He touched the tool panel, sliding it out. The craft shook more violently than before, he lost his footing and collapsed onto the steel grating. The screen flashed red and gravity began to bend as the ship tilted, he pushed himself up, working against it. The ship spoke.

"Warning, steep terrain. Recommend new course line, unable to climb."

J scanned the picture, the mech was attempting to climb the mountain, his original course led them toward it and he hadn't corrected.

"Adjust course to Tremessos."

He felt the machine shift its legs, twisting its torso toward the valley's center. The cockpit leveled and he reached for the open panel, pulling himself to it. He peeked down and

instantly perked up as he reached in and presented himself
with a torch. A green flame shot out when he clicked it on.
Transfixed, his mouth parted, his eyes shook back and forth,
slow at first then quicker as if searching for something. He
shut off the torch, pinched his lips together, then hurdled the
back of the chair and pulled the thruster back. The mech came
to a stop. His eyes explored the screen, a large field sprawled
out before him, the moonlight flashed on the grass as the wind
rushed over it. He tapped on the controls, zooming into the
far tree line, and enhanced the picture. Four mechanized vehi-
cles sat motionless in the dark. He took a deep breath, causing
him to cough, then tilted his head back staring at the ceiling.

"What to do?"

He reached into his knowledge banks, first wishing he had
more, then led his mind through possible scenarios. He began
with the facts. One, he was bleeding internally. *Luckily not
as badly as Ariel.* He dwelled on that a moment, reminding
himself that she had to be okay, his mind wouldn't have it any
other way. He moved on. Two, his friends were captured and
he needed to rescue them. He had no clue how to go about
accomplishing that task. And three, the enemy was awaiting
him across the field, their mechs poised and ready to strike.
He knew those ships, their power and capabilities. He'd seen
them once before today.

"Cybermantis."

He let that sink in. The rockets scattering, the innocent
people Cyrellia tested it on. *His craft was strong, but would it
hold up to such firepower?* He pulled the thruster back and the
machine inched backward, crushing shrubs and rocks with its

huge hydraulic legs. He tapped on the display and a comm box appeared in the bottom of the screen, the word "searching" rotated about. He stared at it, willed it to make a connection, the mech still walking backward.

"Transmission negative, all frequencies jammed. Would you like to try again?"

J's eyes fell to the floor. *Would I like to try again? To what end?* He was alone, something deep inside of him told him that. He stared at his feet, the solid surface of the space boots a dull grey glowed back at him from the dim cockpit lights. He placed a hand on his face pulling the other up with it. He rolled his eyes, his cuffed hand hung limp. *Might as well free my hands.* He slipped out of the chair and acquired the torch, clicked it on. It took him a minute to figure out the solution. He melted the bindings, snapping them in half, the cylindrical pieces remained on his wrists as bracelets. *It would have to do*. He slipped the torch into his pocket and it clanged as it hit something hard. He felt around, pulling out the gold like brick. Dropping back down in the pilot seat, the machine still on in reverse, he watched the landscape flow backward. The trees growing outside, the river flowing underneath. He pressed the thruster forward bringing the machine to a standstill. Closing his eyes, he rubbed the bridge of his nose, pressed air out through his nostrils listening to the sounds as it flowed out. He knew what he had to do. He opened his eyes and the Datacle caught his attention. He twisted his wrist, the map still displayed, the dot flashed. He examined it, squinting as he manipulated the controls, chewing his tongue as he did. Without breaking his concentration, he shouted a command to the mech.

"Mech...ship...whatever you are, set a course for Tremessos. Avoid the field up ahead."

This ship really needs a name.

"Rerouting course."

The ship went silent, J's eyes scanned the ceiling as if the voice would appear overhead.

"Alternate route found, confirm selection."

A map flashed on the screen displaying a blue dotted line circumnavigating the threat area.

"Confirm."

"Course set."

The mech began to turn around, tromping along, its giant feet splashed in the water, the sound of hydraulics breaking through the forest's roars of wildlife. J stared out as the ship marched along. He was happy to be safe inside the machine, the animals he encountered were anything but friendly. He found himself thinking of recent events, tried to make sense of it. Cyrellia had offered to trade him, yet Dillon gunned him down like a common criminal. *Was that the plan all along?* His body trembled. All of the questions, the discussions, they were all gone now. He had traveled across the universe, years, decades to find his father, and in the blink of an eye he was gone. Cyrellia's smug face flashed into his head and he clenched his fists, his lips parted over tight teeth. He wanted to punch something. Revenge was swelling up inside of him. His nose twitched as a tear dripped down onto his bottom lip. His mind flooded with ways to kill her, some quick, others slow and more violent. *She didn't deserve a quick death, she deserved pain, more pain than any death would cause her.*

"Tremessos, 2 clicks out."

J twisted his head from side to side, he'd lost track of time. Cyrellia's tower rose above the trees, its metal and glass structure reflecting the moonlight. He wished the circumstances were different. The beautiful tower, now tainted by the evil within, would have to be removed. He tapped controls requesting the ship to scan for hostiles. Amongst the menus, he stumbled across a cloaking setting. He stared at it a moment. He knew some spacecraft had it, imagined it would work the same for a terrestrial vehicle. He engaged it and the mech flickered then its legs disappeared on the screen, only holographic lines representing where they'd been could be seen. The legs crashed down onto the forest below, the trees tall opposite the mountains to his left. He could see the indents and footprints made by the machine, ominous and ghostly. The city came into view as he walked past a row of trees, he flung his hand onto the thruster pulling it to full stop. Off the nose, Mediators stood guard on a large walled platform, the open field between him and them. He backed up the mech, stopping behind the tree line, and zoomed the screen in, hoping they hadn't spotted him. The metal monstrosities stood at the ready, but unaware. Invisibility came in handy. He coughed once again, the blood a reminder that he couldn't just sit out there all night. His hands slid up his face, rubbed his temples.

"What to do?"

He stood up, moved to the metal storage locker and grabbed a blaster, then strapped it to his leg. Took another and

repeated. He eyed the rifles, trying to determine which one
would best suit his needs, before yanking a snub-nose barrel
off the rack. Dillon had called it a MKIV Badger, perfect for
close combat. He checked the load, full cell, then strapped it
onto his back. J took one last look around to see if there was
anything else that could aid him and, finding nothing, climbed
up the ladder and out the hatch. Spinning around he closed
it, ensured it was locked, then almost tumbled off as his heart
jumped into his throat. There was nothing underneath him,
he stared down dozens of feet at the ground below him. Even
though he could feel it, the craft was invisible, the cloaking device manipulating the light to appear nonexistent. He
took a deep breath telling himself it was an illusion, dropped
onto his hands and knees and swept his hands back and forth
in search of the ladder. His hand grabbed air, but he caught
himself, nearly slipping off. *This was a bad idea.* He found the
first post of the round steel ladder, clasped it tightly lowering himself down. He jumped off the last few rungs, his feet
hitting the ground with a thud, and moved toward the city
seeking cover as he went. The shrubs proved handy. Just larger
than him, they concealed his movements. Had it been a grass
field as before, the path would've been much more difficult.
He pressed forward, arrived at the steel and concrete structure
without notice. Running his hand over the sand-like concrete,
it was perfect, nearly unblemished. *TK must be using local
resources.* J slipped his hand off, began searching for a way in.
He followed the fortification for hundreds of yards and began
to question his choice to go on foot. A blast of air from up
ahead ruffled his hair and he continued the few steps between

to investigate where it had come from. Warm exhaust poured out through steel grating, engulfing his body in a myriad of smells. The mix was hard to describe, but was something like stale bread and socks. He patted his leg pocket. *Good, it's still there.* Concentrated green light shone from the torch and he wasted no time making a hole in the panel just large enough to slip through. Once inside, he found himself engulfed in darkness, the moons' light flickered outside the grate, shunning it. He pulled his rifle forward, clicked on the combat torch, that's what Dillon had called it. He grimaced at the name, every inch of his body hoped he lay dead in that field. J attempted to shake off his dark thoughts, pressed forward down what seemed like miles, cross-sections split this way and that, but he kept straight. Surely it would lead him somewhere. His faith was rewarded when he came upon a ladder leading up. He reached the top, clicked off the light and strapped the rifle onto his back. Opening a storm drain, he slid the top off, exposing his head. The moons had begun to dim, clouds were rolling in too, now fully obscuring the third almost as much as its brothers. An empty street gave him the confidence to emerge and he slipped the cover back onto its home, moved into the shadows, the darkness becoming easier to find. He flipped his wrist up, swiped through menus until he came to a map. Settings displayed a scout function and a shallow tone emitted from the Datacle. J quickly covered it, his eyes searching to see if his position was compromised. His initial scan came up with nothing. Tremessos was displayed in detail, something that surprised J. It was as if it'd been downloaded. He searched for the tower, Cyrellia's tower. If he was going to find what he needed, it would be there. He felt like he was about to cough, covered his mouth muffling the sound. Sneaking would prove difficult. Ever vigilant to stay in the shadows, the Datacle led him toward the tower, the streets empty as if a curfew was in place. He glanced at the Datacle once more and a phrase caught his eye, something he didn't notice before. A large square building sat next to the tower.

Detention center.

CHAPTER TWENTY FOUR

The Moons hung over the planet, a stunning sight. He'd always admired the round white light glowing down on Earth. Here there were three. The windows of the tower sparkled from their light and J stared at it, transfixed. Refocusing on the map, his eyes tracked back and forth between the buildings, his mind following suit, then switched to Ariel or Cyrellia. He clenched his fists, his nose crinkled, bottom lip pressed up. He couldn't overcome his desire for Ariel. As strong as his feeling of revenge had become, she was more important. He changed directions heading to the detention center.

Two Mediators stood guard outside the door. He inhaled through his nose, exhaled through his mouth, a technique he did before every inning to relax himself. Baseball seemed so far away, but he needed to be centered, precise. He flipped up his rifle to his target eye and, aiming at the first Mediator, released a shot. The robot's head exploded into pieces, its body collapsing. Barely moving, he let another shot fly and dropped the second before floating toward the objective, rifle up and ready. Another Mediator stepped out just as he reached the building. J blasted him, hopped over the smoldering wreck that once was an android. He slipped into the complex, his hands tight on the rifle, ready to fire. In the main lobby, two men stood behind a desk. J didn't hesitate, he blasted one, turned the weapon on the other.

"Open the cells containing Ariel, Zane, Tara..." he paused a second, hoping the next name would be there as well. "...and V."

The man raised his hands visibly trembling.

"I'm not going to ask again." J's tone solid, unwavering, his eyes pinched, rifle trained on its target. He wouldn't miss.

The man swallowed moving an arm to the controls. J caught motion out of the corner of his eye and swung the rifle around, blasting a Mediator. Another popped out of the other side, the same fate awaited that one. He fixated back on the controller. The man tapped a sequence of commands into the console. J inched forward.

"What cells?"

The man's eyes flicked down reading the screen then focused back on J. "Three, four, six, and nine."

J continued toward him, his pace quickened. "Lead the way."

The man turned, hands up, and led J down a long hall. A head poked out of a cell then popped back in, they continued forward. The head popped out again, this time its body attached. J breathed a sigh of relief and smiled, his heart paced. Ariel grabbed the man, tossed him into the cell and slammed the door shut. She jumped on J, gave him a hug so quick he couldn't' return it, then ran over to find the others. Zane stepped out, a big grin on his face. Tara appeared after him, but Ariel disappeared into a cell as Zane approached.

"You don't look too good, kid."

J felt his wet lips, smashed them together. His fingers pulled away and blood dripped down toward his wrist. Zane was right, he wasn't doing too well, but there was no time to stop. He caught movement behind Zane. Ariel hopped out dragging V behind her. J hadn't realized how tense he'd been, waiting to see if she was alive, if she was okay.

V squinted, her small eyes almost invisible, before she scurried over to him, her face becoming stern. She grabbed his shoulder pulling his face to hers. "When will you and Ariel ever learn? Been hanging with this guy too much." Her arm extended, fingers stiff and pointing at Zane.

He turned his head to the sky, acting as if his ears were clogged. Her head snapped back onto him.

"Chest hurt?"

J bobbed his head. Not only did his chest throb, but his body had been put through the wringer by those six-legged creatures.

V looked to Ariel. "We need to get him to the medical facility."

She raised her arms, walking over, her brows tightened into a v. "How are we supp—"

A blast shook the building, the entrance doors flipped toward them like cardboard boxes in the wind. Ariel's hair swirled as the current of air from the concussion whipped through the hall. They turned as one, staring at the gaping hole where smoke whirled around obscuring everything but the blue glow behind it. The alarm sounded, lights flickered, spinning in a deep red. Shadowed figures appeared, stalking steadily toward them.

J raised his rifle, he was the only one armed. "Go!" He waved his hand behind him.

Ariel pulled up next to him, hands collapsing around the metal and plastic rifle, her blue irises stared into his, soothing him. His grip relaxed and she snatched the weapon from his hand, flipping it onto her shoulder. The barrel pointed at the enemy, she released a burst of fire. "V get him to medical, I'll be right behind you."

J's jaw dropped, still contemplating what happened, her movement fluid, effortless.

V grabbed his wrist, her tiny hand half way around the shackle, she gave a powerful tug. "You heard her, come on!"

She yanked again and he followed, his eyes still focused on Ariel. Mediators marched through the smoke, their bodies glistening in the spinning lights. Ariel let loose and metal pieces ricocheted off the walls and ceiling, shiny body parts bounced and skipped off the ground coming to rest near her feet. Another tug on his arm. His head snapped around, V was staring at him as they ran.

"No time for gawking, we need to find the medical bay."

They continued down the hall, Zane and Tara running with them. His breath quickened, legs tense, the muscles ripped and fatigued, he could feel his body slowing. V tugged at him, but his pace was maxed out. He trudged along, the cough hindering him. They turned the corner skidding to a stop, the exit was blocked. Mediators stepped forward, raising their weapons. One exploded. J stumbled back, his eyes popping wide. Two others dropped. *The blasts had come from outside.* J and the others froze, not understanding what was happening. A man stepped into the complex, rifles slung on his shoulders, one raised ready to strike, his body and features as shadows in the dark night. V had slipped her hand down, now wrapped around his fingers, and squeezed. He felt the tension in her arm, her body rigid. J glanced down then adjusted his eyes to the man. The light flashed, displaying his face.

J's jaw dropped, eyebrows raised. "Dmitry?"

Admiral Titov stepped closer, tossed a rifle to both Tara and Zane.

V clenched her fist, her nose crinkled, eyes burned with hatred. "Traitor!" She attempted to grab the rifle from Zane.

He pulled it away, not knowing her intentions. "What are you doing?"

V looked back at him, her fist shook at Dmitry. "He's a traitor, he can't be trusted. I told you something was off about him." She stomped her foot, crossed her arms.

Zane held his rifle at the ready, searched her face, then turned to Dmitry. "What's this all about? You imprisoned V and turned us over to the enemy, why help us now?"

"There will be time to explain later. Right now we need to get the jammer in place, it's the only way to save everyone."

J stepped forward, V grabbed him as he stumbled, her eyes staring daggers at Dmitry. "Why should we trust you?" Her lips quivered as she continued her unloving gaze toward Dmitry. J coughed.

"Let's just say it was planned." He tossed the final rifle to J, who released V to catch it. Dmitry stepped closer. "Can we go now? It looks like you could use some medical attention. The medical bay's down the street to the left, building 1820." His eyes landed on each of them, counting. "Where's Ariel?"

As if on cue, she rolled into sight, blasts followed deflecting off the wall behind her. She flipped herself to her feet, running at the others. "I think we pissed them off." She ran past them out the exit.

J and the others turned their attention to the hall where a large mechanized suit appeared, its joints whirring as it stepped its feet pounding the ground, causing the floor to shake. It rotated to face them and a chain gun began to spin.

"I think it's time to go."

J grabbed V's wrist yanking her off her feet, his body's flight response kicked in, weakened muscles an afterthought. He ran out through the door followed by Tara and Zane. The sound of bees hit J's ears louder than anything he'd ever heard. Rounds zipped over and around his body, he dropped to the ground, taking V with him. The sound trailed off, he peeked out, the others all prone on the ground as well. Dmitry pulled himself up to a knee. Raising his rifle, he let multiple bursts go.

"I'll distract him, you guys go."

J hesitated searching for Ariel, she was nowhere to be seen. Dmitry's eyes shifted back to him. "Go!"

He got to his feet searching for the building as they scrambled down the road, its wide concrete floor as smooth as glass, the building dozens of floors high, the street still empty. He heard a scream from behind and the sound of bees rang out again. They turned the corner. *The building should be right there.* He pressed his back into the wall leaning his full weight on it, V grabbed his hand.

"No time to rest, you need medical attention and fast."

Zane popped out from the road, Tara with him, his breath heavy as though he'd just finished a marathon.

"Dmitry's gone. The peacekeeper MarkXII will be here

any second. I suggest we move."

He didn't have to say another word, the pounding of the machine's heavy legs rattled the ground. J searched the streets. The next building was the medical bay, the number 1820 etched above the threshold glowed a dim blue. He pointed it out to the others and Zane grabbed him, pulling him over his shoulder. Tara was able to hack the door panel and they ran into the building, she locked it behind them. V found a treatment room, a surgical table in the center.

"Set him there." She pointed at the table, her motions quick, commands precise. She worked feverishly typing procedures into the surgical equipment. A set of tools, needles and pointy metal devices slid out from the wall. She threw a metal syringe to Zane as he turned around. He caught it, examining the metal item. V continued typing as she spoke.

"Inject that into his chest. I don't have time to program the machine, I'll have to do it manually."

J was weak but still aware, the words causing him to sit up. "Manually?"

The building shook, explosions coming from the front entrance. V strode over. Grabbing one of J's arms, she forced the zipper of his shirt down, turned to Tara. "Help Zane hold him down."

J's eyes flicked over to Tara as she ran over and grabbed his other arm. Zane handed the syringe back to V, he wasn't sure what he was doing and hadn't administered it as requested. He grabbed J's other arm.

His wide eyes staring at his bare chest, his mind running through words, all he managed was half of a "Wha—"

V stood next to him adjusting the needle for the strike, its point aimed under his ribcage. "I'm sorry, J. This is going to hurt like the dickens, but I don't have time to put you under."

His eyes became softballs, mouth still frozen. His arms tightened, fingers clenched. Tara and Zane bore down on his arms. V glanced into J's eyes pressing her lips together then jabbed the needle in. J winced in pain, a growl emerged from his lips, his eyes squeezed shut. His arms struggled, his chest burned, the liquid flowing through his inner cavity. His jaw clenched for a moment and he thought his teeth would shatter, then nothing. All of the pain melted away. He languidly looked over at Tara and Zane, their touch gone, his feet gone, he felt nothing. He stared down at his chest where V pulled out the long needle. She then shoved it into his chest cavity between his ribs. J stared at it as if in a dream, almost like he was looking at someone else's body. V had a set of goggles that allowed her to peer into his body as she manipulated the controls, healing his damaged lungs. She worked fast, but the blasts continued, the intensity increased, the floor rattled. V pulled out the tool for the last time, dropped it on the floor slinging the goggles across the room.

"One of you will have to carry him, he'll be worthless for another twenty minutes."

Zane looked at Tara and shrugged. She shook her head and grabbed him, tossing his limp body over her shoulder.

"Where to?" Tara asked.

J's face hung planted in Tara's backside, he tried to say something before remembering an important fact. His mouth was as immobile as his body. He was baggage for the time being, nothing more. Tara scanned the building, the enemy intruder neared, its bionic movements piercing the room.

"This way."

Tara had found another way out. She led them through several rooms and winding hallways before exiting the building on the far end. *Why do architects in the future always design winding hallways?*

V grabbed Zane's hand. "Where's Ariel?"

J's head spun, in the frantic escape, they'd lost her. *Where did she go?* She ran out, but they didn't see her after that. He began to search in his mind for her whereabouts. *Where would she go?* He had ideas, ones he wanted to verbalize. His body, a prison unto itself, wouldn't cooperate. He hung silently, listening to the other three brainstorm. Eventually, Zane convinced the others to proceed toward the tower, he was sure she'd head there. Tara scanned for a location to rest, getting them off the street, give time for J to recoup. She sat him against the wall of the complex, the structure incomplete, void of life real or synthetic.

J's body tingled, the feeling coming back. V paced, Tara stood monitoring the street, while Zane was busy checking his and J's rifles.

"The tower."

The three of them snapped their gaze to J. He continued, his voice shaky, the drugs still wearing off.

"The tower. We need to plant this."

He tossed the gold bar onto the floor, the metal singing as it hit. Zane walked over and picked it up, the grooves catching his attention.

Tara asked to see it, her systems scanning the bar, her eyes dancing around it as if unable to lock on. She handed it back to Zane. "It contains code to pacify the systems and remove power in Tremessos."

He climbed to his feet, catching himself as he stumbled forward. He figured there was a use for it, though he hadn't known exactly what it was. There had to be a reason Arcturus needed it, J had one piece of the puzzle, now he needed the rest.

"Where do we take it?"

Tara looked at J, her head tilted, brows wrinkled. "Why, the tower of course."

J returned the look. "Figures it'd be the tower, but where? How do we get there?"

Her puzzled look continued and she pointed to his wrist. "You have the map there, it will tell you what you need to know."

J's head pushed back, his chin buried in his chest. He lifted his wrist, the shackles were beginning to chafe his skin. The map was still displayed on his Datacle. "This is just the map of the city, it doesn't have details or the location or how to implant that—"

While he was ranting, Tara strolled over, a slight smile lifted one cheek. She raised his wrist, her finger flicked around, depressed the final button. Holding it a moment while her smile grew larger, her eyes rose up staring into J's.

His mouth opened, his eyes locking onto hers. "Was that there the whole time?"

"Yes."

CHAPTER TWENTY FOUR

He slapped his forehead, rubbing it before dragging his fingers down his face.

Zane walked over, his lips pursed. "Whatcha got there?" He grabbed J's wrist, twisting it for his view, chuckled.

V ran over, curious to see for herself. "What are you guys laughing about?"

J showed her the complex, its sensors, cameras, data on every building, room locations of Mediators. And the kicker, a path to avoid them all and the location to implant the device including procedures to do it.

"You've gotta give it to Arcturus, he knew what he was doing." Zane patted J on his shoulder. "I bet he's amassing troops for a final assault."

J slipped out of his grip, his shoulders sunk. He slumped to the wall, threw his back against it and slid to the floor. He pulled his knees up, bent his head down, eyes gazing through the floor. He'd forgotten, wanted to forget, to pretend it didn't happen, his mind recreated the scenario. Dillon blasting his father, his body collapsing in a heap. He rubbed his fingers together, his body felt empty. Zane approached, squatting down in front of him.

"What's up, J?" His voice serious, like a concerned parent, he waited for the response, not pushing anymore.

J's lip quivered, his eyes had begun to tear up still melting through the steel floor below. He looked back at Zane, his face leaning forward still waiting.

"He's dead."

CHAPTER TWENTY FIVE

Tara manipulated the controls for the door, her small fingers working quickly. They only had a few more seconds before the patrol arrived. They'd made their way to the base of Cyrellia's tower. J hadn't said a word to the others since they left the construction site, he merely plodded along, his eyes focused on the ground, mind elsewhere. Tara had downloaded the data from his wrist and was leading the way, the door lock proved difficult. V bounced on her toes, her head rocking back and forth, side to side, searching for the patrol. The door hissed open, Tara waved the others through. It was a service entrance, one rarely used by her account. She led them deeper into the underlying structure, the crown jewel of the great city of Tremessos. After an elevator ride and trek down a long hallway they stood at a huge metal door, its surface rough to the touch. Cold, indented blocks in a checkered pattern etched into it. Tara went to work again, the door coded and secure. J, still distraught, glanced around. His senses trickled back. *Something didn't feel right, this was too easy.* He panned his eyes over Tara as she entered the final character.

The door shook, a loud sounding motor turned, behind it gears pressed together, the tight fitting fingers slipping, the sound of poorly lubricated metal screeching in his ears. Zane was the first in, stepping past the thick walled barricade now out of sight. He kept his rifle high and tight to his shoulder, V tucked herself next to him, huddling unarmed on his hip. Tara ran in, turned down a row of flashing lights. J's body tensed, his skin tingled, ears twitched. The smell of blood was still on his lips and he turned around, backing into the room. He surveyed the hall, empty. Nothing stirred. His eyes were drawn to the walls. Metal circuits ran in precise patterns intertwined like miniature highways, all covered by glass. Some glowed blue, others green. As he stared at them, the cool colors calmed his nerves, yet something in the back of his mind was warning him. His fingers squeezed the rifle, careful to remove his trigger finger. No need to draw any more attention. He stepped onto Zane's foot. Zane twisted around lifting his eyebrows, J raised a hand, signaling that he was sorry.

Tara broke the silence with a whisper. "You have the chip?"

He tightened his brow, one cheek pushing up, wrinkles stretched out from the same eye. *Chip? Maybe she meant the gold brick.* He produced the metallic object and she took it. Zane stepped back, guarding their exit, V stayed with him. Tara slid the ingot into a slot and J realized something, something he hoped the others knew.

"You said this will remove power from the city?"

Tara stopped typing, her fingers resting on the keypad, her face turned to his.

"Yes, what's wrong?"

She read his face, something was wrong. He pressed his chin up, his eyes reading the equipment, the lights flickered and moved about. "If we knock out the power, how do we get to the surface? Don't the elevators work on power?"

Tara became a statue, J could see here circuits pulsating, data flowing through her head working out the issue. "I can set a delay, five minutes will suffice."

J stood back. Five minutes wasn't a lot of time, especially if they encountered any resistance, but he nodded knowing it was the best solution. Tara finished her data entries, stood up. Not a word was exchanged. Zane felt a tap on his shoulder, his gaze still fixed on the exit. After receiving the signal, he moved forward, his senses heightened, footsteps light. V continued pinned to his side, Tara and J in the back. J felt jittery as he had so many times before, times when lives had been on the line, he knew what was at stake. They stepped into the elevator, his eyes glanced at the control panel as Tara pressed the first floor. The doors closed and J stared at the controls, there was something he had to do, something he had to do alone. The elevator came to a stop, his bodyweight lifting as gravity returned to normal, the panels hissed open. Zane and V slipped out, Tara was next. Zane scouted the path, V spun around as if she had a sixth sense, her eyes locked on J. He pressed the panel, the doors shut. V's eyes widened as she lunged toward him, her mouth open. But, she was too late, the panels merged, the soft muffled sound of rubber cushions bouncing together rang into the lift. Pressure hit J's feet, gravity increasing as he shot up. His fingers massaged the plastic handle of the rifle and he examined the cell, full load, a railgun a weapon J had grown to enjoy, yet hate. He stared at it, the light sound of rubber belts and chains as he zipped up toward his fate. The weapon almost killed him, but saved him as well. This new world presented so much violence, so much strife, fear, anger, and death. He sighed. Taking in a deep long breath, he held it in his chest, tightening it before releasing it fully. He stared through the wall thinking of what he must do. Dillon entered his mind, the blast hitting his father. J's muscles tensed and the rifle shook. Cyrellia was going to pay. The elevator beeped before opening to a lobby of sorts, two more elevator doors sat at the other end and windows adorned both walls, stretching the length of the building. He stepped out raising his rifle, his feet shuffling. The view was magnificent, something he could've spent hours enjoying at another time. The mountains scaled up one of the windows, a vast forest grew out the other, the moonlight illuminating both in a soothing blue. He reached the far set of elevators, spun around, his eyes and ears alert. The sensation was back, his skin tingled, his muscles twitched, screaming at him. The elevator arrived and he backed in.

"Floor please?" the glass box asked.

All four walls were glass, not a speck of metal or bars, only the floor and ceiling were made of an opaque plastic. J turned around, gazing at the city below.

"Penthouse."

"Lady Cyrellia's quarters? Authorized users only, please state your name and request."

J continued surveying the world, this new planet, new city, new life. Acadia, Tremessos. "J, for an audience with Cyrellia."

Silence filled the room, his thoughts redressing his plan. His words were carefully chosen, reciting the conversation, what she could say, what she would say. The city began to pull away, its buildings shrinking as he ascended. He rubbed his fingers together, his leg bounced.

He turned as his ride reached the top, the glass now opening up to her lavish apartment. Above all, as a queen in her castle ruling over the subclasses. The door opened. Cyrellia stood with her back to him, her focus toward the mountains, the ever-present glass of wine in her hand. Stepping out, rifle focused on the target, he studied her.

Her wrist rolled around, swirling the glass. "Isn't it magnificent?"

J didn't answer, just stepped forward, his lips white as they clamped together. He continued to walk toward her and the power shut down, the audible hum surrounding the city faded, the room's lights extinguished. *It was fitting moonlight would be her last.*

Cyrellia shifted her weight onto one foot, her hip kicked out. "I may have underestimated you. You and that band of misfits. Very clever suppressing the city's power." She turned, her eyes locked onto J's. "Arcturus was quite the clever man." She stepped toward him taking a sip of wine, a devious grin grew on her face seeing his pain, J's eyes welling up.

He'd caught her subtlety. "Was." *Arcturus was clever.* He readjusted his grip on the rifle, the crosshatched texture imprinting on his skin. "You're going to pay for what you did to him. What you did to everyone!" J shook as he spoke, his lips quivering but his voice solid, his mind focusing on the words. "With your defenses down, your war is over...surrender."

Cyrellia stopped, raising an eyebrow her cheek pinned up. She crossed her arms leaning back. "Checkmate I suppose?"

Her snarky attitude shone through even in defeat. J's nostrils flared, his jaw beginning to burn as he bore down on his teeth. He tensed at the sound, pulled the rifle in closer its stock grinding into his shoulder.

Cyrellia pointed at his weapon. "And what are you going to do with that? Hmm...we both know you won't shoot, you're but a misguided child, a boy. Not a killer. I'm the only family you have left."

Her eyes burned red and bright, a stark contrast to the surrounding blue glow. He placed his cheek on the stock staring through the sight, three green florid arrows pointing to the weapon's impact sight met his eye. He slipped his finger onto the trigger, its metal chill shooting through his hand and down his arm. The great equalizer, a weapon he had learned to use and with great skill. She was right of course, well half right. He was no killer, but he was no boy. His eyes focused, his ears attuned to his heartbeat, his breathing, listening for a foe to appear somewhere, anywhere. Cyrellia was in his sights, a trigger pull away from ending it. Or at least delaying it, he'd still have the council to attend to.

She swirled the wine, her chin dropping, eyes locked onto him, she mocked him. Her glamorous outfit flickering, its gold trim picking up the moonlight and bouncing it around like a house of mirrors. She placed a hand on her hip tilting her head, her eyes matching the stance. "You still have a choice. You are blood...my blood. You have a choice as we all do, as your father did."

She strolled over to the bar still a dozen feet away, planted the glass on the table, its contents spilling over the side from the violent act. J loosened his grip on the rifle, its barrel falling to the floor, he softened his gaze. Cyrellia pressed her chin up, peering down at him, assessing his actions. He flipped the rifle, strapping it to his shoulder, his hands free to manipulate the Datacle on his wrist. He tapped a button.

"You are right about one thing, Cyrellia."

She turned her face, raising an eyebrow.

"I'm no killer, but that doesn't mean you're not going to die."

He pointed out the window, his head tucked down, eyes boring into her through his brows. Cyrellia opened her eyes wide spinning her head toward the window. Ships began to emerge, fighter craft filled the sky like swarms of locusts, troop carriers landed in the city deploying fully armed soldiers ready for combat.

J smiled. This was the end of TK, the end of Cyrellia. "It's finished. Our forces will eliminate all of your drones...your Mediators, supporters. Your evil will no longer reign, you will hold no power here. TK is finished."

J bowed up his chest, his arms flared out to the side, his cheek pulsed as it tensed. Cyrellia stared out at the city where troops continued flooding in, setting up barricades, searching for enemy positions. The fighter craft scoured the sky in support of the ground forces, their engines glowing as they zipped to and fro. J was caught staring himself, watching the elaborate assault. His transmission worked, the Houzeau still capable and in command of space. Cyrellia began to laugh, a few small sounds spaced out almost as a cough. J ignored it, his attention still outside. Her laugh grew larger, deeper, more sinister, her shoulders jumped, eyes blazing down at the soldiers shouting commands, the ships landing. J turned his head, the sound now undeniable, the source of all noise in the room. His ears pulled back, he shivered as if a cold draft passed through his clothes. Cyrellia hunched over, her head almost touching the glass.

"You naive little boy, you think your late father was the only one pulling the strings, the only puppet master? The prophet? ...you are sadly mistaken. You think you're here by chance, by skill, by divine intervention? You are here because I made it so, because I wanted you to be here. I could have eliminated you at any moment, in front of your dear Carol, with Ariel, with your father. I chose to keep you alive, to let you live. You have no purpose but to reign with me, and in time, you will. You will grow to see things as I see them, to feel things how I feel, to govern as I govern. There is no choice, your destiny was laid out for you when I chose your father."

J stepped back, his legs weak, shaking as if a heavy load had been thrust upon his back. His blood pulsed in his ears with every pump of his heart, his eyes hit the ground, his voice stolen. Cyrellia stepped forward standing tall, her eyes destroying J.

"You think you have defeated me? My army? Think again. I pull a string and your forces are crushed, cut off from one another. Look James, look out to your rescue, your saviors, your end."

J whirled to the glass, his eyes growing large, his stomach clenched. Ships rained down ordinance from the sky, mechs danced out of the tree line, their green blast tearing apart spacecraft, evaporating soldiers. Fighters dropped from the sky like acorns out of a tree, balls of flames popped here and there as ships ignited into flame. His eyes darted about, his body visibly shaking. It seemed all was lost. Nothing to lose, he twisted his body rotating the rifle into firing position. Cyrellia watched, her teeth seen out of the side of her mouth from a smirk. J glowered, his jaw almost shattering, his body tight as a statue. He fired. The bolt zipped through Cyrellia's chest bouncing off of the window behind, her chin tucked in as her eyes fell. J's nose tingled from the scent of burnt leather, his shot impacting a sofa chair. J's arms dropped, incredulous. His eyes trained on Cyrellia, mouth parted. Cyrellia's eyes tilted upward, the knowing smile that had once left was back. J's eyes swept over her body. *What happened?* She was unaffected as if a ghost, no damage, no scorch marks, no blood. And, more importantly his goal was taken from him, no death. Cyrellia stepped forward, her hips swaying, gown dragging behind her.

"You are here on my account because I chose it. I see you are confused, perplexed. I'll make this simple for you."

The lights flickered on, power restored to the building. J shook his head taking in the lights, his eyes squinting tighter than before, restricting the intense fluorescence about him. She pointed toward the bar and a screen solidified. Words swept over it streaming down, red, illegible phrases, words and numbers. They changed to something he knew, something familiar to him. Something he wanted, desired, needed... loved.

CHAPTER TWENTY SIX

Ariel's body hung on a wall, her head down, unkempt hair draped over her body. Blood covered her chest and arms, her clothes tattered and torn. J stared in horror, his arms going lax, the rifle slipping out of his hand. His chest rose and fell heavy, uneven. His knees went weak, unable to hold his weight and he dropped to the ground, his glutes resting on his heels, arms like noodles at his side. His gaze never left the image. Cyrellia pressed forward, closer than she'd been before. His head locked, unwavering, he paid no attention. She scrutinized him, her face resting as before.

"You see, I control everything. One ruler to rule all. If you wish to see her alive, you will come to my ship, pledge your allegiance to me. The council is no more, I am the Kontrollery."

J grabbed the rifle, snapped it up toward the threat and let loose a flurry of blasts, the bolts zipping all around. His vision blinded by the flashes, his voice screaming, shoulder vibrating from the kickback. His finger turned numb, the pressure on the trigger nonexistent. The shots ceased, ammunition cell depleted. Cyrellia stood unharmed, laughing.

"I told you, boy. I control all, I know all. I am a God in this world. You will meet me on my ship, the Harbinger. You will come alone or your love will die."

Cyrellia dissolved, her image gone. J's eyes shifted to the ground, his posture slumped and the rifle lay at his knees. Flashes of light reminded him of the devastation, the calamity outside. He was defeated, his body worn. Ariel was captured, his father dead, his friends God knew where. His Datacle vibrated, he ignored it, strengthening his resolve. The vibrations continued. He stood up, unwrapped the Datacle from his wrist and chucked it toward the window. It bounced off, coming to a rest on the floor flashing. He stared out the window, the blasts still flickering like the Fourth of July, ships attempting to evacuate, cut down by enemy fire.

"J."

His first thought was to ignore it, he had more important things on his mind. He couldn't be bothered, nothing could help, no-one could help.

"J, it's Max. We're getting obliterated out here! We need your help."

J's eyes shifted around the room eventually realizing that the sound came from the Datacle. *Max?*

"J, if you copy, respond."

He could hear the urgency in Max's voice and his protective instincts kicked in. He couldn't let them die, not while he still had breath in his lungs. He shot to his feet running over to snatch the device, twisting the screen around to face him. Max's image glowed back at him.

"J, there you are. You okay? It sucks out here, but I have something that might help. Where are the others?"

J glanced around the room as if they were there standing with him. He rested his head on the screen, eyelids drooping. He was alone.

"Just me. I...I don't know where the others are...but—"

"Hey! Snap out of it, it's not over yet. Not sure where you're at or what happened, but you're alive."

J's eyes slipped away from the screen, the tears building, producing a glimmering clear film. His thoughts on his father, the soldiers exploding, evaporating like paper, his mind told him it was over. There was no hope.

Max's voice snapped, his tone direct, yet soothing. "J, look at me."

He turned his head, a droplet rolling down his cheek, his mouth quivered in silence. Max leaned closer to the screen, the explosions behind him now blocked.

"Listen, J. I know things aren't perfect, but we need you. We all need you. Focus on what you can do. Without you, we're lost. I need to know where the mech is."

He squeezed his eyelids shut, drops trickled down his cheek. He gnawed on the inside of his bottom lip. "Yeah... yeah I know where it is."

Max's head rested back, his eyes tracking, maneuvering his fighter around. "Good, where are you?"

J wiped his eyes with his forearm, the shackles still in place. He sniffled, clearing his nose. "The tower."

"Okay, I see it. There's a platform near the top. I'm inbound, be ready. Won't have time for a second pass, these enemy fighters are no joke."

The screen cut out. J dropped his arm surveying the room. His eyes fell on the rifle, the ammunition cell flashed empty. *Boy, that was dumb, letting my anger get away from me.* He'd emptied the entire contents into the room at a hologram, one so real he never would've known, his emotions driving him to a solution which proved false. He bypassed the worthless weapon running to the elevator and slipped in.

275

"Destination?"

J glanced at the ceiling, a habit he seemed to do nearly every time. "Landing pad."

He shot down two floors, the doors opened. Glass covered the exterior walls, only the elevator shafts blocked any view. The sky lit up then went dark, the bursts of color still dancing in the sky. He tried to pretend they were fireworks, not ships, not people. Not lives. He spotted the platform centered on the adjacent wall, flat, open. Two doors led out to it. He stepped near a sensor calling them open, empty. He looked out on the pad, the battle raging on. His eyes scanned the sky, searching for Max. *Did he miss the ship?* He'd said there'd only be one shot. The pad lit up in a burst of fire. J jumped to the side, sliding on his belly and coming to a stop, arms covering his head. He peeked up, saw the attacking craft continuing upward into the sky, spinning and flipping around adjusting for another attack run. Out of the corner of his eye, he saw motion, too close to be a fighter. Looking closer, he was wrong. A craft popped up over the platform skidding to a stop, the small canopy opened.

"You waitin' for an invitation? Our friends are coming back."

Max pointed at the attacking craft now inbound. J leapt to his feet, sprinting toward the ship, a small tandem seat fighter. At least it was a multi-seat, something about sitting on his lap didn't appeal to him. He grabbed the rail, throwing himself over the edge, his butt plopping down with a thud. Max buried the thruster onto the front stop, zipped away. J scrambled to find the restraints as the enemy's shots flew past.

Max closed the canopy.

"Glad to see you, J."

He tucked the nose of the ship and J smacked into the canopy, his chest and face pressed against it. Max maneuvered the craft, bringing back positive gs.

"Sorry about that. Restraints are the green button on the right wall."

J rubbed his head, his right arm punching the button, straps slipped around his chest, crotch and waist then tightened, pulling him into the seat. The craft spun and pulled more gs. In the past, J would've thought he did that on purpose, but now he looked past it, even if it was intentional. He gathered himself, examining the secondary controls, the display screens, switches and buttons.

"You said we needed the mech. What for?" Max's hands flipped switches on the canopy. Something about the ship seemed older, less autonomous. The other crafts he'd flown in had less switches, dials and buttons.

"You see those mechs down there?"

He flipped the craft over, J looked up to gaze down. Four mechs crawled over the ground, their green blasts evaporating anything they touched. He tightened his jaw.

"Cybermantis."

J could see Max nod before he pulled the craft into a turn.

"Your mech has a weapon on it that can knock those puppies out, but I can't find it."

J's head whipped about as Max continued his maneuvers, spinning and flipping the ship, avoiding multiple engagements. He was puzzled. *Why couldn't Max find it?* Then he remembered, grinning.

"I have the cloaking system on, it's over there." J pointed just outside the city to the tree line he'd left it under.

"You're going to have to do better than that, I can't see you back there. Describe it."

J did his best to describe the location, they went back and forth then Max decided to fly the perimeter and J executed a countdown over the location.

"Three, two, one."

Max rocked back on the throttle slamming it into reverse. The ship stopped, the sudden shift jarring J into his restraints. Max piloted the ship over the site and they touched down less than a hundred yards from the mech, still invisible, untouched. Max slipped open the canopy.

"You sure it's here?"

"Yeah, like I said, invisible."

J slipped out, scouted the surroundings. Whether by luck or some unseen force, that side of the city had seen little action, the main battle was on the far side. Only shrapnel from downed fighters smoked on the forest floor near them. Max stepped down, tossing his helmet into the seat.

"It's over there."

J pointed, beginning to jog, the sense of urgency overtaking him. They tromped through the grass, continuing their push toward the invisible mech. Max, who was matching J's pace, turned his head to address him.

"You sure it's here?"

J didn't have time to answer before Max drilled something hard, fell back landing on his butt. J held back the laughter.

Sweet justice. "Yep."

Max rubbed his head as J approached, the grass crushed near him from an unseen object.

He extended his hand, a smile on his face.

Max eyed him, grabbed J's hand, shaking it off. "Guess we're even."

J chuckled, nodding. He began feeling for the ladder, it proved difficult as the leg they'd run into was not the entrance. Luckily, the second leg they found was. After the very eerie feeling of climbing on nothing, J found the hatch on top, his fear of heights relieved as he dropped into the cockpit. He climbed into the pilot seat, booted up the system. Screens flashed, weapons load-out displayed, he tapped commands. His attention shifted to Max who was comfortably seated next to him.

"What's this weapon?"

Max punched in commands and brought up the inventory then flipped through it, resting the selection on something J had seen before. Ariel had translated it.

"Dragon's fire?"

Max brought up the area map. Ships and ground troops littered the ground and sky, he zoomed onto the mantis mechs.

"Better if I show you."

J pressed the thruster forward and the machine came alive, its large legs howling and screeching as it inched forward, its speed increasing with each step. J followed the map, continuing to drive the mech to their target. He glanced over to Max. "So, where have you been?"

Max worked the controls to target ships, adjusting the

power and shield systems.

"After you were ambushed I headed back to Arcturus, he's the one who mentioned the Dragon's fire. He said there'd be a time to use it, that Cyrellia had some super mechs that could obliterate anything they attacked. He sent me to look for you, you're a very hard man to find."

J opened his mouth then closed it. *Man?* He'd thought of himself as a boy, something he'd always been, something ingrained in his head. Cyrellia had made sure of that. Ariel was captured, tortured, and he hadn't been able to do anything about it. Hadn't been able to kill Cyrellia, had fallen for her ruse. He didn't feel like a man.

Max brought up the final systems menu and his eyes drifted to J. "We're going to have to de-cloak and remove shields to use the weapon, it's going to take all the power we have to charge."

J didn't like the sound of that. De-cloaking was one thing, but pulling down the shields left them exposed to enemy fire, naked in the woods. That didn't sound pleasant. He pursed his mouth as he thought, swaying with the mech's movement, the long legs pounding the ground with each step.

The battlefront came into view; men were scattered throughout the trees, in the city, on the streets. Wrecked hulls of friendly and enemy ships alike lined their path toward the threat. J's eyes picked up the first of the four targets and Max readied the weapon via the control screens.

"Target acquired, locking on. Charging weapon. Okay, dropping cloaking and shields. J, stay the course."

He held the controls, their surface slick with sweat, his

grip tight. Max locked the reticule onto the Cybermantis, its rear exposed to them as it walked away. They inched closer, the thruster still at 75% power. They both focused on the "charge" display, now at 55% and increasing. The enemy mech continued its engagement with the ground forces, missiles whipped out of it into the sky, smoke trailing in elegant circles.

"100%. Fire!"

The target was acquired, power charged, but J had the final say. He pulled the trigger. A hum began underneath them, their feet vibrated and a dim yellow glow ignited in the windscreen. The screen washed out and pure white light shined back at them, momentarily blinding them. J squeezed his eyes shut, but it wasn't enough to block out the intensity of the beam, so he covered them with his hand as well. The light dissipated and the dark, moonlit battlefield came into view, spots dancing in his vision. The mech had disappeared without a trace, the trees behind it gone, smoke rose from the forest in the distance, flames flickered. J spotted the second Cybermantis, they no longer had the element of surprise. Max feverishly worked to recharge the weapon, but they were at the mercy of the system.

"Better hurry."

"Nothing more I can do."

J wanted to request that he work faster, find some way to speed up the process, but he knew Max was doing everything he could. After all, they were in the mech together.

The enemy mech crept forward. J adjusted the controls, sliding the machine to the side, he engaged the thruster to 100%, the mech now scampering sideways like a crab in the sand, its weapon fixed on the target. Trails of smoke filled the air.

"We have incoming!" Max shouted.

The display flashed and the mech's voice declared, "Incoming missile, launching counter measures."

A series of explosions rattled off above J, his eyes chasing the sound. On the screen, the missile trails changed directions, more explosions sounded as the enemy's ordinance took the bait, engaging the countermeasures. Eyes focused back on the charge, ninety nine. His fingers rolled on the controls, his forefinger resting on the trigger. The target flashed at one hundred and he let loose the same yellow glow, the hum, the screen flashing then dissolving back to an empty sight, their enemy vaporized as the first.

Max manipulated the map, the radar scanning for the fourth enemy mech. Sounds of rocks bouncing off of metal tin cans hit J's ears, his head swiveled about. A fighter craft bolted over them. The sound was alien to him now, something he might have heard on Earth, weapons with metal rounds not the laser blasts he'd become so accustomed to. Finding the final target, his voice hurried, his throat tense, Max yelled at J.

"Powering up for the final shot. You're going to have to take it, I'll distract them."

J could see the stress on his body, movements rigid, fighting through fear. J's head snapped around not understanding the situation. His thoughts had been solely focused on their objective, the mantis mech, he'd failed to see something obvious, something right in front of him. Max unstrapped, throwing the seat restraints, the buckles clacking on the plastic chair back. He rolled out and by J whose eyes followed intently. Max opened the weapons locker and extracted a massive hand-held anti-craft weapon known as a Paladin.

He nodded to J. "Good luck, Godspeed."

Before J could speak he was gone, the hatch closing behind him. He stared at the ladder a moment, the machine still plodding toward its foe, the legs creating thunderous noise on the concrete of the city. The rattling occurred again, this time longer, closer, heavier. Realization struck. *He was the tin can*. He swung his head back around, catching his mistake. The weapons store flashed zero, Max had emptied all of their weaponry defending the mech. In a last ditch effort, he was the defense. The machine walked in the open as a mouse in a field, the owls in the moonlight eyeing their prey. Smoke trailed across the screen toward the heavens, a blip on the radar disappearing. He focused back on the target, thinking of the past would do him no good now. The last mantis was two blocks away, his machine now in the streets, two prize bulls on a collision course from which only one would survive.

J adjusted the sights, his weapons expert now gone. He prayed Max would make it, but that was all he could do. He had to focus. His field of view shrank, fingers danced, tapping on the controls, the thruster at half forward crawling through the street. More steel plinking echoed in his ears, the smell of burnt metal, rubber and other debris filled his nostrils, it was a mixture he would never forget. He checked the map once again, less than a block, one building between the two, did the mantis have him targeted as well? There was no time to dwell on that and frankly it didn't matter. The charge hit 100%, his machine still marching, its legs adjusting on each step keeping the cockpit level. His eyes focused on the reticule ensuring it remained locked, the system interpreting the enemy's location through buildings and terrain. A metal leg came into sight, stepping into the road, the mass of it sheltered by a building. It froze, a metal statue. J continued his march, expecting at any moment to spot the rest, but his hopes were short-lived, the mantis never moved. He racked the throttle back to a dead stop, the machine's legs following orders, one hanging in the air mid stroke. J's seat shook, his ears rang from the sound of ripping and shredding metal, the floor next to him gapped open, hydraulic lines spewing their contents onto the steel grating. His head snapped back, moonlight shined in through three large tire-sized holes. The mech screamed the obvious at him. "Hull breach, hull breach, hull breach!"

J threw the thruster full forward, silencing the warning. There was no time for strategy, he was only going to get one shot at this. He verified the settings, the sights still acquiring his target. His seat bounced reminding him of that cobblestone road back in Sector 11 in his truck. He drew in a deep breath, his mind flashing back to the days on the farm, the movies, school, his friends. The mantis stepped out, but J was ready. His finger depressed the trigger, time slowed, he could hear his heartbeat one thump at a time as if each took a second to occur. The yellow glow grew under the belly, the power flashed 100%, smoke trailed out of the mantis like a white spider web blanketing the sky. His ears picked up the warning, a horn beeped, and the machine screamed.

"Incoming, incoming, incoming! Eject, eject, eject!"

CHAPTER TWENTY SEVEN

J depressed the button and a series of audible clicks rang out under and behind his body. The moon glowed on his face, its light nearly as bright as the sun. His butt pressed into the seat, head snapped down, staring at his feet, the g forces not willing to allow him any other view. His strained gaze watched the mech depart beneath him, the yellow glow pulsing out from underneath the silhouette of the ship was the only detail remaining. J closed his eyes, blinded. His ears finally adjusted to the outside world, explosions popped like firecrackers, wind whistled, ships and the now distant mech hummed. Crisp air nipped at his face, its smell tainted by the carnage, the death, a fragrance he would not soon forget. Darkness returned and he began to freefall. His eyes opened, his stomach in his chest, a sensation he loathed. A fighter craft zipped by him, another trailed, nearly clipping his weightless prison. His hands gripped the chair rails and his teeth clenched, his eyes stayed locked shut. He tensed his whole body, conforming to the chair. His mind locked as well and he concentrated on his breath. He felt a kick in the pants and his eyes sprang open like a startled toddler, the chair fired thrusters, slowing his impact. J struck the ground before tipping over on his side, the uneven ground not suitable for a landing. His head lolled side-ways, and he found himself staring at plants unlike anything on Earth. His restraints unlatched and his limp body rolled out, a blast hit above him lighting up the sky, reminding him of where he was. He gained a knee, tall enough to look out over the plants he had become intimately familiar with. He was in a field close to the city, maybe a block or so. He brought the Datacle up to his face and pulled up the map.

"God's smiling down on me."

He stood up, the tree line to his left, and his body screamed at him. Grimacing, he doubled over. The pain from the ejection, pressure from the impact, flowed through his nerves. J rubbed his neck and groaned as he rolled it around. He pressed his hand to his jaw then wiped his eyes. *That sucked, let's not do that again.* He straightened up, scanning the horizon. He had to save Ariel and Max's ship would be the best bet. His mind had been caught up with Max, the whole situation occurred so quick it'd drawn his attention away from it. Now his thoughts were only on Ariel, her tattered body, in the hands of Cyrellia. He ignored the pain, running toward Max's fighter. Ducking into the tree line, the massive trees provided cover, but also slowed his progress as he wove around them. The sounds of war reverberated in the distance, reminding him of the gravity of his situation. He slipped around the final tree and his eyes lit up, the ship was still there. He turned his eyes to the heavens. "Thank you."

His energy returned, his legs stronger, arms loose. He slapped a hand on the canopy, sliding it open, and dropped into the pilot seat, then reality hit. Countless switches and buttons littered the dash. His mouth hung open making an audible sound as he exhaled, the only saving grace was that everything was labeled. He pulled his hair back with both hands, stretching his forehead tight then stopped, dug his fingers into his scalp. His eyes canvassed the interior. *There had to be a start button, right?* One button caught his attention, a little red rocker switch labeled "energizer." He reached over. *Here's hoping.* The ship came to life, the screens flickered on, switches glowed. His fingers searched, something had to make sense. He stared at the screen, resting his hands on the controls. His thumb slipped off the top of the stick and a small arrow zipped across the screen. J sat up realizing he found something. He manipulated his thumb on the control, the arrow following his movements, and found an onscreen manual. After a few minutes of reading, he threw his head back. For a brief second he thought walking to space would be quicker than learning the ship's controls. The ground lit up next to him, dirt spewed into the cockpit as the hum of an engine zipped by. J began reading as fast as he could, hitting switches left and right, some correct, others wrong. The cockpit shut, another blast hit, the ship rocking. Buzzers sounded, flashing damage onscreen. He managed to start the craft then pressed the thruster forward, the gear dragged across the ground creating a long divot. He pulled back, raising the nose, the craft accelerated forward into the sky. Not as smooth as Max, but he was getting somewhere. The ship was hit again and more warnings buzzed, lights flashed. Randomly, he flipped switches, many labeled things he'd never heard of but thought might be useful. Two rockets departed unarmed and J groaned as he maneuvered the ship away from the attacking craft. He pointed it straight into the sky, one of the moons off his nose. The thruster was buried, but the craft began to slow, warnings flickered and digital flags dropped on the screen. One read, "Engage Accelerant". J scanned the switches, frantically searching for the correct one. The ship rattled as it was hit again. He spotted the switch, his finger couldn't reach it fast enough, and flicked it. His body was pinned back into the seat, the only indication of increased speed. Within a matter of seconds, he was in space, the velvet black blanket of stars crystal clear, the three moons stood in stark contrast, their pitted white blue surfaces hanging in orbit, the sun's rays gleamed into the cockpit. He reduced the thruster, realizing he had no clue where he was going. The Harbinger. *How would he find it? Where would he find it?* He reduced the thruster further to full stop, scanned the screens and his Datacle, neither had anything of use. He peered out the glass. In the distance was a large ship, flashes of light surrounded it. He swung his head around, another ship peeked out from behind a moon. Its appearance resembled a sheathed sword, the forward area smooth while the back end was jagged. It wasn't a ship he'd seen before. A light flashed on the cockpit dash, he pressed it.

"This is the Harbinger, identify yourself. You have one minute to comply."

Well, I've found it. Now what do I do? J filled his lungs then exhaled, his cheeks expanding as the air rushed out. He knew it was where he needed to be, yet he didn't want to answer the call. He stared back at the looming ship. *Maybe I'll wake up.* That thought had come to him more than once since he found himself on the other side of the wall, but this time he wished for it more than ever. He slouched in his seat, his arms dropped over his knees and he leaned forward, placing his head on the dash. He placed his hand on the thruster, depressing the comm switch.

"This is J, I've come to see Cyrellia. She's expecting me."

Silence filled the air. His head still rested on the dash, his eyes closed. *Maybe they'd leave him alone, maybe this would all go away.*

"Turn off your thrusters, we will dock you."

J raised his head. Twisting his neck, he winced. The Harbinger closed in, the massive ship engulfing the cockpit, blotting out the moons' glow. The sun began to fade as the ship swallowed him up like a whale. Exposed wires, tubing, and incomplete panels left open greeted him as his craft was pulled into the interior. He found himself in a large hangar and his ship descended by some unknown force, his entourage waiting. The craft touched down. Mediators surrounded him. Soldiers stood behind them in formation wearing green and gold uniforms, perfectly fitting, conforming to each other as clones. They stepped apart as J opened the cockpit and two individuals approached down the lane now created by the soldiers. One a man, the other an E-Rat. J bit his lip, he thought he'd left those in Atlantis. He crawled out, his body throbbing, but he straightened up and fought through the pain. He kept his head high as they approached, the man was young, in his twenties, his hair parted down the center of his feminine face. He stopped at J's feet.

"You are J?"

He nodded, his face wrinkled and misshapen.

"You are in need of medical treatment."

The E-Rat grabbed him, stuck a needle in his neck, then the world spun and J collapsed.

His eyes opened, lights beamed down on him. He felt

groggy, but the clean smell of circulated air permeated his nose. He sat up on a surgical table in a white room with no markings or items other than the table he sat on. He massaged the back of his head, the pain was gone, his memory fuzzy. He was there to see Cyrellia, that much was certain. All of a sudden, his memories flooded back. He slipped off the table and ran to the door. Finding it locked, he pounded on it, trying to rouse his captors. He took a step back as the door hissed open. The man he'd seen earlier stood in front of him holding a uniform on a hanger.

"Your clothes, sir. I will retrieve you when you are dressed."

J glanced down, he was in his underwear...again...his mind so focused on Ariel he hadn't realized it. He snatched the clothes, covering himself. The man's face was expressionless as he stepped back and the door closed. J tossed the outfit onto the table, examined it. Green with gold trim pants with multiple pockets, the top as well, the collar tight and form fitting like a turtleneck. Gold rope adorned one shoulder, the other bearing a symbol he hadn't seen before, a square with two vertical stripes in the center. He unzipped the top, set it aside. Then, staring at the pants, he placed his hands on the table.

"What am I doing?"

Those were Cyrellia's clothes, her army's uniform. *What did she want? Did she really expect him to join her?* His mind felt funny, his memories of her obscured, incomplete. He didn't know how to feel about her, the past week's events like a distant memory, a movie seen long ago where very few details remain. He tried to remember how he got there. *Where was he exactly?* So many missing pieces. He grabbed the pants and pulled them on. A tight, form-fitting shirt followed then the overcoat finished the ensemble. He found auto-boots near the door and slipped them on, their sensors conforming to his feet. He stood up and the door hissed open causing him to jump back, his fists clenched. The young man stood with his hands behind his back.

"Cyrellia will see you now, please follow me."

The man promptly executed an about face and started down the hall. J stepped out, surveying every inch of the ship. His mind worked through solutions to his predicament, thoughts only broken up by Ariel. *Was she okay?* They continued into a large open room, a clear tube divided the three-story room in half. They approached the tube and J watched mesmerized as a door rotated up, exposing a pod with eight seats, four facing another four. The young man stopped, extending a hand toward the transport device. J looked up. Great paneled windows ran the length of the room parallel to the tube extending for what looked like three-thousand yards, its end barely visible. He stepped in, the young man taking a seat across from him. The door closed and the pod accelerated, the room zipped by plants and trees, it felt almost as an indoor park would at night the large window displaying the beautiful stars. They sat in silence, J paying more attention to the room than the man, the pod slowed to a stop and the door opened. The young man stepped out first, turning to wait for J.

"It's not much further."

J shook his head. The young man stepped away, leading them to an elevator at the side of the room, it too was created

completely of glass. They rode it up, facing toward the room.
J could see the layout much better now, and what he saw left
him awestruck. He had to tell himself he was inside a ship and
not a large arboretum. The young man stepped out of the
elevator, J hesitated, still mesmerized by the sight.

"This way, please."

The young man led him down a long, wide hall, its ceiling
arched. Banners hung above sizeable entryways, their contents
hidden behind closed doors. At the far end, they stopped in
front of two lavish metal doors wrapped in textured designs
of vines and flowers, the symbol he'd seen earlier adorned the
center. His guide stepped closer and the massive doors rotated
inward. Skylights covered the roof and moonlight shined in,
adding its ethereal blue to the glowing green walls. Golden
arches crisscrossed the ceiling and walls where soldiers stood
facing the center, their outfits just like his. At the end, Cyrellia sat upon an emerald cushion in a plain, gold, high-backed
chair, her head back, eyes studying him. He sauntered forward,
keeping pace with the young man. They stopped a few feet
away from the long white steps lined with green lighting that
led up toward the chair. J straightened up, his hands clasped
behind his back. His guide placed a foot on the first step.
Knee bent, he bowed his head low to the ground.

"Your majesty, J has arrived. His treatment is complete."

Cyrellia stood up, her arm sweeping down to her side. The
dress sleeve flowed, creating a curtain of greens and golds as
it sparkled in the moonlight. She stepped forward, her gown
dragging behind her, her movements slow and proper, head
held high. She continued down the stairs, the gown now

covering the entire staircase. At the bottom, she waved the young man away.

"Welcome, I am pleased that you decided to join me. Please, will you walk with me?"

J felt a sense of calm at her words and nodded, words failing him. She stepped away and he strolled beside her toward the doors.

"Green suits you. Like Acadia, our empire, it invokes strength, power, resilience."

They continued walking, J's head turning this way and that, discovering more beautiful objects to sip in. His eyes appraised Cyrellia. He struggled with his thoughts, his senses overwhelmed, but his body felt relaxed, the pain had left him for the first time in ages. He remembered that he needed to speak with her about something.

"You have something for me, a deal?"

Cyrellia interlocked her fingers near her stomach, her hands disappearing inside her sleeves. "Yes, you are my son and rightful heir to the new kingdom I have created. The council has elected me to be in charge of the people's well being." She paused, considering him, her expression wistful. "I want you to reign with me. Create a perfect world, a world of beauty and bliss, one where all is right and orderly."

J's gaze fell on the ground, it all sounded good, incredible even. His ill feelings seemed in the past, a distant memory, still there but faded. *A perfect world?* Something out of a fairytale. His eyes danced around her ship. It was like being in a castle, clean, unblemished, something he'd rarely seen before entering this new world. But, something nagged at him. Not something, someone. A name, a person. He continued walking, listening to Cyrellia, her ambitions for the betterment of society, the beautiful new world she painted, as he searched for the person. He remembered and his mind calmed.

"Where's Ariel?"

Cyrellia smiled, her head twisting at him. "She's here, safe, and will be meeting us for dinner. I understand you like dumplings, so I've had my chef make some just the way you like."

J's mind drifted to food. Dumplings sounded amazing. His stomach growled, triggered by the thought of the savory goodness, his mouth watered in anticipation. They continued their walk down the hall, turning into one of the large doors. Its contents revealed an enormous table stretching fifty feet in the middle of the room, plates laid out at each chair, set with elegance, multiple forks, knives, spoons. J didn't understand what they were all for. Cyrellia guided them to the far end and a young man strolled up, pulling a chair from under the table, waving his hand for J to sit. Cyrellia sat at the head of the table, J to the side, his mind preoccupied with the place settings.

Cyrellia angled her head toward the door. "There she is."

J swung his head around, seeking her face. A gentle smile pressed his cheeks up, his breath deepened. He knew the girl, his girl. His heart throbbed and he felt flushed, his skin reddening. He slid out of the chair, his stance proper, hands behind him once more.

"Ariel."

She walked toward him, her face beaming with delight. She wore a gold dress with green trim, a miniaturized version of Cyrellia's. He waited, his knees weak, watching her icy blue eyes flicker in the light. She met him, his body held back, the intensity burning inside, wanting to squeeze her tight. He hugged her, his touch gentle, her return the same. He leaned back then dropped his head in for a kiss. Their lips met, endorphins surged through his body, he was in heaven. A voice rang through his ears, he pulled back, focused on Cyrellia.

"There will be plenty of time for that later. Our food has arrived, we don't want it to get cold."

Ariel scrunched her nose, showing her teeth. She slipped out of his grasp, rotating to the seat across from him. Young men began bringing in dishes of food and J's thoughts drifted to the wondrous smells, the saliva building on his gums. A plate of dumplings was placed in front of him, a glass of red wine, and an assortment of side dishes grew on the table. J stabbed a dumpling, sliding it into his mouth. His eyes closing on impact, his brain sending signals of the pure pleasure from the food. Cyrellia and Ariel began eating as well, silence filled the room while the wait staff tapered off. In no time, he was finished. He wiped his mouth with a napkin, the square emblem representing Cyrellia's reign embroidered upon it. He turned to Cyrellia, his mind attempting to connect the past to the present. He was there for a reason, he had a mission, something deep in his head stirred, unable to be released. Cyrellia swirled her wine glass, her senses telling her that J was watching.

"I know you have questions, and they will be answered soon. I would like to discuss my proposal."

She nosed the wine, taking a sip. J's eyes fell on Ariel, her beautiful face glowed back at him, curls sweeping onto her face and shoulders, the dress snug against her elegant curves. His body tingled, he couldn't help but smile back at her, he was at a loss for words, yet something seemed different. He contemplated the question, looking back at Cyrellia.

"Your proposal?"

She set down the glass and stood up, her chair pushed back automatically. She extended a hand her, long fingers dancing, inviting. He pressed back his chair, took her hand, then she strolled over and did the same to Ariel. With J on one hand and Ariel on the other, she sauntered out into the adjacent room. A huge window, three stories tall and wide, met their vision. She centered them on it. Outside, Acadia sat. Its green and blue glow vibrant, reflecting the system's sun. Behind it, two of the three moons sat motionless, the blue-white spheres reminding him of something he'd seen long ago, another lifetime ago.

"Acadia, our world. Only primitive life inhabited it before we arrived, poised and ready to be made anew. Better than our old planet, with a governing class ensuring the survival of the species, of expansion into new worlds, endless opportunities to better mankind."

The window changed and the city of Tremessos filled the screen, a bird's eye view of the pristine buildings, untouched by weather, decay, violence.

"This is our capital, it will be your capital. But, I need your help. I need a prince, a general, a warrior."

She stepped back, brought her hands together, J's and

Ariel's intertwining, replacing hers. J's eyes locking with Ariel's, she smiled back, her chest rising and falling. J looked back at the city, unblemished, but it didn't feel right. It was like a dream, his love next to him, the perfect city before him, a long lost mother guiding him.

Cyrellia's voice again broke the silence, full of joy, something which sounded foreign to him. "The prince and his bride."

J swung his head around, his jaw open. Ariel turned as well. "Bride?"

Cyrellia grinned, her chin held out. "Yes, you two will be wed. Unless you would prefer not to? Every prince needs a princess."

J's eyes searched for answers, his mind overwhelmed. His muscles tensed and he tightened his grip.

Ariel leaned in. "J, are you okay?"

He looked up into her beautiful blue eyes, earnest with concern for him, wanting to tell her yes. More than anything he wanted to tell her yes, but he couldn't, he wasn't okay. His temples pulsed, the bridge of his nose felt like needles had been shoved through his skull. He stumbled forward, Cyrellia waved aid over and a young man grabbed J, helping him straighten up.

"Take Ariel and J to their quarters, they need rest. It's been a lot to take in."

The young man bowed, escorted them out into the hall. J rubbed his temple, the pain subsiding but not gone. Their escort left them in a room, its window looking out toward Acadia. A king-sized bed on one wall, the other held a painting of Tremessos' tower, Cyrellia's tower.

Ariel helped him to the bed. "Probably just need some rest. I had headaches earlier as well, the rest did me good, cleared my head. Made me realize things I didn't before."

J pressed his head to the pillow his gaze locked onto the ceiling, crisscrossed metal beams creating a diamond pattern reflected down on him. He stared through it, closing his eyes, felt Ariel's head rest upon his chest. The smell of sunflowers and ozone entered his nostrils and his mind drifted off.

CHAPTER TWENTY EIGHT

A man stood next to him smoking a cigarette, he blew out the smoke in a straight line billowing into a cloud.

"I don't think this system is humane. You sure you want to proceed with this?"

Through a window, J watched a man sitting in a chair, staring at a wall. His cell a small five-by-five box, the door hidden behind panels. He examined the individual, his eyes bloodshot, veins wrapped around the whites almost eliminating the absence of color. He reached up, rubbing his temples, his eyes not moving, lower lip hanging over his chin.

His eyes popped open, his arms twitched and he heard a low grumble, his chest heavy. He peered down over his chin, the lovely smell of flowers engulfed his senses. Ariel was asleep. He wiggled his way loose to the sound of a few more grumbles as her head touched the mattress. He faced the window, his bare feet on the floor, and rubbed his eyes, then pressed his hands through his hair. A dull pain still permeated his skull, but not nearly the pain he'd felt earlier. It took him a moment to remember where he was. On Cyrellia's ship, asked to govern with her, his mind still fuzzy as to how he arrived here. He sat on the edge of the bed rubbing his head, staring at Acadia. Memories of his childhood, learning the Earth was flat, saving Earth. Cyrellia helping him against Arcturus, the evil mastermind bent on power and pain. Pieces seemed missing, gaps.

He heard a groan behind him. Ariel rolled over instinctively grabbing a pillow, the sun's beams ricocheted into the room, the ship continuing its orbit around the planet. Finding her still asleep, he turned his gaze from his love down to his uniform. He found a mirror on the wall and left the bed. Posing, standing tall and proper, he held his eyes heavy as if making a great decision.

"That suits you...General."

Caught, his shoulders inched up, his head slowly turned toward the bed. Ariel peeked out from under the pillow, her head cocooned, the hint of a smile as he heard her snicker.

"What do you think?"

Ariel pulled the pillow to her stomach and sat up with one arm extended, her body weight supported. She yawned as she talked. "About what?"

J studied his hands, softer than he remembered, less callused. Not the hands of a farmer. He rubbed a thumb on his palm. "Ruling the planet...marriage..."

Marriage to Ariel, it seemed like a dream. His heart yearned for her, his mind filled with thoughts of their adventures, her warmth, smarts, beauty. He smiled.

"Not sure if I could spend a lifetime with you."

The pillow hit his head as he stood there, stunned. He lunged at the bed, tackling Ariel. She let him pin her and they stared into each other's eyes in silence. J pressed his lips toward her. A buzzer rang and they both looked at the door. It buzzed again. J dropped his forehead to hers, squeezed his eyes closed, and gathered himself. He pecked her lips, rolling out of bed to the door. He pressed the panel and the door hissed open. His escort from earlier stood, proper, hands together.

"I'm sorry to disturb you, sire, but Cyrellia requires you on the bridge."

J glanced back at Ariel. She flopped back onto the bed and waved him forward.

He stepped out into the hall. "What is it?"

"An uprising. Members of the old order have attempted to take over the capital."

He ran to the bridge, his steps light, full of energy. Ariel in the back of his mind, mixed memories filled his head, his experience taking over as a craft on autopilot. The enemy must be defeated, they stood between peace and the common good. His escort opened the final door and he stepped onto the bridge. Cyrellia stood at the center, her arms stretched out, resting on two of the consoles.

"My boy, I am glad you've arrived. Your expertise is needed."

He stepped up next to her, his heart thumping, his body tingling. He rolled his fingers in his hands. "What's the situation?"

Cyrellia brought up a view of the city, soldiers stalked through the streets, buildings on fire, ships passed by dropping ordinance.

"The faction has attacked. I ask you to do what I have always asked. Eliminate the threat, bring peace back to Acadia. We can't have them taking over as they did on Earth, ripping the planet apart, enslaving it."

J heard the door open behind him and a familiar voice. "Orders?"

Ariel stood in full battle garb, rifle slung on her back, her green uniform a bit more fitted than his. She slipped a blaster in her leg holster.

Cyrellia turned her head, her eyes looking back. "You will lead the ground insertion, take squad 5. J, you have the sky, squad 11 is standing by, awaiting your command. We must act fast before the tower is taken."

Ariel skipped out, full running as she hit the door. J took one last look at Cyrellia and she nodded.

"God be with you."

J snapped to it, sprinting out. Body moving autonomously, he hit the elevator, the lift descending into the frame of the ship. A soldier tossed him a helmet and began running with him. Something told him what to do, new memories, old memories, the enemy, the faction.

"Squadron's ready, your ship's fueled and your customized load-out is onboard."

The man running with him was heavyset, in his twenties. His cheeks puffed out as he talked, his voice deep and thick. J spotted his ship. A Tetriack, his Tetriack. He grabbed the rail and, sliding in, placed his hand on the canopy.

"Welcome, J. Weapons systems loaded, fuel cells charged, battlespace uplink initiated."

The ship's female voice amped him up. In some ways, he felt like he was in another body, someone else's mind, something he'd felt before. He glanced up, seeing the large hangar bay doors opening to space beyond, the stars peeked in anticipating the show. The ship lifted up and the squadron checked in.

"Spacewolf 2, comm check."

J clicked through menus while he responded. "Loud and clear, rest of the squadron proceed."

Numbers filled the air, each one responding in turn. He echoed the last statement, his squadron was checked in. The last requirement before takeoff was checking the ground team. On cue he heard her.

"Squad 5 locked and loaded, ready for insertion."

Ariel's voice sounded sexy even on the slightly garbled comm. He wondered why, with all of the technology this crazy new world seemed to possess, the radios were still hit or miss. He pressed the thruster forward and the ship bolted out of the now open hangar. Icons of his squadron in tight formation showed on the map, his eyes scanned around each ship inches from another in a V pattern. Ariel's landing ships followed tightly behind, fifteen of them, fully loaded with combat troops. He rocketed toward the surface, fighter craft appeared out of the atmosphere, ordnance greeting them. J took evasive maneuvers, commanding his squadron to do the same. It came natural to him. The fighters split formation, engaging the enemy craft, and Ariel's ships pushed past untouched. J eyed their descent, watching them glow bright as their hulls barreled through the unforgiving atmosphere. J engaged a ship, shot it down, the explosion in greens and blues, different from most. He adjusted the controls, racing toward Acadia, and called for the squadron to follow. They punched through the atmosphere, fighters instantly engaged them. J spun the Tetriack, avoiding the incoming missiles. His eyes picked up the ground force ships landing, ramps opening, letting out fifty troops each. The ground firefight erupted as he zipped overhead, peering down.

"Need cover fire. Sending coordinates."

Ariel was pinned down. J would take this one himself. He went through his weapons load, selecting anti-personnel ordinance. He adjusted the run, slipping down in between the buildings. The target approached, he pickled the load, and bombs dropped from the open bomb bay breaking into smaller bomblets as they fell, each one acquiring a target. The missiles zipped around in a frenzy and the street filled with smoke and explosions. J pulled up out of the city, the map which once flashed enemy activity went silent. His squad took out the few stragglers in the air, soon reporting all enemy activity had ceased. J circled, searching for Ariel, her squadron sweeping the streets. He pulled the thruster back to cruise, drawing in a deep breath. His mind wandered, body loosened, until the dull pain in his forehead returned.

"Sweep complete, ready for extraction."

The transport craft executed approaches near the ground forces and he zoomed in with his sensors watching Ariel boarding one. This could be his life, a team eliminating the insurgents, protecting the peace, all with a beautiful bride on his arm, a teammate, an equal. He rubbed his temples.

Cyrellia's face emerged via transmission. "I understand that the target is neutralized. Return to base for a debrief. You did well." The picture faded.

He pulled up, spinning the craft around, aiming toward the heavens, and commanded the squadron to follow. Ariel's ship was still there, he could see it on the map. He approached the Harbinger, its doors still open from their departure. It'd been a quick mission and a complete success from what he could tell. He planted the Tetriack onto the pad, opened the canopy. Ground teams swarmed in rolling ordinance racks filled with the anti-personnel missiles he'd just expelled. A man dragged a fuel hose, snapping it onto an open panel beneath the ship. He slipped his helmet off and watched the landing craft enter, the hulls flashed as they went through the shield, something new to him. He waited as the ships' ramp opened, soldiers flooded out, some men, some women. Ariel was the last to appear. She strutted down the ramp after talking to one of the crewmembers, crinkled her nose with a smile as she saw him.

"Thanks for the CAS, made my life easier."

She extended a hand and J took it, her soft fingers melting into his. His breathing slowed as they walked toward the bridge. His mind reverted to the battle, he'd surprised himself. He didn't quite understand why actions seemed so natural, so practiced, so right. The dull pain seeped into his thoughts. *Maybe something had messed with his head affecting his memories.* He stared at the ground as they walked.

Ariel squeezed his hand. "You okay?"

He nodded. "Yeah, just working through a few things."

Ariel chuckled. "You're always working things through. You don't always have to be the best, you know."

He smiled, acted as if nothing was wrong. She did have a point. *What was he doing?* They walked through the ship, a few officers greeted them as they passed. They entered the briefing room, its twenty levels of seating like a horseshoe stadium facing a massive stage with a gigantic screen behind it. A man with glasses tapped on the bottom corner bringing up a map of the city. His large build made J think he belonged in a gym, not working with technology. J took a seat in the front row and Ariel kissed him on the cheek before walking up the stage steps to grab a tablet from the bodybuilder. Soldiers from the attack filtered in, the room stood up at attention as Cyrellia appeared. She took a seat on the top level in the back, waving everyone to sit. Ariel waited for the room to settle, then began.

"Intel placed the insurgents here and here." She tapped on the tablet, the main screen mirroring her movements. She worked through the operations, detailing the enemy locations, their weapons, and their actions. She finished the debrief then dismissed the room. Cyrellia waved the room at ease, but remained seated in the back. J climbed the stairs with Ariel to see if there was anything else she needed.

She eyed Ariel, her bottom eyelids shuttered as she raised them. "Any sightings of their leader, Zane?"

Ariel set the tablet in a rack off to the side and it slipped in, disappearing from sight. She turned back to Cyrellia, shaking her head. "No, he wasn't part of the attack. We eliminated all forces as requested, no survivors."

Cyrellia stood up to leave. "Very well, be ready for another attack. I feel another will be coming...soon."

She walked out, her gown flowing beneath her. J stared at the green silk cloth, the gold reflecting the ship's lighting onto the chairs and ceiling. *Zane, why did that name sound so familiar?* He felt his hand squeezed.

"I need a shower."

J smiled, he needed one as well. His body was on overdrive during the combat, and as well as his uniform breathed, teenage boys still sweat profusely. They headed to their room. J sat on the bed and slipped his boots off, wiggled his toes, the freedom was glorious. As comfortable as the boots were, nothing beat free toes. Ariel had hopped in the shower first, his old-fashioned beliefs still part of his being. The water hissed in the background, steam trickled out like a magical fog. He plopped his chin on his hands, elbows now supported by his knees, his back arched. He became lost in his thoughts and worry filled his mind. Memories danced half-finished through his head and he attempted to make sense of them. The pain was still present, so he rubbed his temples, closing his eyes. The ship zipping through the sky, the firefight on the ground, the farm, Earth, Exodus, the gaps remained open. He looked at the stars as if they could speak, to give him his answers.

"All yours."

He turned. Ariel stood in the bathroom doorway holding a towel over her body, another wrapped around her hair. J gawked, his mouth open. She winked, dropping the towel from her head.

"Better get in there or I'll drop this one as well."

J blushed, his eyes snapping to the floor. He scurried to the shower, shutting the door behind him. He laid his hands on the sink, leaned toward the mirror on the wall. His face appeared ragged, which was odd, he didn't know why he'd need sleep. He worked his clothes off, turned on the shower, and slipped in letting the water run over his body. He lowered his head, the shower spraying over his neck, both hands on the wall supporting his weight. The water felt warm, relaxing, necessary. His body was recuperating and healing, his mind a wreck. He tried to lose himself in his thoughts, but nothing came. It was as though his memories were stolen, a feeling which shook him to the core. He shivered under the hot water. Closing his eyes, he concentrated on Ariel, Cyrellia, the ship, his past. He squinted, concentrating. A man popped into his head, a man he'd seen before but now couldn't place.

He stared into J's eyes. "You'll do well, it's in your blood. Trust your instincts."

His head began to throb and he grabbed his temples, collapsing to the ground. The pain shot through his body, the water pooled around him as he lay on the shower floor. He tried to think of something else, anything else, but the pain was overwhelming.

CHAPTER TWENTY NINE

A hand swept over his head, caressing his hair. He breathed out a groan, his head still throbbing but much less than before. His forehead drawing down, a tear slipped out of his eye and ran down his cheek.

"Hey. It's alright, I'm here. You okay?"

He opened his eyes. Ariel sat on the bed, his head in her lap. Her eyes glowed, the moonlight intensifying their icy blue details. He breathed in, taking in her scent, the pain continued to subside but never completely vanished. He sat up and noticed that Ariel wore a tight, military style t-shirt, and he was shirtless. He caught himself staring and turned to the wall.

He placed a forefinger and thumb on the bridge of his nose, pinching and pulling his cheeks up. "Yeah, just a slight headache, you?"

She tilted her head, one eyebrow raised. "You sure? You've been a little...off, since we got here."

He placed his fist on his forehead twisting his head toward her. It was time to come clean, or at least tell her some of it. *What did she know? How was she feeling?* He dropped his hand, sliding a knee toward her.

"What do you remember?"

Ariel snickered, looked out at the stars then back toward him. "That's a pretty vague question. I think you're going to have to be more specific."

J looked down at the bedding, its white silk fabric soft to the touch, pleasant under his hand. "Before you arrived on the Harbinger. What do you remember? How did you get here?"

Ariel shook her head, pressing her chin into her throat, her eyes flicking back and forth. "We were on a mission, I got cut off from my squad. They sent an extraction team to pick me up."

"And you were the only survivor?"

Ariel paused a moment, her gears turning, attempting to recall. She responded, her answer slow. "Yes."

J sat back on both arms, his gaze shifting to the ceiling. He needed to find some common ground, something they both would be able to recall, something simple, something they'd never forget. He sat up, leaning forward he slid his hand onto hers.

"How did we meet?"

Ariel closed her eyes, laughing under her breath. She scrutinized his face. "Isn't that a question I'm supposed to ask you?"

He snapped his head back not ready for the deflection. He searched his memories, it was fuzzy, but there. He recalled it, his test turned back on himself. "You shoved me into the Tetriack on Atlantis."

She smiled, leaning toward him, lifting her hand interlocking his. "There was a little more to it than that, but I'll call it a pass?"

He frowned. *A pass?* That was good and all, but he needed more, more details. "What else happened that day?"

Her eyes rolled to the ceiling, searching for an answer. She popped her lips as she opened her mouth. "Let me see...we were chased by Mediators, ended up meeting up with Dillon... umm."

J stopped her. "Dillon?"

The name was familiar, a picture of him almost came into focus, but the pain increased. He rubbed his temples, his mind shifted to Ariel, the pains decreased. The door buzzed again and Ariel popped up. J stared at her backside as she strutted to the door. The metal plate opened, revealing the same young man from before.

"Cyrellia has a mission for the two of you. Please come with me to the bridge."

J stood up, searching for his top. He snatched it off a hanger at the same time Ariel found hers.

On the bridge, they found Cyrellia standing, arms crossed. A ship displayed on the screen, a short bald man holding a tablet was discussing something with her. She shooed the man away as she noticed them enter.

"We have had some luck. It seems that during a previous engagement we damaged the fusion cells of the Houzeau. Reconnaissance reports that their leader, Zane, is on board and the ship is running out of fuel. If we secure the ship, it will provide the crippling blow needed to stop the insurgents and bring back peace to the planet."

J's leg shook. *Zane. Was that how he knew the name? The leader of the insurgents? It felt like something more.* His eyes paced back and forth.

Cyrellia approached him. "When you return, we'll discuss my proposition. Once void of insurgents, peace will settle in. We will rule Acadia with a singular focus, bringing heath and prosperity to the masses."

J bit his lip, his inner voice in conflict, hesitant to accept.

The pain rushed through his head, he pushed through, ignoring it. He looked away and Ariel grabbed his arm.

"Are you sure you're okay? Maybe we should go see Dr. Medelev, he could fix you up."

J grimaced, nudging her off. He was tired of her asking if he was okay, of course he was okay. He spun around, walked out, his head throbbing. "I told you, I'm fine."

Ariel lifted her hand up as he twisted out of her grasp, her lips puckered. Cyrellia touched her shoulder. "Give him some space, his mind needs to figure things out, to get right, to heal."

J heard the comment as he left the room. He squeezed his hands. He didn't need to figure it out, he already figured it out, or so he told himself. Ariel met him in the hangar where soldiers were donning spacesuits. J grabbed a set slipping one on.

Ariel stormed up next to him. "What was that all about, huh? I'm worried about you. If you need help, tell me. If not, fine, but don't get snippy with me."

J ignored her, zipping the suit up he slipped his helmet on, snapped it into place, his thoughts on the mission, on Zane. The insurgents must be removed, they were parasites. He was beginning to remember, no feel it. His head continued to pound like a bass drum beating in his ear, his memories vibrating as such. He strutted onto the troop transport, climbing into a seat. A soldier walked by, dropped a pulse rifle in his hands. He checked it, the cell full, the sights prepped for close combat, the stock collapsed. He slapped the side ensuring the cell was locked in, it didn't budge. His cheek bulged as

he looked up. Ariel sat across from him, her stern face glaring
at him. His eyes moved to the ramp, the solid, ribbed metal
panel closing locking them in. The huddled mass of troops sat
awaiting the drop, some of them chatting, others silent, one
joked while another discussed the mission details. J was one
of the quiet ones, he knew the mission, what was at stake. The
ship rumbled into the air, the forward thrust evident as the
entire cargo compartment rocked sideways, the two rows of
combat seats on the outskirts facing the middle. J's body drifted back to neutral, his eyes locked on the flooring in front of
him. He glanced up multiple times only to be met with Ariel's
serious face. The soldier next to him checked his charges, ship
cutters he heard some of men call them, designed for breaching
the hull of a ship. He glanced up toward the cockpit, the ship
stable he couldn't even tell they were in motion. A commander
walked down checking each of their restraints, after adjusting
his neighbors, she stopped at J. She leaned toward his helmet
her hand sliding onto his waist.

"Better double-check you. Don't want anything happening
to the nice body of yours." She winked at him giving the seat-
belt a tug. He groaned from the pressure, attempting to keep
a straight face. The commander chuckled, passing to the next.
Ariel growled at him, her eyebrows drawn, he looked away. He
could tell what she was feeling, her eyes told the whole story.
At that moment, he didn't care, couldn't care about anything
but the hammers pounding on his skull. The ship announced
five minutes out, the commander ran by them toward the
cockpit, she tripped, stumbling, glanced back then continued
on her way. J looked toward Ariel, her face sporting a devi-

ous grin, his face remained constant, no acknowledgement. The ship shouted again, one minute. J checked the rifle, the ship rattled, the sound of shields deflecting ordinance flooded through the cabin.

"Deploy, deploy, deploy," the ship announced.

The first set of seats dropped out of sight, shooting them downward. They continued in sequence, his head swung to Ariel, she disappeared as his body was thrown into the shoulder straps. Blasts skipped by, fighter craft zipped underneath, his chair rotated and the Houzeau flexed into view. The thrusters bolted him toward the enemy ship and he watched the others, their chairs departing, their bodies reaching the hull. The breachers worked on placing the ship cutters, two were gunned down by a strafing fighter, another blew up with the explosives. J's chair ejected him and he adjusted the controls, his vector straight for the hole in the ship. He readied his rifle, troops began pouring into the hull, he popped in, blasts trailing above, nearly ending him. The zero g was still found in the ship, red lights flashed, his eyes danced around looking for the next exit. He felt his shoulder skip backward, his body spun. He manipulated the controls, stopping the spin, and found the culprit. An enemy soldier fired another shot, the second sparkled in his glass visor. He fired back, his aim off, then thrust himself to the door, his aim still on his target. Two more shots bolted out of his weapon, the second finally making the connection. The soldier spun out of the hole into space. J turned his attention to the door, the control panel flashed red. With no airlock, the ship had gone into lockdown. A hand reached by him.

CHAPTER TWENTY NINE

"Care for some help, jerk!"

Ariel began tapping on the control pad, attempting to break the code. A round skipped off her helmet her head snapped to the side. J pushed himself around, vanquishing the enemy target. He looked back at Ariel, she was still working her magic like nothing had happened, her fingers dancing on the keyboard, air was squealing out of a hole in her helmet. The door hissed open and J pushed her toward it. Falling behind her, one of their soldiers approached, J glanced at Ariel, punching the controls, the door slammed shut. The panel flashed yellow then green, their bodies plummeted to the ground in a heap, gravity had returned. J scrambled to her, removing her helmet. Her eyes were closed. He sat her up against the wall.

"Ariel."

There was no response. He twisted his helmet off, tossing it aside. He worked on his gloves, pulling them off, which was much harder than he remembered. He slipped his hand onto her neck, his heart racing, his breath vibrating. "I'm sorry, I'm so sorry, Ariel." His fingers found a pulse as he leaned toward her.

Ariel peeked back under her eyelids. "You'd better be."

He grabbed her, squeezed her tight, then pulled himself back. He opened his mouth to speak, but was cut off. The door at the end of the hall squealed open, both their heads snapped toward it. Two soldiers stood with rifles aimed at them. They both raised their arms as the soldiers crept toward them, weapons at the ready.

"On your feet."

J obliged, but Ariel hesitated, then she groaned. J peeked back down and she gave a sly wink.

"She needs medical attention."

The first soldier grabbed J's hand, pulling it down behind his back, the other kept the rifle aimed at Ariel. J was cuffed and pushed toward the open door, the second moved to Ariel, kneeling down.

"Your turn sweetheart."

He grabbed her wrist, but she slipped out of it. Grabbing him, she flipped him down to the ground, pinning his head to the floor. J kneed the other one in the stomach, his attention drawn to the commotion. The soldier jabbed back. J's eyes glowed as a blast hit him square in the chest, dropping him to the ground. He heard a crack, realized that Ariel knocked out the other. She searched the body for the cuff key and found it, pulling the square card from his belt, she tapped it on his cuffs. They released instantly.

"We'd better move, more of them for sure."

She swiped through her Datacle and took off through the open door. J stood a moment scrunching his face, the throbbing which had subsided was now back. Ariel yelled for him and he shook off the pain running after her. He tried to focus on his actions, the intensity of the situation seemed to alleviate the pain even if it was temporary. Ariel led them through the ship, encountering enemies as they progressed. She managed to find some less-traveled areas making the journey quicker. They soon found themselves on an elevator below the bridge.

Ariel planted her hand on the panel, looked toward J. "You ready?"

He checked the pulse rifle, his cell low, but sufficient. He nodded. The lift shot up, the doors spread open wide, and they stepped out. The bridge was a frenzy of activity. Soldiers ran about, working on different consoles, commands were shouted, the large screen flashed. The battlespace displayed the moons glowing behind flashes of light as weapons fired, hitting ships between the stars. J inched forward, his rifle pressed to his ear, the scope adjacent to his eye though not in use. Ariel mirrored him, their target in sight. Locked on, they wouldn't miss.

The man turned and his jaw shifted to the side, eyebrows raised in surprise. "J?"

CHAPTER THIRTY

The man took a step toward them, raised his hands showing his palms. "Ariel, J...what's going on? Where've you been?"

J didn't answer, just continued to study the room. He guessed there were twenty or so total, his weapon could handle that. Ariel pressed forward a step, her weapon fixed on the man's head.

"Let's keep this simple, she just wants you, Zane. We'll leave the others, no need for more bloodshed."

At her voice, the bridge stopped as if a time bomb went off, freezing everything inside. Eyes and heads snapped toward the two intruders, the flashes of the battle outside became the only motion as ships continued their dog-fighting. Zane laughed, his large frame bouncing as he did. Ariel stepped forward, her face unwavering.

His laugh died off and he pointed a finger at each of them. "You're serious?"

J inched forward, panned the rifle around the room. A smaller girl stepped up next to Zane and he locked his weapon onto her. "Don't move!"

Zane pinched his eyebrows together as he put himself between them and the girl. "Now you're threatening V? What is this? What's going on?"

"You heard her, you're coming with us. Cyrellia only wants you. There's been enough death, I don't want to see any more."

He stiffened his jaw as flash of pain wrapped around his head like a turban. He blinked his eyes, refocusing.

"J, you need medical attention. I'll take you to the med

bay and we can fix you up."

J shook his head. "No! I've had enough of that for today. Now, for the last time, come with us peacefully or we will force you to."

Zane shook his head, chuckled. "Okay, let's see where this is going. Commander, you have the bridge."

A younger soldier responded in the affirmative. Zane walked forward, V followed.

"Just you." Ariel stared daggers at Zane.

He stopped, glanced down softly at the petite teenager. "If you're taking me, she comes, too."

J growled, his fingers tightening on the rifle. "Very well."

Ariel twisted around, scanning the elevator. J kept his focus on the prisoners as he backed into the lift, Zane and V followed their arms held high. They attempted to relax, but were met with resistance. Ariel cuffed them as the lift descended.

Zane turned to J. "So, what's the plan? You infiltrate the Harbinger?"

J rocked his jaw, biting his cheek. He pressed the barrel into Zane's side. "Another word and I'll blast you. I'd rather deal with Cyrellia than your mouth."

Zane buttoned up, his lips pursed, eyes assessing. They exited the elevator and headed toward the hangar, the only words exchanged came from a couple soldiers questioning the cuffs. Zane played it off as a ruse. They boarded a small cargo ship in a hangar littered with damaged fighters, men scrambling to fix broken panels, reload weapons. The sounds of war could be heard outside, the doors opening enough for craft to enter and exit. After locking the prisoners into the cabin, Ariel climbed into the pilot seat, J hopped in next to her. She fired up the engines, the hum not doing much for J, distracted by the overwhelming headache. She opened the hangar doors and blasted through into the firefight. Ariel maneuvered to avoid as many engagements as she could, J worked the weapons systems for defense only, they didn't want to attract unnecessary attention. One fighter was persistent, trailing them until they reached target range of the Harbinger. The screen flashed an incoming message and J flicked a switch displaying it on screen.

Cyrellia gazed intently back at them. "Did you capture the objective?"

"Yes, but he wouldn't come without another. A girl named, V."

Cyrellia leaned back. "Bring them to my quarters."

The transmission screen dissolved leaving the Harbinger engulfing the whole screen. The hangar bay door crept open, Ariel engaged auto-land and leaned back. J fixated on one of the ships on the deck, a Tetriack.

"You think we're doing the right thing?"

Ariel turned her head, pulling up half her mouth. "Yeah... why?"

J continued his stare, his pain dwindled. The dull stage was becoming tolerable, but his body tingled as if something was wrong. He hesitated, he didn't want to seem weak, or crazy. *How would memory loss be dealt with?*

"I just...I just feel weird about the whole situation, the insurgents, Zane, Cyrellia. I'm trying to piece it all together, but I'm having trouble remembering things."

He awaited the blowback. *What would she think? How would she react?* The ship touched down, the hydraulics squeaked, bouncing like overused shocks. He felt a hand on his.

"After this is over, we'll get you fixed up. We'll adjust those memories good as new."

J stood up, he hoped she was right, the gaps in his brain were troubling. He knew it had something to do with the pain, but what? They escorted the prisoners through the ship by way of the tunnel, zipping past the trees, the indoor greenhouse before arriving at Cyrellia's quarters at the very front of the ship. The doors opened, J hesitated a moment thinking he would float away. The ceiling and walls transparent, invisible, the starry sky greeted them, two moons in the distance the third peeking over Acadia. Cyrellia stood admiring the view.

"It never gets old. This view is so peaceful, serene."

She turned. Gazing at the prisoners, her eyes hardened and she stepped toward them. Zane and V were pushed forward still in cuffs, Ariel and J relaxed their weapons. J slipped his hands behind his back, resting his arms, fingers locked together. Ariel's hip kicked out, the same arm resting the rifle on her shoulder, both of them watching the interrogation.

Cyrellia approached, her stance aggressive, arms straight at her sides, hands hidden beneath the sleeves of her dress. "Where is he?"

Zane looked down, his chin tucked in. "Who?"

Cyrellia's left eye twitched, her nostrils flared. "You know who, Arcturus. He needs to end this foolishness."

He glanced over at J. "He's dead."

Cyrellia rocked back laughing then twisted around, her dress flowing as she walked away past leather sofas and chairs toward the point of the ship. "Don't lie to me. The grand puppet master is not dead, I know his plans, the way he thinks... more intimately than you realize. It is pointless to continue this conflict, resources are at stake, people, the most precious of all."

She turned her head to the side, her voice steady, even, unwavering. "Now, where is he?"

Zane glanced over at J with a slight shake of his head, his brows raised. J glared back, his eyes passing through him, his mind contemplating the words. Zane turned his attention back to Cyrellia realizing J was no help. He kept his head held high, V tucked next to him. His mouth began to open, the words building on his lips, but a picture appeared floating in space, a woman standing on the bridge.

"Lady Cyrellia, there is an urgent incoming transmission."

Cyrellia scowled as she continued toward the picture. "Patch it through."

Her face lighted, head tilted back, her back arching, shoulders up straight and tall. "Arcturus, back from the dead."

J squinted, the man looked unfamiliar, yet something told him he was. The others all remained silent watching the exchange.

"I understand you have something of value to me."

Cyrellia glanced back at J, eyes heavy, before she pushed them back to the image. "Yes, if you want him, we must meet, in person. My prisoner for a truce."

"The terms?"

Cyrellia's hands locked together, she leaned back, her face firm, her nose twitched once. "I return him, you leave. Back to Earth. I will not pursue you."

Arcturus leaned back, his face stoic. "Very well. I'm on Acadia, I'll send the coordinates. Bring only yourself and my property."

The picture dissolved, Cyrellia visibly relaxed, inhaled heavily through her nose. J continued to stare at the spot where the man, Arcturus, had been. The others seemed to be in the same state of confusion or contemplation, the room silent.

Cyrellia regained her composure, started a brisk walk toward the exit, her face intent. She passed J, her dress flowing behind her. "Ready the ship, we go to Acadia.

J snatched Zane's shackles, pushing him along.

"This part of the plan?"

J didn't listen, his head throbbed as he pushed the prisoners into the elevator.

Zane leaned down, trying to connect with J. "Hey, kid, you've been acting awfully strange. What's going on?"

"Please let me take a look at you, you don't seem yourself," V added.

J leaned back against the far wall. *What did they mean he wasn't himself?* Other than the pounding in his head, he was fine. He knew the world, knew his place, his position.

"Ariel, tell him. Stop this acting, both of you. I don't understand what's going on here, but it's time to stop."

Ariel rifled a fist at his stomach, his back smacked the wall.

He bent over, wheezing, sucking in air. His nostrils flared like a bull's, expelling a mixture of snot and air, he threw himself into Ariel pinning her to the back wall. J flew in with a right hook to Zane's face, it snapped to the side, saliva spewing out. Zane pushed himself off the wall, Ariel groaned from the pressure of being crushed. He lunged for J, he'd dropped his weapon, his stance that of a boxer's, he side-stepped Zane's juggernaut charge. Zane hit the wall, convulsing, his body crumpling into a ball. J's eyes snapped to Ariel, her arm extended holding a shock pistol, her butt and free hand planted on the floor. She swept it over to V, huddling in the corner, her lip quivering, her eyes wet locked onto Zane.

"Don't you move missy."

"Why are you doing this?! He's your friend! The closest thing you have to family!"

Ariel stood up, still aiming the weapon at V. "I don't know what you're talking about, but you're going to get the same treatment if you don't shut your mouth. Now."

J trained his attention to the mass of a man crumpled in a ball lying motionless on the floor. "Great. Hope you have a way to carry this beast." J ran his hand through his hair pausing at the top.

Ariel holstered the pistol. "Thought you could carry him, you are the muscle. I'm the brains."

He couldn't help but chuckle, her face holding back a smile. V continued her disbelief, motionless.

The lift's doors parted and Ariel waved an open hand to the room beyond. "See, things have a way of working out."

Two soldiers stood there awaiting the elevator and Ariel

ordered them to drag Zane to the drop ship. The rest of the
walk was quiet, J and Ariel both in their own thoughts. He
continued running V's questions through his head. *He didn't
seem himself. Zane's our friend? Our family?* He felt that he
knew more about them, deep down, he knew that was true,
but it was like looking through smoky glass, he couldn't seem
to grasp the details. Cyrellia was already onboard, the pilots
firing up the engines. J and Ariel stepped aboard the ship,
much fancier than any drop ship he'd been on. The interior posh, all leather seats, the steel floor grating covered in
textured plastic. Cyrellia buckled herself in, her outfit more
modest, less dress to maneuver.

"You two run into trouble?" She eyed Zane who was
tossed into a chair and buckled, his arms fixed in his lap, still
unconscious.

"Nothing we couldn't handle."

J nodded with Ariel after she spoke, the doors closed and
the ship lifted off, departing into space. J searched his memories still, attempting to associate Zane and V. *They seemed
like they were close, were they?* He tilted his head up. Ariel
had fallen asleep, something he wished he could've done,
maybe sleep would fix his head. He was too awake, sifting
through things, though his body felt worn down, his mind
hazy. Cyrellia remained silent, her eyes closed as if meditat-
ing, her head bobbing gently with the rocking of the ship. The
pilots announced the approach. He vaguely recalled Acadia,
his mission to quell the uprising, the first and only in recent
memory. But he felt strange, he had to have been there before.
That couldn't have been the first time. The ship rattled as

it touched down, the metal chirping as the gear compressed under the craft's weight. The engines spooled down, the hum dwindling. Cyrellia unbuckled and stood up, placed a hand on Ariel's shoulder nudging her awake then turned to J.

"You stay here. I'll call you when you're needed."

J started to argue, not clear why she asked that of him, but she raised a finger and he slouched back into his seat like a scolded child. His eyes danced around as the ship's door opened. Ariel disappeared first followed by Cyrellia and one of the pilots. The moonlight bounced onto V's face, glowing from her position nearest to the door. Her eyes focused on Zane, her eyebrows lifted. She moved them to J, slow he could see them clicking along their path as they did.

"You don't remember us, do you? You don't remember anything? Your memories are gone."

J unbuckled, something drew him to her. He approached and knelt down. *Did he open up to her, to a stranger, an enemy?* The dull pain still threatened his thoughts. He looked her in her almond eyes and she gazed back, her concern as a friend seeing another in pain, someone she loved in anguish, strife, evident on her face.

"Who are you?"

V swallowed, sucked her lips together glancing down a moment. "A friend. Someone did something to you, something unlawful, horrible. You must trust Zane and I. We're your friends, Ariel's friends. Not that woman out there. She is pure evil, do not fall for her tricks, her schemes, her lavish plans to bring you into the fold, to make you like her."

J sat back onto the adjacent seat. *Was she a friend? Was she right? Was Cyrellia really pure evil?* He questioned everything, the haze making it difficult to concentrate, on anything. He rubbed his temple.

"How do I know you're the one telling the truth and not filling my head with lies?"

V took a long breath, leaned in as close as she could still strapped to the seat. "Think of how you came to be on Cyrellia's ship. Do you remember? Do you remember anything before that? Your adventures with Ariel? Growing up on Earth?"

He stared at the ground focusing on remembering. Remembering Ariel, how he came to be on the Harbinger. He felt there was something there, his body tingled, his memories just out of reach, teasing him along. His arm buzzed and he lifted up the Datacle, a message flashed across the screen.

"Ready for you. Come alone."

J stood up, eyed V. "I'm needed outside."

CHAPTER THIRTY ONE

J stepped out onto the plateau, his hand under V's. The flat ground stretched for a thousand feet in all directions, mossy plants covered the stone and the adjacent mountains peeked back at him from various positions all around. Steep cliffs surrounded their meeting location, Cyrellia stood facing four silhouettes, their visages obscured from the distance and the night, the moon behind them. The enemy ship broke up a quarter of the moon, an outline he thought he recognized from somewhere. Ariel stood next to Cyrellia, her rifle locked onto her shoulder, a deadly appendage ready to strike. He pressed forward, moving V along, her small short steps impeding his progress. But he didn't force her, something about what she'd said still swirled in his mind. *Friend.* If she was a friend she didn't deserve to be treated poorly. He stepped up beside Cyrellia and the men came into focus. Arcturus, the man on the screen, among them. He stepped forward, the other three remaining back.

"Send him over. I will leave as agreed." He outstretched a hand toward J, his head shifted down.

J gaped at Cyrellia, his eyes quizzical. He swallowed the painful lump in his throat, before asking, "Me? He wanted me? Why?"

Cyrellia's eyes bored into his, imploring him to listen, then turned her head toward Arcturus.

"Listen to me very carefully, J. Arcturus has been manipulating you. He plans to ruin everything I have built, everything I have done for mankind. He has modified your thoughts, your dreams, your motives, your beliefs. I need you to see through all of the horrors that he put into your head. I mean to end this once and for all, but I need you to do it."

She extended her arms and produced a locket, the symbol of a moon etched on a steel plate smaller than his palm. He bent his head so she could hang it around his neck, then she placed a hand over it on his chest and spoke low so only he could hear. "This locket is a key to my vault on Earth. Once he knows it, he will want nothing else. Give it to him. When the time is right, you'll know what to do."

She ran her hand up his neck and placed two fingers on his chin, lifting it toward her. "Your memories will return and this will all make sense. You just need time. Time that I wish I could give you, but we've run out. You are my son, my blood, my legacy. My love."

She released her hand, pressed on his back, steering him toward Arcturus, her eyes locked onto him. J turned toward the man, his arm still extended. He sucked in air, wrapping his top lip over the bottom before glancing back at Ariel, still poised to strike. She smiled as if she knew the outcome, but he was unsure, his steps cautious. He marched on, straightening with every step, his rifle slung over his shoulder, metal clad boots pounding the ground. He reached Arcturus.

"Don't worry about Ariel, we'll free her. Cyrellia knows how to manipulate the mind, but there's nothing that we cannot undo. Come, we have some planning to attend to."

He slipped an arm around J's shoulder, ushering him toward the craft. They loaded and J took one last look at Ariel as he did. *Was he doing the right thing? Was Cyrellia telling the truth? Was time really the answer to his memory loss and the headaches?* He sat down staring at the wall, Arcturus across from him. The compartment was void of windows, so J's only indication that the ship was climbing away was his stomach dropping, backside pressing into his seat. Arcturus crossed his leg flipping his robe on top, his gaze fell on the locket.

"What's this?"

J pinched his chin back, grasping it with his hand. "Cyrellia's locket. She said there were things I might need on Earth."

Arcturus tightened his eyes, head rocking, chin lifting to his upper lip. "May I see it?"

J removed the locket. *Once he knows it, he will want nothing else.* He held it, spinning in front of his eyes. J focused past it. He could see the want, the lust for it in Arcturus' eyes. J dropped it into Arcturus open palm and he handled the locket examining the features.

"I'll hold onto this, we will need to run some analysis on it to ensure it is what she says it is. She is crafty and shrewd, I'm sure she filled your head with stories."

J's head continued its monotonous ache, but he didn't want to reveal it, didn't know who to trust. He leaned back, his full weight in the chair, his shoulders sank. Arcturus clasped the locket around his own neck. J closed his eyes, maybe he could get some sleep now. Then thought better of it, snapping to.

"So, who are you?"

Arcturus studied him, deadpan. He didn't speak for a moment, only stared. J tilted his head leaning forward.

"Cyrellia." Arcturus' head swung to the front of the craft.

"Machiavellian."

J pressed his head back against the headrest, chin to his chest, eyebrows questioning.

Arcturus swung his head back, his eyes bouncing off the floor. "What did she tell you?"

J wasn't ready for the questioning, his lips parted, but no sound was released. He bit his bottom lip wandering his mind through the foggy vault that it was.

"The leader of the insurgents, or one of them. Zane is another—" J continued to ramble on about the little facts that he could piece together.

Arcturus cut him off. "Insurgent! Well, I suppose you could call us that. Resistance, rebellion, there are many names. We are attempting to remove Cyrellia from power, her thirst for it is unquenchable. After Earth, she needed more. And now here we are on Acadia, a new world which will end as the last if we don't stop her."

J's heart raced. The tone, the words, Arcturus has awoken something inside of him. He felt the need to save the planet. He rubbed his finger on the rifle. *Cyrellia, evil, manipulative?* He still wasn't sure. He'd only just met this man, Arcturus. *Or had he?* He felt the ship slowing. Arcturus looked to the front of the ship, unbuckled and walked to the cockpit. J sat drowning in his thoughts, overwhelmed by the data he'd just received. Had he been a computer, he would've processed it already, determined a course of action. But, he was not, he was human, a boy.

Arcturus returned, buckled in. "We are landing at an outpost on the far side of Acadia. You should get food and rest before we proceed."

"Proceed? Where? With what?"

"All in due time."

The ship touched down and the ramp opened, sunlight hit his face. He raised a hand, squinting, the brightness overpowering his senses. The smell of pine trees wafted into the craft and the engines quieted, leaving room for the sound of whistling. He stepped out into the light, the wind whipped around him. He felt something touch his hand and glanced down at a pair of blue tinted sunglasses resting in his palm. He slipped them over his eyes, the world came into view. He was in a meadow surrounded by trees, a cave entrance was carved into the mountainside. Dozens of people worked on an assortment of craft both in and outside. His glasses adjusted to the light, the irritation gone from his eyes. Icons popped up on items as he scanned the area identifying what he was looking at. Some he recognized "human", "stone", but others were new. What he thought was a pine tree was labeled "Tamatukus". Arcturus walked away toward the cavern, once again leaving him with questions. At that moment, J noticed that the person who handed him the glasses still stood next to him, he jumped back.

"Well, hello to you too, J."

J pressed his head backward, his mind no longer focused on the glasses. A young woman with dark brown hair and deep tan skin stood holding out her hand.

"I'm Zeline. I'll be getting you prepped for the operation."

J shook her hand, followed her into the mountain. The area was enormous. Ships of all sizes sat in various states, some in very bad shape, sparks rained down from welding torches and plasma cutters. He spun around more than once as they walked, taking it all in. They strolled into a briefing room, a round table in the center, but not a chair in sight. A three-dimensional hologram of Tremessos hovered above, so real it looked like a model. Arcturus was tapping at one end of the table, the city shifting. Men and women gathered in various types of clothing, not uniformed like Cyrellia's forces. Four-teen men and women of various ages stood awaiting Arcturus' lead. He pulled the city toward the table, shrinking its size, the surrounding mountains coming into view.

Arcturus pointed at the open field near the city.

"Thanks to J, Cybermantis no longer protects the western front. We will use that as a starting point for the invasion, a distraction. Talon, you take the 1st and 2nd squadrons and suppress any enemy forces on the north, drawing them to us. The plan is not to defeat them, but to distract them."

He twisted his head, focusing on J, his eyes intense.

"J, you will come with Zeline, Dillon and I to infiltrate the tower. I know you've been there before, so you will need to guide us to Cyrellia's quarters before she can escape. 3rd squadron, you are to keep cover over the area at all cost, no ships are to leave the city. We will only get one shot at this, our numbers are few, and I know we will lose more."

He turned, walked toward another screen, and began to scroll through menus. The others mingled, discussing things J couldn't hear, his focus on Arcturus. A man stepped in front of him.

"No hard feelings, right?"

J tilted his head back examining the bearded man, he felt

he should recognize him. J shook his head from side to side.

"That's right. Arcturus said Cyrellia messed with your head. Seems to do that to the best of us, probably better you forgot a few things." He handed J a pistol. "Name's Dillon. Don't worry, it'll come back. You hungry?"

Right. This wasn't the first person to tell him that his memories would come back, yet his past was still a mystery. He was hungry and could use a leisurely meal, it seemed he'd been moving nonstop ever since setting foot on the Harbinger. J nodded his head and Dillon escorted him to the dining hall. It was smaller than J would've guessed for all the personnel he'd witnessed meandering through the tunnels. The food was fresh, the smells of fruits and meats tickled his nose. He shuffled through the line after Dillon, taking a few small portions of everything, including a piece of a pie. He wasn't sure what kind it was, the contents resembling nothing he'd ever seen on Earth.

Dillon found a table, set a jug down beside them. "So, you've been in the tower?"

J had already said grace and was stuffing a piece of bread in his mouth. He chewed, trying to get it down. With a small piece left to swallow, he nodded, mumbling "yes".

Dillon tore a piece of bread, dipped it in the juices from the tender pink meat resting on his plate. "Beats rations. So, Cyrellia's quarters, they on the top floor like Atlantis? That's what the blueprints say."

J, anticipating the question, left his hands in his lap. "Yes... Do I know you?"

Dillon swallowed the piece of bread, pulled a knife from

his hip and began cutting the meat. "Yep, Ariel introduced us. How's the girl doing these days? Didn't leave on such great terms, she around here somewhere?" Dillon looked around as if expecting to see her come in through the door.

J would've welcomed that. He felt alone, surrounded by strangers. Ariel was his constant, the one thing that couldn't be erased from his memory. He followed Dillon's lead, cutting a piece and holding it up to his face, examining it. "No, Cyrellia has her."

He slipped the slice between his lips, the taste of perfectly cooked beef rolled around his mouth. He closed his eyes remembering the farm, he was happy to still have those memories.

Dillon stabbed what looked like a purple carrot with a knife. "Damsel in distress, that's a mission worth doing." He crunched off half of the alien carrot, his cheeks bulging out as he chewed.

He was right about the mission, but J would hardly call her a damsel in distress. He'd seen her fight, she could hold her own. If anything, he was the less skilled of the two.

Dillon slid the jug over to him. "You're a farm boy, you'll love this."

"What is it?"

"Try it, then I'll tell you."

The contents looked white, like milk. He smelled it, the rustic odor of unpasteurized cream hit his nostrils, and he shrugged his shoulders then took a sip. He closed his eyes as the liquid drowned his tongue, taste buds shouting to his brain. He set the jug down. "Cream from a cow?"

Dillon chuckled. Leaning back, he placed a hand on J's shoulder. "You'd think that. Naw, it's an animal from this planet. The nerds call them Hipotymous, the rest of us just call them hips. This side of the planet is crawling with them, that meat there is hips too."

J took another piece of the meat contemplating, a cow on another planet. He tried remembering what Hollywood depicted alien animals like, but for some reason couldn't get past the blob. He held in a chuckle, he didn't want to explain it to Dillon. J twisted his head to peer at Dillon. "You think Arcturus is right? This the best plan?"

Dillon nodded, his mouth full of food. Dillon swallowed, his bottom lip smooshed into the top, one eyebrow peaked. "Yeah."

J stroked his chin, resting his elbow on the table. "Is he right for the people? Can we trust him to do what's right for the people?"

Dillon tilted his head, expression locked. "Of course, why do you ask? Cyrellia putting nonsense in your head?"

He turned, continuing to eat his food. J shrugged his shoulders grabbing the fork to pick at his meal. He decided to not pursue the question anymore, Dillon's responses weren't making his memory any better and the pain in his head was back. Talking hurt, thinking hurt, living hurt. They finished up and Dillon steered them toward the ammo dump to acquire a few more weapons. He gave J a pair of anti-grav boots, something he vaguely recalled. Dillon laced his pockets with detonators, insisting J do the same. He only took a few, he wanted to be light on his feet, recalling running tended to be a common occurrence. They met Arcturus at the ship, he was already seated inside, the small craft able to hold four and the pilot. J slipped into his seat, a woman with a katana blade sat beside him. Young, her face glowing, she smiled as he entered, but said nothing. J sat down across from them, Dillon filled in the final seat.

The ship rattled off, Arcturus leaned toward J. "You are the key, your DNA should allow us access. Information from our insiders revealed that most of the tower is empty, Cyrellia has been pushing her combat troops to the exterior. Once inside, we will remove her from power."

J nodded. *Right, like it would be that simple.* The massive headaches informing him it would be anything but. He closed his eyes, the hum of the engines comforting him like a sweet lullaby, the pain dwindled, nearly gone. He sat there the whole trip, basking in the lull in activity. Dillon had made an attempt to disturb him, but Arcturus steadied his hand.

"Five minutes out."

J opened his eyes.

Dillon was checking his weapon, he clicked off the safety, grinning at J. "Time to get some."

J pushed his lips together, popping out a breath. He slipped his finger off of the safety, the weapon armed and ready. The pilot announced one minute and the ship began to shake, executing an approach. J hadn't asked where they'd be dropped off, but he imagined it would be the executive pad near the top. His body shifted forward, the craft stopping abruptly. A loud thud crackled through the cabin and the door opened. Dillon and the female poured out, J and Arcturus

right behind them. He was correct, the pad was clear, only
a few stories under the penthouse. On instinct, he glanced
up. Cyrellia watched them, her eyes locked onto J. He shrank
under her scrutiny and ran under the awning, disappearing
from her view. Dillon shouted for him to open the door. He
planted his hand on the control panel. A quick beep and
the door slid open. They stepped inside. J felt déjà vu as he
surveyed the glass walls and elevator shafts greeting him. He
wasted no time finding the correct elevator, the four of them
piled in. J commanded the lift up, his body felt the rush of
speed as they ascended. The ride stopped, the elevator doors
opened and J planted a foot out, he was in the lead the others
trailing him. Only a few steps in, he halted, a rifle aiming
at his head, Ariel at the other end of it. Cyrellia stood still,
gazing out at the city below.

CHAPTER THIRTY TWO

"You came as well, surprising. Having known you all of these years, I would have bet you'd send the boy to do your dirty work...Arcturus."

She spun around, her gown flowing around her. She hadn't changed from earlier. Her movement was elegant, refined. Her hands clasped together, the large sleeves falling toward the ground, the gold trim sparkling. She strolled toward them, her head high, lips pinned together.

"I'd offer you some wine, but as I recall, you have trouble holding your liquor." She offered a smirk, continuing toward them.

Arcturus stepped next to J, his hands resting behind his back. J examined him out of the corner of his eye, standing proud, upright, ready to deal. J flicked his eye to Ariel. Her face locked onto him, her rifle accompanying it, his own just above the hip, the position he entered with. He wanted to lower it, but could feel the tension rising in the room, his body hot, skin tingling.

"It seems we are always at odds, you on one end, I on the other."

Cyrellia stopped a yard away. The female from the ship stood behind J, Dillon behind Arcturus, the six of them in a standoff. J's eyes swept across the room assessing everybody and everything. He couldn't believe Cyrellia would only have Ariel for protection, there had to be more security somewhere. Arcturus picked up on it, too.

"I only see two people, Cyrellia. If that truly is the case, you have made this all too easy."

Cyrellia tilted her head back showing her teeth, her lips stretched thin in a smile. "Oh the grand planner, the architect, the builder, and scientist. There is one thing you did not account for, something you failed to notice. See, you are not the only one playing chess. You may have me in check, but it is far from checkmate."

She eyed J, her head still facing her opponent. J peeked at Ariel, she gave a slight nod toward the others. He ran through scenarios in his head, thinking of possible outcomes, a pivotal moment, a turning point in the game the decisive point. He knew that he had to make a decision, he had to act fast. If only he had more time, more information, more knowledge. He raised the weapon to his shoulder, his torso twisting to Arcturus, his aim resting on the man's chest. Dillon's mouth opened in shock, Arcturus' eyes widened though he was quick to reel them back. Ariel shifted her aim onto Dillon, her nose wrinkled.

Cyrellia tilted her head sideways. "Sometimes blood is thicker than any concoction you can make, even with your technology, your dream machine."

Arcturus turned his head toward J, his left eyelid twitched. "J, you must not listen to her, she has manipulated you. She is power hungry, she left Earth to die, to destroy itself, her only thoughts on power on conquest, on pain. She is making you a pawn. Remember. Remember the dreams, the treachery, the—"

"Lies!" Cyrellia shouted, arm outstretched, pointing at Arcturus. "That man is the con-artist. How did you gain your knowledge of me? Think of how I was portrayed...through dreams, nightmares. He is the one manipulating you. He has filled your head with ideas, falsehoods, engineered realities. Think of his technology, his equipment, his planning. He is *not* your father. Would I have relations with him? Did that fit my motives in his world? Think, J. Your memories will return, your real memories, not those manufactured by a megalomaniac. Then you will see, you will understand the lies he filled your head with. The truth of Flat Earth, how he stole you from me, how he took you until he was ready for his war, his coup, his...rebellion. I am your mother, blood, kin. You are so precious to me. I have set you free, but you must accept it."

J lowered his weapon, stared at the floor, the dull pain in his head a constant reminder that it wasn't right. Someone screwed with his memories. *Who was the manipulator, the engineer?* Cyrellia had been kind to him since he arrived onboard the Harbinger. Arcturus, though remote, had done the same. He needed the missing pieces, the Rosetta stone, to his memory. His chest constricted, body tensed, the blood crawling under his skin. The sound of the conditioned air sweeping into the room, the smell of plastic and steel, a hint of solder in his nose. J's eyes zipped between Cyrellia and Arcturus, he stood frozen.

His ear picked up the sound of metal sliding along wood and he twisted his head, the world slowing down. The woman drew the sword out, spinning the hilt with both hands, thrusting it toward J's head. Ariel extended her support hand lightning quick, punching him in the chest, his body rocketing backward toward the ground. The razor sharp tip of the blade missing its mark, but finding a new target in Ariel's shoulder. She spun her body, unloading round after round. Dillon grabbed his shoulder, falling to the floor. Arcturus collapsed unharmed, the follow through ending on the woman's body, five rounds penetrating her torso before she hit the ground. Ariel's face twisted and distorted with pain. J plummeted, his arms flailing in the air, his legs bent at the knees, boots bolted to the floor. His head impacted the ground, body following, bouncing twice before coming to rest. Ariel grabbed the katana, pulling it from her limp shoulder. She growled in pain, her face flushed. Snarling, she tossed the bloody blade to the ground, the steel clanging as it impacted the marble flooring, rolling to a stop at J's feet. Ariel trained her weapon on Arcturus, her damaged arm still hanging limp, blood dripping off her middle finger pooling underneath her. Arcturus raised his hand, slowly rising to his feet. Dillon lay on the ground growling holding his shoulder.

Ariel listened intently as J moaned, her eyes and weapon locked on the threat. "How you doing, babe?"

He sat up rubbing his head, eyes still closed. His eyelids fluttered as he opened them and he caught sight of the woman's lifeless body. Climbing to his feet, he shook his head. "Tara? What?"

His eyes moved around the room. Growling, his hand snapped the rifle up, ready to strike. "Dillon," he spat, his teeth clashed together.

He caught a glimpse of the man next to him, his weapon dropped from his hands. "Arcturus?"

Like a lightning strike, it all came back to him, his memories, the chaos, the terror, the joy, the fear. He couldn't move, his mind cycling through memories like a movie binge. The dreams, the tasks, the missteps, his successes, and failures.

Arcturus gained his feet, eyes focused on J. "You must end this, you must end *her*. I can see it in your eyes, I can tell you remember her cruelty, her malice, her evil. She was the one who tore down society, the one who ravaged the planet for resources, all for power. Finish this, finish her. We can set this planet free. Remember the dreams, my reality. I implanted them for you to understand her true character, not the deceitful web she is spinning before you now. Remember Cybermantis, the rockets, the day she murdered those people in the test facility."

Cyrellia stepped forward, her hand clenching in a fist, unseen under her robe yet felt by the ridged shake of her straight arm. "Yes, remember that day, that dream, J. Remember it. I've seen what he placed in your head, the deceit. Now watch the true exchange, the true reality, not his manufactured one."

A screen flickered on the window, the glass becoming opaque. The picture depicted the view from high on the wall of the test facility observation deck, he recognized the armored glass looking down onto the test floor the large mechanized machine standing motionless, people grabbing hoses and cables, dragging them away from the beast. He watched Cyrellia enter and approach the window, Arcturus and Zebulon in trail. Cyrellia placed her hands spread out along the window sill, scrutinizing the machine.

"And this...Cybermantis, will be capable of defending

Tremessos?"

Arcturus placed his hands behind his back. "Is that what the council has chosen for the name of the capital of Acadia?"

Cyrellia smirked still surveying the project, the rest of her body a statue, dress draped over her body. "You were the one to submit the name, are you surprised? We both know the council favors your opinions."

"Sir, Ma'am, the Mantis is ready for the demonstration. With your approval, we'll begin with anti-armor missiles, the new AN/23AAMs," said Zebulon.

Arcturus turned his head toward Cyrellia.

"What's the target?" she asked.

"Ma'am, a M6A8 Hover tank, factory built, all systems operational."

She nodded and Zebulon approached the viewing area, ensuring the target was positioned.

"Commence the demonstration, ready thunderbolt missiles, fire when ready."

"Commencing demonstration in three, two, one."

Sounds of weapons firing, a loud booming explosion shot out of the screen hitting J's ears, he winced remembering the tank breaking apart, only scraps remaining. Cyrellia and the others stood unwavering, their eyes focused on the carnage.

"If you are ready, anti-personnel cluster bombs up for demo," Zebulon announced.

Arcturus shot a hand into the air, his fingers raised indicating for Zebulon to stop. He exposed a Datacle on his right wrist, tapping commands into it.

"Those are your targets!?" Cyrellia declared, her head

turning to Arcturus. "You can't do that, this is a weapons demonstration, not mass murder."

"I wanted to see the demonstration on humans. I have chosen some. Do not worry, they are all criminals and could prove useful for my research."

Cyrellia released the window standing tall, turning her whole body toward Arcturus, her nose twitched as her face tightened.

"I will not allow murder during a demonstration, we are better than that here."

Arcturus raised a hand in the air. "Commander Zebulon, commence the test."

Zebulon turned his head toward the officer near the back of the room "Fire angry hornet swarm, lock onto all available targets."

The muffled sound of ordinance exploding reverberated off the glass. Zebulon stared at Arcturus with a slow nod. Silence filled the air and Cyrellia whirled toward Arcturus, her eyes locking onto his, her dress flowing over from her aggressive body motion.

"The council will hear about this. You had better step in line. Once we land in Acadia things will be different, if you desire to remain on the council you better temper your more zealous *experiments*."

She stormed out, disappearing into the elevator.

The screen switched off.

Arcturus whirled to J, pointed to the screen, his face distraught. "That is the manipulation, think of the truth."

His arm shook as his stern words flowed from his mouth.

J looked back, his memory recalling a different exchange between the two in the observation deck. His head was clear, the haze gone, the headache finally nonexistent. He could concentrate, yet he was more confused than ever.

Cyrellia stormed forward, her arm raised in the air, an item clenched in her fist. She threw it toward him, the contents skipping on the ground sliding to a stop at his feet. He bent down to examine it.

"That is the manipulation. A device, a program, a restraint to control humanity. Created by him."

J picked up the device and found a tiny electronics chip, hair-like wires dangled from it. J's mind flashed to Carol ,to Earth. His eyes zipped to Cyrellia, her stance forward, shoulders down, arm still holding position after the throw. He glanced to Arcturus, his face blank, no response. Behind him in the window, he could see craft shooting by.

J gained his feet. "Is that true? Was this your device?"

Something came over him, his mind now questioning the dreams, their validity. He stepped toward Arcturus raising his rifle once more. "Why did you create this?"

"It was at her request. Remember the dreams, my reality... our reality, I—"

Cyrellia straightened her spine, her eyes burning with rage, locked onto Arcturus.

"You pitched that...abomination to the council. You pushed it, not me. You were the one to rain down fire upon Sector 5. I spoke to the council about another chance, but you were the one to deliver the ultimatum, to execute the orders."

Arcturus turned to J. "She is filling your head with more

lies, more deceit."

"Then how did he get the scar on the back of his head? I left it there as a reminder for him of your foul, evil ways."

Cyrellia turned to J her face softening. "Feel the back of your head, the scar, the device's sinister home. Ariel had one, Zane, the others. His plot is much larger than you could fathom."

J slipped his fingers along his neck toward the back of his head, the tips brushing onto skin, raised, bald, where hair should have been. His eyes snapped to Ariel, her focus still on Dillon.

"How did he react when you told him about the locket? I don't see you wearing it," Cyrellia said.

J glanced at Arcturus' neck, the locket hidden under his robe, the chain barely visible on his exposed shoulder. J's eyes drifted to the ground, he had to figure something out, the sounds of the battle outside closer than ever. He had to stop this, he had to choose. He didn't want to choose, he wanted things as they were, simple, the lines between good and evil clear, not this jumbled grey that now engulfed him like a wool blanket on a winter's day. He needed help, someone he could trust, someone who had been there for him since the beginning.

"Ariel?"

His vision shifted to her and she glanced over toward him, her icy blue eyes glowing from the explosions outside, the battle encroaching on the tower. He opened his mouth the words forming on his tongue. She could help him, she had to help him. A flash of light burst onto her glossy retina, J's

347

eyes still focused on her. Ariel collapsed and J's head snapped toward the source. Dillon stood glowering over the sight, rifle at the ready. J lunged toward Ariel, dropping his weapon, catching her with both arms. He studied her body, the scorch mark in the center of her chest, the suit absorbing the brunt of the blow, but not all. Her coverings burnt, exposing her charred and bloody skin. She lay in his arms, clenched her teeth together holding in a groan.

Arcturus swung his attention to Dillon. "Shoot her!"

Dillon pulled the weapon up to his shoulder, digging it in deep, his eyes adjusting to the target. Cyrellia's head fell, her eyes bending to J. He grabbed Ariel's rifle, releasing a burst of shots at Dillon, who stumbled back, falling to the ground. J climbed to his feet, the weapon tucked into his shoulder, the rifle's empty barrel pointed at Arcturus. He strode forward, his muscles tensing, body trembling, his eyes filled about to burst.

"Why did you do it?"

Arcturus straightened up, his hands slipping behind him. "For you J, for you."

J fired, the bolt cutting Arcturus down. J stared at the empty space, gazing out the open window, his view now clear. He took a deep breath, still questioning his decision. He squinted, attempting to magnify the outside world. A ship was headed toward them, the impact imminent. He scrambled ,jumping onto Ariel. The building shook, glass shattered scattering throughout the room. He covered his head, body surrounding Ariel's. His exposed skin felt the heat of the explosion, his eardrums vibrating from the shockwave. He laid

there, ears ringing, blood flowing around his neck, small pieces
of glass littering the floor. He pressed himself up, watching Ariel. She was still alive, her breath shallow. J stood up
surveying the carnage.

Cyrellia was holding her head, her gown torn, burnt. She
stumbled to her feet. "We need to get to the Harbinger if
there is any chance to save her."

She worked her way to standing, her hand on her knee.
Her hair, once tightly woven on the back of her head, now
a flowing mess around her face. J lifted Ariel into his arms,
stumbled toward Cyrellia through the wreckage, burning ship
parts filled the room, the sound of war now audible with no
glass to obstruct it. Cyrellia trudged toward a central pedestal,
placed her hand on it. It glowed red and the floor collapsed
underneath them, an elevator system taking them down.
Below the floor a ship came into view, its engines pointing
their way. It was small, shaped like a wedge, with a total of
four square engines along the rear edges. Cyrellia stepped off
the platform, stumbling as the structure shook once more. J
braced himself, legs out, knees bent.

"In here! I hope that fall didn't mess with your piloting
skills." She ushered him in. The small ship housed six seats,
four in the mid-section, two in the front, the engines taking up
the rear.

He rested Ariel on one of the seats, strapping her in, leaned
over and kissed her forehead. "Hang in there." Then hopped
into the pilot's seat. The opposition continued to bombard the
tower, the intervals tightly spaced. They had to be close now.
He began the startup sequence, systems buzzed on, the engines

came alive, the hum warming J's mind. *Hang in there Ariel.*
The controls were natural to him, like other ships he'd flown.
With his memories restored, it came naturally, like he was an
old pro. Had he the time, he would have reminisced about
his past, his other life. The wall slid open and he slammed
the thruster forward, the walls disappearing behind them, the
night sky engulfing the craft and the blue moonglow dancing
off the windscreen. The windscreen lit up, washing out the
mountains in the distance.

"Warning ! Shields, shields!" the ship screamed.

He checked the display, 90% flashed back at him. His
fingers swiped through the weapons load-out and found only
bare bones available. He selected the auto-canons, that would
at least provide him the time needed to bug out. He pulled the
controls back, initiating a climb and departing the atmosphere,
one ship on his tail. The cannons engaged and blasts of light
trailed, zipping past the assailant, the accuracy less than ideal.
He engaged the autopilot, the course set for the Harbinger,
then switched over to manual weapons mode as the trailing
ship fired and hit the rear of the craft. The shields glowed,
the ship continued its nagging and J silenced it, focusing on
the enemy craft. He locked on, letting a barrage of fire fly.
The ship ignited into flames, spinning out of control toward
Acadia. He saw the pilot eject, the body flipping through
the air like a ragdoll, falling lifeless toward the ground. The
battle, the war. *Hundreds...thousands of people dying for what?*
Supremacy over Acadia? To rule as they see fit? Was it truly over
control or one man's search for power? He looked back at Ariel,
her body slumped in the chair, and remembered his question to

CHAPTER THIRTY TWO

Arcturus, the answer.

"You said he controlled more than just me and Ariel?"

Cyrellia leaned toward him, her forehead wrinkled. "Yes.
My intelligence sources relay that nearly his entire army is
under one form of mind control or another. He either has
them fooled, duped, or he controls their every decision...their
memories."

J flashed his eyes to the moon ahead, pulled his lips in
against his teeth, and breathed in deeply through his nose.
His hand slapped the panel, unlocking the manual control
and, flipping the ship, pulling it around in a loop to aim back
toward the planet. Cyrellia was pinned back into her seat. J
heard her groans from the g forces he brought upon them. He
released the pressure, forcing the craft to level off, then added
power to the thrusters. The ship rocketed forward, their speed
creating a shockwave, the sonic boom echoed around them.
The darkness of night began to fade as he approached the
planet, a sunrise he would've loved to stop and admire slowly
emerged, the beautiful beams of light wisping through the
atmosphere in all shades of colors. Cyrellia worked her eyes
toward him, the forces now relaxed.

"Where are you going? Ariel..."

"You said he was controlling people, which means he must
have something like a mainframe set up to manipulate everyone. I need to eliminate it."

Cyrellia's eyebrows pinched together, she grabbed his
shoulder. "What about Ariel?"

J twisted his head toward Ariel, his eyes roving over the
face that had become more dear to him than his own life.

Stomach tingling, he pulled his gaze away and turned to Cyrel-lia. "This is bigger than one person, I know that now. I'm leaving her in your hands, trusting you to save her."

Keying a sequence of buttons, he climbed over the seat, passed Cyrellia, and leaned in to kiss Ariel. "This is for you."

CHAPTER THIRTY THREE

He pressed his hand on the ceiling, the other hovering near the door controls.

"Ship's on autopilot to the Harbinger. Save her, she means everything to me." He pressed the button and was sucked out into the air, his body spun as his arms flailed about.

"Dorothy." He clicked his heels together and the boots came to life, slowing his spin. He clicked them again, adjusting for the freefall, the trees like carpet, the mountains piles of sand. Scanning, he picked up his target, Arcturus' cave. Acadia continued to expand, his vision losing the curvature of the planet, the ground now beginning to rush toward him. He manipulated his body, becoming an arrow, his sights set on the entrance. Just before impact, he kicked himself around clicking his heels, the boots slowing his fall for a gentle touchdown. He hit the ground running, adjusting his rifle as he swept for targets. None appeared. At the entrance, there was a distinct lack of commotion, the ships were gone, the flurry of activity he'd seen, absent. One man meandered out of the cave, spotted J and leaned forward to get a closer look. J continued his sprint, weapon ready for engagement. The man stopped, his empty arms hanging to his side. J flipped a hand up, two fingers out in a loosely tucked hand into the air. The man stared, his mouth open as he nodded, following J's path. Inside, J found more of the same. He skidded to a stop, the hangar revealing four doors. *Which one?* He gazed down the barrel of the rifle catching a glimpse of the Datacle on his support arm. He dropped the weapon its weight falling on his shoulder, the strap clinging like a nagging spider web. He worked through the menus, his cheeks lifted, eyes widening, as the map of the facility appeared. He scanned through it, but nothing looked familiar. Just then, a man with a tablet walked in, his stare contemplating J's presence in the cave.

"J? Where's Arcturus?"

It was Arcturus' assistant. *He would know, he had to know.* J moved toward him, his slow walk became brisk. Time was wasting, he needed to figure this out and quick.

"He's on his way back, sent me to adjust some of the equipment."

The assistant's arms dropped, his head tilted, one eyebrow raised over his glasses. "Equipment?"

Jeffrey was shorter than he remembered from the dreams. *The dreams. When this was all settled, Cyrellia had some explaining to do.* He shook off his thoughts, distracted. "Yeah, there's a problem with the control module for the chips.

The assistant pressed his chin upward, shook his head slightly. "Chips?" Then quickly glanced down at his pad, tapping commands into it.

J's heart raced, his leg began bouncing, eyes shifting about.

The assistant looked up. "Ah yes, the chips. You'll need to see the mainframe. This way."

J followed him into a series of tunnels, his eyes checking the tablet as if it were updating him on something. Deeper into the mountain they went. Each door felt smaller than the last and he began to feel claustrophobic, his chest tight, field of vision seeming to shrink. The assistant finally came to a door, opened it. J peered at him, the man smiled, his face retreating to neutral. Tucking his chin, J took a step toward the door, peeked inside. Something felt off, wrong. He stopped, examining the room from the outside.

The assistant looked down at his tablet once again. "It's behind the back wall, there's a secret panel to access it."

His voice fluctuated, uneven, strained, not what J remembered from the dreams, something was definitely wrong. J stood up, his hand sliding onto the rifle behind his back, his eyes fixed reading his guide. "You first."

The assistant glanced down to check the tablet once more, but J had enough of the man's evasion and grabbed it with his free hand, spinning it around. The top right read "intruder", the word flashing. It displayed a map of the complex, icons glowed indicating troop movement, they were close. He heard a shout from down the hall behind him. Knowing that he didn't have much time before they were discovered, he shoved the tablet into his pants, flipping up the rifle, the barrel pressing on the assistant's neck.

"No more games. Which way?"

The assistant shook, his words frozen in his throat. J's ears picked up a buzz zipping by his ear, a ball of light preceding it. He wrapped an arm around the assistant, pulling the weapon around as he spun toward his attackers. He fired down the hall, the aggressors ducking to the side, then pushed his prisoner forward. He could feel his body shaking, his muscles resisting direction. He strengthened his hold, dragging his prisoner away from the fire. One of the soldiers ducked into the hall, let fly a few shots. J ducked, his instincts taking over. The shots found their mark on his prisoner, the searing heat warming his arm. His eyes darted around as he dropped the man, jumped over his lifeless body. Another few shots zipped past him as he hugged the wall and he let loose, creating his own cover fire. One of the soldiers popped his head out, J hit his mark, one down, he gritted his teeth pressing his lips together. *Was he controlled, too?* He didn't have time to contemplate he had to find the controls. The other man exposed himself and J finished him off. But he wasn't unscathed, pain radiated from his hip. He glanced down, found his waist charred, black, sizzling. He pushed through the pain continuing onward. After another room, he slapped his back onto the wall, sliding down onto his butt. He pulled out the tablet, his eyes devouring it, and located the mainframe. The assistant's tablet was highly detailed, something told him that made sense. He examined the route. "Get up J, get up."

He popped up holding his hip, the burning sensation growing, and he winced as he straightened up, placed the tablet back in his pants. *Always bring a backpack on adventures.* As he entered the hangar again, a flurry of shots zipped around him, his eyes adjusting to the sunlight streaming in. His plan to sneak in was shot, though it could've been worse. He exchanged fire, moving between large storage containers, boxes with hoses protruding from them like octopuses. He slipped through another door, tapping a command to lock it behind him. Limping down the hall, his hip irritated, slowing his progress. He grunted, trying to distract his mind, but it was no use, the pain continued its onslaught. He stopped once more, leaned on the wall, the pressure off his wounded hip, and checked the tablet. *Almost there.* The device showed three more soldiers between him and the mainframe.

He pressed on, dispatching one of the three along the way. Rounding the corner, his eyes focused on the final door, closed, steel, cold. Behind it, freedom. He input the code, referencing the tablet, and the door hissed open. Two children played with a ball, the one mid-throw, the other awaiting the ball. They both stopped, stared at him. The ball bounced off of the second child's head, but J didn't know if he should laugh or not, he didn't understand the situation. Between the children was a large metal box. The room glowed eerily from red lights high above, but the box shined blue and green creating a strange aura around it, the colors clashing, hot vs. cold. He stepped forward, the children following his every movement. He tried to shoo them along, but they stood stock still, their heads rotating to follow him. J glanced left and right, examined the mainframe by sliding his hand along the surface. A panel folded down revealing a keypad and he began typing.

A small voice chimed from behind him. "What are you doing?"

He turned his head to see the child walking toward him, head tilted, its face stagnant save for its raised eyebrows.

"Are you allowed to be here?" the other asked, its expression identical to the first.

"Father wouldn't want you playing with his stuff." The first child inched closer.

"Yes, it is only for him," the other agreed.

J tried to ignore them, his fingers frantically typing commands. He pulled out the tablet, searching for instructions, directions, any clue on what to do. He found nothing.

"You should leave," said the first child.

"Yes, leave or we will call father," the other instructed.

J stepped back and found the children within striking distance, he backed a few steps toward the door.

"Who's your father?"

"Arcturus," replied the first.

"We protect his equipment," announced the other.

"You must leave," declared the first.

"Yes, you must."

J's eyes slipped back and forth between the two. *What was he going to do? Who where these children? Did they really belong to Arcturus?* He shook his head and thought of Ariel, the battle raging, the lives already lost. Resolve found, he stepped forward. He had to shut down the system. Running to the box, ignoring the pain, he began tapping on the keyboard once again, hoping to find something. Pain shot through his lower back and up toward his shoulders. Screaming, he fell into the controls. Another shot of pain came from the other side, this time the blow had been aimed at his kidney. He fell to the ground. Flipping around, he saw the two children standing with their hands balled into fists, eyes glowing an unnatural red. One lunged at him, J ducked his head to the side, the small strike smacked the mainframe. A metal clang reverberated around the room. The other child attempted the same, but J threw up his good leg striking the child in the face, its body bouncing back onto the ground. The first attacked again and J rolled away. Gaining his feet, he flipped up the rifle.

"Don't come any closer...I'll shoot."

J backed away from the children. *What were these things? Children, clones, or something else? The strike sounded metallic, not organic, not human.* He'd heard that sound many times before, with the replicants, E-Rats...Tara. The first child jumped at him, J fired, the blast glowing bright nearly blinding him in the dimly lit room. His target dropped to the ground. J crumpled over as a flurry of punches landed on his oblique. He swatted the other child away. Stumbling toward the machine, his empty hand caught the keyboard, using it for support. He swept the room. The first child, its chest smoking, climbed to its feet. The other was in better shape and doing the same.

"Father said no intruders," stated the smoking one.

"Yes, no intruders," repeated the second.

"Intruders don't survive," declared the first

"Don't survive," affirmed the second.

J's hand slipped off the keyboard. Brushing his pant pocket, the sound of Chinese Baoding balls chimed. He glanced down as his hand found the fastening then glanced back at the children. Hobbling away along the keyboard, he slipped his hand into his pocket, his other still maintaining a grip on the rifle. "Okay, I'll leave. You can tell your father I left."

The children continued stalking toward him, J split his attention between the two, not sure which would attempt a strike first. He fumbled in his pocket, his hand finding the round metal sphere and his finger slipped over a switch.

"Too late, intruders must be eliminated," intoned the first.

"Eliminated."

J had reached the end of the mainframe. He swallowed,

his whole body shouting at him in pain. "Well, that's too bad. I thought you could continue your game of catch."

He flipped one of the balls in the air, the children studiously watched it fly, it's arc aimed at the damaged one. Jumping away, he covered his head, he wasn't sure what was going to happen. His chest hit the stone floor and he slid. A concussion struck his eardrums, the floor shook, dirt trickled down on him like snow. The room went silent. He peeked under his arm and saw one of the children push itself up, its glowing red eyes locking onto him. J rolled onto his side, positioning his weapon. The child sprinted toward him, his finger squeezed the trigger, exerting all the force he could, attempting to steady the rifle as it sprayed fire like a garden hose. His teeth felt like wooden planks in a hurricane about to snap from the pressure, his upper body shook violently. His aim stayed true, but the child careened toward him as if immune to the weapon's blasts. The firing stopped, the cell flashing empty, and the child collided into him. He closed his eyes on impact, awaiting pain.

A moment passed, his muscles loosened, his eyes peeked under heavy eyelids. The child lay lifeless on top of him, its body hot, almost burning him through his suit. J groaned. Pushing his attacker off of him, he rolled onto his back stared at the ceiling, one arm resting on his chest. "I need a vacation."

He coughed, pulling himself onto an elbow, and searched the room. Still. His chest pushed out one heavy breath, his heart thumping like a ticking clock. He shifted his body weight, wincing as the pressure hit his hip, gained his feet, his posture bent, crooked like an old man. The mainframe stood intact. He gazed down at the child, its chest gone, a metal skeleton exposed, wires flickered with sparks. Relief washed over him, he didn't know if he could've lived with himself had it been a real child. He hobbled over to the mainframe and found the other in pieces, missing an arm, a leg. He inspected the rifle, the cell sill flashing empty, and dropped it wondering why he wasted the energy to carry it. He smacked both palms onto the keyboard, lifting his face to the small screen, eyed it a moment. *How do I stop you?* He examined the letters, the words on the screen, nothing seemed to make sense. He felt his waist, the tablet was gone. His eyes scanned the floor, the tablet lay at his feet, the screen cracked, the display unreadable. Leaning forward, he bumped his head on the mainframe, his eyes staring past the keyboard to the floor. He looked through it as if focusing on the other side of Acadia. *What was he going to do? He needed Ariel and not just to hack the system.* His eyes drifted to his pant leg, a bulging pocket catching his attention. He snapped up straight, reaching in and pulled out a detonator. Holding it up in the dim light he shook his head. "Wish I'd listened to Dillon."

But that was the past, he had only taken two. One saved his life, he prayed this would save more. He searched the mainframe, there had to be a hole or service panel, some way into the system. He scoured the entire box, the panels smooth, no seams, a piece of art in its own right. J stepped back, staring at its entirety. Then it came to him, a last ditch effort, an idea. He stepped forward and jumped as high as he could, one leg lifted up high and bent at the knee. He thrust his boot down like a hammer on top of the keyboard. His foot glanced off, his shoulder impacting the metal surface. He crumpled to the ground. Rolling over, he looked up at the keyboard, his mouth hanging open at finding it still intact. He snapped his head forward chin into his chest, exhaled with a groan and picked himself up. *Now what?*

His movements slow, he started a new search to find any weakness in the structure. His ears pushed back and his eyes popped open. The keyboard had moved, hardly an inch, but it moved. J executed his jump again, this time minding his balance better, his hip burning, shooting pain as he struck. On the fourth attempt, the board snapped off. J thrust his fist into the air like he just scored the winning run. While not the same on any scale, it felt like a win nonetheless. He preened at his prize, a square hole large enough for the detonator. He extracted the device and, clicking the switch, tossed it in. So proud of his accomplishment, he almost forgot to duck. At the last second, he dove toward the door, hands on the back of his head. The room erupted in a series of explosions, smoke filled the air, an acrid smell entered his nostrils causing him to sneeze. He heard the hiss of a door and two sets of heavy steps hit the ground. J didn't want to look, he just kept his arms over his head.

"You okay down there?"

"Whoa, what happened in here? Are those kids?"

J heard one set of footsteps run past him as he felt a tap on his shoulder.

"Hey buddy, you okay?"

J placed his palms on the floor, pushed his head back. A man looked back at him, resting on one knee.

"You okay? What happened?"

J climbed to his feet, the man watched, his rifle still slung, his face concerned.

J smiled. "I'm okay, there was a malfunction with the mainframe. I'm going to go report it."

The man looked past him scratching his head. "Mainframe?"

J stepped past him and the two men started talking back and forth, the first informing the other that the children were replicants.

J snickered. *Killer replicants.* He hobbled down the hall, passing a few more people who simply gave him a curious look. One stopped to tell him where the medical bay was. He thanked them politely and continued on. He had somewhere to be. He stepped out into the hangar and found it empty. J stopped hobbling and rubbed the bridge of his nose, closing his eyes. *How was he going to get back?* The hum of an engine caught his attention and his head perked up, scanning for the source. A single fighter flew in, landed on a parking pad. J shuffled over nearly at a run, his face grimacing as he did. The cockpit opened and the pilot slipped out. J ran to him, the man tilted his head analyzing him.

"You okay?"

The man stared down at J's hip.

J assessed the man's ship. "What happened out there?"

The man massaged the back of his neck. "Not sure. The captain just called off the attack. I happened to be the first one back, I guess."

J moved his attention to the pilot. "Your ship damaged at all?"

The pilot pinched his eyebrows together, twisting his head.

"No...she's low on fuel, but fine—"

J took off toward the ship, the pilot yelled after him, "You'd better fuel it! You won't make it very far."

J hopped in, firing the engines and grinned. He checked the fuel, 10%, then worked his way through the ship's computer finding the Harbinger. J shook his head, it would be close, but he could make it. He lifted the craft, hovering it out into the bright sunlight. Placing the thruster full forward, the ship rocketed off. It climbed nearly straight up, he could conserve fuel once he left the atmosphere. The sky shifted into darkness, the stars brightening by the second, and the moons came into view, their white-blue glow glaring off the windscreen. He pulled the thruster back setting cruise power, it wasn't the fastest, but it would get him there. He relished the sound, silence but for the light soothing engine hum. Resting his head against the seat and closing his eyes, he took a deep breath. He couldn't wait to see Ariel, prayed she was alright. He pushed out any negative thoughts, she had to be alright, he didn't know what his world would be without her. He thought of what it might be like now that the war was over. *Would it be simple, like his life on the farm? Nothing could ever be that simple.* J almost dozed off, but the ship brought him back, the speakers beeping. He glanced at the fuel system, 1%. Out the windscreen the Harbinger was coming into view. He tapped on the fuel display like he used to on his old Chevy and the screen zoomed in, not the effect he was going for. The engines cut out. J smacked his head back against the seat, shoulders sagging. A new tone sounded and J thrust his head forward, looking up at the screen. The display informed him there was an inbound call.

"Hey kid, glad you made it."

Zane seemed even more chipper than usual, if that was even possible. He leaned in, pushing one eye closer to the camera. "You don't look so hot, I'll have V meet you in the hangar."

J shook his head looking down, his shoulder hung limp, a reminder of his situation helped pain creep back into his head. He bit his lip, his eyes off into space. "Well...you might have to come get me."

His last few words spoken with a grimace, Zane chuckled. "What, you run outta fuel?"

J tried to hold in a laugh, but couldn't. He peeked up at Zane. "You know me too well."

Zane chuckled, standing up, his stomach in the shot. "I'm coming for ya."

The transmission switched off and J realized he didn't ask about Ariel, he needed to know she was alright. He placed a hand on his hip, immediately regretting it, the nerves screaming at him to stop. He leaned back placing his hands behind his head, watching the stars and the Harbinger. After a few minutes the ship's hangar opened, a cargo cruiser appeared adjusting its trajectory toward him. As the ship neared, J switched on the Harbinger comm frequency, he could hear other ships landing back in Tremessos, others enroute to the Harbinger like himself. Another transmission came in and J switched it on screen.

Max's arrogant face shined back at him smirk and all. "Zane says you're pretty banged up. I'll give you a day then I

ACADIA

want another round of crud."

J laughed. "Sure, but only if I get Ariel on my team."

Max's smile dwindled and he looked away from the screen. J's heart sank, his eyes searching for an answer, his lips rubbed against each other, the words not coming out of his mouth. *Ariel had to be alive, she just had to be.* He worked up the courage to ask, Max beat him to it.

"I'm just kidding, she's recovering from surgery. V said she'll be fine, but she needs a few days rest, she was pretty messed up. How you holding up?"

J wanted to reach through the screen and strangle him, his fists clenched, knuckles transparent as paper. "Don't ever joke like that again." J's eyes were stern. "I couldn't..." He blew out a deep breath. "I'm fine, not sure if I'll ever walk right, this hip is killing me."

Max finished loading J's ship into the cargo bay then flew back and landed safely in the Harbinger. J commanded the cockpit open. He attempted to crawl out once, but fell back into the seat, his body not functioning, shutting down.

CHAPTER THIRTY FOUR

Three moons watched over him, gently nudging him awake. His eyelids, still heavy from much needed sleep, fought back, the call of night still upon him. The moons battled back, reminding him it was time to wake up, it was time for his new world to take hold. He fluttered his eyes, squinting, letting them adjust in increments, the blue-white glow flooding into the room. His nose picked up a scent he remembered, enjoyed, loved. Thinking of it now made him laugh inside, burnt air and sunflowers. His eyes focused on a large glass window covering the entire wall, welcoming him back to life. He rolled over and saw Ariel reading a tablet.

"Morning."

She peeked an eye over at him then pretended to read. J sat up, attempting to focus on the recent events. He whipped his head to Ariel, grabbing her and pulling her close. She dropped the tablet and placed her hands on his cheeks, their lips merging. He closed his eyes, his body melting into hers. He absorbed her essence, her being, his body felt new, reborn. A heavy burden lifted, the curtain drawn back, stepping into heaven. She pulled away, their foreheads touching, her skin soft, smooth, comforting, her eyes reflecting the moonlight. He wanted to speak, to say something, something meaningful. His eyes searched hers, he didn't want to spoil the moment.

She placed a small kiss on his lips, pulling away she ran the back of her hand on his cheek. "Now that's a good morning."

J smiled in agreement, his skin tingled, he still tasted her on his lips. He slid out of the bed. Gazing down, he realizing he was wearing a t-shirt and lightweight sleeping pants, his shoulders relaxed. He was happy to finally wake up in more than just his underwear.

Ariel must have noticed because she snickered. "You like the pants? Picked them out myself, slipped 'em on ya, too."

J blushed. He kept his head toward the stars. He felt vibrations on the floor, light footsteps approaching.

Ariel threw her arms around his waist, squeezing tight, her head resting on his upper back. "Beautiful, isn't it?"

J rotated around, coaxing her in front of him, both of them holding each other peeking at the moons. "They are." J tightened his embrace. "You think they're hollow?"

He loosened his hug. Ariel pulled back, gazing up at him, she didn't answer, but her lips creeped up into a smirk. She slipped out of his arms, walked toward the bathroom, her nightgown hugging all her curves. He gawked as her hips swung from side to side until she disappeared through the doorway.

"Better get dressed, I told the others I'd bring you by once you woke up. Your clothes are hanging next to the bed."

He turned around and found a military style suit, pressed, the green bright like new though it was the same uniform he'd worn before. He sauntered over, his steps light, his body riding high, almost floating. No tasks to perform, no items to find, no planet to save. He felt whole, free. He slipped on the pants, shaking his hips as he pulled them past his waist.

"Woohoo."

J turned to see Ariel leaning on the door, zipping up her top. The uniform the same as his only there were more gold ropes around her shoulder. J zipped his pants up quickly, pinching his finger, he winced. Ariel chuckled and J began shaking his finger, placing it in his mouth.

"Why do you have more ropes than me?"

"It's complicated."

He heard her holding in a laugh as she responded, decided to let it be. He was sure he'd find out soon enough. He slipped on the top then his boots, Ariel opened the door leading them out. She offered her hand and he took it, lively swinging it as they went. Ariel grinned calling him a goof. J's body warmed, it was the goal of his act, to see her reaction. They meandered through the ship, taking their time. J examined the walls, the rooms, furniture, fixtures, it all seemed like a futuristic lavish hotel. If he didn't know better, it could've been on Earth or Acadia, the stars hidden from view in most of the halls. One, however, was laced with glass, the ceiling nearly one singular panel running the length of it. They ended up in the transport room and rode the tube toward the bridge. J enjoyed the view, watching the normal-sized trees as they zipped past. They stepped into the final elevator leading to the bridge and Ariel leaned her back against the wall, her lips pressed out, her eyes on his.

"Kind of a trip, huh?"

J studied her, that was probably the best way to describe it. He was still sorting through everything. He had so many questions, but right now he was on such a high he didn't want to think about it. He bit his bottom lip looking at the elevator door. "Yeah, definitely a trip."

The door hissed open and Ariel stepped out grabbing his

hand. Two soldiers snapped to attention as they sauntered past. Ariel put them at ease, J attempted to figure out what just happened. He twisted his head toward the large control screen and saw Cyrellia, standing with her palms resting on the console, overlooking the ship's crew.

"Awake are we?"

She rotated, slid her arms into her sleeves, her blue dress catching J a little off guard. He squinted trying to read her face when he was crushed. Huge arms wrapped around him, then released. He turned to see Zane smiling back at him.

"How ya feelin', kid?"

J took a moment, decided to downplay his emotional high. "Good. You?"

Zane turned his head looking out the side of his eye. "You sure just good? You did just win a war, you gotta be doing better than good."

J tightened his eyes. *Did he though?* His gaze returned to Cyrellia. He was conflicted still, in all of the dreams, she was the enemy, the Kontrollery, the mind control. He was attacked again as V latched onto him, then released him, sliding in beside Zane.

"Looking good, J."

J smiled, his cheeks almost sore from being overworked. He knew he owed V his life, more than that she'd saved Ariel and Zane countless times. None of them would be there without her, he bowed his head slightly looking down at her.

"Thank you. Thank you for reminding me, for never giving up, for saving me, and Ariel, and all of us. I'm forever in your debt."

V's cheeks lifted and she blushed. She glanced over at Ariel. "I'll work on you two anytime. I should be thanking you though, you set me free."

J drew in a breath at the comment. *Did he set them free?* He didn't want to think about it, he was happy the way things were. It seemed when he thought he understood the world, he was uprooted, transplanted. He prayed that this was the last time. J searched the room, coming back to Zane. "Where's Max?"

Ariel piped in, her response a bit snarky. "Playing crud in the bar."

J didn't need any more information, seemed like he was doing just fine. He smiled admiring his friends, his family.

Cyrellia approached, her face light, a soft glow about her, much different from his dreams, from his memories of their encounters. She placed an arm around his upper back, leaned her head toward him. "Walk with me dear boy, I know you must have many questions. I will not have all of the answers, but I will do my best."

J stared into her eyes, they were sincere, truthful. He nodded, pressing his lips together and she slipped her arm off of him, holding it in the air to signal for the others to stay. She kicked her foot forward, her gown flowing outward. J matched her speed as they proceeded forward. Stepping into the elevator, she turned to face him, commanding the bottom floor of the ship.

"I will begin with a question, then a statement. Afterward, you can ask your questions."

He placed his hands behind his back, biting his bottom lip,

and nodded, accepting the terms. Cyrellia smiled for a reason only known to her at the moment. She began.

"What is reality? Reality is different to everyone. My reality is different than your reality. We could be in the same room, doing the same things, hearing the same people talk and each of our realities could be drastically different. I may perceive something to be horrible, you may find it good. They are the same, yet different realities. Arcturus used that to his advantage, he utilized the inherent flaws in our minds to manipulate reality to what benefitted him. When you met Ariel, it was by his design. He knew she was already betrothed to you and he found it beneficial to use her. Do you think she would have been able to infiltrate so many security measures without her royal blood? Why do you think she survived countless encounters, pure skill? She is an amazing fighter, but my orders were for her to be brought back alive. This brings me to the reality of what you thought to be the Kontrolery. They never existed, it was a creation of Arcturus' playing on what he himself was doing, controlling all. He was a puppet master, his chips designed to help us keep peace on Earth turned against us. Humans are drawn to conflict, to strife, persecution. Arcturus designed the chips to remove that from the people of Earth. Then he turned it into something sinister. We were to leave Earth and remove the restraint when we did, leave them to do as they pleased. Our society had enough conflict, we have evolved, but not enough to eliminate that completely. Arcturus is proof enough of that. Thousands of years ago, we adopted a royal system like the lands of old, but with countermeasures to ensure humanity's interests were met.

The council you know as TK is mine, they support me advise me. If I make a misstep, they correct me or remove me from power. They are a council yes, but not TK's council. I know some of what was put in your head, we have archives of all those meetings and you can access them whenever you please."

The elevator stopped, the door hissed open and they walked out onto a suspended bridge running the length of the ship. Ten feet below, the belly wrapped in glass panels, a sea of stars filled the view, Acadia peeking in. They continued to walk, J speechless, attempting to download it, to process it. His face wrinkled as they continued, he twisted his head to Cyrellia.

"Was he my father?"

Cyrellia held in a laugh, her face dropping into sadness. "No, no he wasn't. Yet another ruse. Your father was royalty, something Arcturus could never be. I think in some ways that was what created him, he couldn't handle seeing others in power. You will come to find out, J, it is not all sunshine and rainbows. There are tough decisions to make, sacrifices to choose. Earth, for example. It was true we were going to bring everyone with us, but the materials wouldn't allow it. The most beneficial decision was to split the population, Earth was not supposed to destroy itself, it was to be sustainable for thousands of years. Arcturus fabricated the failures to push you here. I tried to have you come with us, even rescued you in hopes of having this decision on the other side of the universe...twice. It seems Ariel was more cunning than I anticipated. More reason to like her."

She turned her head, winking at J. It drew a smile to his

face. She was clever, her mind years ahead of his. He bit his lip as they strolled, his hands still interlocked behind his back.

"You remind me of him. You have his devilish good looks, the posture, your hands behind your back, the way you bite your lip while thinking. Those are all traits you share with your real father."

"What happened to my father?"

"He was murdered by Arcturus when he stole you from us. I lost you both that day. But I was determined to find you, to get you back." She stopped and turned to him, staring earnestly into his eyes. "That's why I created the watchers. But no matter how many people volunteered to look for you or how many resources we dedicated to it, I suspect that Arcturus knew and planted someone in their ranks to keep you hidden from me. I worried that Arcturus was also using that person to keep tabs on the Earth, but couldn't bring myself to stop the watcher program, even if there was only the slimmest hope that we would ever find you."

Her eyes fell to the floor. J could feel her pain so stayed silent, giving her time. Cyrellia angled her body away from him, her hands extending, grasping the rail. She gazed down onto Acadia, J mirrored her position.

"What a beautiful planet," she sighed, a small smile on her lips. She lingered there, taking it in, then took a deep breath and faced J. "We should get back to the bridge, I have an announcement to make. And before I do that, you should talk to Ariel ...alone. My suggestion? Tell her your true feelings for her." She lifted her arms to embrace him, but hesitated and settled on patting him on the shoulder before strolling back toward the elevator.

For a moment, J watched her go. He realized that they had a lot to work on when it came to a mother-son relationship, but for the first time in a while, felt lighthearted about the future and what it could bring. Twisting around to stare out at Acadia a moment, he reflected on that future... his future... with Ariel. *True feelings. He knew he loved her, but he'd never said it before, not first, not with true conviction.* He shivered, goosebumps rising on his arms. He spun around and jogged to catch up to his mother, his mind circling through his memories. He still had questions, but some were difficult to find now that another weighed on his mind. Deep in his thoughts, the walk seemed to progress faster and in no time they were at the lift. They headed up, exiting back onto the bridge. As they walked, Ariel marched toward them.

Cyrellia leaned into J's ear, whispering, "Take her for a stroll."

J glanced back at her, then snapped his eyes back to Ariel. He extended his hand, Ariel took it and he tugged her into the elevator. The ride was silent, but his brain was going a mile a minute. *His mother knew how he felt about Ariel without asking. Did anyone else? He loved Ariel, she was right, he needed to tell her.* But, he was hesitant, worried about her reaction. The elevator stopped and they exited at the bottom floor, Ariel's face lit up. J smiled at the reaction, he could tell she'd never been there and he was secretly proud that he was the one to show it to her. He gave her hand a tug as they moved along the walkway, their pace slow, deliberate. J glanced over at Ariel, her beautiful hair knotted at the nape of her neck, small tendrils escaping to frame the face that had become so precious to him.

"Did you know that Arcturus—"

"Yep."

"And that he—"

"Yep."

"That reality—"

"Yep."

"I love you."

"Yep...wait, what?!"

She stopped, tugging on his hand, her eyes becoming glossy. J pressed in toward her, his face glowing. He enjoyed her reaction, it was perfect. She was perfect. He pulled her in close as a single tear grazed her nose. Her eyes locked onto his.

"I love you, too."

J felt like his body disappeared, floating over the glass, the walkway gone, nonexistent. He pulled her in, locking them together in a kiss. The world disappeared and only space remained; the starry sky, the moons, Acadia. He drew in the memory, knowing he would do anything to keep it, to make more. They released, still facing each other, all of Acadia watching on. The ship's speakers came to life and Cyrellia's voice echoed in all areas of the floating world.

"Attention citizens of Acadia. This is Cyrellia, Lady of the Quilin Empire. The war against the insurgency is over; we have achieved victory over the megalomaniacal tyrant who attempted to control our every thought, decision and the very essence of our lives. Henceforth, today will be known as our Day of Peace and it will be celebrated annually as a reminder of not only the victory, but the lives lost. To commemorate this auspicious occasion, tonight we will have a royal feast, one for the ages, and a wedding between my son, J, and his warrior bride, Ariel. As a wedding gift, I bestow upon them...Acadia."

END OF BOOK THREE

FLAT EARTH SERIES

If you enjoy sci-fi action adventure join my newsletter where I release info on upcoming books, answer questions, and give you a glimpse into my future works. Sign up for my mailing list.

or visit my website at:

www.g11wingedhussar.com

or E-mail me at:

g11wingedhussar@gmail.com

I would love to hear from you and don't forget to leave a review!

About the Author:
Brent Golembiewski is a U. S. Air Force veteran with 20+ years of
service. He started his career as an enlisted troop, working as an
Electronic Warfare Technician, and completed it as an officer, never
working a day as a Helicopter Evaluator Pilot, flying the mighty
UH-1N "Huey". After retiring from the USAF, he began Valkyrie
Air, providing aircraft charter operations for people who find value
in time. He met the love of his life in the second-worst place he'd
ever been stationed and she's still on active duty. Together they have
two boys (the terrible Ts) a giant Yetti, a miniature ThunderCat,
and one old caricature of a dog that will never die.

For more information and to subscribe visit
www.g11wingedhussar.com

Made in the USA
Monee, IL
23 November 2020

49309867R00236